THE BODY TRANSPLANT

Elisabeth Link, M.D

The Body Transplant

The Body Transplant

*

A Medical Mystery

Elisabeth Link, M.D.

First published in the United States of America
by Monasteria Press LLC, San Francisco, USA

ISBNs
Paperback 978-1-958277-20-1
Hardback 978-1-958277-21-8
eBook 978-1-958277-22-5

DEDICATION

For my colleagues and friends
at the Stanford medical humanities program.

Acclaim for Elisabeth Link

"I couldn't book this book down. I just had to read what happens next."

"Captivating storyline with strong female role models."

"This story masterfully combines elements of suspense, medical mystery, and thriller genres, providing a unique reading experience."

"I liked the author's voice and her knowledge of the subject matter, how she interwove it into fiction."

"Elisabeth Link's writing is compelling and evocative, creating a reading experience that lingers long after the final page."

"You don't love someone for their looks, or their clothes, or their fancy car, but because they sing a song only you can hear."

— Oscar Wilde

The Body Transplant

*

A Medical Mystery

Elisabeth Link, MD

PROLOGUE

Silicon Valley University of Evolutionary Computation (SUEC) was established in 2025 in the hills above Redwood City, California. SUEC realized a new model of public–private partnership between the state of California and major tech companies, such as Apple, Google, Meta, Intel, Walt Disney, HP, Cisco, and many others. This unique collaboration fostered innovation within SUEC's research-focused environment, pushing the boundaries of cutting-edge technology. With an endowment of sixty billion dollars and generous corporate funding, SUEC had a larger budget than any other university in the world. Many innovations developed and explored at SUEC were years ahead of what was available anywhere else.

To provide convenient medical services, SUEC owned a hospital, which was located in nearby Redwood City and was open to the public. The two-hundred-bed university hospital provided medical emergency care, general medical care, and a variety of medical specialty services for both adult and pediatric patients. The pride of the hospital was its capacity to deliver the most advanced specialized medical care across various disciplines, such as surgery, neurology, cardiology, oncology, and pediatrics, among many others. The neurosurgery department was the most famous in the world, with pioneering discoveries in minimally invasive surgeries, robotic-assisted surgeries, brain chip technology, and brain–computer interfaces. The most famous faculty and the brightest students from around the world worked at SUEC Hospital, generating billions of dollars in donations and revenue.

As the center of technological innovation in the world, SUEC naturally drew intense interest from the US government. This crown jewel of technological innovations became a constant target for spies, thieves, and other criminals. To safeguard its discoveries and patents, SUEC had a large security team and sophisticated surveillance systems. In addition, the US government deployed undercover FBI and CIA agents to protect SUEC's assets of national interest and to identify activities that might impair national security.

- 1 -

ANNYA

Monday, November 8, 2032, 8:30 a.m.

Annya briskly pushed through the silver double doors into the operating room. The heavy weight of the doors hissed shut behind her as an orchestra of beeps and hums greeted her. Before her lay two bodies draped in emerald green against steel tables, encircled by two surgical teams. The air, sharp with chlorine and a tang of adrenaline, seemed to crackle with unspoken prayers. The neck of the woman on the first operating table glistened with iodine. The highly classified, first-of-its-kind surgery was about to begin.

The two operating tables were placed side by side, each surrounded by two surgeons, two nurses, and an anesthesiologist, all in green gowns, head covers, and face masks. The team was small, chosen for their discretion and unwavering loyalty to SUEC's clandestine agenda. Annya's gaze landed on the lead surgeon, Dr. Triveda, who stood in front of the operating table on the right. She looked briefly at Annya, her brows furrowed. She and Annya had tackled their fair share of challenging cases in the ER together, but nothing like this. Annya nodded at her colleague reassuringly. She nodded back briefly, then returned her focus to the draped body in front of her. Her hands trembled slightly as she adjusted the delicate instruments hovering over the patient's neck.

Annya could not see much of the patient. Layers of green shrouded the woman's body, leaving only the neck area and a pale hand exposed. She had been placed into the usual neurosurgical sitting position, a position where the head was transfixed with holding devices and the upper body was half-elevated. The patient's head was covered by a helmet that emanated a chilling mist from its vents. This device induced hypothermia and minimized damage to the brain. The EEG monitor beside the table showed periods of high-voltage electrical activity alternating with periods of no activity, confirming that the patient was under deep anesthesia.

Annya instinctively shifted closer for a better glimpse of the patient. Beside the surgeon, a stern-faced charge nurse raised a hand in a gesture of disapproval. He pointed toward the upper end of the two operating tables. "You can observe there, Dr. Segond," he said in a resolute voice. Annya nodded and went to the assigned spot. From here, she had a pretty good view of both tables. Her heart raced in anticipation. She was about to witness a procedure that would make history, the culmination of months of grueling research, of sleepless nights and nervous energy. A body transplant, a bold move into a new era for humankind.

Compelled by the intricate process, Annya leaned slightly forward as the procedure unfolded. On the other table, the donor's spinal cord was cooled through coiled tubes that snaked their way into and out of the patient's spinal canal. A perfusion machine pumped frigid solution into the spinal canal, bathing the delicate spinal cord in an icy embrace. Like the recipient, the donor was prepped for surgery in the neurosurgical pose. Secured by a network of stabilizing straps and bolts, her upper body was elevated on an adjustable surgical chair, creating a half-sitting position.

The two surgical teams around the patients looked like mirror images of each other, their eyes carrying the same steely focus, their scalpels flashing, their masks concealing their apprehension. In meticulously practiced coordination, the lead surgeon at each of the two operating tables created a circular cut through the neck tissues in front of them, carving through layers of skin. They carefully dissected every muscle and marked them for future reconnection. With practiced ease, they isolated the arteries and veins on either side of the neck and secured them with sutures. Then, they dissected the trachea, the rigid tube that channels air from the nose and mouth to the lungs, and the esophagus, the muscular tube that connects the mouth with the stomach. Next, they carefully dissected the nerves along the neck, marking them as well. The assistant surgeons and nurses followed every move of their lead surgeon, anticipating each need, instruments ready and gleaming.

After the soft tissues of the neck were dissected, the lead surgeons removed the posterior arch of the vertebral columns of the fifth cervical vertebral body. Removing this bony section provided access to the spinal cord, the vital bundle of nerves encased within the spinal canal. The surgeons meticulously ligated the vertebral artery, a crucial blood vessel that ran along either side of the spinal column, ensuring minimal blood loss during the following steps. Then, they dissected the anterior part of the vertebral body and opened the dura, a thin membrane that surrounded the spinal cord.

The nurses moved microscopes on robot arms over the surgical area and handed ultrasharp microsurgical blades to their surgeons. The chief surgeon at each table looked up and met the others' gazes to make sure that the next step would be employed in perfect coordination. The surgeons quickly transected the spinal cords of the patient in front of them under microscopic guidance. Annya held her breath. This was different from a spinal cord injury where the spinal cord was severely damaged. In this case, a clean cut would allow for severed nerves in the upper spinal cord to fuse with their counterparts in the donor's lower spinal cord.

The charge nurse lifted the head of the recipient. Annya had read her medical record. Her name was Grace, and she had widely metastasized breast cancer. She would receive a new body today. Grace had been the ideal candidate for the highly classified procedure. A neuroscience researcher trained at SUEC, loyal to the university and its mission, ambitious, psychologically stable, single, no human attachments. A smart and courageous young woman caught in the grip of an incurable cancer. Grace had signed the consent form for an experimental body transplantation without hesitation, grabbing the opportunity of a second life with both hands.

Annya stared at Grace's head. It was suspended in the air, awaiting a new union. The charge nurse exsanguinated it by perfusing it with a clear liquid solution. A rebellious curl of brunette hair escaped from beneath the head's blue drape, framing delicate brows above eyes closed in slumber. Tubes snaked from Grace's mouth and severed neck, whispering of a life suspended.

The head nurse at the other operating table lifted the head of the donor. Annya had read her medical record as well. A twenty-eight-year-old nurse who had committed suicide by shooting herself in the head. Her head had thick, gaping, blood-encrusted wounds at each temple. Her eyes were severely swollen and surrounded by dark red and blue hemorrhages. On one side of the head, the calvarium had been blown away, providing a direct view of blood-covered meshed brain tissue. That brain was clearly beyond revival.

Both heads were hanging in the air above the patients now. The surgeons stepped back. The nurses unlogged the surgical tables, moved the table with Grace's metastases-consumed body out of the way, and rolled the table with the healthy body toward Grace's released head. The chief surgeon and his team closed in again and carefully adjusted Grace's head toward her new body.

Annya's eyes followed every move as she watched gloved hands fusing the two spinal cords with precision, utilizing chitosan-polyethylene glue to reconstitute damaged cell membranes. The assistant surgeons helped to stabilize and fuse the vertebral bodies with orthopedic plates and screws. The crucial part was done. Grace's brain was connected to the donor's spinal cord.

The assistant surgeons connected the vital vessels—the carotid artery, which carried blood from the heart to the head, and the jugular vein, which carried blood back from the head to the heart—a pivotal step to enable the donor's blood circulation and provide blood to the transplanted head. Clamps to the vessels were released, and the new heart pumped blood from the transplanted body into Grace's head and brain.

Holding their breath, everyone stared at the screen that

showed the patient's vital signs and EEG. The monitor first showed steady lines, then a rhythmic pulse and brainwaves over all brain areas. The waves were still shallow, suppressed by anesthesia and hypothermia, but the curves held.

A collective exhale and a tremor of disbelief rippled through the room. The entire team applauded. Annya joined in. The chief nurse wiped pearls of sweat from Dr. Triveda's forehead as the circulation of the patient was established.

The assistant surgeons, a gleam of victory in their eyes, turned their attention back to Grace. They meticulously closed the trachea, the esophagus, and the delicate network of nerves along her neck. The last phase mirrored the first—they reconnected every severed muscle, recipient to donor. Finally, they sewed the final layer of skin. It was done. The procedure had been successfully completed.

Annya watched with fascination as final sutures bound flesh to flesh. The head and body had become one. She wondered how Grace would cope with her new existence. She had been desperate to escape her fate's bitter grip. Would her head govern the new body, or would the new body change her brain activity? Nobody knew that.

- 2 -

GRACE

Thursday, November 11, 2032, 9:30 a.m.

Grace forced her eyes open. A harsh bright neon light struck her with brute force. Piercing beeps from monitors amplified the dull throb in her head. The air stung with antiseptic smell.

White ceiling. White walls. Starched sheets. A hospital bed. She remembered. It had been done. A drop of sweat formed on her forehead, clinging for a moment to her right eyebrow before slowly snaking down her temple.

"She's awake!" cried a women's voice to her left. A nurse, perhaps. Grace caught a flurry of movement in the corner of her vision, followed by the hollow thud of disappearing footsteps. Grace willed her head to turn, but it remained stubbornly fixed where it was.

I can hear her. She tried to calm her racing mind. *I'm alive.* But she did not *feel* anything. Her body was gone. At least, the sensation of it. She tried to move her arms. No response. She tried to move her legs. Nothing. She summoned all her strength and fought to move, but her body refused to obey. *Her* body? Or the body she borrowed? Either way, she couldn't feel it at all. There was only the harsh press of fabric against her cheek. Hopefully there was a body. Grace tried to lift her head. She couldn't move at all.

Panic crashed over her. Had the body transplant not worked? Did she have a new body she couldn't feel? Was she completely paralyzed? More sweat erupted on her forehead, cascading down her face. The beeps of the monitors accelerated, morphing into a frantic staccato.

"Hello, Grace!" A figure materialized above her, bathed in fluorescent light, like an angel against the sun.

It was Dr. Triveda, her surgeon. "Welcome back." A warm hand adjusted the pillow and brushed her cheek. "No need to panic. Everything went according to plan. You are better than new!" The surgeon chuckled.

Well, I can't move! Grace wanted to cry. But even though her mouth opened and closed, the words wouldn't come out.

Dr. Triveda's gaze softened. "Grace, you need to be patient," she murmured. "As I said, everything went fine. Now your body needs to heal. That will take some time—and a lot of hard work."

Grace's eyes widened. She remembered. Dr. Triveda had explained it. Months of rehab. But fear had silenced her questions. Too much information would have crushed her courage to go through with the procedure. Now she craved more clarity. There were so many details they hadn't discussed. Such as waking up completely paralyzed.

"As I said, everything is fine," Dr. Triveda reassured her again. "We kept you in a drug-induced coma for three days to help your brain adjust and recover. Your EEG and EKG look good, considering the circumstances. Your heart and brain are working fine. The lab function tests for your organs look good as well."

But I cannot move—and I cannot talk! Grace opened her mouth, but words would not come out.

Dr. Triveda held her intense glare. Grace could see in her eyes that she understood her terror. "We inserted a tracheostomy tube to help you breathe," she explained with a soft voice. "It's just for the transition period. I'm sure we can remove it soon enough. We also checked your peripheral nerves with nerve conduction studies, and the response of your muscles with electromyography. All tests were positive. You will be fine, Grace. You made it!"

Grace closed her eyes. The beeps settled into a steadier rhythm, but fear still gnawed at her. The surgeon's words felt like a lifeline. She sounded so sure. Or did she just want to calm her down?

Grace had no choice but to believe her. The alternative was too bleak to contemplate.

"Did she get her sedative?" Dr. Triveda asked calmly. "She needs time to heal."

"She got the last dose at 6 a.m.," another woman's voice answered, presumably the nurse again. "I can give her another dose, if you want to put in an order?"

"Yes, she needs to get some more sleep," the surgeon answered.

Grace's thoughts started to soften. But her worries continued to flutter around in her mind, refusing to surrender to slumber. Then, another familiar voice drifted through the haze of her mind.

"I got your text that she woke up. How is she?"

"Hello, Annya," Dr. Triveda responded. "She woke up briefly but fell asleep again. We completed extensive tests, and everything looks good. But nerves don't mend overnight. It will take some time."

Grace strained to lift her heavy eyelids. But even the smallest flicker felt like a monumental effort.

"When will you start her rehab program?" Annya asked.

"As soon as she's ready," the surgeon's voice responded. "Tomorrow, if she's up for it. Baby steps, of course."

"The sooner she sees tangible progress, the better. She is a neuroscientist. Seeing results will energize her."

"Agreed. We'll begin with breathing and basic motor skills, building from there."

Exercise? I cannot move! Grace thought, her monitors picking up speed again.

There was a brief pause.

"I wonder why she did it," Annya said.

"Well, you can ask her soon enough. She confided in me a little before the surgery. She felt trapped in her dying body and desperately wanted to live. An unsatisfied hunger for life. She asked me many questions about the surgery. The technical details seemed to hold a strange allure for her."

Hunger for life? Grace scoffed internally. *I am the center of a world-altering scientific discovery.*

"The audacity of defying death with a revolutionary surgery likely outweighed her fear," Annya said.

Exactly! Grace thought. The emergency physician understood her better than the surgeon. Grace remembered her. Dr. Annya Segond had sat beside her at a recent faculty dinner. Now she checked on her in the intensive care unit. What a coincidence. Or had their encounter been orchestrated, a subtle nudge toward this very moment?

"Perhaps she was intrigued by the groundbreaking nature of the procedure before the surgery," the surgeon said. "But when she woke up today, she was very anxious."

"Of course she was. Who wouldn't be in her situation? Relearning basic functions like speaking, eating, and walking will take a lot of grit. Does she have close family or friends who could support her during this recovery period?"

"Unfortunately, her parents both died of cancer. A genetic predisposition in her family. She has no siblings, and her boyfriend left her. Her lack of attachment contributed to her selection for this project. She has nobody who will ask too many questions. But I agree with you—it makes rehab more difficult."

"Poor thing," said the emergency physician. "Will you work with her during the recovery?"

"I'm eager to see her progress and will swing by every day, but I have a very busy surgery schedule. I cannot hold her hand every day. I just don't have the bandwidth."

The silence that followed hung heavy in the air.

A tear, warm and unwelcome, escaped Grace's eye, tracing a path down her cheek. She was reborn yet still alone. Why did they talk about her like that? She wished they would leave.

"Perhaps I can help. I can visit her before or after my shift every day and help her with her recovery," the ER physician said. "I have a busy schedule as well, but I can carve out the time."

"That is very generous, Annya. You know her secret. Having someone she can truly confide in will make a huge difference."

I have a friend, Grace's mind echoed.

A warm breath tickled her cheek. "One breath at a time, one step at a time," Annya's voice whispered into her ear.

The words settled over her like a soothing balm. She drifted into a deeper slumber, repeating this mantra of hope against the tide of uncertainty.

- 3 -

GRACE

Friday, August 5, 2033, 9:30 a.m.

Sunlight streamed through expansive windows, bouncing off the polished linoleum floor of the rehabilitation ward. It was her first day without crutches. Closing the door to her tastefully decorated patient room, Grace inhaled deeply. The air was crisp and faintly scented with rosewater. The surgery had sharpened her sense of smell, making the subtle fragrance more noticeable. After all, her nose and the olfactory nerve resided in her head that still felt wholly hers. With a self-conscious tug, she adjusted the silky scarf around her neck—a veil concealing the angry red scar. She grabbed the gleaming handrail and navigated down the wide, brightly lit hallway toward the neurosurgery ward in the main hospital. A slight limp lingered, but her legs obeyed her commands. She felt a sense of pride and accomplishment.

The neurosurgery ward was on the second floor. Habit would have steered her toward the elevator, but Annya's voice echoed in her mind: *Challenge your body every day. One breath at a time. One step at a time.* Grace decided to take the stairs today. Taking a deep breath, she approached them. One by one, she mastered each step. It went better than she had thought. People around her, mostly staff, rushed by without sending her a second look. Grace took silent comfort in their indifference; it meant her movements, though slow, weren't alarming. She would practice the stairs more over the next weeks. With a relieved sigh, Grace conquered the last step and made her way to the neurosurgery clinic. The receptionist greeted her at the entrance and led her to an exam room.

She sat on the edge of the exam table, a smile playing on her lips. She felt strong and powerful after seizing the stairs. When Dr. Triveda rushed in, she raised an arm in a casual wave, the simple gesture a world away from the agonizing weeks and months of dependence.

"Good morning, Grace," Dr. Triveda exclaimed. "No crutches, huh? I spotted you from down the hall. You are a miracle in motion!"

Grace smiled. "I know. I've come a long way."

"May I see your scar?"

Grace's fingers trembled slightly as she lowered her scarf. It felt like a silent surrender.

Dr. Triveda inspected the scar and palpated it with a professional touch. She carefully tilted Grace's head, assessing the range of motion. Finally, she stepped back, a hint of satisfaction in her eyes.

"The scars are healing beautifully," she declared. "There's bound to be some stiffness with the plates and screws we used, but your pulse is strong. Overall, this looks very positive."

A soft knock echoed through the room.

"Come in," Dr. Triveda called out.

A young physician in a tailored white coat entered. Grace was surprised. Her monthly checks were always private.

Dr. Triveda caught her gaze. "This is Lu'lu, one of the junior surgeons who assisted with your surgery," she explained. "She's eager to learn about your progress. Would you mind answering a few questions?"

Grace's stomach clenched. Annya's words echoed in her head: *Keep all information about your surgery confidential.* She shifted uncomfortably on the table, her eyes darting between the two women. "I'm not sure," she answered.

Dr. Triveda offered a reassuring smile. "Lu'lu already knows everything about your surgery, Grace. I fully trust her, and I believe you can too. These follow-up exams are crucial for years to come, and while I'm always here for the big check-ins, having another skilled surgeon like Lu'lu on board ensures continuity of care."

Grace studied their faces, searching for a hidden motive. Lu'lu's expression mirrored the eagerness for knowledge that often accompanied those early in their medical careers. Grace would have preferred one-on-one meetings with her surgeon. But she didn't have an option here, did she? Perhaps discussing her progress with Lu'lu wouldn't be so bad. With a hesitant breath, she met the surgeon's curious gaze. "What would you like to know?"

Lu'lu eagerly perched on a rolling stool, her electronic notepad ready. "Can you tell me about the transition after the surgery?"

Grace's breath hitched. Her memories flooded back, a torrent of emotions engulfing her. Cancer surgery, radiation, and chemotherapy. Then, complete paralysis. The sudden loss of any control over her body had been a new dimension of terror.

"It was," she began, her voice barely a whisper, "a different kind of hell. I couldn't breathe, I couldn't speak, I couldn't move. For months, I was dependent on others for even the simplest tasks."

The young surgeon's brow furrowed. "I understand," she said gently. "That must have been difficult."

Grace's gaze drifted away. *No, you don't understand anything*, she thought. *You have no idea.*

"What were the steps back to your recovery?" Lu'lu asked.

Grace felt overwhelmed. Tears welled in her eyes.

Dr. Triveda interjected, sensing her struggle. "We started with breathing training," she explained. "To get her off the ventilator. Then, she received speech training and slowly learned to formulate words and speak again. We implanted a pacemaker to support her heart until her autonomous nervous system recovered. Her body functions had to get coordinated as well. Holding and emptying her urinary bladder, her bowel movements. From there, movements of the hands and arms. Moving her legs, moving her body. But Grace pressed through all of these challenges with deep determination." Her gaze lingered on Grace, a mix of pride and something else, perhaps a hint of awe, in her eyes.

Grace shifted uncomfortably under the scrutiny, feeling more like a study subject on display than a human being. She longed for the privacy of her room, where she could be more than a collection of scars and test results. Yet, here she was, laid bare under the junior surgeon's watchful gaze.

"What about your sensations?" Lu'lu asked, her youthful enthusiasm missing the undercurrent of tension.

Grace cleared her throat to regain her composure. "At first, I didn't feel anything at all," she whispered. "Then, I started to feel tingling sensations in different body parts. A slow creep of sensation, like a thousand ants awakening on my skin. My body was a foreign attachment I couldn't navigate. A few weeks later, the pain hit. Agonizing needles burrowing deep into different parts at random. Torture from within. The nights were the worst—endless stretches of searing pain punctuated by chilling numbness. I lived on pain meds for months. Thankfully, most of it was temporary."

"Does she still require pain medication now?" Lu'lu asked Dr. Triveda, her brow furrowed in clinical curiosity.

The surgeon nodded. "We've managed to wean her off morphine, but she still needs other pain medications. She's also on immunosuppressants, standard protocol after transplant procedures."

Lu'lu nodded eagerly. "I read the papers from Xiaoping Ren," she said. "His team grafted the head of a mouse onto another mouse's body; the grafted heads survived up to six months, thanks to immunosuppressants. I also read about the experiments by Robert White and team. They transplanted the head of a rhesus monkey on the body of another, and the animal lived for eight days."

Grace felt a shiver running down her spine. She wasn't a lab rat. As a neuroscientist, she had of course studied the experiments in animal models as well. Several scientists had transplanted the head of one animal onto the body of another. Experiments in mice, rats, dogs, and monkeys. Many early experiments had failed due to rejection of the transplanted head. Hopefully, that would not be her fate.

Dr. Triveda nodded. "Sergio Canavero was another pioneer in this field. He conducted many experiments in small and large animals, and he published a protocol for human head transplantation. But he never conducted the procedure himself. Our team substantially advanced his approach, addressing many challenges related to immunosuppression and neuroprotection."

Lu'lu nodded, her eyes gleaming. "That surgery was so much work. I remember how exhausted I was. Each severed nerve, like frayed threads, had to be meticulously rejoined. Motion control, sensory feedback—all woven back together."

Grace looked from one surgeon to the other. They were not talking with her; they were talking about her. It felt dehumanizing. Annya's words echoed in her mind: *Text me if anything feels off.* She reached for her phone and typed a single message to Annya. *SOS*. Her phone was linked to Annya's through a tracking app. The surgeons continued their hushed praise, oblivious to the silent rebellion happening under their noses.

About two minutes later, it knocked at the door and Annya's head peeked through the opening.

"Hi," she greeted them. "I have an appointment with Grace now. Are you finished here?"

The two surgeons exchanged a surprised glance. Dr. Triveda cleared her throat. "We are in the middle of her exam."

"With Lu'lu present?" Annya raised an eyebrow.

Dr. Triveda bristled slightly. "She was cleared to participate in the surgery."

"No disrespect"—Annya turned to Lu'lu, her smile turning cool—"but all information about Grace's case is classified, isn't it?"

Lu'lu flushed. "I just wanted to get her perspective for a case report," she stammered. "This could be a shoo-in for the New England Journal!"

Annya's gaze snapped to Dr. Triveda. "Please handle this." Extending a hand toward Grace, she added, "Shall we go?"

"Yes, please," Grace replied, her voice trembling slightly. She wasted no time following Annya out of the office.

"Calling me was the smartest thing you could have done," Annya said. "Tea? This will be my treat."

She had remembered that Grace didn't drink coffee. "Are you sure you have time?" she asked.

Annya's smile held a hint of mischief. "I am a workaholic, remember? Plenty of colleagues owe me a favor. And one of them is covering for me now."

A wave of gratitude washed over Grace. With Annya, any problem seemed solvable. Grace had always admired the attention garnered by the ER physician, both from patients and staff alike. Her emerald eyes held a captivating glint, her fiery red hair crackled with untamed energy, and she moved with a quiet confidence that turned heads wherever she went. Now, Grace found herself receiving similar looks, which she found invigorating—a newfound sense of being noticed.

Together, they descended the stairs, their steps echoing faintly against the sterile silence of the stairwell. They walked through the main hall and pushed through the double doors that led to the hospital garden. A refreshing morning breeze welcomed them. The sun in the dark-blue California sky cast a long shadow of the hospital building onto a perfectly manicured lawn. They followed a small path through lush rhododendron bushes, which led them to a charming kiosk nestled amidst the greenery. Annya walked over and emerged with two iced teas and a pair of mini chocolate brownies, a delightful treat to savor the moment. They settled on a nearby bench overlooking a bustling playground. Children chased each other amidst colorful swings, their laughter echoing like wind chimes.

"That was your monthly exam?" Annya asked.

Grace nodded.

"How are you feeling?"

Grace looked at the ground. "I've regained full movement, which is amazing," she said. "But there are still challenges. My arms and legs feel numb."

"Do you feel like the body belongs to you?" Annya asked gently.

"Yes and no. I feel literally as if my brain took control over a new body. The body resisted at first. But step by step, it decided to comply."

"That's a powerful way to see it," Annya said.

Grace nodded. "I've been learning about my donor," Grace continued. "Bianca. She was incredibly kind and donated her organs, even during her struggle with depression. I want to do my best to make her sacrifice count."

"That's a noble purpose," Annya acknowledged. "To honor Bianca's sacrifice. Have you managed to accept her body as yours?"

A hint of sadness crept into Grace's voice. "The hardest part is the way people react when they see my scar. I knew recovery wouldn't be easy. But I thought there would be a finish line. This seems more like a constant uphill battle."

Annya squeezed her hand. "You should be proud of yourself, Grace. You've pushed your body beyond anyone's expectations."

"I know. I'm ready to leave the hospital," Grace said. "Who knows how long this new life will last? I want to live it while I can."

Annya studied her thoughtfully. "I believe you need a few more weeks, Grace, to improve your head–body connection and mental resilience. You thought the encounter today was awful? Brace yourself. If word of your surgery gets out, the intrusion will be far more intense."

Grace circled the dark-red scar around her neck with her index finger. "Everyone stares at my scar," she whispered.

Annya nodded. "I know. I think the scarf is a good idea for now. You need to keep your surgery confidential."

Grace's jaw tightened. "They've drilled that into me."

"It's just . . . complicated." Annya sighed. "There could be ethical concerns, media frenzy . . . For your safety, it's best to keep this under wraps."

A beat of silence hung between them. "And there's something else," Annya continued, a concerned look in her eyes. "Before you leave, I think it's crucial that you receive self-defense training."

Grace blinked, surprised. "Self-defense?"

Annya nodded. "We don't know what you might face out there. We can arrange for a trainer to come to the hospital gym in the evenings. You'll learn valuable skills—how to protect yourself without drawing unnecessary attention."

Grace hesitated. "Is that necessary?"

Annya offered a small shrug. "Better safe than sorry, right?"

- 4 -

ANNYA

Tuesday, November 8, 2033, 11:30 a.m.

Annya's heart drummed against her ribs as she rushed toward the extension building of the hospital.

The loudspeaker's monotone voice cut through the air. "Code blue in the rehabilitation center."

Please not Grace, she prayed.

Grace had continued to make a marvelous recovery from her postsurgical paralysis—a true miracle. Now a code blue? It couldn't be her. Not after all they had gone through. Did hoping it wasn't Grace mean wishing ill on someone else? The thought chilled her. But she couldn't bear to lose Grace after watching her fight so hard.

Footsteps tapped closer, followed by a cheery, "Hey, Annya, I'm coming to help you!"

Annya sighed. Julius. While his enthusiasm was admirable, his lack of experience often caused more harm than good. The last time they had worked on an unconscious patient together, Julius had arrived first at the scene and forgotten to check the pulse of his patient. He had administered chest compressions on a patient with a normal heart rate, who had been merely inebriated. Julius's unwavering confidence contrasted sharply with his gaps in medical knowledge. She had often wondered if he had completed medical school based on pure merit, or if something else, like family connections, had paved his path. But one thing was undeniable: Julius possessed a genuine kindness that shone through even in his moments of professional uncertainty.

Bursting through the automatic doors, Annya scanned the

panicked faces in the lobby. An unconscious man on the floor. Perhaps in his mid-thirties. Scrubs, dark hair with wispy hints at the temples. Definitely not Grace. A nurse. A small crowd had assembled around him.

Annya kneeled beside him. No pulse. "Get a defibrillator!" she yelled at Julius, who had mirrored her action, kneeling on the opposite side of the unconscious man. Annya started chest compressions, her movements practiced and efficient.

"Are you sure he needs it?" Julius asked.

The unconscious man on the floor lay still, his face pale.

"Yes, I am very sure." Annya raised her voice. "Defibrillator!"

Julius, looking slightly panicked, fumbled with the buttons of his white coat. "Do you know where it is?" he stammered.

"Right there, Julius!" she barked, gesturing toward the elevator. "There's a bright orange box with a big red light next to the elevator. You can't miss it! Bring it here, fast!" Her gaze flickered between the unconscious man, his breaths shallow and his skin clammy, and Julius, who stared at the scene. Finally, he sprinted toward the elevator.

Annya fought the urge to run after him, but she knew she couldn't leave the patient. She continued the chest compressions. Hopefully Julius would bring back the box. Time seemed to stretch, each tick of the clock an accusation.

He finally returned with a plastic case. Annya reached out and opened it. She quickly checked the device's charge and ripped open the man's scrubs. Tattoos covered his clammy chest—two large dragons and a circular symbol of a snake devouring its own tail, an ouroboros. Annya attached adhesive pads to the head of one dragon and the ouroboros. A tense silence descended upon the crowd around them as she analyzed the heart rhythm displayed on the defibrillator's screen.

Annya spoke clearly. "Charging, step back."

Another brief hum, and then a firm yet reassuring voice from the device announced, "Ready to deliver shock."

Taking a deep breath, Annya pressed the button, sending a jolt of electricity through the patient.

The man's body flung upward and crashed back onto the floor.

Annya scrambled, her fingers flying to his carotid artery, searching for a flicker of life. Nothing. Dread settled in her stomach. She repeated the procedure, but the rhythmic beeps of the monitor fell silent, emanating a chilling emptiness. The man lay still, his eyes showing a cold, glassy emptiness.

Hurried footsteps echoed against the pavement. Two paramedics emerged, hauling a stretcher into the foyer.

"He's dead," Annya announced.

A collective gasp rippled through the crowd around them, followed by a flurry of hushed whispers.

One of the paramedics came closer and checked the pulse of the man on the floor. He nodded with a grim face.

Julius helped the paramedics lift the man's lifeless form onto the cold canvas. The man's extremities hung limply, his eyes closed. Annya provided the paramedics with a brief report. They made a few notes. Then, they wheeled the body away. The rhythmic squeak of the wheels echoed through the hospital foyer as she watched them go.

One by one, the spectators drifted away, leaving behind a heavy silence.

"Are you okay?" Julius asked.

Annya closed her eyes, a knot of worry tightening in her stomach. She couldn't afford to crumble. "I'm fine," she forced out, willing the nausea to subside. "Go back to the ER, Julius. I need to check on another patient."

Julius's brows furrowed. "Annya, you look as white as a sheet. Are you sure you're okay?"

Annya gave him a wan smile. "Just a long shift. Thanks for covering for me."

He nodded, his worry lingering in his eyes. But he turned around and disappeared through the double doors.

Annya took a moment to steady herself. She was an experienced ER physician. Yet this one—a young patient, a nurse—had slipped through her grasp. Why had she lost the man? Did he have an underlying heart condition? This did not make sense.

A prickling sensation pulled her gaze upward. Across the bustling foyer, a figure emerged. Grace. Her worn jeans were far too short and wide for her new frame. Like relics of a past existence that clung stubbornly to her new physicality. The fabric of her T-shirt stretched subtly over her curves and toned muscles. Thousands of hours of exercise and self-defense training had sculpted her.

Heads turned toward Grace, drawn by an invisible magnetism. Was it the dark-red scar that circled her neck like a morbid necklace? She had embraced her new identity and left the silk scarf behind. When people stared at her too much, she told them that she had tried to hang herself. Her low voice added to the theatrical effect and repelled the curious. Her cold response was a shield, a way to control the attention, even if it meant pushing people away. But Annya knew that, beneath the mask, Grace yearned for genuine connection, for someone to see beyond the scar and recognize the strength it took to carry it openly.

And Annya felt another force emanating from Grace. A remarkable intensity in her eyes, sharp and deep as if they had seen beyond the veil. A deep-seated confidence, unfaltering even under the weight of curious stares. It was the aura of someone who had wrestled with death and emerged transformed.

A young man attempted to weave his way into her orbit. But Grace remained a steady star, her gaze fixed on a distant point. The man retreated, shoulders slumped in defeat. A glimmer of amusement danced in Grace's eyes. Her self-sufficiency held a quiet power. She didn't need anyone's validation.

Annya's heart swelled with pride. She waved and approached her protégé. The woman returned the gesture, a faint smile on her lips. Just a few weeks ago, Grace had been full of self-doubt. Now, she exuded a captivating elegance.

"Hello, Grace. Did you witness what just happened?" Annya asked.

Grace nodded. "There's something I need to tell you, but we can't talk here," she whispered. "Too many ears. Can we go to my room?"

"Sure." Something was not right. Her sixth sense was rarely wrong.

They walked side by side, their steps muffled by the smooth tiles. Sunlight streamed through the expansive windows lining the hospital corridor. They had walked this path countless times. From the confines of a wheelchair to the tentative support of crutches, to the halting steps of recovery, and finally, to the newfound elegance of Grace's stride.

They reached a pair of double glass doors marked Rehabilitation Center. Grace swiped her ID card, and the doors opened with a soft hiss. Stepping through, they entered another corridor, this one adorned with vibrant modern paintings that offered a welcome splash of color against the sterile white walls. Grace stopped at a bright-white door on the right with the number 733. She pushed the door open, revealing a warmly lit room. Annya followed her inside, and Grace gently closed the door behind them.

Annya knew the room from countless visits. It held a sterile air despite the attempts at comfort. A hospital bed stood opposite the door, its crisp white sheets contrasting with the dark-red leather of two large armchairs flanking a coffee table. In the corner, a small workout area featured a sleek indoor bike and a yoga mat.

Grace gestured toward one of the chairs. "Would you like to sit down?"

"Sure." Annya lowered herself onto the cool leather and Grace settled beside her.

"Is something bothering you?" Annya asked.

Grace hesitated, her gaze flickering toward the door as if seeking privacy. "It's about the man . . . the one who had the heart attack."

Annya met Grace's gaze. "The nurse we tried to save? What about him?"

Grace looked back at Annya, contemplating.

"I can't help you if you don't tell me what's going on."

Grace took a deep breath. "I guess he worked here."

"On this ward?"

Grace nodded. "The weird thing is, I've been living here for months and I know everyone on staff personally. They're all carefully vetted. But I only encountered this man a few days ago. No one introduced us and I never saw him interacting with any of the other staff."

"That's strange indeed. Did he try to make contact?"

Grace nodded. "He came to see me multiple times over the past few days, whenever I was alone in my room. Each time, he'd offer to bring me a coffee."

"That was nice?"

"I only drink tea, Annya. Everyone here knows that. It felt . . . off. He had clearly not been instructed by anyone. And I'm supposed to prepare my tea by myself to train my fine motor skills."

Annya shrugged. "But this person was new?"

"That's what I first thought as well. But he was very insisting and even brought me drinks unannounced. I finally decided to take on the challenge and agreed this morning."

Annya looked at her with wide eyes. "The nurse who had a heart attack brought you your morning tea today? Did you notice anything unusual?"

"I surely did. Remember, my sense of smell has been heightened after my surgery. The tea had an unfamiliar fragrance."

Annya looked at her in awe.

"The man carried a mug as well. I feigned a problem in the bathroom," Grace whispered. "While he was occupied, I poured his tea into the vase on the table and replaced it with mine."

Annya stared at her.

"He wished me a good day and left with his mug. A few

minutes later, I heard someone gasping for breath in the hallway," she continued, her voice trembling slightly. "It was him. His face was twisted in panic as he stumbled into the foyer. I followed him at a distance. He stood for a while in the middle of the hall and stared at people who were making their way through. Then, he broke down and someone called the emergency team. You know the rest."

Annya studied Grace's face. She sat before her, tense and poised, her fists clenched at her sides. Had the surgery twisted Grace into something darker, something more volatile? Or was this sudden aggression merely a desperate attempt to protect herself?

"Where is your cup?" she asked.

Grace looked at the empty coffee table in front of them and shrugged. "My cup was here when I left the room. Someone must have removed it."

Annya tried to think. There was no evidence to support Grace's story. But it seemed implausible that she had fabricated it. What was going on?

- 5 -

GRACE

Tuesday, November 8, 2033, 12:15 p.m.

Grace shut the door behind Annya, a wave of relief washing over her after sharing the incident with the man. Annya, with her sharp mind and meticulous approach, was her best bet to find out what was going on. "We will run a full tox screen on the man," she had promised. "His rapid cardiovascular breakdown points to something specific, not a random poisoning. I will find out what killed him."

Memories of the man flashed in Grace's mind. His casual smile when he'd offered her tea, the sudden panic in his eyes, the sickening thud of his body hitting the floor. Why would he bring her poisoned tea? This had to do with her surgery. He was gone now, but she couldn't shake a gnawing sense of unease.

As she stepped back into her room, she caught her reflection in the mirror, her gaze lingering on her lean yet curvy shape and toned muscles, sculpted by weeks of disciplined workouts. Her previous body had been stocky. Not fat, but not lean either. Short neck; short, plump arms; and short legs. She had always worked out, but there was only so much you could do. Her face remained average as well. Not ugly, not pretty. Nobody had ever given her a second look. Now, a halo of curly blonde hair framed her face, a tangible change brought by the unexpected gift of the donor's bone marrow. She hadn't known that a bone marrow transplantation, which she had essentially received with the body transplant, affected the texture of her hair.

But the best part was her restored breasts. Grace remembered the ugly scar that had replaced her amputated breast after the cancer surgery, a stark line that had severed her femininity. It had chipped away at her sense of self, leaving her feeling damaged, incomplete. Her fingertips traced the gentle curves of her new breasts, a deeply satisfying sensation. They weren't just restored, they were perfect, a tangible symbol of her transformation. She had been reborn into a new existence, and she would defend it by any means possible.

Her gaze drifted downward, taking in her toned legs. All her life she had yearned for long legs like that. Her baggy jeans, relics of a past life, hung loose above her ankles. She definitely needed new pants as soon as she could get out of here. Her eyes fell on the intricate tattoo on her right ankle—a swirling serpent, its body forming a perfect circle by biting its own tail. It wasn't her style, yet somehow, on her new body, it was cute.

A smile tugged at the corner of her lips, not just from the physical change but from the sense of accomplishment it represented. *One breath at a time. One step at a time.* Each drop of sweat and each aching muscle were a testament to her dedication, a reminder of the strength she had cultivated to take command over her new body. Heads turned toward her now. This hard-won new existence was hers to cherish and protect by any means possible.

The phone's shrill ring sliced through the quiet, and the caller ID displayed *Tina (Boss)*.

Grace's stomach clenched—a familiar ache. Taking a deep breath, she answered, "Hello?"

Tina's voice, brisk and laced with a hint of impatience, filled Grace's ear. "Hey, Grace. Just checking in. I heard you're back on your feet. You cannot imagine the gossip in the lab here. Your colleagues thought you were dying. But I just learned that you got through intensive chemotherapy and are completely tumor-free now. Good for you!"

Her usual monologue offered no room for Grace to respond or interject.

"So, I wanted to check in to ask when we can expect you back in the lab. We're swamped with the deadline for our DIPUSTS project, and your skills are much needed here."

Unbelievable. Grace's hand strangled her phone. This was Tina's first call after a year? Worried about her *project*? Tina had not sent her a single get well card. Not even a text. Grace wouldn't have welcomed a pity visit, but the silence of the woman she'd worked for for four years had felt deafening. Grace pushed the thought away, focusing on the call at hand.

"I understand the urgency, Tina," she said coldly, choosing her words carefully. "Unfortunately, my recovery is taking longer than expected. I need to prioritize my health right now."

Tina didn't seem to notice the irritation in Grace's voice. "Honestly, Grace, you're making this more difficult than it needs to be. You've been out on sick leave for months while the rest of us are pulling double shifts. Have you considered how your absence affects everyone else? Frankly, we're all replaceable, but wouldn't you rather earn your living with dignity instead of relying on welfare? Just get over yourself and get to work!" Tina's voice carried a hint of anger.

That was enough. Grace loved being a scientist. She'd always had. But she couldn't endure that pressure cooker again, Tina's relentless scrutiny, the constant feeling of being on edge. Visions of late nights fueled by caffeine, missed dinners with friends, the gnawing sense of sacrificing everything for this career flashed before her eyes. Was this the life she truly desired, or was there another path, one that offered fulfillment without the suffocating pressure?

Grace's gaze fell on her figure in the mirror. Yes, she was a scientist. This time, the experiment was her own body, and the results were yet to be explored. She felt a renewed excitement, a childlike wonder at the possibilities that lay ahead. Maybe it was time to rewrite her own narrative.

"I quit," she said loud and clear, the words tasting like freedom on her tongue. This was her declaration of a future she dared to dream of.

Tina scoffed. "You are out of your mind, Grace. For your own sake, I haven't heard this. You are clearly not well. Talk with your shrink. I'll give you another week and then check in again. You have nothing, Grace. No family, no money. You need a job. I'm just trying to help."

A click echoed in Grace's ear. Tina had hung up. But her intimidating manners, once potent weapons, now felt like hollow echoes.

Grace smiled. She was far from desperate. She had just fought off an assault on her life. And she would continue to fight off whoever would attack her. Annya, her new friend, was such a wonderful role model. Smart, confident, and self-sufficient. Annya had trained her in self-defense. *That* was the support she needed. Grace felt strong and powerful. And the university pension, a lifelong reward for her brave surgery, freed her from the shackles of a draining job. She could afford a new life of self-worth and fulfillment. From now on, her circle would be filled with people who inspired her and made her heart sing. She would live her new life on her own terms.

- 6 -

JULIUS

Tuesday, November 8, 2033, 6:15 p.m.

Dr. Julius Philopator Zhang eased his yellow Lamborghini up the familiar stretch of driveway leading to his family residence in Atherton, California. After a stressful day, he found solace in the embrace of the towering cypresses that lined the driveway. He ascended a gentle rise, past meticulously manicured lawns and a gaggle of geese that were quacking excitedly. At the crest, the pristine white Georgian mansion, his home, emerged from the lush greenery.

Sliding into his habitual spot, he noticed his father's silver Lexus already parked beside him. He got out of the car and hurried up the stairs. Ever since his mother succumbed to cancer when he was a child, dinner with his father had become a sacred ritual, a space for them to connect after a busy day.

Carlos, the house manager, greeted him at the entrance. Julius handed his coat to him with a curt nod and strode purposefully through the grand entrance hall, his footsteps echoing on the polished marble floor. The scent of freshly baked bread and jasmine wafted from the formal dining room. A crystal vase, filled with delicate white blooms, graced the polished mahogany table. Two place settings, adorned with fine china, awaited their occupants.

Nathanael Zhang, CEO of OrchidBio, the largest biotech company in California, sat across the room in front of the French windows that overlooked the manicured gardens. He held a sleek tablet with a holographic display of the *New York Times.* On the table beside him, a crystal glass held a verdant liquid cradled in ice. A Green Dragon cocktail, no doubt. Tonight's menu had to be Chinese, then. Matching his drink to the cuisine was a tradition his father cherished. In the Zhang household, details held a special significance.

"Hi, Dad. I'm sorry I'm a little late," Julius said.

Nathanael Zhang glanced up briefly and adjusted his thick glasses. "What is your excuse today?" he asked with an edge of disapproval.

"We had a complex case. Cardiac arrest." A beat of silence hung in the air. "We weren't able to save the patient."

"Well, that's unfortunate. I'm sure you did the best you could."

Julius nodded slowly. His father's words, delivered with a practiced indifference, felt like a cold splash in the face. The weight of countless disappointments—low math scores, disappointing med school results, the struggle to secure a residency—crashed down on him once more. He felt like a constant failure, forever falling short of his father's expectations.

"I think I prefer business over medicine," he said. "Perhaps I should quit and start a new career. This is too nerve-racking for me."

His father met his gaze with an intensity that made Julius squirm. "We've spoken about this, Julius. Business requires a foundation. The medical field can provide you with valuable experience. You will remain until you've established a successful venture within this environment."

"I did start a business. I created robots for kids on the pediatric oncology ward."

Nathanael's expression hardened. "You mean, you hired someone to build them? And then you gave them away for free?"

"Well, yeah. I had a computer scientist and designer help, but I came up with the idea! And the kids loved them, Dad. They brought a lot of smiles to their faces."

"That's good to hear, son. But a real business needs to turn a profit. You cannot live off of charity. How do you want to support yourself when I am no longer around?"

Julius mustered a smile. "Dad, you're healthy and in great shape. I'm sure you'll live to be a hundred."

"I hope I will. But remember your mom. Fate does not always play your way."

Julius let out a long sigh, the sound echoing in the tense silence between them. "I'm exhausted, Dad. I want to move on from medicine."

Nathanael leaned back in his chair, steepling his fingers. His gaze, cool and assessing, lingered on Julius. It held a familiar weight, laden with unspoken expectations. He wanted his son to excel more, to embody a sharper, more accomplished version of himself.

"Well, I might have a business opportunity for you," he finally said. "If you can work this out, you can quit medicine and become the richest man on the planet."

"What is it?"

Nathanael Zhang waved toward the opulent armchair beside him. "Please sit down."

"With pleasure." Julius settled next to his father.

Carlos approached and quietly placed a chilled glass of diet tonic water in front of Julius, his usual pre-dinner drink. He took a long, contemplative sip.

"I've got some inside information," his father said, his voice low and conspiratorial. "SUEC has cracked the code. They've found a cure for cancer."

Julius scoffed. "Really? That's news? Isn't every research institution chasing the same dream?"

His father, undeterred, leaned forward, eyes gleaming. "Perhaps. But SUEC has crossed the finish line. This is, quite literally, huge!"

"But why haven't I heard anything about this? There'd be news everywhere if it were true."

"They're keeping it under wraps. Why, I have no idea. But with you working there, you have a unique opportunity to find out."

Julius stared at his father. "You want me to spy for you?"

His father took a sip from his cocktail. "Spy is a harsh term, son. Think of it more like . . . sharing valuable information with your old man. Apparently, a woman with terminal cancer has been cured. Now, if you could discreetly find out more about her—"

"Then what?"

"If we know what drug cured her and, most importantly, who developed it, we can offer SUEC a deal they can't refuse. We'll solve whatever's holding them back, and then"—his voice dropped to a near whisper—"we will launch the business of the century. Millions of lives saved, billions of dollars made." A thin smile played on his lips.

Julius looked at his father, thinking. He wanted to be a hero who saved lives. And he could do that from the comfort of a business office rather than the cold floor of a hospital hall. The allure was undeniable. "And how should I find that woman who was cured? People with cancer go into remission all the time."

"This is different. Apparently, this woman had incurable cancer and was left to die. But she got some wonder drug and is completely free of the tumor now. I have to know what that drug is. At all costs. You need to find out who she is and how she was treated."

"Couldn't your informant tell you that?"

"Well, she disappeared."

"What?"

"She was a physiotherapist at the rehabilitation center. She previously worked at OrchidBio and sent me an email about the cure. She wanted a cut of the business. But then she disappeared—and her email as well. I went to SUEC Hospital to find her, but her colleagues said she'd moved to Australia. My network's vast, son, but even they couldn't find her there."

Julius thought about the man with the cardiac arrest in the rehabilitation center. "What do you think happened to her?"

"Maybe she ruffled some feathers at SUEC or with the authorities. Makes you wonder, doesn't it? If something this big is true, who decides when the world's ready for it?"

Julius studied his father, a knot tightening in his stomach. "And now you want to drag me into this? What if *I* disappear?" He looked at his father, searching for a flicker of empathy, a hint that his safety mattered.

His father's brows furrowed, carving deep lines across his forehead. "There's always a risk involved, son, in anything worth doing. But whoever pulled this stunt will think twice about crossing me. I want you to lead the biggest business of the century. *That* would make me proud!"

Carlos entered the room with a plate of oysters. "Dinner is ready, sir," he announced.

They both rose from their armchairs and walked over to the dining table. Julius gnawed on his lip. He was so ready to quit medicine. If he had to find a new business first, this might be a good assignment. He was good with people; they loved him. He could uncover a secret. That was one of the few things he was good at. Perhaps he could finally meet his father's expectations.

"I'll see what I can find out," Julius promised.

His father patted his shoulder. "That's my son."

- 7 -

ANNYA

Wednesday, November 9, 2033, 8:30 a.m.

Annya gestured to the open door of the shared physicians' office in the ER of SUEC Hospital, her hand hovering in a welcoming invitation. "Come in, Angus," she said.

The FBI director hesitated. "Are you sure you have time to see me before your next shift starts?" he asked her, his voice laced with concern. His perfectly ironed suit, crisp and professional, couldn't fully contain the hints of defined muscle it skimmed. But it was his eyes that captivated her. They were the serene blue of the Pacific Ocean, pulling her in like the tide.

"For you, I'll always make time," she whispered, placing a lingering kiss on his lips. Angus gently pushed her into the office and tried to embrace her for more, but she pulled away. This was not the appropriate place or time. They had to talk about business. His gaze followed her, a silent plea lingering in his eyes. Their bond had blossomed despite their demanding careers and the relentless scrutiny of the CIA and the FBI. Their superiors disapproved that they were dating, but what could they do?

Annya smiled. "I'm on the nine a.m.–six p.m. shift today. So we have about thirty minutes." She closed the door behind them with a soft click and waved toward the single desk in the middle of the room. It was overwhelmed by a hulking computer, two chairs facing each other across it. "Please sit."

They settled into the cold metal chairs.

"Did you find out who the man with the heart attack was?" she asked. "He didn't work as a nurse at SUEC, that much is clear."

"He operated as a contractor on the dark web, offering a range of services—theft, betrayal, intimidation, you name it. He had two arrests on his record and spent a year in jail. However, murder was not on his list of offenses. Perhaps that's why he was unsuccessful in assaulting Grace. He appeared to be a minor player, not on the radar of federal authorities."

"And did the forensic lab find out if he was poisoned?"

"Yes, his bloodwork confirmed traces of belladonna. We placed an undercover FBI agent in the kitchen of the rehab center after the incident. He intercepted another attempt to poison Grace's food before it reached her. We haven't identified the culprit. Not yet."

Annya had grown fond of Grace over the past few months, visiting her every day and witnessing her remarkable recovery. The news of a threat to her struck her like a personal offense. Who in their right mind would want to harm her? Well, there were probably a million reasons. Pharmaceutical giants desperate to protect their profits. Politicians eager to capitalize on her cure. Foreign powers hungry for a medical marvel. Annya met Angus's gaze. "She needs to be relocated," she said with a resolute tone. "I'll speak with Dr. Triveda to expedite her discharge. I think she's ready."

Angus nodded. "Make it a surprise to the criminals. If they suspect we're on to them, they will think of other modes of attack."

"Do you have any suspicions who is behind this?"

Angus shook his head. "Not yet. We have to consider both domestic and international threats."

"Until we identify the attacker, she cannot return home," Annya replied, her voice firm. "We need to find her a safe haven, somewhere secure and discreet."

"We could move her to a safe house?"

"That could be an option if the situation gets worse. However, for the time being, it's crucial for her to receive follow-up exams here at SUEC. She's still experiencing significant sensory issues.

"So, you want to locate her somewhere close? Where?"

"I don't know yet. But I will figure something out."

There was a knock at the door. Then, it opened slowly.

"Hello, Annya, can I come in?" It was Julius.

Annya sighed. "Of course," she said with a hint of sympathy. This was a shared office, and he was at the end of his 1–9 a.m. shift, the least popular shift in the ER. He surely was eager to get home.

Julius entered the office with a fuming coffee in his hand. "Hello, Agent Weber," he said cheerfully. "What brings you by? Should I be worried?"

Angus smiled back. "Well, Julius, I'm not looking for your boyfriend this time, if that's what you mean."

Julius gave him a probing look. Annya remembered that his boyfriend was a wanted cyberhacker, a stark contrast to Julius's own moral compass. Julius bent the rules when necessary, but he never crossed the line into illegal territory.

"Are you looking for the woman who was cured of terminal cancer?" Julius asked casually. He took a sip from his coffee.

Annya and Angus stared at him.

"Who told you about a woman who was cured of terminal cancer?" Angus asked with an intimidating tone.

Julius's gaze bounced between them, his voice dropping apologetically. "Sorry if I misspoke. I can't recall who mentioned her, but it sounded like a remarkable story. What drug did she get, again?"

Annya exhaled. Julius had a vast circle of friends, and he had apparently picked up something. The staff on the rehabilitation ward talked about Grace's amazing cure all the time. But none of them knew the secret of the body transplant. The official story was that she had received high dose chemotherapy and spine surgery for metastases. She had slowly recovered from both and was in complete remission now. Perhaps Julius had talked with one of the staff.

"Her name is Grace. Would you like to meet her?" Annya asked lightly.

Julius's tired eyes widened. "I would be delighted," he said.

Angus looked at Annya. "Why would Julius want to meet her?"

"Julius lives in a highly secured mansion in Atherton," she

explained with a sly smile. “A place with high fences, security cameras, and a single guarded entry. I think he can help us with our problem.”

Julius looked from Angus to Annya. “I don’t understand what my home has to do with anything?”

Annya gestured towards an empty chair beside Angus. “Please sit down. We have a proposition for you.”

- 8 -

GRACE

Wednesday, November 9, 2033, 11:45 a.m.

Grace looked out of the window of Julius's roaring Lamborghini. Excitement bubbled in her chest, tinged with a prickling unease. The bucket seat felt strangely confining, the leather cool against her worn jeans. Julius navigated the winding driveway with practiced familiarity, the manicured landscape around them a stark contrast to the dusty streets in San Francisco, her previous home. The air was heavy with the scent of wealth. Flowers, perhaps, or blossoming trees? In the distance, a colossal white house materialized, its grandeur both awe-inspiring and intimidating. This was the pinnacle of privilege, a stark contrast to the cramped apartment she had shared with her ex-husband.

Grace's gaze drifted to the young ER physician beside her. He was perhaps three years older than her—or five years if she counted the age of her new body—and ridiculously attractive. A physically fit young man in his early thirties, with short dark hair that framed a face etched with the beginnings of laugh lines. The crisp lines of a tailored jacket hinted at a refined taste, while his worn leather satchel on the back seat whispered tales of past adventures. When he glanced at her through his sun glasses, a spark of rebellion peeked through his impeccably composed demeanor.

She pointed at a herd of snow-white birds on the sun-drenched lawn. "Are there geese on your property?" she asked. Some of the birds grazed diligently. Others held their heads high, eyes fixed on the approaching car.

"Yes, they are better guards than dogs," Julius explained.

"They are very territorial and make loud noises to frighten off intruders. And unlike dogs, they are completely incorruptible. Offer one a stale cracker, and you'll get a serenade that'll wake the dead."

"Fascinating!" Grace exclaimed.

Julius chuckled. "We mostly let them loose at dusk. During the day, they have a designated area to roam, but they still keep a watchful eye. Trust me, they don't miss a thing."

Grace found herself drawn to his disarming smile that sometimes emerged beneath his stern expression. It was both mischievous and refreshingly youthful. She somehow sensed that he, too, had weathered his share of hardships. When they'd met at the rehabilitation center, he had invited her for a coffee. Grace had been reluctant at first, given her recent experiences. But Annya had assured her that Julius was trustable. While Annya prepared the discharge paperwork, they had gone to the coffee shop next to the hospital and instantly connected. They both had lost their mothers too soon, they fondly recalled their time at SUEC, and they discovered that they both yearned for something new, not sure yet what, exactly.

Julius hadn't been briefed on her body transplant. That was too risky. Instead, Annya had explained that Grace had undergone an experimental new chemotherapy and needed to be discharged. Recently divorced, she required a temporary home with a physician overseeing her recovery. Her treatment might attract media attention, but SUEC wanted to keep it confidential until more data about her recovery were available. Julius had surprisingly few questions and immediately offered her to stay at his home for a few days. They had plenty of space.

That had been an understatement. The Georgian mansion before them was a colossal masterpiece. Its symmetrical façade was adorned with delicate fretwork that gleamed in the sunlight. Tall mullioned windows framed with mahogany shutters were perfectly spaced across the front. As they came closer, a grand portico, supported by a row of imposing Doric columns, came into view. Above, a series of dormer windows punctuated the steeply pitched roof, which was covered in slate tiles that shimmered subtly in the light. Ivy climbed gracefully up one side of the mansion.

Julius pulled the car to a stop with a soft hiss of brakes. He exited the car, strode purposefully around the vehicle and opened the passenger door. With an outstretched hand, palm up, he offered Grace a silent invitation. She quickly pinched her arm to confirm it wasn't a dream. Steeling herself, she grasped his hand and climbed out of the vehicle.

They ascended the broad staircase. At the top, a man in a tuxedo materialized from the shadows.

"Hello, Mr. Zhang," he said. "Who is gracing our presence today?"

"This is Grace." Julius turned toward her. "This is Carlos, our house manager."

"Nice to meet you!" She smiled at the man, extending her hand in greeting.

The man inclined his head slightly and gracefully swung the double doors wider. "Welcome to the Zhang residence."

"Grace will stay with us for a few days," Julius explained.

"Certainly," Carlos answered. "Shall I fetch her luggage?"

"She doesn't have any," Julius said. "This was a spontaneous decision. She was just released from the hospital."

The manager's gaze swept over her with a hint of disapproval. Her worn-out jeans, while practical and comfortable, seemed a world away from the formal elegance here.

"Perhaps I could contact Ms. Walker to arrange some suitable attire?" A faint crease deepened between his brows as his eyes snagged on the circular scar around Grace's neck.

Grace felt a flush erupting on her face. She bit her tongue to swallow her usual sarcastic comment. Perhaps it had been a bad idea to come here after all. She felt completely misplaced.

Julius pretended not to notice. "Great idea," he answered. "Something that covers her scar, please. Ideally before the dinner tonight."

Carlos nodded, exchanging a knowing glance with Julius. "Which room would you prefer for Miss Grace to stay?"

"The guest room beside my suite, please. Then, she can easily reach me if she needs anything."

"Certainly," Carlos replied smoothly. "I'll have it prepared immediately."

Julius guided Grace into the grand entrance hall, where golden light poured in through stained glass windows, casting a warm glow on the polished marble floor. They passed a magnificent V-shaped marble staircase, flanked by ornately carved columns, and approached a small mahogany door at the back of the room. Julius opened it, revealing a surprisingly cozy family room with expansive French doors at the far end. Beyond the glass, a small terrace overlooked a lush garden. Inside, a cream leather sofa, its cushions invitingly rumpled with a tapestry of pillows, sat nestled before a crackling fireplace. Floor-to-ceiling bookshelves, overflowing with well-worn leather-bound volumes, flanked the hearth. The air was heavy with the comforting aroma of woodsmoke and freshly baked bread.

Julius collapsed onto the sofa with a sigh. "Would you like some ciabatta?" He gestured toward a large plate on the coffee table. "Or should I ask Carlos to prepare us something more substantial?"

Grace couldn't suppress a smile as looked at the assembly of about twenty ciabatta pieces. That could feed an army. "This is perfect," she said, settling beside Julius. Here, amidst the warmth and inviting aromas, the imposing marble hall felt like a world away.

Julius reached for the tomato bread. It toppled over, scattering tomato bits all over his pristine suit and the sofa. "Oh no," he exclaimed.

Grace handed him a napkin, chuckling. "No big deal," she said. "Looks like you have plenty of backup, don't you?"

They both laughed. Together, they picked up the fallen pieces and Julius fetched another slice.

"So, you're in complete remission now?" he asked between two bites.

"Yes, I am," Grace admitted. "I see it as a second chance. Honestly, I didn't think I'd make it."

"What did they give you to achieve such a remarkable recovery?" Julius asked lightly, his gaze lingering on her.

She felt a wave of unease. "I'm afraid I can't discuss that."

"Why not?"

She hesitated, her mind racing. She hadn't prepared for this conversation and struggled to find a way to explain the scar without revealing the truth. Fortunately, they were interrupted by a woman in a designer suit who entered the room. Her sharp eyes, framed by tortoiseshell glasses, scanned the room, pausing briefly on Grace before settling on Julius.

"Hello, Mr. Zhang," she greeted him. "You requested my assistance?"

"Hello, Fay. Yes, indeed," Julius responded. "This is Grace. She'll be staying with us for a while. Could you please arrange a selection of suitable attire for her? We'll need something appropriate for daytime, something elegant for dinner—perhaps a party if the occasion arises—and a comfortable nightgown."

"Certainly, Mr. Zhang," Fay replied, a smile playing on her lips. She extended a hand to Grace. "It's a pleasure to meet you, Grace. We haven't had a lady visitor in quite some time. Please follow me and we'll get you settled in."

"I'll catch a nap in the meantime," Julius announced. "I just finished a long night shift." He sent Grace a tired smile. "We'll convene in the dining room at six p.m. Fay can show you where it is. I'll introduce you to my father."

A knot of apprehension tightened in Grace's stomach. The mansion with its service personnel was overwhelming. The butler at the door eying her with his critical gaze, the designer seizing her up like a dress form. Julius' mention of his father added another layer of formality.

With a curt nod, Julius disappeared down the hallway, leaving Grace stranded on a plush island in the cavernous room. The opulence seemed to press in on her: The high ceilings, the stucco moldings, the ornately framed paintings on the walls, and the kind of delicately patterned rug she'd only ever seen in magazines.

But Fay didn't leave her much time to contemplate, ushering her up the stairs.

- 9 -

JULIUS

Wednesday, November 9, 2033, 5:30 p.m.

Julius felt refreshed after his nap. He stretched and pushed himself out of the embrace of the chaise lounge. The afternoon sun had begun its descent, casting long shadows across his room. He walked to his desk and brushed against a familiar imperfection in the smooth surface. Finding the disguised compartment, his fingers extracted an unregistered burner phone. A memorized number later, he was connected to Rolando

"Hey, Julius, what's up?" said Rolando's familiar deep voice. Julius winced internally. Their bond was a whirlwind—passionate encounters punctuated by chilling absences that stretched for weeks. A purely physical tie, undeniably thrilling. But Julius yearned for stability, a connection beyond stolen moments.

He remembered Grace's excitement when they'd driven up the hill to the Zhang residence, her infectious laughter, the way her eyes seemed to crackle with unspoken energy, and the fleeting brush of her fingers against his arm. He hadn't reacted, but he had noticed. He wished it had been Rolando.

"I haven't seen you for weeks," he said. "I miss you."

"I miss you too, Julius," Rolando said flatly. "I'm sorry, I'm working on an important project."

"What is it this time?"

"Believe me, you don't want to know. It's for your own safety. Let's just say I'm taking steps to redistribute the scales between the rich and the poor a bit."

Julius sighed. Rolando was a cyberhacker who considered

himself a modern Robin Hood. That was part of the problem. He was constantly on a mission.

"My father's throwing a gala for his investors tomorrow night at the California Palace," Julius said. "It will be a big event, and I thought maybe you could join me?"

A beat of silence stretched between them. "I'm sorry, Julius," Rolando finally said. "The FBI is still hot on my heels. I cannot risk that kind of exposure."

"There will be hundreds of guests, Rolando. Do you really think you are so important that the FBI will single you out among a crowd?"

"Yes, I do, Julius. Especially when I'm done with my new gig here."

Julius released a frustrated sigh. "How can we have a future if we can never be together in public?"

"We will have a future, Julius," Rolando replied, his voice softening slightly. "We just have to be smart about it. I'll come see you as soon as this is done, I promise. It won't take much longer."

"Whatever you say." Julius felt a cold anger swelling in his chest. "Just don't be surprised if I find other company in the meantime."

"Julius, don't act like a child. I promise I'll come to see you before the weekend."

"I'm sick of empty promises," Julius spat, and hung up. Perhaps it was time for a change.

He threw on a fresh white shirt and stomped down the marble staircase. A sweet yet melancholic melody drifted from the dining room. Chopin, perhaps? The familiar notes were a stark juxtaposition to the raw intensity of his phone conversation. The music captivated him somehow, washing over him like a gentle tide.

In the dining room was a woman he hardly recognized. Grace, transformed. She stood in the center of the dining room, bathed in the chandelier's warm glow. A sleek scarlet cashmere dress clung to her curves, its high neckline a stark contrast to the vulnerability he'd glimpsed earlier. Gone was the woman in cheap jeans; in her place stood a woman of elegance and quiet power. Her hair, meticulously styled in an updo, framed her face, a few tendrils escaping in a touch of playful defiance. There was a hint of scarlet on her lips, and golden earrings cascaded down her neck.

Grace was engaged in a lively discussion with his father, their conversation a blur of animation. Julius was surprised by the ease with which she conversed with his dad. His father had apparently forgotten his pre-dinner drink. Grace's unexpected appearance had clearly stolen his attention. As Julius entered, their conversation faltered, both heads turning toward him.

"Julius, I am delighted to meet your new friend," his father said with a broad smile.

Was that admiration in his gaze? "The delight is all mine," Julius answered, looking at the transformed woman in front of him. "Grace, you look amazing!"

"Your designer did a great job!" She beamed. "I feel beautiful!"

"You *are* beautiful!" he exclaimed.

Carlos arrived with a set of china cradled in his arms. "Forgive me, Mr. Zhang," he murmured, "but I wasn't certain Miss Grace would be joining you for dinner this evening."

Julius met Carlos' gaze. He'd explicitly mentioned Grace staying over, yet the mahogany table held only two place settings.

"Thank you, Carlos," his father said with practiced nonchalance. "Would you take a photo of Julius and Grace, please? I think they look great together!"

"Of course." The manager set down the china and walked over to them.

Grace's smile bloomed as she looked at Julius. He felt a bit uncomfortable. His father was a man of calculated gestures, not affection. But he played along. He stepped closer to her and gently placed his arm around her shoulders. Grace leaned in slightly, the subtle contact sending a surprising jolt through him. Carlos's phone flashed once, twice, thrice, capturing the carefully constructed tableau. With a shared sense of awkwardness, they retreated.

The music changed to a slow melody of cello intermixed with Chinese glides and the erhu. The tunes felt magical, old and wise.

"Is this Tan Dun?" Grace asked. "'Crouching Tiger'?"

"Grace, my dear, your knowledge of classical composers is truly impressive!" His father's voice boomed.

"I find this music quite captivating," Grace mused. "It has a healing quality to it."

Nathanael Zhang turned toward Julius, a sharp glint in his eye. "Should we keep this as our accompaniment to dinner tonight? What do you think, Julius?"

"Sure, great idea." Julius looked at his father. Music hadn't accompanied their dinner since his mother's passing. Now, his father was orchestrating a charade.

"So, you two met in the hospital?" his father asked cheerfully.

"Yes, we did," Grace confirmed, her gaze lingering on Julius. A playful smile tugged at the corner of her lips as she tucked a stray strand of hair behind her ear.

"Are you also a physician?"

"I am a neuroscientist. But I recently quit my job."

"Is that so?" Nathanael Zhang gave her a probing look.

Julius felt a surge of protectiveness wash over him. He knew Grace's dream was to take a break, to savor life after her grueling battle with cancer. But revealing that here felt like inviting ridicule.

"Grace was a patient at SUEC Hospital," he explained. "She had terminal cancer and was cured. She is in complete remission now and is taking some well-deserved time off."

"She is a cancer survivor?" Nathanael looked at Julius. "Do you mean *the* patient who survived?"

"Yes, she is," Julius confirmed, his voice tight.

"Fascinating," Nathanael Zhang said slowly, leaning forward.

Grace darted a confused look at Julius.

"Tell me, Grace, what cutting-edge treatment did SUEC

employ to achieve such a remarkable recovery?" Nathanael asked.

Grace's gaze shifted to him, her smile faltering. "I'm sorry, I don't want to talk about it," she said curtly.

Nathanael winked conspiratorially: "Everyone's buzzing about SUEC's advancements. A hint wouldn't hurt, would it?"

Grace exhaled sharply. "I'm sorry, this is a personal matter and I'm not comfortable discussing it."

"Of course," Nathanael Zhang said with strained cheerfulness. "Let's move on to something lighter, shall we?" He glanced toward the corner, where the house manager had retreated discreetly. "Carlos," he boomed, "wine for everyone!"

The house manager uncorked a bottle of white wine and poured it into their glasses. Then, he left the room, only to return moments later with a large tray. He carefully placed a shimmering platter of oysters on ice at the center of the mahogany table. Beside it, he arranged a crystal bowl overflowing with glistening mignonette sauce, speckled with fresh herbs and a hint of red pepper, alongside a dish of shaved horseradish.

Julius had had this starter countless times, yet he enjoyed watching Grace's wide eyes take in the splendor. Her gaze flicked to him, seeking reassurance. He offered a subtle nod, and a warmth bloomed in his chest. This shared pleasure felt good.

They ate for a while in silence, the classical music weaving a tapestry of ethereal melodies in the background. The gentle strains of a flute drifted through the air, carried on the warm undercurrents of the cello.

Grace finally broke the silence. "This is absolutely delicious!" she exclaimed, her voice tinged with genuine awe.

Julius couldn't suppress a smile. She was a breath of fresh air.

Carlos reappeared with a silver platter that held a glistening sea bass, surrounded by a colorful array of vegetables. The air hummed with the aroma of garlic butter and a hint of lemon. With a flourish, he placed the dish on the table. "Our main course," he announced, "pan-roasted sea bass."

Grace eagerly accepted a large piece and Carlos ladled a generous portion of yellow sauce on it. Then, he served Julius and Nathanael. He walked back to the kitchen and brought a dollop of creamy mashed potatoes, their scent infused with the earthy aroma of truffle oil. Finally, he presented a bowl overflowing with a vibrant medley of sautéed green beans and sugar snap peas.

Nathanael continued the conversation. "This latest political squabble at the senate is a farce," he declared, swirling the golden wine in his glass. "All bluster and no action. Reminds me of a bull in a China shop."

Grace met Nathanael's gaze with confidence. "The optics are certainly poor," she conceded, "but perhaps it's more than just grandstanding. Maybe there's a deeper reason for the impasse. Have you considered the recent Supreme Court decision and its potential impact on the proposed environmental regulations?"

Nathanael's amusement faltered. "Interesting point, Grace. I hadn't connected those dots. Maybe the environmental bloc is digging in their heels in anticipation of the court challenge." He cleared his throat. "Anyway, I'm more concerned about the stock market. It's been a rollercoaster lately."

Grace leaned forward. "Indeed. It seems the tech bubble might be showing some cracks."

Julius watched, captivated by the intellectual dance unfolding before him. Grace wasn't just holding her own; she was engaging his father in a stimulating conversation, seamlessly weaving in references to recent political events, economic reports and potential market shifts. He had rarely seen his dad so impressed by someone outside his inner circle.

The conversation shifted, encompassing the recent exhibit at the San Francisco Museum of Modern Art. Grace spoke of the bold brushstrokes and thought-provoking themes, her words revealing a genuine appreciation for the artist's vision. Nathanael, a self-proclaimed traditionalist, listened intently, occasionally interjecting with his own opinions on art and its place in society.

As the night wore on, Julius couldn't help but feel a surge of admiration for Grace. Her ability to navigate this high-powered environment, to seamlessly converse with his intimidating father on a wide range of topics, was truly impressive.

As the last morsels of the sea bass disappeared, Grace dabbed her lips with a linen napkin and rose gracefully. "Excuse me, gentlemen," she announced, and stepped out of the room.

Nathanael, ever the opportunist, seized the moment. Leaning forward, he lowered his voice to a whisper. "This is *the* cancer survivor we talked about?" he inquired, his eyes twinkling. "The one who was cured with that miraculous treatment?"

Julius glanced briefly toward the open door. "Yes, that's her," he confirmed, a touch of pride coloring his voice.

Nathanael's eyebrows shot up. "Extraordinary! Cognitive problems after chemo are an issue, but she is remarkably sharp. It reflects well on the treatment, doesn't it? How did you secure her presence here tonight?"

Julius smiled. "Let's just say," he replied, "my negotiation skills have improved considerably."

A hint of skepticism flickered across Nathanael's face. "There's more to it, Julius," he pressed. "You haven't magically acquired the Midas touch overnight."

Julius met his father's gaze, frustration welling up in his chest. His father's comments held a constant undercurrent of dismissal. But before he could respond, the gentle click of footsteps cut through the air.

Grace reappeared with a radiant smile and resumed her seat. "The flowers in the restroom are exquisite," she said. "A true feast for the eyes. And they smelled so good!"

Julius noted a predatory glint in his father's eyes as he looked at her.

"Julius just told me about your miraculous cure from cancer." Nathanael Zhang leaned forward. "SUEC has some truly groundbreaking treatments in the pipeline, wouldn't you say?"

Grace offered a hesitant nod. "So I've heard."

"You battled metastatic cancer, spread throughout your entire body?"

Grace's jaw clenched slightly. "Yes, that's correct."

"You received a completely novel treatment?" He leaned in further, his eyes gleaming. "That's absolutely fascinating. We're honored to have you here, Grace. Perhaps a little more information wouldn't be out of the question?"

Grace shifted uncomfortably in her chair. "I'm truly sorry, Mr. Zhang," she said, her voice firm. "As I said earlier, my treatment is a private matter."

Of course, of course," he said lightly, waving a dismissive hand.

Carlos arrived just then with a tray of three chocolate mousses. Nathanael raised his hand. "Not for me, Carlos, thank you," he said, his gaze shifting back to Grace. "I have some tasks that require my attention. But by all means, please enjoy your desserts. I'll leave you two to catch up."

His eyelids fluttered slightly as he cast a quick glance at Julius. Julius inclined his head in a barely noticeable nod, a glint of shared understanding passing between them. The assignment was clear.

- 10 -

WASSILY

Thursday, November 10, 2033, 9 a.m.

Weaving through his cramped apartment in the Mission District of San Francisco, Wassily entered his miniature kitchen. His and Grace's kitchen, to be precise. Her name was still on the renter's contract as co-tenant, but she had left more than a year ago and never returned. He had moved her belongings to a few boxes in the basement, just in case she needed them. Not that there was much to begin with. Certainly nothing valuable.

Sunlight slanted through the grime-streaked window above the sink, illuminating a sliver of a narrow street and a solitary palm tree struggling for life. Wassily snagged a mug with a faded SUEC sign from the drying rack. A quick rinse under the faucet, and it was ready for duty. With the practiced efficiency of a man who knew his limitations in this shoebox, he cranked the faucet to hot. There was no space for a water heater, so he had gotten used to bypassing the kettle.

While the water ran, he rummaged through a dented tin canister beside the sink. He found a lone tea bag and a crumpled sugar packet—liberated treasures from his latest hospital visit. Every penny counted. With a swirl, he mixed it all together and the familiar scent of black tea filled the tiny kitchen. Carefully, Wassily balanced the mug and a chocolate chip cookie in a napkin to the living room.

He settled on his futon, the worn fabric a familiar comfort. Cradling the mug in both hands, he felt the warmth radiating through the ceramic, chasing away the chill of the San Francisco morning fog. With a contented sigh, Wassily kicked his feet up on the coffee table and propped his iPad against an empty pizza box.

He hated his tiny apartment. It mirrored his life—cramped and devoid of the luxuries he craved. He couldn't afford anything nice.

He glanced at the overflowing bookshelf across the room. Seven dog-eared copies of *The Art of Selling Anything* sat nestled amongst biographies of famous socialites and self-help gurus. They were his weapons in a war he wasn't winning.

His parents, with their brood of seven, had offered a simple message when it came to college: "Get a job." It felt like a betrayal, even now. Balancing study and work had been a nightmare for most students, and especially for him. Grace had made it look easy, but then again, Grace was a genius. He wasn't.

For a while, Wassily had embraced the bohemian artist life. Like his namesake, Wassily Kandinsky. His grandma had given him ten dollars every time he'd shown up with a painting at her nursing home. He'd hoped to expand from there by taking a painting class, creating oil paintings, and selling them online. It hadn't been as successful as he had hoped.

He gazed at a particularly violent-looking abstract oil painting propped against the wall. It resembled a road rage incident more than a landscape. But didn't Kandinsky's paintings look like that as well? It wasn't the art itself; it was a matter of how to sell them. But unfortunately, his signature wasn't quite as recognizable.

He led out a frustrated sigh. His application to change his last name to Kandinsky had been a brilliant plan—a shortcut to artistic fame by feigning descent from the master himself. But the city of San Francisco demanded ironclad proof before allowing the change. This city didn't support artists like him. Perhaps one day he'd move to Las Vegas and try again.

For now, though, a more immediate problem loomed. Rent was due, and Zuri, his new girlfriend, wasn't exactly a financial windfall. Her trust fund had been a temporary balm, but her personal philosophy was keeping, not sharing. Those endless questions about his artistic endeavors were starting to grate as well. Zuri's usefulness had reached its expiration date.

Wassily smoothed his hair. His charm was a finely tuned weapon honed over years. It was time to find a new roommate, someone less inquisitive and more pliable. Zuri could pack her bags.

"Times are tough for everyone," he muttered. "A man can't be expected to go it alone." He needed a woman who appreciated having a man like him by her side. He would make her feel special and ensure she had a good time. In return, she could move in and help with the rent. It was a fair transaction, really – a service with a side of financial security.

But where could he find a woman who could afford the life he deserved? Wassily tapped a search into the browser on his iPad: *richest people in the bay area.*

An update from the Zhang family popped up on the OrchidBio blog—an investor party at the California Palace. The Zhang heir and his glamorous date were prominently featured. The woman looked somehow familiar. He clicked on the accompanying photo and zoomed in. His disbelief morphed into astonishment. *Grace?* That was his ex-wife in a hot dress, new hair and all. She looked amazing.

A pang of regret lanced through him. It hadn't been his finest hour, getting caught with Zuri while Grace was supposedly at the clinic. He'd thought that chemotherapy took all day. Why had she come back early? A cruel twist of fate, that was all. Clearly not his fault. He'd tried. He'd offered a shoulder to cry on. But a man had needs, and Grace, bless her brilliant mind, had been far too focused on battling her own war to understand his.

The divorce, swift and merciless, still rankled. Not much of a loss since she was as broke as he was. He'd naïvely expected a scientist at a prestigious institution like SUEC to be wealthy, only to discover she wasn't faculty. He had learned the hard way that academia rarely led to riches, even for professors. It had been better to move on.

A few weeks ago, Zuri had told him that Grace had been cured. He had shrugged it off. Good for her. But now he stared at her photo on his tablet. He hadn't expected a *transformation.* SUEC had claimed most of her time during their marriage. Now, it had done something good after all. This wasn't just a change in hairstyle or wardrobe; his ex-wife looked like an entire new woman. Better than new. Perfect figure. Sexy haircut. Expensive dress. And she must have done a lot of exercise. Grace had never been a looker, but that woman there could make a lot of money with her appearance. As a model, actress, social media influencer. The possibilities were endless. *That* was the opportunity he'd been waiting for. The article mentioned a charity event tied to the investor party. He had to go. Zuri, with her social circle, could get him in. But he had to find a way to use her connections without taking her along. He would win Grace back.

- 11 -

GRACE

Thursday, November 10, 2033, 9 a.m.

Silence reigned in the house. Nathanael Zhang and Julius had both left for work early in the morning. Grace had slept long, enjoying her luxury bedroom. Or perhaps suite was a better expression for the expansive room, which was bathed in sunlight. The crisp sheets and plush comfort of her canopy bed had provided a much more sumptuous sleep than the sterile confines of the hospital bed that had been her companion for the past few months.

Grace burrowed deeper into the pillows, closing her eyes. This all still felt like a dream. Images of Julius flickered in her mind—the sharp angles of his face, the warmth in his dark eyes, the way his smile crinkled the corners just slightly. He was undeniably handsome, but that was just the surface. It was the way he made her feel seen, truly seen, that sent a delicious shiver down her spine. When they talked, he held her gaze and responded with thoughtful comments, revealing that he'd truly listened. Unlike his father, who seemed to constantly test her. And unlike her ex Wassily, who offered only absent nods and wandering eyes during her stories. Julius remembered her family's quirks, her passion for neuroscience, her favorite colors, and her preference for tea instead of coffee. Even though she'd only known him for a short time, the bond they were forging felt timeless.

But what was it? Friendship? Soulmates? Or more? Grace had tested the waters with playful touches—a brush on the hand, a casual bump of the shoulder. He hadn't exactly reciprocated. Yet, he'd invited her to his father's party tonight. That was a spark. Their connection was undeniable, a feeling Grace was certain Julius shared.

A sharp buzz shattered the tranquil morning. Grace's phone vibrated on the nightstand, a name flashing on the screen. She reached for her phone, the name on the display burning into her eyes. Tina. Her old boss. A scoff escaped her lips. The woman hadn't bothered with a call in a year, yet here was her text message. *Grace, I need to talk with you.* Well, that feeling wasn't mutual. Grace had quit, walked away from a life of bullying and intimidation. With a decisive flick of her wrist, she silenced the notification, shoving the phone aside. She wanted to leave the past behind and focus on her new self.

Her gaze swept across the room. What would she do today? To her left, a plush chaise lounge invited her to unwind with a book. A discreetly placed flat-screen TV was nestled beside a compact desk. She could watch a movie or start writing her memoir. But the view beyond the expansive windows was most captivating: a crystal-clear lake with a gaggle of geese enjoying their morning ablutions. A curious squirrel peered down at her from a nearby pine.

With a swift move, Grace got up from her bed and flung open the windows. The crisp air washed over her like a cool wave. She inhaled deeply, the scent of pine and roses filling her lungs. It was good to be alive! With a rustle of anticipation, Grace turned around and appraised her new clothes in the wardrobe. She slipped into a blue turtleneck sweater and gray pants, a simple yet elegant ensemble thanks to Fay's keen eye for style. As she caught her reflection in the mirror, she noted a new spark in her eyes. This wasn't just new clothes for a new body; it was a new version of herself. A life free from the mundane worries that had always weighed her down. Excitement bubbled in her chest, a promise of a future brimming with possibilities.

As she opened the door to the hallway, she was greeted by the rhythmic clatter of dishes and the scent of brewing coffee. A faint melody with Latin vocals drifted up from below, likely emanating from the kitchen where the house manager was busy at work.

She went down the marble staircase to the kitchen. The opulent dinner still sat heavy in her stomach. A cup of tea, not a full breakfast, seemed the most appealing way to greet the day.

The kitchen stole her breath as she entered. It was larger than her entire San Francisco apartment, a vast room with polished marble countertops, tall windows draped in elegant fabric, soaring ceilings and intricate moldings. Sunlight streamed through the windows, casting a warm glow over gleaming copper pots and pans. The rich aroma of freshly brewed coffee mingled with the sweet scent of cinnamon and freshly baked goods.

Carlos, dressed in a tailored uniform and an apron, stood at the stove, arranging a tray of steaming pastries. He glanced up as she entered. "Good morning, Miss Grace. Would you like some coffee?"

The phrase somehow reminded her of the nurse in the rehabilitation center, the one who had died of a heart attack.

"Good morning. Would it be okay if I prepare my own tea?" she asked.

"Of course," he said smoothly and waved toward a cupboard at the other end of the room. "Everything you need is over there."

"Thank you!" She fetched a cup and filled it with hot water from the sink.

"The pot for proper brewing is over there, if you'd like to experience the full flavor," Carlos offered.

"Thanks, I'm fine," she mumbled, already drawn to the ornately carved box labeled Tea on the counter. Lifting the lid, she found a dazzling array of loose-leaf teas. Her gaze darted around until she spotted a lone tea bag tucked in a corner. That would do. Dipping the bag into the mug, she inhaled the rising flavor of hibiscus.

"Do you have a bit of honey, by any chance?" she asked.

The house manager stood rigid at the other end of the kitchen, his arms folded tightly across his chest. His gaze flickered from the open tea box to the cup in her hand.

"Of course," he said slowly. "It's in the cupboard above the tea box."

Grace ignored his stare and opened the cupboard. Inside was an array of gleaming honey jars that would make any connoisseur swoon. She reached for one of the jars, plunged a spoon deep into the golden liquid and watched with satisfaction as the honey clung to the metal in a thick, glistening glaze. Three twirls released the excess back into the jar. With a swift motion, she lifted the spoon's cargo into her mug. A single amber strand of the golden glaze left a glistening trail on the counter.

Carlos glared at her, his head tilted.

"Can I have a pastry as well?" she asked. The smell was too good to resist.

"Certainly," he said curtly.

"Thank you!" She grabbed a brioche raisin snail, turned on her heels and walked back up to her room.

A fragrant breeze of roses and the cheerful chirping of birds greeted her through the open window. With a satisfying click, she closed the door, retrieved the holographic laptop from the desk, and settled onto the soft chaise lounge, sipping her tea. Julius had given her the password for the computer. She opened the browser and searched for Bianca.

Bianca's profile on the SUEC home page came up first. She had worked as a nurse practitioner in the department of surgery at SUEC Hospital. There was not much more information. A Facebook page under Bianca's name had a few public photos. In one, Bianca stood between an elderly man and woman, presumably her parents, their arms wrapped around her. Their smiles were genuine, a candid moment of unconditional love. Another photo showed Bianca in a beautiful white wedding dress, embraced by a young man in a dark suit. Their expressions exuded happiness and contentment. Next, there was a photo of Bianca cradling a baby in her arms. The tenderness in her gaze and the innocence of the child conveyed a deep sense of maternal joy. There were no more photos after that.

Grace clicked on the next search result. Her heart sank as she realized it was Bianca's obituary. The notice celebrated her as a dedicated professional, a loving daughter, a blissful wife, and a nurturing mother. The obituary also mentioned that she had joined her daughter in the afterlife. Grace felt a chill inside her borrowed body. Bianca must have lost her baby. Perhaps that was part of the reason she had committed suicide.

The obituary also stated that Grace's funeral would take place at the Holy Cross Cemetery in Menlo Park. That had been about a year ago. Grace closed her laptop and rose from her chaise lounge. Suddenly, she knew exactly what she needed to do today—she would go and pay her respects.

She shrugged into a lightweight cardigan and walked down the marble staircase. She wasn't too eager to meet Carlos again. No need for pleasantries if he had some kind of issue with her. She bypassed the grand entrance, opting instead for the side door that led directly to the driveway.

The sun blazed down from the cloudless California sky. A glint of chrome caught her eye—a sleek bicycle propped by the side entrance. That would do. Without a second thought, she swung her leg over the seat and propelled herself down the path, leaving the imposing Zhang residence behind.

- 12 -

GRACE

Thursday, November 10, 2033, 11 a.m.

Grace steered her bike down the path, the crunching gravel a satisfying counterpoint to the rhythmic whir of the wheels. Towering oaks, their leaves a tapestry of emerald and jade, cast dappled shadows across the path. Her legs pumped in a satisfying rhythm. How had nature grown two legs at exactly the same length? Their effortless coordination felt like a miraculous gift, a stark contrast to the horrors of her past paralysis.

A gaggle of geese honked and squawked beside her on the emerald lawn. She picked up the pace and their calls faded into the background. Gratitude surged through her. The simple act of being alive, of experiencing the world in this way, filled her with a deep appreciation for life's beauty. With a deep breath that filled her lungs with crisp air, she pushed on, the sun warm on her back and the open road stretching before her.

The ride to Menlo Park was more exhausting than she had expected. Twenty-minutes in, her energy was already drained. Months of pedaling stationary bikes in the sterile confines of the SUEC gym felt utterly useless compared to the demands of the open road. Yet, a pleasant ache settled in her legs, a welcome contrast to the numbness she had felt for so long.

She parked her bike at the gate, locked it with a soft click and stepped into the embrace of the cemetery. Sunlight dappled through a canopy of ancient oaks as she walked though rows of tombstones, each a testament to a life lived. She pressed forward onto the winding paths that led deeper into the heart of the Holy Cross. Finally, she spotted what she'd come for—an unassuming plaque adorned with a fresh bouquet of flowers and etched with the name Bianca, her donor.

Grace stood in silence before the plaque, paying her respects to the woman who'd gifted her a second chance at life. Bianca's decision to sign an organ donor card had been an act of profound selflessness and generosity. Bianca could have simply departed this world, consumed by her own struggles. Instead, in her darkest hour, she had extended a lifeline to a stranger.

The air around her was still, the only sound a mournful whisper of leaves. Their hues, a dying ember's kiss, echoed the somberness within her. Grace looked at the soil beneath her feet. Deep beneath the surface lay the remains of her old body. That thought was both unsettling and surreal.

She remembered her old body, a vessel marked by imperfections and scars that held tales of childhood adventures, scraped knees, and her mother's gentle touch after her appendectomy. The old body had been less than flawless, but it had been hers. She felt a sense of deep sadness, a bittersweet feeling of saying goodbye to her former self.

So many new experiences had happened to her since she had abandoned her old body and received the body transplant. Was her old self still in there, piloting this stranger's body? Or had she become someone entirely new, a Frankenstein's monster stitched together from memory and borrowed flesh?

Grace was so occupied with her thoughts that she didn't hear the crunch of approaching footsteps.

"Bianca!"

She whirled around, her heart hammering against her ribs. A young man in jeans and a worn leather jacket was rooted to the spot, his eyes wide with startling recognition.

"I . . . I'm sorry," he stammered, the apology laced with a tremor that sent shivers down her spine. Their gazes locked in a breathless moment. "You just look so much like her," he finally managed to say, his voice barely a whisper. "For a moment, I thought

I saw her ghost."

"I apologize if I startled you somehow," she said.

"You came to see Bianca? Do you know her?" he asked. His gaze up and down her body felt unwelcome.

"I'm a friend," Grace lied. "Who are you?"

"Karim, her husband."

A jolt shot through her like a bolt of lightning. Bianca's husband. Would he recognize his wife's body? No, that was impossible. Many women shared similar figures.

"Nice to meet you, Karim," she said, forcing a smile.

He continued to scrutinize her, his gaze intrusive and distant at the same time.

Grace searched for a hint of recognition in his eyes. But his gaze remained fixed on her body. His face, pale and marked by deep lines, revealed nothing.

"How did you know her?" he asked. "I don't remember seeing you before."

Grace hesitated, her mind racing. "We both worked at SUEC," she offered, the vagueness a shield against unwanted scrutiny. "But somehow, we lost sight of each other."

He sighed. "Grace pulled away from everyone. She'd battled chronic depression all her life."

"I'm sorry." Grace glanced at the man. He wasn't conventionally handsome—his build was more solid than athletic, his face weathered and his hair a bit unruly. Yet, there was a magnetism about him, a spark of vulnerability in his narrow eyes that was quite captivating.

"Did Bianca not seek professional help?" she asked.

The man shook his head. "She did see a psychologist, but it didn't help much."

"The family couldn't support her either?"

"We tried, so did her friends. I'm a hospitalist, and I helped her through some rough patches. We'd known each other since kindergarten. But she distanced herself more and more from me."

"That must have been hard," Grace said softly.

His eyes glistened with tears. "Just before . . . before it happened"—his voice trembled slightly—"I was so caught up at the hospital that I didn't talk to her enough about what she was going through. I had no idea it was that bad. Then I got the call that she had died."

Grace just stood there, not sure what to say. The man made a deep impression on her. Whether it was the way his voice dipped and rose, weaving a subtle spell with its rhythm, or the way he held himself with quiet assurance, she couldn't quite pinpoint it.

"I always wonder if I could have saved her if I had just tried harder," he continued. "Why did I work so much? In the end, I lost what was most precious to me—my wife, my soulmate, my best friend."

Grace nodded. "I was consumed by too much work too. I'm a scientist and worked around the clock to develop a new drug. My husband got bored and started an affair. Then, I got cancer. I wondered so many times, why I had worked so hard? For what?"

"I'm sorry," he offered sincerely.

"Don't," Grace replied, her tone gentle. "I'm okay now. But it's humbling to realize that what truly mattered slipped away: time."

"Exactly," he responded. "I've often wished I could turn back time and begin anew. If I would get another chance, I wouldn't squander a single moment with those I hold dear."

There was a pause, filled with unspoken thoughts. Grace looked at the bouquet of flowers in front of the tombstone. Red roses, their fragrance almost unbearably sweet.

"When I caught sight of you from afar, for a fleeting moment, I thought you were her," he confessed. "Would you care to join me for a coffee?"

Grace eyed the man cautiously. Coffee? What an eerie conversation at a cemetery.

Before she could answer, a figure materialized from the rows of headstones. A trench coat billowed around the approaching figure, the brim of a hat obscuring his face. A flicker of recognition sparked in Grace's memory. Angus Weber, the FBI agent from the hospital.

"Hello, Grace," he greeted her. "How are you doing?"

"Hello," she said. "Did you come to pay your respects, or did you want to pick me up?"

A smile played on Weber's lips. "Both."

Karim's gaze flickered from Grace to Angus. "Looks like Bianca got lots of visitors today," he said.

"He's my uncle," Grace explained, looking anxiously at Angus. Hopefully he would play along.

Angus nodded in agreement.

"Your uncle, hm?" Karim said, and extended his hand. "Nice to meet you, Mister . . .?"

"Weber," Angus finished for him. "We're actually due at a family luncheon soon, so I came to pick up Grace."

"Of course," Karim said. He turned to Grace. "It was a pleasure meeting you, Grace. Perhaps we could chat again sometime?"

Grace's throat tightened. That was probably not a good idea. But she liked the guy and felt a deep sympathy for his loss. She stole a glance at Weber. His expression was unreadable.

Karim checked his watch. "I'll be here again on Friday at eleven a.m. Perhaps you'd care to join me then?"

She found herself saying, "I'd like that." Caught by her own boldness, she turned around and followed Agent Weber down the graveled path. Her mind reeled. Agreeing to meet Bianca's husband again felt completely illogical, given the circumstances. But the raw pain in his eyes had struck a chord within her, leaving her unable to resist the unexpected pull.

When they were out of hearing distance, she asked the FBI agent, "Why did you follow me?"

The agent smiled. "I wanted to keep an eye on you."

Grace glared at him. Was she under surveillance?

"Can I drive you home?" he asked.

Grace nodded. That was the least he could do. "Thank you. If you can squeeze my bike into your car, that would be great."

"We will find a way."

They continued down the path, passing weathered headstones. At the gate, Grace fetched her bike while the agent opened the doors of his Mercedes with a smooth double chime.

"I'm glad I came to look after you. You should stay in the Zhang residence, Grace. That is the safest place for you right now," he said with a stern expression.

"What was I supposed to do there? I cannot sit around all day."

"Consider it a vacation," Angus said. "It's not the worst of places I heard. And it is well-protected. Someone out there wants to harm you. You can resume your endeavors when he or she is behind bars." His gaze flickered across her face.

"I'll do my best. But I need to know who is behind the attack at the rehab center. Perhaps this is related to Bianca somehow."

"You can be assured that we're leaving no stone unturned finding that out for you," he said. He started the engine and it hummed to life with a soft purr.

"Actually," Grace interjected, a new thought striking her, "I have a medical appointment at the hospital this afternoon. Since you're practically babysitting me, would you mind giving me a ride?"

"Using the FBI as your personal taxi?"

"It's the best way to ensure my safety."

He shook his head in a mixture of exasperation and admiration. "Sure, why not."

- 13 -

ANNYA

Thursday, November 10, 2033, 2 p.m.

Annya burst into the cramped exam room at SUEC Hospital. Harsh fluorescent lights hummed overhead, putting a spotlight on Grace, who was perched on the examination table. The familiar antiseptic scent was oddly tinged with a hint of something floral, like rosewater. Annya gave Grace a probing look. The rapid dismissal to the Zhang residence had been good for her. A rosy flush bloomed on Grace's cheeks, and she wore a new cashmere shirt that covered her scar and suited her well.

After the unsettling incident with Dr. Triveda, Grace had requested that Annya perform her follow-up medical exams. Dr. Triveda wasn't pleased, but she had reluctantly agreed, on the condition of a full report. Annya couldn't blame her—Grace's case was unlike any other. The near complete recovery from a spinal cord transection, followed by an apparently seamless integration with a new body, was nothing short of miraculous. Perhaps the most significant medical breakthrough of the century.

Annya had ordered a series of medical tests for Grace, including a blood draw, x-ray, EEG, ECG, and a thorough neurological examination. Stepping forward, Annya offered a warm smile, hoping to ease some of the tension. She settled onto the stool beside the examination table, checking the results on the electronic medical record.

"Hello, Grace, your medical exams look great," she said. "How was your first day out there?"

Grace leaned forward, an unreadable expression crossing her

face. "Thanks for asking. I feel stronger and stronger every day. But I still have problems with my sensations." She flexed her hand experimentally. The movement seemed a bit unnatural.

"Yes, I noticed that in the neurological exam results," Annya confirmed. She checked Grace's chart. "Reduced sensation in your extremities, except for the palms and soles. Does that cause problems in your daily life?"

Grace pondered for a moment. "No, I don't think so. Occasionally, I might bump into something without realizing it." She lifted her pant leg and pointed at a faint bruise on her shin. "Surprise souvenirs," she added with a wry smile. "But they are not painful. Overall, I'm managing well."

Annya leaned in, her voice softer. "How does the new body feel, Grace? Does it feel like yours?"

Grace's gaze drifted to the floor. "Honestly, it's very confusing. One moment, I'm incredibly grateful. The new body is so strong and beautiful, everything mine could never be." She ran a hand down her arm. "But it also feels a bit unreal. Like I woke up in a different body. Sometimes I look in the mirror and wonder—is that really me?"

"It's completely all right to feel conflicted, Grace," Annya said, her tone reassuring. "A new body is a lot to take in, physically and emotionally. You're still you at your core, but with exciting new possibilities."

Grace nodded, determination in her eyes. "Of course. This new life is a chance I never thought I'd have. I've come this far, and I won't let anything stop me now."

Annya's gaze lingered on Grace. Medically, her physical recovery was phenomenal. But as a seasoned CIA operative, she worried that Grace's emotional struggles presented a vulnerability. It could render her susceptible to manipulation and exploitation.

"It's fortunate that Julius invited you to stay at their gated residence," she said. "That will add a layer of security and give you some time to process your situation."

Grace nodded. "Yes, I am very grateful for that. I really like him."

Annya smiled. "When would you like to go back to your work at SUEC?" The closer Grace was, the easier it would be to keep an eye on her.

"Well, I quit my job."

"Really? I thought you were a passionate scientist?"

"I still am. But my supervisor was terrible. She pressured me to produce results that were not there. She overcriticized my work when in fact her drug simply didn't work."

Annya looked at her. "That sounds like a difficult situation. You were investigating a new drug? Which drug was it?"

Grace smiled. "Tina asked me to suggest a name for it. I called it DIPUTS, an acronym for drug-induced protection from uncontrolled tumor spread. Tina liked the name and kept it."

"That's a great name, indeed!"

"I'd say it's fitting. It didn't work as well as we'd hoped. Results were modest at best. I'm so glad I don't have to deal with it anymore."

"You could move to a different lab or a different university?"

Grace shook her head. "With my history of cancer, it will raise too many questions. Either they won't believe that I'm cured, or they'll want to know what cured me. I'm already getting questions from everyone who knew me at SUEC—especially the Zhang family. Curiosity is one thing, but it can feel intrusive after a while, you know?"

"I understand."

"And besides, I love the Bay Area. I grew up here. I don't want to live anywhere else."

Annya gave her a reassuring nod. "The Bay Area has a special way of holding on to its own."

"And I absolutely love the Zhang residence!"

Annya smiled. "I knew you would. But remember, you cannot stay there forever. It's only for a limited time, until the FBI has found the person who wants to hurt you."

"I know that."

"With your health on the mend, maybe it's a good time to explore new activities. Have you thought about what kind of work might be fulfilling for you?"

Grace's eyes sparkled. "I don't *have* to work anymore. My pension from SUEC takes care of that."

"So, if you could do anything in the world, what would it be?"

"This whole experience, becoming Human 2.0, is exhilarating! I can be the subject and researcher at the same time. I want to document my progress, charting my neurological progress firsthand, a living record for the world when it's ready for it." Her voice vibrated with excitement. "There's so much we don't understand—the way my body integrates, the impact on my neural pathways."

Annya watched her closely. Grace's excitement was both inspiring and concerning. Was she her own worst threat to the privacy of her clandestine surgery? Could she keep this monumental secret to herself?

"Documenting your progress is a wonderful idea, Grace," she said gently. "Just remember, discretion is paramount for now."

Grace's smile faltered. "Of course. I already started a journal, and I'll keep it private for now." Her voice regained its cheerfulness. "And I'll live my life to the fullest! Who knows how long this amazing new body will last, right?"

Annya leaned back, her gaze steady on Grace. Was it possible for her to establish a sense of normalcy? Perhaps it would be healthier to develop interests beyond the transplant. "Outside of documenting your experiences, Grace, what brings you joy? Leisure activities, hobbies . . .?"

Grace thought for a moment. "Honestly, everything feels so new. Taking a walk through the gardens at the Zhang residence, observing the sunlight catching the dewdrops on the roses, patterns on the leaves I never noticed before. It's like seeing the world's beauty for the first time." Her voice trailed off, a hint of wonder coloring her tone. "And my mind feels much sharper somehow. Images come alive in my head, stories begging to be told. I even considered writing a novel, something I never dared to do before."

"Oh, fiction. What genre are you interested in?"

"Perhaps a thriller."

"A thriller?"

Grace smiled. "A thriller about a woman who kills her husband who abandoned her."

"Hm, that's interesting," said Annya. "Make sure it remains fiction."

Grace's shoulders straightened. Was there a hint of defiance flickering in her eyes?

"It's just a thought. But speaking of leisure activities. Julius invited me to a gathering tonight. An investor party at the California Palace."

"An event at the California Palace? Didn't we just discuss keeping a low profile?"

Grace nodded. "I know, but this event is really important to Julius. He's been incredibly supportive and I cannot turn down his invitation. Besides, you just asked me what brings me joy. This is it. I want to experience the good things in life. Don't I deserve a little normalcy after everything I've been through?"

"You surely do. But you also just escaped a poisoning attack. Someone is trying to kill you, Grace."

"Of course, I understand the risks. And I cannot disappoint Julius. I will be extremely careful. And there will be lot's of security. A millionaire's party is hardly a setting for an assassination."

"You don't know anything about these things, Grace." Annya felt a sting of annoyance. "I'll be there to keep an eye on you."

"I appreciate your concern, Annya. But I can handle myself. Remember that self-defense course? The last guy who tried to kill me didn't fare too well. I'll be cautious, and I owe it to Julius to attend this event."

"Don't tempt your luck, Grace."

- 14 -

ANNYA

Thursday, November 10, 2033, 7:10 p.m.

A quick glance in the staff bathroom mirror confirmed the need for repairs. Taking care of a traffic accident victim had stolen precious minutes from Annya, leaving no time for a home pit stop. Thankfully, she'd managed to stabilize the patient, a man with several fractured ribs and a pneumothorax but no life-threatening injuries.

She had informed Angus about Grace's plans to attend the Zhang party, and he hadn't been thrilled either. But what could they do? Grace was an adult and free to go wherever she liked. And they, Angus and Annya, had to keep her safe. She was a national treasure now. They would both attend the party as well.

Angus had offered to pick her up at the clinic. Fortunately Annya kept a dress in her office for occasions such as this. She reached into the lowest drawer of her desk, retrieving a smooth emerald dress that mirrored her eyes. Thankfully, chiffon held its shape well, a silent blessing in the hurried change that followed. Moments later, Annya stood transformed, the vibrant green cascading around her. A touch of rouge, a swipe of mascara, and a twist of hair into a chic updo. Ready to dazzle, she burst out of the hospital doors.

Outside, Angus leaned against his sleek gray Mercedes, a flicker of worry softening into a slow smile as he lowered his sunglasses to meet her gaze. His ex-wife had always lamented his tardiness. Now, it was Annya who kept him waiting. Fortunately, they were both driven by their work, so he understood and never complained.

"Sorry I'm late," she gasped, the adrenaline from the day

leaving her breathless. A quick peck on the cheek, and she practically tumbled into the passenger seat. "Let's go."

"You look fabulous." His eyes crinkling at the corners as he smiled at her. He started the car and pulled away from the curb, the engine purring as he merged onto the bustling US 101. The steady hum of traffic filled the car. The city lights began to twinkle in the distance, a promise of excitement.

"How is Grace doing?" he asked.

"Healthwise, she's doing amazingly fine. No signs of a tumor recurrence or transplant rejection."

"The SUEC team transplanted the whole body, so why would she have a tumor recurrence?"

"Patients with metastasized breast cancer can develop brain metastases. But Grace underwent thorough pre-surgical screening and consistent MRI monitoring. Her brain is clear as of now, and I'm optimistic we're far enough out to avoid this complication."

"What about a transplant rejection? Can the body reject the head or vice versa?"

"Yes, Bianca's body produces white blood cells that could reject Grace's head. We carefully matched immune markers of donor and recipient to minimize that risk. Grace is also on medication to suppress her immune system."

"Does that mean that she can contract infections more easily?"

"Correct. Her risk of infection is increased. She's been taught to identify potential infections in others, she practices excellent hand hygiene and she's up-to-date on common vaccinations. Rejection is still a real threat. We can't predict how much time she has."

"What happens if the head gets rejected?" he asked.

"Rejection is a serious complication. It can lead to a variety of problems, including death."

"Is she aware of that?"

"It has been disclosed to her as a possible complications of the transplant surgery. She already knew this from her neuroscience research."

"So, her time may be limited. Perhaps that is the reason she quit her job and doesn't want to start any new long-term activity?"

Annya nodded. "I guess so. She might have many years, or only a few months. Nobody knows that. It's understandable that she wants to enjoy her life now."

The San Francisco skyline was sprawled to their right. Angus took the exit toward Octavia Boulevard and drove up Fell Street. The streetlights illuminated colorful Victorian houses to either side.

"Have you found out more about who wanted to poison her?" Annya asked.

Angus shook his head. "Hitting dead ends everywhere. Like I said, the man at the hospital wasn't a big player. But there must be a bigger network out there that orchestrated the attack. We tracked a black van that's been tailing Grace. It was unregistered. We have no idea who we're dealing with."

"Did you check out the members of the surgery team? If someone leaked information? It must have started with an insider."

"They were all vetted carefully. However, there was a surprise. The chief surgeon got a ten-thousand-dollar check for consulting services with OrchidBio, the largest biotech company in California. And do you know who the CEO of OrchidBio is?"

A blue Jeep suddenly stopped in front of them, its backlights flashing. Angus slammed on the brakes. A figure exited from the passenger side. Angus swerved around the Jeep and accelerated down the street.

"Do people in San Francisco have a death wish?" Annya gasped.

Angus sighed. "Sorry, they do this all the time here."

Annya looked at him. He drove on as if nothing had happened.

"Nathanael Zhang, Julius's father, is the CEO of OrchidBio," she said. "Why would he give Dr. Triveda a check? I know her well, and I can't imagine her being involved in anything improper. She's more motivated by fame than money."

"Well, people surprise me all the time."

"What did she get the check for? Did you ask her?"

"Of course I did. She said Mr. Zhang wanted to know everything about her cancer research. She told him about her novel robotic surgical techniques, but she didn't tell him anything about the body transplant."

"This is bad, Angus. Nathanael Zhang is actively digging for Grace's secret. Julius adores his father, and he could be influenced to pry information out of her. Should we remove Grace from their home?"

Angus shook his head. "She seems to be safe there for now. And where else would we put her?"

"You mentioned a safe house before?" Annya asked.

"That would be remote. It might be better to have a close eye on her. Plus, you need to check on her clinically, right?"

"Yes, that's correct. She does need close medical follow-ups at least once a week."

Angus looked at her sideways, a playful glint in his eyes. "See, there are not that many options. Unless you want to host her."

"Me?" Annya laughed. "You know I live in a one bedroom, no space for company."

"Exactly. The Zhangs have not committed any crime as of now. Julius or his father might want to know her secret. But I don't think they will hurt her. And even if they are up to something, they will protect their own home from negative publicity."

They had reached Thirty-Fourth Avenue, a residential street with a dense mix of Victorian houses. They passed stucco villas with intricate fretwork, stoic Edwardians with wide porches, and vibrant Mexican houses painted in cheerful colors. Angus pulled into Legion of Honors Street, which climbed steadily uphill beneath a canopy of towering trees. Streetlights filtered through the leaves and created patterns on the asphalt. A fresh scent of eucalyptus filled the air.

"If anyone else wants to get to her, the Zhang residence might be the safest place for her right now," he continued. "If they are after Grace's secret, they'll shield her."

Annya nodded. "You may be right. But their little detective stunt with the chief surgeon makes me nervous. Mr. Zhang is an American citizen, but he has close ties to China. His company has a subsidiary in Shanghai. I don't want this to bloom into an international affair. We should have a close eye on them."

"We can do that right now," Angus said.

Before them emerged the California Palace. Floodlights bathed the monumental Beaux-Arts building in a warm glow, creating a majestic silhouette against the darkening sky. A line of cars snaked across the crest of the hill. Young people in crisp uniforms directed vehicles into the few remaining parking spots. Angus joined the queue. Annya felt impatience creeping in as the minutes ticked by.

- 15 -

GRACE

Thursday, November 10, 2033, 7:30 p.m.

With every step, Grace felt a growing sense of anticipation. The grand arched entryway of the California Palace loomed ahead. A lone violinist serenaded the arriving crowd, the sweet melody weaving through Greek pillars around them. They passed Rodin's iconic bronze sculpture *The Thinker,* which sat in deep contemplation within the courtyard.

Grace stole a glance at Julius, her heart skipping a beat as she admired him in his tailored dark-gray Armani suit. She felt a rush of confidence in her own attire—a long, dark silk dress adorned with delicate golden embroidery, reminiscent of intricate lace. The modest high neck concealed her scar and her hair was elegantly swept back in a half-up style, forming cascading loose waves that added to her air of poise and sophistication.

They reached a line in front of a metal archway, which mirrored the security check at an airport. A uniformed officer stood at the front, checking IDs and gesturing guests toward a humming radiation machine that scanned bags and purses. This was a minor inconvenience, but it also offered extra protection.

They passed the security gate and walked toward the entrance of the main building, which was flanked by colossal white marble columns. Julius smiled at her and offered his arm, the admiring gazes of onlookers following their every step. Despite the weight of scrutiny, Grace held her head high, feeling a sense of pride and gratitude. Every ache, every tear, every grueling session of rehab—all of it melted away in the brilliance of this moment.

It was all worth it, she thought.

Inside, the foyer hummed with people engaged in sophisticated conversation. Soft light emanated from strategically placed sconces, casting dramatic shadows across the polished marble floors. The alluring strains of the violin echoed through the ornate halls, drawing guests deeper into the museum's captivating embrace.

Julius navigated them through the crowd to the Rodin Galleries, which had been transformed into a stunning event space with carefully arranged seating areas and elegant décor that complemented the sculptures on display. Guests mingled and admired the sculptures as they sipped on champagne and enjoyed hors d'oeuvres. Grace caught Julius's gaze. Pride danced in his eyes, a silent compliment that sparked a dazzling smile across her lips. She leaned closer to him and whispered, "It's wonderful here."

In the center of the room, Nathanael Zhang held court, his conversation flowing easily with two sharply dressed men and their accompanying women. The men, likely in their sixties, exuded formal elegance, while their female companions were both stunning and half their age. One a brunette in a crimson gown, opulent gold necklace, and dramatic makeup. The other a blonde in a daringly short black dress and sky-high heels, leaning against her partner with a champagne flute held high. Grace studied the scene with a flicker of unease. Was this the world she'd envisioned for herself—the realm of wealth and influence, where partnerships seemed to follow a familiar script?

Nathanael spotted them across the hall, flashing a wave before returning to his conversation. Grace waved back, and Julius sent a curt nod in his father's direction. "Perhaps drinks first?" he asked. "These folks seem . . . unremarkable."

Grace chuckled. "Funny you should say that," she admitted. "I just thought the same." They executed a smooth about-face, heading down the hall in the opposite direction.

A discordant screech shattered the elegant evening. "Grace!" An elderly woman with dull gray hair materialized from the crowd. Her ill-fitting dress hung a bit too loose, revealing a décolletage that belonged decades in the past. A young man seemed to linger at her side, his gaze flitting around the room. When his eyes met Grace's, he retreated into the throng.

Tina approached Grace with a determined gait, her lips pressed into a thin line. "Hello, Grace," she rasped. "Missing work for months, but plenty of time to dress up and party, I see." Her beady eyes flicked to Julius, taking in his confident demeanor. "New boyfriend? Do you want to introduce me?"

Grace's smile faltered for a brief moment, but she recovered quickly. "My lab director," she whispered in Julius's ear.

Julius stepped forward and extended a hand. "Hello," he said evenly, "I'm Julius Philopator Zhang."

Tina's gaze narrowed as she assessed him. After a beat, she offered a curt nod. "Nice to meet you," she muttered. "Julius Zhang. Are you Nathanael Zhang's son?"

"Yes, I am."

"Good," Tina said, her voice gaining a steely edge. "Then perhaps you can deliver a message to your father. I've developed a new cancer treatment that can save millions of lives. We called it DIPUTS, an acronym for drug-induced protection from uncontrolled tumor spread. Your father seems to be dragging his feet on signing the contract. We've been negotiating with him for a year, and he assured me over the phone he was ready. Now, radio silence. No response to my calls. That's highly unprofessional, wouldn't you say?"

Grace's blood ran cold. She'd spent years toiling away in Tina's lab, and there had been no breakthrough. In fact, their most recent attempt hadn't shown much promise.

Julius remained composed. "I'm afraid I'm not privy to my father's business dealings," he said evenly. "Perhaps you could try contacting him again, or maybe approach him yourself over there." He gestured toward Nathanael, who was still engrossed in conversation.

Tina's face contorted in frustration. "His security guard wouldn't let me near him! But you, you can get through, right? This is important, young man. Lives are at stake!"

Julius hesitated, visibly torn between courtesy and a growing unease. "Of course, I'll mention it to him. But if you'll excuse us now, this isn't exactly the place for business discussions."

"No?" Tina's voice cracked. "What do you think all these fancy suits are here for? Sightseeing? They're here for deals, young man, deals that could save lives!"

Ignoring the curious stares from nearby guests, Julius offered a strained smile. "It was a pleasure meeting you, Tina," he said curtly.

Tina leaned in closer, her voice dropping to a conspiratorial whisper. "Or maybe your dad found a better offer? From a competitor? But let me tell you something, sweetheart. Their drug is nothing compared to mine. He cannot let me down like that. He's playing a dangerous game here."

"I'm sorry. You need to talk to my father directly," Julius said.

Tina's eyes darted between Grace and Julius. "Or did someone here feed him lies?" she shrieked. She spun on Grace, her face contorted with rage. "Did *you* try to sabotage my work, Grace?"

The murmurs around them had died down, replaced with a stunned silence. All eyes were glued to the unfolding drama.

A security guard materialized beside them. "Ma'am," he addressed Tina in a firm voice, "it seems you've had a bit too much to drink. Perhaps it's best if you get some fresh air outside."

Tina bristled. "I won't go anywhere! These people need to hear the truth!" she bellowed, her voice echoing through the hall.

Another guard appeared, and together they gently but firmly took hold of Tina's arms. "Let's just take a step back, ma'am," the other guard said. "You can rejoin the event when you've calmed down." Despite Tina's protests, the guards ushered her away from the stunned crowd and disappeared through the door.

The tension slowly dissipated. After a few stolen glances, the people around them resumed their conversations. But Grace felt mortified by her supervisor's outburst. What an embarrassment. "I'm so sorry," she finally managed to say.

Julius offered a reassuring smile. "Not your fault, Grace," he said gently. "Neither of us deserve to have our evening spoiled by this."

She took a deep breath, trying to steady her racing heart. "It's just . . . *my* lab director."

"And *my* father's business practices. We should not be dragged into this. We deserve a better night. Perhaps a fresh start?" He extended a hand toward her.

Grace met his gaze. "I'm so glad I met you," she whispered with a genuine smile.

Julius smiled back at her. "And I," he replied, his voice taking on a deeper tone, "I'm glad I met you."

- 16 -

GRACE

Thursday, November 10, 2033, 8:30 p.m.

The evening at the California Palace unfolded with a formal program. The mayor of San Francisco gave a brief speech, lauding OrchidBio's legacy and its valuable contributions to the city. Then, several company executives showcased their most successful product launches with a holographic presentation. The air crackled with a quiet energy as attendees in black ties and glittering gowns leaned in to absorb the company's new developments. The program culminated in a much-anticipated address by Nathanael Zhang. His voice boomed through the hall, detailing OrchidBio's vision and future endeavors.

With the formalities complete, a gentle wave of movement rippled through the crowd as they were ushered down the grand marble staircases to the café downstairs. Strategically placed lamps cast a warm golden glow, bathing the spacious dining hall in a welcoming ambiance. In the center, a lavish buffet awaited the guests, a feast for both the eyes and the stomach. Open glass doors led to a walled patio, inviting cool night air and the lively sounds of a band playing just outside. The formal atmosphere softened.

Grace and Julius shook a blur of hands, warm and dry, clammy and cool, young and old, all seeking theirs. Grace stole a glance at Julius by her side. He managed each encounter like a practiced dance: smile, shake, exchange pleasantries. Grace followed suit, but felt a dull ache in her palm after a while. She hadn't encountered this level of attention before. Every handshake was accompanied by a barrage of glances, curious, appraising, sometimes even envious.

Julius's charm was selective. Even though their encounters

appeared random, Julius actually navigated them through the crowd, avoiding the formality of traditional guests and gravitating toward creative eccentrics.

They finally lingered with a group that was fun to talk with: an opulent opera singer with a long velvety stola draped around her shoulders, and two men with matching purple hair, their laughter as vibrant as their dye jobs. "Partners in crime," they declared with a wink, leaving Grace to playfully pry into their business. A shared chuckle erupted when the revelation turned out to be a romantic partnership. Instead of asking her the somewhat mundane "what do you do?" question, these people asked her about her personal interests and passions. Laughter bubbled up easily, a refreshing change from the previous stilted pleasantries. The evening unfolded with a delightful ease. Grace found herself basking in Julius's presence, the formality melting away with each passing interaction. Even as they were both engaged in conversations with others, she caught him stealing glances at her, his expression softening into a smile.

A cry pierced the air. "Grace! You look incredible!"

Grace whirled around, her heart leaping into her throat. Another relict from the past. A man with a crudely shaved face, clad in a white shirt and worn-out suit, charged toward her with arms outstretched. His grin stretched unnaturally wide, revealing a series of uneven teeth.

"Wassily?" Grace breathed. What a nightmare. She leaned toward Julius and whispered, "That's my ex-husband."

Before Wassily could reach her, a towering figure materialized between them. The security guard. Wassily skidded to a halt, his eyes darting from Grace to the imposing man.

"Hey, come on, don't you recognize your old buddy?" Wassily cast a lecherous look at Grace, his grin faltering for a moment. "You look . . . amazing! How'd you get so tall?"

Grace's voice snapped with a cold fury. "Perhaps," she hissed, "you've gotten smaller."

A flicker of unease crossed Wassily's features. "Come on,

Grace," he wheedled, "we agreed to leave the past behind. We need to celebrate your miracle cure! The doctors said . . . well, you know, the end of the year. And here you are, looking better than ever! How did SUEC pull that off? This is a real miracle!"

Grace rolled her eyes. How did she ever fall for this guy?

Conversations around them sputtered to another halt. Curious stares turned into open gawking. A camera flashed in the semidarkness, capturing the bizarre scene.

Julius intercepted smoothly. "I suppose you're Grace's ex-husband?" he said loudly.

"Yes, I am. And you are?" Wassily responded, oblivious to the growing tension.

Julius's smile remained fixed, but a hint of steel flickered in his eyes. "A friend," he replied, the single word leaving no room for argument.

"Is that so?"

"Welcome, Wassily," Julius said smoothly, and extended his hand. "Why don't we all have a drink at the bar?"

Wassily hesitated, his eyes darting between Grace and Julius. A slow, unsettling smile spread across his face. "Sure," he finally said.

With a nod to the guard, Julius steered Grace through the dispersing crowd. Wassily followed closely behind. As they moved away, the watchful gazes around them seemed to lose interest. Julius ordered three champagnes at the bar.

"That guy is gay," Wassily whispered in her ear.

"That's none of your business," she whispered back. "And not everybody is binary these days."

"Well, until we know what *he* wants, can I invite you for a dance?"

Julius turned around. Had he caught that? He handed them their flutes, each adorned with a single bloom for recognition. Wassily got a yellow chrysanthemum and Grace got a white peony. She locked eyes with Julius in a silent exchange.

"Shall we dance?" he asked.

Grace beamed. "I'd love to."

They put their champagnes on a nearby table.

"Can you watch these?" she asked Wassily. "It will just take a few minutes."

Wassily forced a smile. "Sure, no problem. I'll wait here."

Grace and Julius walked over to the dance floor. The air thrummed with the low notes of a new song, the rhythm encircling them. Julius extended his hand, his eyes twinkling. Grace, a smile playing on her lips, slipped her fingers into his. He pulled her close, and she melted into his embrace. They fell in step, letting the rhythm control their movements. Grace felt the watchful eyes of the crowd on them. From the corner of her eye, she saw Nathanael in the doorway, sending her a satisfied nod. But then she leaned in and let the world around them dissolve. Her body was acting well to her commands, no chains to hold her back. She relaxed and wrapped her arms around Julius's neck. She just wanted to feel this moment.

My God, he was a dancer. Grace couldn't remember the last time she'd done anything like this. She'd taken dance lessons as a teenager—why had she ever stopped? Wassily hadn't been into it. She looked into Julius's dark-brown eyes. Would a gay man dance like this? The thought quickly vanished. Labels didn't matter on the dance floor, only the exhilarating rhythm pulling them closer.

Julius swung her backward, dipped her low, then soared her into the air, the flashing colors around them momentarily blinding her. She touched the ground again and skidded to a smiling, breathless halt. A blonde tendril fell over her eye. He delicately tucked it behind her ear, and her eyes twinkled back at him. The crowd applauded.

She whispered, "You are an excellent dancer."

"I know," he responded with a confident smile. "You're a natural yourself."

Other people joined them on the dance floor. Julius and Grace continued to dance, too lost in the music to halt.

Finally, the music stopped. The band took a break.

Grace and Julius laughed at each other. "That was fun!" she

exclaimed.

They walked back to the bar. To her dismay, Wassily was still there. Grace had hoped he might walk away, but he was not so easy to get rid of. Beside him stood a new woman, cascading dark hair, dark almond-shaped eyes, and a dress that left little to the imagination.

Of course, the moment Grace turned around, there was another woman at his side. Nothing had changed about this guy.

The woman's gaze lingered on Julius.

His composure stiffened, and he adjusted his cufflinks.

"Nice suit, Julius," Wassily drawled, his grin lingering a beat too long on Grace. "Though, Grace usually prefers a more relaxed style, wouldn't you say?" He grinned at her.

Better to shut him up. Grace grabbed the champagne flutes and handed one to Wassily and another to the woman. There was only one left. She looked at Julius.

"I'll get another one from the bar," he said. He gently placed his hands on her shoulders to guide himself past her toward the bar, leaning in to whisper into her ear, "Get them drunk. Perhaps we can escape then." They both chuckled, and he disappeared into the crowd.

"Let's celebrate!" Grace raised her glass. Their flutes met in a perfunctory clink. She didn't feel inclined to cheer with Wassily on anything—or that unwelcome woman. Every fiber of her screamed to hurl her glass against the wall beside the cheater, but the need to maintain composure held her captive. She watched as they both took a large gulp, setting her own glass down untouched. Her gaze wandered through the crowd, searching for Julius. Hopefully he would be back soon.

A choking sound led her attention back to the woman beside Wassily. Did her face flush? She'd sported a porcelain-like complexion moments ago. Perhaps the champagne? The woman let out another choked gasp. Then her face continued to flush to a horrifying crimson red, panic flickering in her eyes. Her hand flew to her chest, knuckles stark against the fabric of her flimsy dress. Her breaths hitched, shallow gasps that seemed to struggle for air. Before anyone could react, her body crumpled. Wassily lunged, arms flailing in a desperate attempt to catch her, but she slipped from his grasp like a broken doll tumbling to the floor.

A collective gasp rippled through the crowd around them. Security materialized with unnerving swiftness, two burly men scooping the woman up in a practiced maneuver. Her panicked breaths were barely audible as they disappeared through the door, hundreds of curious eyes following them.

A beat of silence hung in the air. Grace spotted Nathanael Zhang at the other end of the room. "Just a lady who had a little too much champagne," he said cheerfully. "Be careful to not follow suit!"

The crowd laughed and the music continued.

- 17 -

ANNYA

Friday, November 11, 2033, 10:30 p.m.

When they saw the woman collapsing, they decided on the spot. Annya would find out what had happened to her. Angus would watch Grace and keep her safe. Annya followed the security guards to the restricted staff room. She flashed her SUEC emergency physician ID at the entrance, and they let her in. Inside, the woman lay on a stretcher, two paramedics flanking her. Her eyes stared at the ceiling, wide pupils in a flushed face. Annya's hand snapped to the woman's neck, her fingers instantly finding a frantic pulse. One of the paramedics was in the process of intubating her.

"An ambulance is waiting outside," the other explained.

"We had a recent incident of belladonna intoxication," Annya offered.

"We have atropine in the ambulance," the paramedic grunted. "We will get her to the hospital as quickly as possible."

They lifted the gurney and disappeared through a swinging side door. Annya's stomach clenched as she watched them leave. A single chilling thought echoed in her mind: *Too late. Again.*

She went back to the event hall. The music played on as if nothing had happened. Couples twirled obliviously on the dance floor. Others chatted in animated groups. Angus, Grace, Julius, and Nathanael Zhang stood huddled at the table where the woman had broken down, their faces etched with concern. A few curious glances followed Annya as she made her way to them. The man in the cheap suit was gone.

"How is she doing?" Angus asked.

Annya shrugged. "The paramedics took her to the hospital. I'm not sure if she'll make it."

Angus's brows furrowed. "Intoxication?" he asked.

Annya's gaze flickered to Grace, who stood strangely composed. "It could be anything. But yes, I am concerned about it."

"I believe she had my champagne," Grace said calmly. "I remember the white peony on the rim of the glass."

Annya stared at her. How could she be so composed? "You should leave immediately," she said.

"Can any of you explain what's going on?" Julius asked, looking confused from Grace to Angus and Annya.

"There's a possibility," Annya whispered, "that someone intended to poison Grace."

"Why would anyone want to harm her?" Julius asked, a bewildered frown creasing his forehead.

"We cannot explain that here," Angus said. "For now, her safety is paramount. We have an FBI van waiting outside to get you home safely."

Julius nodded curtly. "Will you arrest whoever did this?"

Nathanael Zhang, a forced smile plastered on his face, interjected. "Hold on, Julius. Let's not jump to conclusions. Maybe it was just an allergic reaction, right? After all, this is a high-profile event, and creating chaos wouldn't be good for anyone's image."

Julius's gaze narrowed. "If someone wanted to harm Grace, I want justice."

"We'll handle this discreetly," Angus intercepted. "Security's already questioning everyone who was near the champagne table—a simple precaution."

"Except that ex-husband of Grace. He vanished," Julius said.

"No worries, I'll get to him," Angus said calmly.

Annya's gaze lingered on Grace. *Who tried to kill whom?*

- 18 -

GRACE

Friday, November 11, 2033, 10:30 a.m.

Grace lay on her bed at the Zhang residence and stared at the ceiling. Despite the luxurious surroundings, a suffocating tightness gripped her chest. Her eyes traced the intricate patterns of the ornately carved ceiling, yet her mind whirled in turmoil, Annya's chilling words echoing: "Dead. The woman was dead."

Grace choked on remorse. It had been her champagne, after all, the one she'd offered to the unsuspecting woman.

I couldn't have known, she told herself, trying to soothe the nagging voice of guilt. *How could I have possibly predicted that someone would spike my drink? It wasn't my fault.*

But even as she tried to push away the guilt, another voice rose within her, relentless in its questioning. *But it was my champagne*, it taunted. *I offered it to her. I saw the white peony. I knew it was my glass.*

Her fist clenched, the sheets twisting in her grip. *I didn't know that the champagne was poisoned*, she tried to reassure herself. *I didn't know . . .*

Why had she relinquished her glass? It had been a fleeting impulse, amplified by the woman's unwelcome presence. But the line between precaution and a calculated move blurred in the harsh light of the morning. Beneath it all, she couldn't deny a dark sense of satisfaction. *Had she wanted her to drink it? Had she wanted to see what would happen?* Uncertainty gnawed at her. Who was *she* in this web of tragedy and unspoken motives? Was her new body creating new feelings? Bianca had committed suicide because of an inner darkness that had overwhelmed her. Did her body produce hormones that clouded her judgment? Grace squeezed her eyes shut, fighting back tears. She craved clarity, a desperate yearning to untangle the knotted web of emotions that choked her from within. The silence around her was suffocating, heavy with the weight of her actions.

A sudden sharp rap against the window shattered her self-talk. Grace whirled around to see a raven sitting on the ornate windowsill, its ebony feathers catching the sunlight.

A shiver ran down her spine. *Was she safe here?*

The bird tilted its head, its intelligent gaze locked with hers. Then, in a flurry, it launched itself into the air, its fleeting shadow disappearing into the vast blue sky.

Her ruminating thoughts flashed back at her. *Who spiked her drink?* She replayed the scene at the party in her mind. Julius had materialized with the flute of champagne, his smile as dazzling as the crystal bubbles. Had his hand lingered a beat too long on the stem of the glass before passing it to her? But he had nudged her toward the dance floor, away from the very drink he'd presented. Was it a genuine attempt to draw her into the festivities, or a calculated maneuver to allow someone else to access the drink?

Nathanael Zhang had watched them dance, a satisfied smirk playing on his lips. He seemed to be pleased by her presence. There had been a glint of something more complex in his eyes, maybe even predatory. He'd certainly had the opportunity. While Julius had drawn her attention to the dance floor, Nathanael could have easily walked over to their table and slipped something into her drink.

The woman was merely an innocent bystander, undoubtedly in the wrong place at the wrong time. If she'd been involved in any way, she wouldn't have consumed the deadly liquid. But why had she joined them in the first place? Was she truly innocent?

And Wassily? Grace had known him for years, or so she thought. He was a cheat, but he was not a murderer. Could a skilled cardsharp like Wassily be hiding a much darker side? Perhaps the woman had stumbled upon a secret he'd desperately needed to keep buried. But she, Grace, had handed her the flute. Wassily had been clearly shocked by the woman's sudden collapse. The whole ordeal made no sense whatsoever.

There had to be a far more cunning player lurking in the shadows. Grace clenched her jaw, a cold fury replacing the initial panic. Whoever it was, they'd underestimated her. She'd deflected their attack twice. Was this a game to them? A twisted test of her resolve? One thing was certain—they wouldn't find her waiting. Grace straightened, a newfound determination hardening her gaze. This predator was about to meet their match.

Her gaze drifted through the French windows, taking in the manicured perfection of the lawn outside. Immaculate flower beds, bursting with vibrant blooms in geometric patterns, led down to a glimmering lake. Perhaps she should go for a walk to clear her head. But as much as she enjoyed the Zhang residence, she knew every squirrel's hiding spot by now. Besides, Carlos was off duty today. He lived in a cottage at the rear of the estate, and she had no desire to cross paths with him. His hostility had only intensified since the incident. Instead of treating her as someone in need of protection, he regarded her as the threat itself. It was clear—he wanted her gone. So, better not run into him while father and son Zhang were out at work.

Grace rose from her luxurious canopy bed. She couldn't stay in this room all day. She had undergone the surgery to embrace life again, to experience the world around her. *One breath at a time. One step at a time*, she repeated in her head. Whoever sought to harm her hadn't managed to breach the security of the Zhang residence. And it was highly unlikely that they would linger at the gate, waiting for her to venture out. So, why not embark on a brief excursion? And if they did show up again, she would get rid of them once and for all. She was not an easy target. Annya had trained her well.

Where could she go to clear her head? Her curiosity had been sparked by the man at the cemetery. Bianca's husband. What was his name, again? She didn't remember. But she longed to learn more about Bianca, the woman whose body now housed her own consciousness. A nurse haunted by depression, driven to take her own life. Was there a connection, a shared darkness that could explain the recent threats against herself? Without wasting another moment, Grace grabbed her jacket and hurried out of the Zhang residence.

- 19 -

GRACE

Friday, November 11, 2033, 11:00 a.m.

Grace's footsteps echoed softly on the cool pavement of the Zhang driveway as she approached the wrought-iron gate that marked the entrance to the property. A man in a dark jacket with large yellow FBI letters leaned against the brick booth beside the gate, tapping away on his phone. He glanced up as she approached. It wasn't Angus Weber, but another FBI agent. She remembered seeing him before.

"Good morning," she ventured, pausing a few feet away.

The man tucked his phone away and offered a curt nod. "Ms. Grace, would you like to leave the property? Can I take you somewhere?"

"Yes," Grace replied. "To the cemetery, please."

The agent's gaze flickered briefly. He picked up the phone again and talked with someone in a low murmur. A tense silence stretched between them as he waited for a response. Finally, he pocketed the phone with a curt nod. "I can take you there."

He gestured toward a black van parked behind the booth. Grace followed him. He slid into the driver's seat and started the engine. Grace joined from the passenger side. The gate swung open, and the agent steered the van out onto the street.

The manicured perfection of the Zhang estate gave way to a more natural landscape. They passed other grand entrances guarded by gates like watchful metal jaws, then ventured into a street lined with a row of smaller houses, each with its own mismatched mailbox. A child's bicycle lay abandoned on a neatly trimmed lawn, a single red balloon tethered to its handlebars. Here, the carefully controlled world of the wealthy seemed to loosen its grip. But the mystery of the poisoned tea and poisoned champagne loomed large in Grace's mind.

She disembarked at the front gate to the cemetery, feeling somewhat apprehensive as she made her way down the gravel path to Bianca's grave. A chill breeze rustled through the canopy of leaves above. Grace scanned the path ahead, her heart hammering against her ribs. Then, a flicker of movement caught her eye. Beneath the sprawling branches of a magnificent oak sat a lone figure on a weathered bench. As she came closer, the familiar silhouette sent a jolt through her—it was him. Dressed in a simple blue sweater and well-worn jeans, he leaned back against the worn wood, his head tilted toward her.

"I'm so glad you could make it!" he said with a broad smile.

A shy shrug escaped her shoulders. "I don't know why," she said. "I guess I was just bored."

"Whatever brought you, I'm glad you made it."

Now she remembered his name. Karim. He looked at her differently than Julius did. Julius always looked deep into her eyes, as if to read her mind. This guy didn't look into her eyes at all. His gaze roamed up and down her body. It felt a bit uncomfortable, but also exhilarating in some way she couldn't explain. Physical, perhaps.

"You look stunning," he said, his eyes lingering on her.

"I have a boyfriend," she countered, defiance in her voice.

"Of course you do." He chuckled. "Would you like to join me?" He gestured toward the empty spot beside him.

She hesitated. "Maybe a walk would be better? I've been sitting around all morning."

"Perfect," he agreed, rising to his feet. She couldn't help but notice the faint coffee stain on his shirt.

He pointed toward the man standing discreetly a few yards away. He had swapped his FBI jacket for a more subdued dark-gray blazer. "Who's that? Another uncle?"

"Just someone making sure I don't get into trouble," she replied coolly.

"A bodyguard, huh? You must be very important," he teased, a playful glint in his eyes.

She shrugged. "Let's just ignore him."

They strolled through the cemetery, the path beneath their feet uneven, weathered by the marks of time. Row upon row of moss-covered tombstones stood sentinel on either side of the path. The air carried the faint aroma of ancient trees around them and a gentle breeze rustled through the leaves.

"So, you were a friend of Bianca?" he asked casually.

"We were acquaintances," she lied. "We often went to lunch at the same time and ended up at the same table. We connected over common interests and started grabbing lunch together."

They navigated around a freshly turned mound of earth. Silence stretched between them, heavy with unspoken questions.

"I was wondering why she did it?" she asked.

"You mean why she committed suicide?"

Grace nodded.

He looked at her sideways. "Well, Bianca had been struggling with depression for a long time," he said. "But I'm also wondering if someone pushed her over the edge."

"*Someone* pushed her?" Grace asked. "What do you mean?"

He sighed. "She signed an organ donor agreement with SUEC shortly before she died. Organs are in short supply. Maybe someone needed one and helped a little."

Grace felt a shiver running down her spine. She shook her head. "SUEC works to the highest ethical standards," she said, attempting to assert confidence. She knew all too well that SUEC had ventured into unethical territory, transplanting a body without explicit approval from the donor or family. While Dr. Triveda had argued that Bianca had consented to donate all of her organs, Grace couldn't shake the feeling that transplanting an entire body was a fundamentally different matter altogether.

"If someone dies and donates their organs, SUEC will gladly accept them. But they wouldn't commit murder," she added.

But the conversation had ignited doubt in her. Hadn't it been quite a miracle that a young woman with a perfect immune match had committed suicide exactly when she'd needed a new body? Organs were transplanted all over the world to unite them with immune-matched recipients. But here, the perfect donor had ended her life just a few miles away from the hospital, at the exact moment her body was needed for transplantation. Just a few weeks later, Grace would have been dead and SUEC would have lost the opportunity to do the clandestine procedure of the century on one of their own scientists.

Karim's lips curved into a knowing smile. "You have doubts," he mused. "You work there and you have doubts as well."

Grace shook her head. "Look, I am a scientist. I don't work at the hospital," she said firmly. "I don't know what they do there. And conspiracy theories won't bring Bianca back. Can we talk about something else, please?"

"Of course," he replied with an apologetic smile. "I'm glad I met you. You remind me so much of her."

"Thank you." She returned the smile.

His gaze went up and down her body again. "It's almost as if she is standing beside me right now."

She glanced back at the FBI agent who was following them at a discreet distance, exchanging a silent understanding.

"Will you go for a coffee with me today?" Karim asked.

The FBI agent stepped closer. "I believe we have to leave now, Ms. Grace," he said in a polite but resolute tone.

She sent him a thankful look. "Sorry," she said to Karim, "maybe another time."

"Of course," he replied, offering her a hand.

Grace felt a small folded piece of paper press into her palm. His voice dropped to a low murmur. "Contact me when you feel like it. I know I messed up with Bianca. I will not make that mistake again."

"Thank you," she whispered, genuinely touched by his words.

With a final glance at Karim, she turned and followed the FBI agent toward the parking lot, the small note burning in her hand.

- 20 -

JULIUS

Friday, November 11, 2033, 11:00 a.m.

Julius pulled into the driveway of the Zhang residence. Today was an unusual day—Annya had sent him home, a rare deviation from her usual insistence on punctuality and diligence. Normally, she was adamant about him not missing a single minute of his duties. Yet today, she had arranged for a replacement and instructed him to go home and look after Grace. He didn't ask for an explanation; he welcomed the opportunity to leave.

Julius liked the idea of being a physician, and he genuinely wanted to help others. But the grueling hours, scarce breaks, subpar cafeteria food, and constant shortages of both staff and supplies left him feeling exploited by the system. The constant feeling of inadequacy fueled his frustration. The sheer number of therapeutic drugs to memorize, the endless tests to conduct, the mountain of diseases to understand—every patient stared back at him with a different kind of pain. Medicine was not his forte; that much was clear. He longed for the approval of his father to quit this part of his life and start a new chapter.

But his father's pharmaceutical empire was an intimidating mountain to climb as well. It hinged on the relentless pursuit of new pharmaceuticals and their patents—a fleeting game where novelty was king. His father excelled at churning out the latest miracle cure, and Julius had to prove himself capable of maintaining that legacy. He remembered his father's unsettling comment—Grace could be the "solution."

A solution for their business or a solution to his loneliness at dull parties? Julius couldn't suppress a smile. She was charming. Her warmth was a welcome respite from the Zhang household's relentless pursuit of profit. Yet, Grace could also be the key to his independent future. Uncovering her secret wouldn't harm her—quite the opposite. Once his father's machinery took over the drug that had cured her, any adversaries would think twice about targeting her. His father held far more power and influence than a naïve young woman.

A glint of chrome caught Julius's eye—his father's Lexus, parked in front of the house. Why wasn't he at work? It was the second time this week that his father had come home early. Curiosity gnawed at Julius as he parked his car and hurried toward the house. Hopefully nothing bad had happened.

As he walked through the entrance hall, unfamiliar sounds emanated from the family room. He pushed the door open, and his jaw nearly hit the floor. There, on the couch, sat his father with a ball of fluffy beige fur at his feet—a playful puppy yapping excitedly at Julius. A Labrador retriever, maybe?

Julius couldn't believe his eyes. He knelt, his hand reaching out cautiously. The puppy, a whirlwind of energy, bounded toward him, sniffing his fingers before launching into a flurry of excited jumps. Julius looked at his father in disbelief.

"I thought we were too busy to take care of a dog?" he asked.

"Well, we have a woman at the house now," his father responded with a mischievous smile. "Don't you think Grace will like him?"

Julius scratched the fluff ball behind his right ear. The dog leaned in, looking at him with his big dark puppy eyes. "I'm sure she will," he said. "He's adorable. Where did you get him?"

"Well, I had my assistant order one." His father smiled. "I'm not sure where she found him. Perhaps online."

"Dad, you can't just order dogs from Amazon," Julius scoffed.

"Details, details," his father said with a broad smile. "The point is, she found one fast. Good on her."

"But why now?" Julius asked. "I've been asking for a dog forever."

"Like I said, we both are busy," his father explained. "But now Grace can take care of him. If she sticks around, of course."

Julius felt a prickle of jealousy rising in his chest. Had Grace, with her effortless intelligence and ability to converse on any topic, captivated his father in less than a week? The way his father beamed at her comments was a sight Julius had never managed to evoke.

He sat on the couch beside his father, the puppy nestling on his lap. He gently stroked his fur. "What's his name?" he asked.

"Let's just call him Puppy. No need to get too attached."

"Why not?"

"Just in case he doesn't stay for long."

Julius glanced at his father. He always had an agenda, always.

"Did you introduce him to Grace yet?" he asked.

His father shook his head. "Grace is out for a walk. The FBI agent took her to the cemetery. I called him and he told me they'll be back shortly."

"The cemetery? What is she doing there?"

"I heard both her parents died some time ago. Perhaps they are there."

"I see." Julius reached for a piece of bread on the coffee table.

"Wait," his father interjected. He snatched a slice himself and offered it to the dog, who gobbled it down in one bite.

Julius stared at his father. "Dad, what are you doing?"

His father petted the dog's head. The eager pup sniffed at his fingers, searching for more.

Realization hit Julius like a punch. "Are you using the dog as a food taster? He's a living creature, not a lab rat!"

His father's smile faltered. "Well, the woman at the party had a poisoning incident. Better safe than sorry."

"Dad, you cannot do that. The poor dog."

"All right, calm down, Julius. As I said, it's just a precaution. Hopefully, we're safe here. I asked Carlos to be extra vigilant with our food. But Grace handed the drink to the woman. What if she poisons people? Maybe if she knows we'll test the food first on the puppy, it'll scare her off."

"Do you really think Grace would try to poison us? That's absurd. We took her in. She wouldn't destroy her own sanctuary."

"Maybe it's someone else. The FBI will figure that out soon enough."

"And why test the food? Someone poisoned her drink, Dad."

"Of course, we'll be cautious with our drinks too. Carlos will only bring us unopened bottles of water and wine. But if someone plans an attack, they won't use the same method twice. Next time, they'll target the food, because we're vigilant about the drinks."

"And what if that's true?"

"Then the dog takes the fall and not my son."

Julius stared at his father. Was this what love looked like?

- 21 -

ANNYA

Friday, November 11, 2033, 11:30 a.m.

The emergency room had been bustling with activity since the early-morning hours. Patients streamed in, minor scrapes mingled with life-threatening emergencies. The waiting area was packed with anxious faces and worried murmurs, occasionally interrupted by sirens outside. Annya hurried from one patient to another, tending to their needs. She thrived in high-pressure situations such as this, where quick thinking and rapid decision-making were essential. She wanted to make a difference in people's lives in their most critical moments, providing them with the best possible care. It helped her rewrite her own history.

She finally found some time to slip into the bathroom. As she washed her hands, she caught her reflection in the mirror. She moved her fiery-red bangs to the side and traced the scar on her forehead with her fingers. She remembered the searing pain and the metallic tang of blood when she'd arrived in the ER, bleeding from a gunshot wound. She'd been shot by her ex-husband, a Russian assassin who had discovered her secret life as a CIA operative. An ER physician had been her hero that day, pulling her back from the brink of death. Now, Annya wielded her medical expertise as an act of defiance. It was her way of paying it forward, each life she touched a testament to her own strength and resilience.

She rearranged her bangs. The past was the past. She probably only had a few minutes until the next crisis. She left the bathroom and made her way to her office. The well-worn leather chair welcomed her with a familiar creak as she settled into it. She swiftly unlocked her phone and dialed Angus's number.

"Hello, Angus, any updates on the woman?"

"Yes, we did an autopsy and found traces of belladonna in her system. We also found traces of belladonna in her champagne flute."

Belladonna, also known as deadly nightshade. "Were nightshade bushes on the property?" she asked.

"Yeah, a few," Angus confirmed. "But frankly, no sane adult stumbles upon nightshade berries by accident. And the amount of belladonna in her system looks like a homicide."

"Who was she?" Annya asked.

Angus sighed. "A young journalist from the *San Francisco Chronicle*. Apparently, she was trying to get close to the Zhang family, digging for a scoop on Grace and her miracle cure."

"Do you think she was targeted?"

"We can't rule it out," Angus admitted. "But she was more likely collateral damage. Several witnesses reported that she took a glass of champagne from Grace."

"We know that already. Grace told us herself. But she only fetched it after it had been sitting unattended on the table for at least twenty minutes. Did you find out who spiked it? Did you check the surveillance cameras?"

"Of course. We combed through all security footage. Live videos, guest recordings, the whole lot. But there were too many people in the room. The view on the table was blocked most of the time. Whoever did it, covered it well."

"What about the other champagne flutes?"

"Two shattered on the floor. Forensics didn't pull anything from the shards. The fourth one that Julius got from the bar was clean."

"So, Grace's glass was the only one tampered with?"

"Correct. But we haven't discounted the buffet yet. We're still analyzing everything."

"Grace was attacked previously. Most likely, someone tried to poison *her* again."

"That's also our assumption."

Annya hesitated. "There's another angle. Grace mentioned wanting revenge on her ex-husband for his betrayal. Could she have targeted him instead?"

"She handed the glass to the woman. If she'd wanted to target her husband, he would be dead by now."

"True." Annya tapped her finger on the desk, her gaze lingering on the delicate orchids adorning the thank-you card from Grace, a memento from her discharge day. "And the ex-husband? He vanished after the woman broke down?"

"Right. He had the opportunity and a motive. He doesn't have a job and urgently needs money. Grace hasn't submitted the divorce proceedings yet, and SUEC provides significant life insurance benefits. But circumstantial evidence only gets us so far. I'm building a case and will visit him later today."

"This is the second poisoning attack. I cannot shake the feeling that it has to be tied to Grace's surgery. Did you look into the hospital staff who had access to her before the incident?"

"Of course. We are following all leads. One of the nurses on Grace's surgery team previously worked for OrchidBio, Nathanael Zhang's business. She contacted Nathanael Zhang to sell information about the surgery. Our team intercepted and relocated her."

"So, we've got two assassination attempts on Grace, a dead assassin at SUEC Hospital, a dead journalist at the Zhang party, a broke ex-husband with an opportunity, and a business magnate with ties to China . . ."

"Exactly. Someone's playing a dangerous game out there," Angus said. "Maybe it's beyond our jurisdiction."

"The feds? What do you mean?"

"Well, Nathanael Zhang is a first-generation American citizen with close ties to China – a business subsidiary in Shanghai. If this spirals into an international incident, it'll land on the CIA's doorstep."

"But Nathanael Zhang wouldn't want to poison Grace?"

"Probably not. Unless he considers her a threat to his business. Imagine a new era with a cure for metastasized cancer. A single surgery, a definitive solution. The entire pharmaceutical industry reliant on treatment drugs might crumble."

"Does Nathanael Zhang's company sell cancer drugs?"

"He has some in his portfolio. But he's a smart businessman. He might be up for a bigger venture. If he gets wind of Grace's secret, he could exploit it much more. He could establish a secret network for head transplantation, catering to wealthy individuals seeking to extend their lives or to transplant their heads onto healthier bodies."

"What a nightmare."

"True, but his ties to China worry me even more. What if the Chinese government gets wind of the body transplant technique? Imagine super soldiers with enhanced skills, created for war. Or a macabre form of punishment, a horrifying control tactic."

"Any government with twisted morals could weaponize this."

"Exactly. Cartels, rogue states . . . The world isn't ready for this, Annya." Angus let out a heavy sigh. "Maybe this surgery shouldn't have happened at all."

Annya searched for the right words. "If we hadn't taken the leap, someone else would've done it. We must be at the cusp of new technologies. It's the only way we can steer new discoveries and their responsible applications—and prepare for the consequences."

"Maybe. But Pandora's box is open now. Leaks about this technology could trigger an international race the likes of which we've never seen. Every power player will scramble to get their hands on it. We need to mitigate the fallout before all hell breaks loose."

"I'll remind Grace that she has to keep her secret at all costs. Meanwhile, we have to find her attacker—that's the key to unraveling this web."

A sharp knock at the door interrupted their conversation. The charge nurse poked her head in, a worried crease between her brows.

"Annya? We have a polytrauma coming in. They need you in the ER stat."

"I'll be right there," Annya replied calmly.

The nurse nodded and retreated.

"Can I see you tonight?" she whispered into the phone.

"I wish I could, but this case is eating up all my hours. I need to find Grace's attacker before someone else gets hurt."

Annya sighed. "Two heroes for the world, no time for us."

"I'll make it up to you, I promise."

"Of course. I love you."

She hung up the phone. The reality of their busy lives felt overwhelming. They were constantly saving others, leaving little time for themselves. A part of her accepted it, but another part longed to pause the world, to hold him close without constant emergencies. She wondered if their extraordinary lives would ever align or forever keep them apart.

- 22 -

GRACE

Friday, November 11, 2033, 11:30 a.m.

Grace sat on the couch next to Julius in the cozy family room. The Zhang residence, with its antique furniture and framed family portraits, felt like a place where time slowed and worries dissipated. The grand fireplace crackled with life, enveloping them in a warm cocoon of comfort. In her lap, she gently stroked the soft fur of the massive pup, her fingers sinking into its plush coat. The Labrador retriever gazed up at her with an innocence and affection that melted her heart. Its wet nose twitched with curiosity and nudged Grace's hand in search for more attention—and food, of course.

"So, you've always wanted a dog. And now your father just brought you one? Why now?" she asked. "You both work full time, and Carlos made it clear that he doesn't like pets."

Julius nodded. "I was as surprised as you are. Apparently, Dad thought you could handle walks with him for now."

"Of course I'll help. But what happens when I'm not around anymore?"

The dog's ears perked up as if listening intently.

Julius met her gaze. "We'll figure it out," he said calmly.

"Of course." She nodded, stroking the pup's fur. "So, what's his name?"

"We named him Puppy for now. Dad doesn't want to get too attached. He always thought that dogs cause unnecessary costs and mess. He believes the dog might be good for our safety for now, but he's uncertain if we'll keep him long term."

The Labrador tilted its head, as if understanding the weight of the conversation.

Grace patted the dog's head. "Well, Puppy it is, then," she said, looking at the dog with pity. "Though, I think you deserve something more special."

The dog wagged his tail excitedly, and Grace offered him a gentle scratch behind the ear. "Don't worry," she murmured. "We'll figure this out together."

Julius shifted uncomfortably on the couch, his eyes darting away from hers as if searching for the right words. "Look, my dad isn't a bad man," he finally said. "His generation has a different view of dogs than ours. They weren't seen as companions so much as working animals." He glanced at her as if searching for understanding. "Maybe that's why he's hesitant to get attached."

Grace frowned. "I don't understand what you are trying to say, Julius," she said. "What are you worried about?"

Julius ran a hand through his hair, a troubled look on his face. "Let's just say it will be good for us to keep an eye on him."

"On the dog? You scare me! You cannot seriously think that someone wants to harm him?" Her gaze lingered on the pup, his tail thumping a happy rhythm against her thigh. She felt uneasy. Julius smile seemed strained. He was holding something back.

"Do you think Carlos might want to get rid of him?" she asked.

Julius laughed. "Carlos? Get rid of a dog? Grace, he wouldn't hurt a fly. He's devoted to our family, maybe a little too much sometimes. Perhaps I'm overreacting. Just keep Puppy out of trouble, all right?"

"You bet I will." There was more to this than Julius was letting on, and she was determined to find out what it was.

A key scraped in the lock, turning with a metallic click. Julius's eyes darted to the back door.

"Is your father coming back early?" Grace asked.

"No, my father works long hours at OrchidBio and usually doesn't come home before seven p.m. This is Rolando, a friend."

The door swung open to reveal a young man with a dark mustache and a shock of wavy hair. His posture exuded a quiet confidence despite his worn clothes. He casted a curious glance at Grace.

"I thought you had the place to yourself, Julius," he said. "Who's this?"

Julius's smile faltered. "No worries, Rolando," he said, waving a dismissive hand in Grace's direction. "This is Grace, my new stepsister."

A pang of hurt shot through Grace's chest. Last night's dance had a different energy than newly minted stepsiblings. She stole a glance at Julius. His expression was unreadable. Across from them, Rolando stood rigid with a forced smile. An awkward tension hung heavy in the air. His eyes darted between Grace and Julius, sharp and assessing, like a hawk eyeing a threat.

"So, you two . . ." Grace searched for the right words. "You two are a couple?"

Rolando's jaw clenched. "That's none of your business," he snapped.

Julius got up from the couch and stepped toward him. "Rolando, as I said, she's practically family. She won't say anything."

"How do you know that?"

"Because she owes me a favor. We took her in to provide her with a safe home." Julius turned to Grace. "Right, Grace?"

Grace lifted her chin, a flicker of defiance in her eyes. "Yes, I am a rescued damsel," she said curtly. Was this all their connection amounted to? A debt to be repaid? Her fingers dug into Puppy's soft fur, the warmth a small comfort in the face of the sudden chill that had settled over the room.

"Can you please forget that you saw Rolando here?" Julius said with a conspiratorial smile. "He's not on the best terms with your FBI friends."

"Oh, why's that?" she asked.

"Well, he is a wanted cyberhacker."

"A cyberhacker?" Grace tried to mask her concern with a casual tone. "That's none of my business, indeed. As long as he does not mistreat any women, children—or puppies."

"He doesn't," Julius said quickly. "He helps them. Like a modern Robin Hood."

"That's interesting company you keep, Julius," Grace said coldly. "I have no interest in learning more about it."

"Right," Julius said, a touch of defensiveness creeping into his voice. "Can we leave you alone for a few hours?"

"Of course. I'm not a child."

"Excellent." Julius offered a strained smile, his eyes lingering on hers a beat too long. He crouched down to Puppy, his voice dropping to a conspiratorial whisper. "Be nice to her."

The two men exchanged a silent look. Then, in practiced unison, they turned and walked out, the door clicking shut behind them with a finality that echoed in the sudden silence.

Grace stared at the closed door. Maybe they thought they could just leave her here like a piece of furniture. But she would surely *not* sit around. She could take care of herself. Her fingers brushed against the crumpled piece of paper in her pocket. Karim did care about her. Was it desperate to call him so soon? She didn't want to appear needy. Perhaps she would give it a bit more time.

A surge of restlessness propelled her to her feet. "Let's go for a walk," she said to Puppy, who was sitting expectantly at her side. She grabbed the leash hanging over the couch, and the fluffy ball leaped with joy. Together, they headed out the veranda door.

- 23 -

WASSILY

Friday, November 11, 2033, 11:30 a.m.

The ring of the doorbell shattered the silence in Wassily's apartment. He shuffled down the narrow hallway, the peeling wallpaper a constant reminder of the renovations he couldn't afford. He yanked the door open a crack, leaving the security chain fastened. Standing outside was a man in a perfectly ironed dark-gray suit. Wassily recognized him. That was the FBI agent from the party—the same one who'd materialized moments after the woman's shocking collapse. Wassily had departed immediately. He knew better than to get mixed up in whatever trouble the FBI was sniffing out.

"Hello, Wassily, may I come in?" the man asked, his voice clipped with authority.

Wassily hesitated. "Can I say no?" he asked.

"You could, but it wouldn't exactly dispel any suspicions."

Wassily's mind churned. He had nothing to hide. Yet, the man's very presence made him nervous. What was the play here? Denying entry could escalate things. He forced a smile.

"Sure, come in," he said, opening the door.

"Thanks." The man brushed past him. There was a slight hitch in his stride. A gun? Wassily swallowed.

He led the man toward the living room, each creak of the floorboards echoing in the tense silence.

The agent's gaze flicked across the room. A breakfast cup and a pizza box still littered the coffee table, and empty beer bottles stood on the desk under the grimy window. Wassily wished he had cleaned up earlier this morning.

"Would you like to sit?" he stammered, kicking discarded socks under the sofa.

"Sure, thanks," the agent replied. He settled into the chair opposite the sofa, his eyes on Wassily's face.

Wassily sank back onto the cushions, the worn fabric offering little comfort.

The agent leaned forward. "Do you recall the woman who collapsed at the party yesterday? The one who choked?"

"Of course."

"She's dead."

Wassily's breath hitched in his throat. "I'm sorry to hear that," he stammered, forcing a neutral tone.

The agent's gaze narrowed. "Did you know her?"

Wassily shook his head, his inner voice screaming at him to be cautious. "No, I didn't."

"You talked with her while Julius and Grace were on the dance floor."

"Yes," he admitted, trying for casual. "Pretty hard to resist a friendly conversation with a beautiful woman, wouldn't you say?"

"What was the topic of your conversation?"

"She asked me if I knew the woman on the stage. I told her that she was my ex-wife. She asked me about Grace's cancer."

"So, the conversation wasn't just about pleasantries, Mr. Wassily?"

Wassily felt a bead of sweat roll down his temple. "Correct," he admitted. "I told her that Grace's cancer had been pretty bad. Like she wouldn't have much time left."

"And then what?"

"Well," he hesitated. "I did tell her the story. About a year ago, Grace mentioned a new treatment at SUEC, some kind of breakthrough. I didn't believe it at the time. We separated and lost touch. But at the party, she looked like a new person. Cured." He forced a chuckle. "Amazing, right? Makes you wonder what they did to pull that off."

"Did you know that the woman was a reporter, Mr. Wassily?" The agent's voice held a sharp edge.

Wassily forced a smile, feeling the corners of his mouth twitch. "I figured something like that. She was certainly quite nosy." He remembered the way she'd hovered near him, peppering him with questions. Maybe he'd been a fool to indulge her. "I'm sorry she choked on something. I saw an ambulance arrive."

The agent's gaze remained steady. "She choked and died."

"My condolences. Life's not fair, that's for sure. One woman battles cancer and pulls through, the other chokes on champagne and dies."

"You were supposed to watch the champagne flutes. Did you see anyone adding something to the champagne?"

"You mean someone spiking the drink?"

"Yes, exactly."

"I didn't notice anything like that. Parties can be distracting, though. I was chatting with a lovely lady. I can't exactly keep my eyes glued to a glass of bubbly the whole night, can I?"

"Did you ever wish her to be out of the picture?"

"Me? What are you suggesting? I told you I didn't know the woman. I just had some small talk with her, that's all."

"I mean your ex-wife, Mr. Wassily. Technically, the divorce isn't finalized, is it? Grace filed and you signed. But she hasn't submitted the paperwork yet."

Wassily felt his palms growing slick. *She* didn't sign? "I didn't know that," he said. "We separated and I never got the finalized documents from her lawyer. But I assumed Grace had handled it."

"Inconvenient that she survived her cancer, wouldn't you say? Did Grace have a life insurance policy with SUEC?"

The agent's words hit him like a blow. "You're the FBI. You tell me. I may not have all my ducks lined up, but I'm not a murderer. In fact, I want her back. I could help her become an influencer. We could start an online channel selling health tips to cancer patients."

"Mr. Wassily, contact with your wife is currently off-limits. Any attempt to meet or communicate with her could be misconstrued and result in your arrest. Understood?" The agent's voice was firm, leaving no room for debate.

Wassily puffed out his chest. He was an expert bluffer and could smell a bluff a mile away. "I've done nothing wrong. I'm a free man and can do what I want." He pushed himself up from the couch. "Is this all, or do you actually have something to charge me with?"

The agent got up as well, holding his gaze. "Not yet, Mr. Wassily. But that window can close quickly."

"Then I guess we're done here."

Wassily led the FBI agent through the narrow hallway and pushed the door open just enough for him to pass. The man brushed past, leaving behind a faint whiff of expensive cologne. Wassily closed the door shut. What a week.

He fetched a Diet Coke from the fridge and flopped back onto the couch, the worn cushions sighing beneath him. But the familiar fizz failed to settle the disquiet in his gut. He tried to think. Something about Grace was different. Way different.

He fetched his phone, went online, and searched for photos from the party. There were multiple chats and tweets about the Zhang heir and his new flame. Wassily scrutinized the photos. Grace's usual bohemian style was gone, replaced with a sleek sophistication. But that wasn't all. Her hair was dyed blonde and she was noticeably slimmer—exercise, maybe? And her figure. She had much fuller breasts now. Perhaps her new millionaire beau had bought implants for her. The most baffling detail, though, was Grace's height. In the past, she had been similar in size to him—easily a good ten inches shorter than the rich guy. Yet in these photos, she and the man stood like perfect equals. Had Grace sprouted several inches in record time? As an adult? Something was not right. What had happened to his ex-wife?

He remembered that Lu'lu, a young surgery resident at SUEC, had told him that his ex-wife had been in the intensive care unit for weeks. He remembered Lu'lu. They had met at a university party. A young woman with a style of comfort and practicality, a far cry from

Grace's newfound glamour. But she had liked him. A lot. A wry smile touched Wassily's lips. He looked at his watch. Eleven thirty a.m. A cafeteria visit wouldn't hurt. With a little luck, he could run into her there and find out more. He grabbed his jacket.

- 24 -

GRACE

Friday, November 11, 2033, 12:30 p.m.

Grace rummaged through the dusty storage room behind the kitchen, uncovering a weathered wooden box. She fetched two of the soft blue towels from the bathroom and transformed the box into a cozy bed for Puppy. Was it indulgent to use designer towels on the dog? A little voice told her the Zhangs wouldn't mind. The Labrador retriever watched her with glazed eyes, struggling to stay on his paws. It had been a whirlwind of fallen leaves outside. Fortunately, the geese had been safely tucked away in their daytime kennel. Now, his eyes drooped, his legs trembling.

Grace carried the dog bed to the family room, Puppy trotting after her. She tucked the dog bed neatly beside the sofa. The pup swayed slightly, nearly collapsing face-first. With a gentle nudge, Grace guided him to his new bed. He curled up and almost immediately drifted off to sleep. Grace felt a pang of sympathy as she watched the pup. His vulnerability was almost heartbreaking. She padded him softly, then sank onto the sofa and flipped open her laptop. A nagging curiosity gnawed at her. She wanted to learn more about Bianca, the woman whose body had given her a second chance at life.

She googled Bianca's name. Her obituary topped the list. With a heavy heart, Grace clicked the Images tab. Several other photos popped up. Some of them showed Bianca at SUEC Hospital, likely taken during her time as a nurse on the surgery ward. One stood out. Clad in a crisp white uniform with a light-blue trim, she stood united with her medical team. A hint of fatigue lingered in her eyes, yet a genuine smile played on her lips. Her colleagues, a diverse group, mirrored her weary yet determined expression. A young man with a mischievous grin rested a casual hand on Bianca's shoulder. Grace zoomed in. She recognized the man. It was a younger Karim, the man from the cemetery, Bianca's husband. He wore a white coat and a SUEC ID badge. That was a surprise. Karim had mentioned that he was a hospitalist, but not that he worked at SUEC. Maybe it was her fault for not connecting the dots.

A chime from her phone interrupted Grace's detective work. It was a text message from Tina. Grace sighed. She had sent Tina a written note of resignation and considered this chapter closed. Apparently, Tina felt differently.

Grace looked at the message. *You never delivered the data from your latest experiment for the DIPUTS drug. I need that data urgently.*

Would it calm Tina down if she responded? Grace looked up the files on her computer and forwarded them. Back to Bianca's history.

Another chime. *The mean data between the treated mice and the untreated controls are not significant.*

Grace exhaled deeply and typed back, *Yes, that's correct.*

Another text. *You did not work diligently. Other fellows in the lab got significant differences.*

Grace's jaw clenched. Other lab members were probably pressured in the same way. But she didn't work for Tina anymore.

I'm sorry, this is what I got, she typed.

Back to Bianca. Perhaps she had been driven into suicide by an evil supervisor.

Another insistent chime. How annoying. Perhaps she should turn the phone off.

You are at the Zhang residence now, right?

Grace told herself to ignore it. But the allure was too strong. She was proud to live in a millionaire's home now.

Yes, why?

They put the contract for my new drug on hold. Did you talk bad about it to Mr. Zhang? I need this contract!

Grace shut the phone down. Not her problem. This woman had harassed her for years. Today would be the end of it.

Back to her investigation of Bianca's past. Grace adjusted the search by selecting "past two years" on the toolbar. Now a more recent photo came up—Bianca with her medical team members at a more informal event. The team, all smiles and relaxed postures, basked in the sun-dappled park. Remnants of a picnic were scattered around them: a crumpled red blanket, a half-eaten burger on a checkered table, and whisps of smoke from a nearby grill. With a beaming smile, Bianca was again in the center. This time, Karim was not part of the group. Grace's jaw dropped. Beside Bianca stood Wassily. He was embracing Bianca, his arm draped around her waist, mirroring her smile.

The world seemed to stand still as Grace tried to process the scene before her. She knew that grin on her ex-husband's face. It was as if she had stumbled upon a secret moment, catching them in flagrant intimacy, a stark reminder of a love that was once hers. She slammed the laptop on the couch table, startling a yelp from Puppy, who looked up at her from his bed. But she did not pat the dog this time. The betrayal twisted too much in her gut. When this photo had been taken, Grace had been confined to her hospital bed, battling cancer. Meanwhile, that rogue had not only betrayed her once but with two women? Or who knew how many.

A grating groan from the back door ripped through the silence. Was Julius back already? He'd said it would take a few hours. Heavy footsteps came toward them, and Puppy lifted his head with a guttural growl. Grace stared at the door. A figure emerged from the shadows, tall and broad-shouldered, framed by the dim light filtering through the doorway. A man with a neatly trimmed dark beard, his face obscured by the gloom. He wore a curious mix—faded dark jeans and a dark suit jacket sharp enough for a boardroom.

"Good afternoon," the man said with a smooth voice, accented with a British lilt. "I apologize for the surprise entrance. I'm Charles, the new butler."

"Really?" said Grace. "Nobody mentioned you."

She looked at the man's hands. White gloves.

"Would you like a coffee?" he asked.

A shiver ran down Grace's spine. The same phrase again. The man had just entered the building and this was his first question? "No, thank you. I just had one," she responded politely.

"How about a sandwich?"

"No, thanks," Grace replied, her voice a touch firmer. "I had a late breakfast and am not hungry."

The man tilted his head, his expression unreadable. "Well, you must eat something. Recovering from cancer requires proper nourishment. Wouldn't you agree?"

She looked at the man. How did he know that she had recovered from cancer? Puppy, sensing her rising irritation, let out a low growl that rumbled in his chest.

"Maybe later," she said lightly. "I need to walk the dog."

She leaned down to pick up Puppy, her fingers brushing against his collar.

"Well, if you insist." The man took a half step back, seemingly accepting her response. But as Grace straightened with Puppy in her arms, he leaped forward and grabbed her neck from behind, encircling her throat with his hands.

Grace gasped for air and dropped the dog to the floor. Puppy barked frantically. The man produced a plastic syringe from his left pocket. It contained some kind of clear liquid. He snapped a cap in the air and held the syringe in front of her gasping mouth. Instinctively, Grace clenched her jaw shut. Her mind screamed, *Poison.* But her nose failed to deliver the air her frantic lungs craved. The world seemed to slow down, her vision starting to blur, the barks from Puppy a distant rumble. She would lose consciousness soon.

With a strength born of desperation, she slammed her elbow squarely into the man's ribs. The impact ripped a gasp from him. The man loosened his grip.

Annya's voice echoed in her mind. *If you are attacked, there's no room for mercy. It's your life or his.* Grace jerked around and pushed her thumb hard into his right eyeball. He cried out and clutched his eye. The syringe dropped to the floor. In a swift movement, Grace fetched it, held it in front of the man's mouth, and pushed. The man stared at her, swallowing in reflex, one eye wide open, the other a bloody hole. Then, he spit the rest of the liquid on the floor.

They both exchanged a gaze of understanding. Whatever was in the syringe, he had swallowed most of it. Grace turned around, grabbed Puppy, and ran toward the door. She jerked it open and ran out of the house, down the stairs toward the path that led to the front gate. The security guard had to be there.

The man leaped after her. She could hear his pounding feet gaining on her with each heavy step. She clutched Puppy to her chest. The furry impediment bounced against her as she sprinted down the driveway. The loose gravel beneath her sneakers skittered. Her lungs burned and her vision blurred at the edges, but a primal fear pushed her further. The man's heavy breaths came closer and closer. Then, a brutal yank at the back of her sweater sent her flying backward. They both crashed to the graveled path and Puppy landed on the ground. He barked frantically.

The man reached for Grace's throat again, his large hands encircling her neck. She tried to scream in terror, but only a pathetic gasp came from her lips. Panic clawed at her mind. *This is it,* she thought. *I'm going to die here.*

To her surprise, the man's grip loosened slowly and the pressure on her throat eased. He stumbled back, a look of dawning horror replacing the predatory gleam in his eyes. He wheezed, clutching his chest, his face contorting in sudden agony.

Grace stared at him, momentarily frozen. This had to be the poison setting in. Finally, her primal instinct roared back to life. She lunged for a large, jagged rock on the path's edge and slammed it against the man's head with a sickening thud.

He sank to the ground, a single wide eye staring accusingly at the ragged tear in her turtleneck. Grace realized that it had been torn during the fight. She fumbled to fix it, her heart hammering against her ribs. The man's gaze shifted to the vast blue California sky above. A rattling breath escaped his lips, and then . . . nothing. Stillness.

Gasping for breath, Grace scrambled to her feet. Was he dead? The silence stretched, heavy and suffocating.

Her neck throbbed, and tremors wracked her body. Had the struggle reopened her wounds? She palpated her neck. There seemed to be no new wound there. Ignoring the pain, she flexed her legs, arms, and hands. They worked. Her right thumb and entire hand were full of blood. Probably the man's blood. Her left hand was clean.

Puppy darted around her and the man, barking frantically. Apparently he hadn't broken anything, a small miracle in the chaos of the struggle.

Grace tried to focus and calm her mind. The guard at the entrance gate. Every fiber of her screamed for sanctuary. Pulling from the last reserves of her strength, she stumbled toward it. The few hundred yards seemed like an eternity. Just across the gate, a solitary figure in a dark jacket leaned casually against a shed, a puff of white smoke curling from an e-cigarette. As she stumbled toward him, his eyes widened in alarm. Grace collapsed into his arms.

- 25 -

ANNYA

Friday, November 11, 2033, 2:00 p.m.

Annya practically flung herself through the doorway of her office at SUEC Hospital, the door snapping shut behind her with a satisfying thud. She collapsed into her chair and let out a long, weary sigh that ruffled the papers on her desk. Today had been busy. She craved a moment of quiet, a cup of coffee that didn't get cold before she could finish it, a chance to push the pause button on the relentless tide of adrenaline rushes in the ER. She loved her job, making a difference in life-or-death situations. But sometimes, it was too much all at once, especially when a life slipped through her grasp.

Annya checked her phone. There was a text from Angus: "Man who attacked Grace arrived at SUEC an hour ago. Call me ASAP."

A new flicker of urgency replaced her exhaustion. She dialed Angus's number.

"Annya, thanks for calling. Our agent on duty thought the man was dead?"

"Yes, we pronounced him dead on arrival," she confirmed. "Who was he? He had no ID on him."

"He was a construction worker from San Mateo, no connection to Grace or Bianca, no violent history. We don't know how he gained entry to the Zhang residence. The security guard swore that no one passed through the gate."

"Perhaps he managed to climb over the fence even though it has razor wires on top?"

"Perhaps. Oddly, the geese were locked in their pen. Julius claimed it was because of their new dog, to prevent a fight."

"Julius locked the geese away?"

"No, Carlos, the house manager."

"Hm, and the man who attacked Grace was not a professional killer?"

"Doesn't look like it. But we're digging into his background to find anything that might tie him to Grace or explain his motive."

"Perhaps I found a clue," Annya said. "I examined him carefully and found a tattoo on his forearm—an ouroboros, a snake eating its tail."

"And why did that pique your interest?"

"It might be a coincidence. But the man who tried to poison Grace at the hospital here had the same tattoo."

"Do you mean they could both belong to some group?"

"Exactly. Can you check if any local group uses an ouroboros as their mascot? A science club, fringe group, biopunks, a cult, a gang . . .?"

"That could be a lead. I'll look into it."

"Did you run a background check on Nathanael Zhang?" Annya asked.

"Yes, of course. I did that even before I agreed to let Grace stay at his home. He did not communicate about her with anyone through channels we can trace. He is far too experienced for that."

"His company, OrchidBio, has major business in cancer therapy?"

"That's correct. That made me wonder: Wouldn't a cure for cancer ruin their business? If there's a pilot patient who was cured of incurable cancer with a new technology, perhaps their survival must fail?"

Annya thought about this possibility. "Nathanael's wife died of cancer. He raised his son as a single father. He and Julius must have a personal grudge against cancer."

"I see."

"Grace told me that both father and son are pestering her about the presumed drug that cured her. I think they are trying to get to her secret in order to make a business out of it."

"What about a competitor?" Angus suggested. "Grace's supervisor made a scene at the party. Her multimillion-dollar contract with OrchidBio was stalled because OrchidBio is after a competing product. That could be Grace's presumed miracle drug. What if Tina is trying to kill Grace in order to eliminate her competition?"

Annya leaned back in her seat. "I heard that she is quite a bully. But there's a line between bullying someone and killing them."

"You never know how far people will go. Desperate people do desperate things."

Annya sighed. "It might not hurt to look into her connections. There could be a link that we don't see yet."

"What if there's a bigger network at play, a web of powerful interests in the pharmaceutical industry who profit handsomely from the status quo? They might see a cure for cancer as a threat to their billion-dollar empire. Eliminating Grace would ensure that there's no living proof of a cure."

Annya thought about it. This idea could only exist in a world where profit was more important than healthy citizens. "I'm afraid the pharma industry isn't the biggest player here," she explained.

"Who is the biggest player?"

"The health insurance industry in the US is about two point six trillion US dollars, the pharmaceutical industry eight hundred fifty billion. This makes the insurance industry roughly three times larger than the pharmaceutical industry," she explained.

"So, Big Pharma cannot hide a cancer cure?"

"Exactly. If the insurance industry believed for a second that the pharma industry was defrauding them of hundreds of billions of dollars, they'd squash them like a bug. The insurance industry could create a totally new pharma industry with their profits. That's how much bigger the insurance industry is."

Angus processed the information. "Okay, we've got an ex-husband in need of cash, a businessman chasing profit, a jealous lab director out for revenge, and two dead assassins with a matching tattoo."

"It seems that we have to follow the tattoo," Annya concluded. "It's a long shot, but for now it's our only lead."

"Consider it my top priority. I'll dig into every facet of that ouroboros symbol. We need to know who's behind it, and fast."

- 26 -

JULIUS

Friday, November 11, 2033, 3:00 p.m.

Julius stretched, his bones popping in the stillness of Rolando's VW campervan. Sunlight dappled through the curtains, gently illuminating the makeshift bed of blankets and pillows. The world seemed to blur into insignificance as he basked in the tranquility of the moment.

Julius couldn't tear his gaze from Rolando. His dark fathomless eyes held him captive, their intensity amplified by his untamed wild hair. His mustache added a touch of sophistication. But what truly captivated Julius was the undeniable aura of danger that clung to his lover. It was a constant undercurrent that kept him on edge, a delicious thrill coursing through him every time he looked at him.

Julius's world was a suffocating spectacle, where every move was on display all the time. Rolando's secret hideaways were like a breath of fresh air, an escape from the constant scrutiny, the never-ending spotlight. Here, amidst their whispers and knowing glances, Julius found a sense of exclusivity, a world just for him. It was both thrilling and intoxicating.

Julius took a deep breath. Today he would do it. Today he'd propose to Rolando. The thrill of commitment coursed through him, the promise of forever. He craved more than just a crush. He wanted a life together, building a nest. He yearned for the comfort of coming home to Rolando every night.

Of course, he knew that Rolando had to hide. He was a wanted hacker. Perhaps a nomadic existence, a love nest that moved from place to place, was the answer. As long as their bond was solidified, Julius could adapt.

He had found the perfect ring. First, it was out of necessity. He could hardly measure Rolando's finger. But it also resonated with Rolando's knack for technology. It was an adjustable wedding band in simple gold, with three large diamonds on it. It could be squeezed to any size. Remarkable.

Julius reached for his jacket to pull out the small velvet box. He would have preferred a more romantic setting, but stolen moments with Rolando were rare. He would do it now.

The shrill ringtone of his cell phone pierced the air. Julius flinched, his gaze lingering on Rolando for a heartbeat longer. Just one more moment.

The phone rang again.

"Julius, your phone," Rolando grunted.

With a reluctant sigh, Julius dug it out of his pocket and glanced at the caller ID. The security guard. He braced himself as he took the call. "Hello?"

Rolando leaned closer, his brows furrowing.

"An intruder tried to kill Grace. You need to come back immediately," the guard urged. "The police want to talk with you."

A jolt of terror electrified him. They shouldn't have left her alone. "I'll be right there," Julius answered curtly.

Rolando scoffed. "I knew that woman was trouble."

"She's my new stepsister, Rolando," Julius said for the tenth time today.

"And what does that mean to you?"

"I like her. We connect on a level I haven't experienced before. Dad likes her too. And right now, she needs me."

Rolando furrowed his brow, his gaze locking on Julius. "Listen, Julius. If this woman truly has been cured of terminal cancer with some miracle drug, she's a walking target. Greedy vultures who leech off current treatments won't hesitate to silence their competition. People kill for far less, Julius. And you're right in the middle of it."

Julius squared his shoulders. "Rolando, you put yourself at risk all the time for what you believe in. Now, it's my turn. Grace needs my help, and I want to keep her safe."

Rolando shook his head. "You're not me, Julius. How do you want to protect her? You've always relied on your father's staff. You don't have a gun, and you lack the guts to use one."

"You're right. I don't intend to hurt anyone. I'll find a way to keep Grace out of trouble, that's all."

Rolando turned around, a dark spark flashing in his eyes. "You want to play hero? You'd rather chase after some dame you barely know than spend time with the man you claim to love?"

Julius looked at him, pleading. "Rolando, you know that I love you, right?" His eyes searched Rolando's face for understanding. Should he confide that he had just wanted to propose? No, that would take the magic away. They deserved a more romantic moment.

Rolando shrugged. "You do what you need to do. If she's that important, then the feds will roll in any moment. Time for me to vanish."

Julius flinched. "Rolando, please don't leave like that. I'll take care of Grace and then I'll be all yours again, I promise. Where can we meet again?"

"I cannot risk getting mixed up with this. The feds would throw a party if they found me in your backyard."

"Anywhere else, then. I'll come wherever it's safe. Just name it." Julius's voice held a desperate edge.

Rolando looked at him, thinking. "I've got a cabin up in Tahoe. You can come find me there at the weekend. But this address must stay between us, Julius. I've grown fond of the place."

Julius beamed. "You have a good heart, Rolando!" He leaned in and placed a passionate kiss on his lips. A weekend in Tahoe. That would be a much better setting for a proposal than the back of a van.

Rolando scribbled something on a scrap of paper. He tore it off and held it out, his eyes locking with Julius's. "Remember this."

It was an address in North Lake Tahoe. Julius knew what would come next. He stared at it, trying to etch it in his mind.

Rolando produced a lighter from his pocket, ignited it with a metallic snap and held the flickering flame to the paper scrap. It caught the flame with a sinister hiss. He tossed it into his empty coffee mug. A wisp of smoke curled upward before the scrap vanished into ash.

"No word of this address to anyone," Rolando said. "Do not enter it into your GPS. Print a map, follow it, and find the place."

"I will!" Julius exclaimed. What a wonderful adventure! He embraced Rolando once more. Then, he threw open the van doors and sprinted toward the Zhang residence.

He found Grace in the dining room, perched on a chair with forced composure. Puppy sat in front of her, his large head on her lap, gazing suspiciously at the uniformed officer beside her. Her dark eyes locked with his as he entered, a spark of relief igniting within them.

Julius felt as if a knife had cut his heart into two pieces. The turtleneck of her sweater was torn, partially revealing her dark-red scar and a blooming red bruise around it. She had pulled back the long sleeve over her right forearm, which revealed a web of bloody scratches and oozing blood.

Julius rushed toward her and inspected the bruises. Fortunately, nothing was broken. He felt a surge of protectiveness. Grace had battled cancer, only to be betrayed by her ex-husband and lose her home. SUEC had treated her with a wonder drug, which had dragged her into the spotlight. Why had a maniac attacked her here? She didn't deserve this.

The policeman politely asked him a few questions. "Sir, were you home this afternoon?"

Julius felt a bead of sweat trickle down his temple. "Yes, Officer. I just took a walk around the park."

He stole a glance at Grace. Her expression was a mask of cool composure. There was this fascinating connection between them. They could communicate without saying a word. From the depth of her eyes, he knew she hadn't mentioned Rolando. Relief washed over him.

The officer scribbled something in his notebook, his brow

furrowed. "Did you see or hear anything unusual, sir?"

Julius forced a confident smile, his heart hammering against his ribs. "No, Officer. I was down by the lake behind the house, listening to a podcast. I must have been too far away to hear anything happening here. Everything seemed quiet." His voice held a slight tremor that he hoped went unnoticed.

The officer nodded curtly. He asked him a few more questions, his eyes fixated on him, observing. Finally, he rose and muttered a perfunctory, "Thanks for your time." He gathered his things and exited the room.

Julius slammed back in his chair, exchanging another glance with Grace. Her expression remained composed. But before they could speak, another commotion erupted at the door. The officer's voice, clipped and professional, mingled with the familiar voice of Julius's father.

A minute later, Nathanael Zhang strode in. His gaze landed on his son, a storm brewing in his steely gray eyes.

"Are you okay?" he asked.

"I'm fine," Julius responded. "I was not attacked. Grace was."

Nathanael looked at Grace. "Who was this man?" he asked, his voice sharp.

"I don't know," she whispered.

Nathanael's composure shattered. "You don't know?" he boomed, a large vein pulsing at his temple. "This clearly relates to your treatment. What cured you, Grace? You live in my house and put us all in danger. We deserve to know."

Julius came to her rescue. "It was not her fault, Dad."

Nathanael Zhang ignored his son. "You tell us right now or you must leave!"

Grace looked at Nathanael, calm and composed.

"And where should she go?" Julius asked.

"Wherever she came from."

"She left her ex-husband and moved out of their home. Then she lived for months in the hospital."

"Seems you know a whole lot about her sob story," Nathanael scoffed. "But not the details that bring danger to this house!"

Grace rose slowly. "I understand," she said with a firm voice. "I wouldn't want to put anyone at risk. And honestly, after what happened today, I don't feel safe here anymore either. Perhaps it will be best for me to leave, indeed."

"Where would you even go, Grace?" Julius asked. "You cannot just run away. You must have a plan."

The light filtering through the window seemed to pass right through her, amplifying the pallor of her skin. She was injured and had no family, no home. "I don't know yet, Julius. But I will figure it out," she said with determination.

"You don't even have a car, do you?" Julius said softly.

"I'll find a way," she said. "I can take a bus, a train, a rental car. The whole point is that nobody knows."

"We cannot help you out there," Julius objected. "You could be attacked elsewhere, no security guard close by."

"I know it's risky," she admitted, "but I can't stay here."

"I agree with that," Nathanael interjected with a resolute tone.

Julius's gaze darted between Grace and his father. Grace filled a void in his heart he hadn't known existed. He remembered her gasp of delight as she settled into his Lamborghini, her wide eyes as she explored their vast home, her laughter as she played with Puppy, and the magic of their dance. In those moments, she seemed to shed all inhibitions, immersing herself fully in the simple pleasures of life. But just like Rolando, she was tethered to secrets and danger.

His father stood tall, hands in his pockets, a monument of pragmatism. Every decision he made was a calculated move driven by years of business acumen. He'd provided security and predictability for Julius, emotions rarely clouding his judgment. Grace had brought warmth, a vibrant counterpoint to his father's controlled world. She approached life with a passion that was both inspiring and uplifting. He couldn't lose her.

"Perhaps we can go together," Julius said, a hesitant smile

playing on his lips. "I've planned a weekend getaway. You can come along if you like."

Rolando's cabin in Tahoe—that could work. It was isolated and off the grid. Nobody would find them there. And if someone did, then Rolando would be far more capable than that useless guard. Besides, this would give them more time together. Rolando was jealous now, but Grace was no competition for him. He would come around.

"Really?" A spark of gratefulness came into her eyes.

"Pack a few things," he said. "We might be gone for a few days. I have a friend at the car rental in Palo Alto who can get us a car without entering our names into the electronic system. I'll pay cash to make it harder to track us. We'll leave in three hours. Can you be ready then?"

She nodded and rushed up the stairs. Julius wanted to follow her, to pack a few things of his own. But his father's hand clamped on his shoulder, holding him back.

"Get that secret out of her," he whispered. "I canceled a major patent deal with her supervisor because of her miracle treatment."

Julius met his father's gaze. "Dad, Grace was just attacked by an assassin. Our priority is to get her to safety, not exploit her!"

Nathanael's eyes narrowed. "Of course. And you stay out of any fight. Whoever wants her, they don't want you. Get the information, then call me immediately."

"The information about her drug?"

Nathanael nodded. "I talked with her ICU nurse. Grace had incurable cancer, metastases everywhere. Then all of her organs were clean. This is revolutionary. A company with this cure will be printing money. You could be at the top, Julius."

Julius felt a wave of nausea. "What about Grace? You just want to use her and toss her?"

"If she cooperates," Nathanael said smoothly, "I'm fine crediting her. There's no existing patent. She has access to her medical files and could claim it as her own invention. We'd license the patent and fund a clinical trial to solidify the idea with other patients. And with that, OrchidBio will be at the core of the business."

"What if Grace and I get killed first?"

"The assassin's gone. Maybe there's another, but the FBI is involved now. That Agent Weber is sharp. Lay low for a few days and let him clean things up. Then, you come back with the formula, and we make our move."

Julius stared at his father, a bitter taste lingering in his mouth. Grace wasn't a lab rat, and this "revolution" felt more like exploitation. Yet, her miracle drug could save millions of lives. He couldn't deny the allure of leaving medicine and starting a business that would eliminate cancer once and for all. Perhaps he could steer this in the right direction and convince Grace to share her secret on her own terms.

"All right, Dad," he finally conceded. "I'll see what I can do."

His father clapped him on his shoulder. "That's my boy."

- 27 -

GRACE

Friday, November 11, 2033, 3:30 p.m.

The afternoon sun slanted through the French windows, casting long shadows across the room Grace was emptying. In ten minutes, her suitcase held the bare necessities: clothes, a scarf, a toothbrush. She paused, briefcase in hand, and gazed out at the sprawl of gardens. The meticulously manicured lawns were lined by a riot of color, the fragrance of red roses and delicate white lilies a bittersweet reminder of an afternoon spent reading by the lake. Even the geese, their honks once a source of amusement, now sounded melancholic. A restless breeze rustled the leaves outside, mirroring the turmoil churning within her.

Who wanted to harm her? Grace tried to analyze the situation like a scientist. Only Julius had known that she'd been alone at home. Had it been naïve to accept his invitation to stay at the Zhang residence after she had just met him? She had placed her trust in him on Annya's word—and her gut instincts.

No, Julius was on her side. She just knew it. He had defended her multiple times. But his shady friend Rolando was a different story—a wanted hacker with an aura of pure danger. Yet, he had been truly surprised to see her at the Zhang home. The attack with a syringe full of poison had been meticulously orchestrated. No, it hadn't been planned by Rolando either.

What about Nathanael Zhang? If he found out about the body transplant, he would consider her a threat to his wealth. What if he knew about it already? Was his fury about her secrecy genuine or a carefully crafted mask? He couldn't be dismissed.

And what about Carlos, the house manager? Their mutual dislike was no secret. But was that grounds for an assassination attempt? The ever-present manager had conveniently claimed a "free day" today. Was that a coincidence or calculated absence? Could Carlos be part of a sinister plot against her?

Grace's thoughts got derailed by a flurry of barks. Those weren't playful; they were accusatory howls echoing from the bathroom. Grace rolled her eyes and shuffled over, already picturing the disaster. There was the massive pup, planted regally in front of the tub. A puddle shimmered at his feet, mirroring his judgmental stare.

"Seriously?" She groaned. "Sorry, I completely forgot to take you for another walk." She grabbed some toilet paper and cleaned up the mess. At least the smart pup had not relieved himself on the carpet. She grabbed the dog and his leash, tiptoed down the stairs, and slipped out through the back door. Two more hours to kill before their departure.

The geese waddled purposefully toward her, and Puppy launched into a barking frenzy. With a sigh, she quickened her pace, skirting toward the front of the house.

Suddenly, a figure in a gray suit emerged in front of her. Angus Weber, the FBI agent, looked at her with an unreadable expression. Where had he come from?

"Hey, Grace, ready for another adventure already?" he asked.

She pointed at the dog, who pulled at his leash. "He needs a walk," she explained. "Would you like to join me?"

"Sure."

As they rounded the corner, Grace saw Agent Weber's Mercedes parked directly across from the mansion. "How could he have known she was leaving? Was she under his personal surveillance?"

"I wanted to visit the cemetery one more time," she said. "Would you take me there?"

He locked eyes with her. "Do you want to see your friend there again?" he asked. "Bianca's husband?"

She shrugged. "I don't know if he'll be there," she responded. The truth was, she didn't know what she wanted. Part of her craved the connection with a familiar face. Someone ordinary, not a millionaire. But another, more cautious part recoiled at the potential for disappointment. "I'm not supposed to contact my old friends or colleagues who knew about my illness. I don't know if I can trust the Zhang family. Karim doesn't know me. To him, I'm just Bianca's friend. That's nice. A little normalcy in a chaotic life."

"Can you do me a favor?" Agent Weber asked.

"What is it?"

"He wanted to invite you for a coffee. Accept. There's a little cafe at the north end of the cemetery. Order a café latte—Bianca's favorite. He likely will too. I need a glass with a smooth surface."

"You want his fingerprints? Why?"

"Just a routine check. Nothing specific at this time. We just check everyone who was in contact with you."

Grace frowned. "I'm not sure I want to see him if he's a suspect."

"We don't have anything on him specifically. Everyone who interacted with you in the last few days is a suspect. It's standard procedure. If you don't go, I cannot check him out. That might be worse."

She thought for a moment. "All right. Fine," she finally agreed.

Agent Weber stepped towards his car and unlocked it with a blip. She slid into the backseat and Puppy leaped onto her lap with an enthusiastic woof. The FBI agent shut the door and settled on the driver's seat, his silhouette etched sharply against the blinding afternoon sun. The engine growled to life, its vibrations resonating through her. She absentmindedly stroke Puppy's fur. Was it right to accept Karim's offer only to get his fingerprints?

They drove the familiar route to the cemetery in silence. Grace stole a glance at Weber in the rearview mirror, her unease deepening with every passing moment. She typed out a message on her phone:

On my way to the cemetery again. Care to join?

A beat of silence followed. Then, her phone buzzed. *On my way.*

"He'll be there," she informed the agent.

Angus Weber grunted in acknowledgment. "Just play it cool. Routine check, remember?"

Grace couldn't shake the suspicion gnawing at her. Why the secrecy? Why not just ask Karim directly to provide his prints? Well, that would require a lot of explanation and expose secrets *she* wasn't ready to reveal.

They parked in the previous spot beside the entrance gate. Grace and Puppy exited the car. She kept the leash short, not sure if dogs were allowed in the cemetery. But there were no signs to the contrary. She followed the path to Bianca's grave, taking a seat on the bench where they had met yesterday.

It took about ten minutes until she saw his figure emerging in the distance. She waved, and he waved back. A rare sense of normalcy washed over her. With his ordinary look, worn jeans, and refreshingly normal life, Karim was a breath of fresh air.

His smile widened as he approached. "Hey, Grace, good to see you again."

"You too," she replied. A knot of guilt tightened in her stomach. She needed to get him cleared, but the idea of manipulating him to get his fingerprints felt wrong.

"Oh, who is this giant baby?" Karim said, crouching down to meet Puppy's inquisitive sniff. A playful glint lit up his eyes as he rummaged in his pocket, producing a crumbled piece of cookie. The pup gulped it down, then sat expectantly, tail wagging.

Grace and Karim both laughed. The heavy weight in her chest seemed to ease. It felt good to do something so profoundly normal.

"Coffee?" he asked.

Grace nodded, battling her apprehension. "There's a charming little cafe at the other end. I know the way."

He smiled. "Excellent!"

They walked down the cemetery path, Puppy trotting happily

beside them. Grace felt a sliver of worry—she hadn't noticed a cafe on her previous visit. Hopefully she would find it. Her gaze darted around, searching for any sign—a banner, perhaps, or an awning peeking through the trees. The path narrowed toward a stand of towering trees, their branches meeting overhead like a somber canopy. At the end, a wrought-iron gate loomed, casting a long shadow.

In the distance, a splash of blue and white emerged behind the trees. The gravel path crunched pleasantly beneath their shoes as they made their way towards it. As they drew closer, they could see a white-painted brick building with a cafe sign and blue awnings over the windows. Outside, bistro tables were bustling with patrons. The café's cheerful facade beckoned them in like a warm hearth.

Grace pushed open the heavy oak door with a gentle creak, Karim following close behind. A wave of enticing aromas—coffee, cinnamon, and freshly baked bread—washed over them. Grace stepped toward the counter and ordered a cafe latte. She glanced at Karim and noticed his eyes lighting up. He echoed her choice, adding a cookie to his order.

"A special treat for your furry companion," he said.

She smiled at him. How thoughtful.

They settled at an outdoor table, Puppy happily claiming a spot at Karim's feet. The afternoon sun cast a warm glow as they chatted about dogs and their shared love for alternative rock music and Italian food. Simple pleasures. The last weeks and months seemed like a distant nightmare. What had she been doing in that opulent mansion? She didn't belong there. She stole glances at the cafe patrons. They had no idea how precious moments like this could be.

The warmth of the latte enveloped Grace's hands, the steam carrying a comforting aroma. She lifted the cup, her eyes meeting Karim's for a fleeting moment before she took a tentative sip. The coffee, smooth and creamy, danced on her tongue. She took another. She usually preferred tea, but this was delicious. She leaned back, savoring the moment.

Across the table, Karim chuckled. His eyes, warm and inviting, crinkled at the corners. "Excuse me," he said softly, leaning towards her.

Grace looked at him, wondering what he wanted.

A playful glint lit up his face. "You have a little . . ." He gestured toward his own mouth, then back at her. "Foam," he clarified.

Grace felt a warm flush on her cheeks. She reached up self-consciously, when Karim's hand gently intercepted. With slow deliberateness, he extended his thumb, his eyes holding hers with an unspoken question.

Grace nodded slightly, a silent permission that felt like a surrender.

He smiled and gently wiped the foam away. His touch sent a jolt through her, a spark that made her breath hitch.

"There," he said, "all clean."

Grace could only manage a breathless smile, her gaze flickering away from his intense stare.

A disgruntled woof erupted from underneath the table, shattering the unexpected intimacy between them. They both laughed.

"Oh, right!" Grace exclaimed.

Karim reached for the cookie, a playful glint in his eyes. "Looks like someone's getting impatient," he said, breaking the treat into bite-sized pieces.

Puppy, sensing his chance, thumped his tail excitedly against the floor. With eager anticipation, he watched Karim's hand descend, then snapped up each proffered morsel in a flash. When the last piece was gone, Puppy paused, his hopeful gaze flitting between Grace and Karim. When it became clear that the treat session was over, he nudged against Grace's leg and settled contentedly underneath the table.

Karim grabbed his own coffee mug and took a long sip.

His fingerprints will be all over it, Grace thought, feeling a twinge of guilt.

He leaned back in his chair. "So, you and Bianca were lunch buddies?" he asked.

Grace met his gaze with a flicker of apprehension. How much

did he already know? "Yes," she confirmed. It was perfectly reasonable to ask about their connection.

"How come you weren't at her funeral, but you came to her grave now, nearly a year later?"

She couldn't think of a good excuse. He had probably seen the news as well. "I had a struggle of my own," she explained. "I had metastasized cancer. I was in the hospital when Bianca died."

"I'm sorry to hear that," he said, his voice sincere.

"I underwent an experimental treatment and am fine now," she added quickly. "I'm incredibly grateful that I got a second chance."

He nodded slowly, his gaze lingering on her face. "I can see that." The expression in his eyes held a hint of something deeper, a quiet defiance that mirrored something within her. She felt a connection with this man. It wasn't the comfortable warmth she shared with Julius. It was more raw, a connection based on pain and resolve.

"Maybe, we appreciate the little things more when we've stared into the abyss," she whispered.

The raw honesty in her words hung in the air between them.

Karim leaned forward slightly, his eyes holding hers. "The abyss can leave its mark," he said softly, "but it can also teach you to fight back."

The weight of his words settled on her, a quiet understanding passing between them. They had both walked through darkness and emerged on the other side.

When she glanced back at Karim, she found his gaze fixed intently on her outstretched leg. Self-consciously, she followed his line of sight. She admired her new body—the long legs and delicate feet. But now, the small circular mark on her right ankle seemed to stand out. A snake, its body forming a perfect circle by biting its own tail.

"What's that?" he asked.

The question sent a jolt though her. She was walking around with Bianca's body. He must have recognized the tattoo at exactly the same place where his wife had it.

"Oh, just a tattoo," she replied a tad defensively.

"How did you get it?" His eyes held a colder glint now.

She tried to think fast. He might know where Bianca got hers.

"Bianca showed me her tattoo and I thought it looked cool," she said. "I decided to get one as well. The right ankle seemed perfect."

"You chose the same spot and the same serpent?"

"It's a striking design, isn't it? I thought it was both mysterious and elegant."

A beat of silence stretched between them. His gaze locked onto hers, his eyes probing for any sign of deception. A single mote of dust, caught in a sunbeam, hung motionless in the quiet air.

"Bianca never mentioned you," he finally said, his gaze sharp.

"We only met a few times for lunch in the SUEC cafeteria. I was already very sick then. I promised to visit her when I was better. But then she died."

"The tattoo was a homage, then?"

Grace forced a small smile. "Exactly. To Bianca."

"Really?" He looked at her suspiciously. "Do you know what it means?"

"Well," she admitted, "I just thought it looked beautiful." The answer seemed hollow even to her own ears.

"I see." He looked at her with a weird expression in his eyes, a mix of sadness, hurt, perhaps a flicker of danger. The magic moment seemed to dissipate.

"It's getting late," she said, rising from her chair. "Maybe we should head out."

Karim nodded and pushed back his chair, the scrape echoing in the quiet that had settled around them. Most other customers had left. In the distance, a man in a gray suit leaned casually against the wall of the building.

They walked back to the cemetery in silence. Their conversation had left an unspoken tension in the air. As they passed the iron gate, Grace felt a strange mix of disappointment and unease. Here she walked Bianca's body beside her grieving husband towards her grave. How bizarre was that. They continued down the path, each lost in their own thoughts.

Rays of golden sunlight filtered through the leaves of towering oaks above them. The air hung heavy with the scent of damp earth and moss. Puppy, oblivious to the undercurrents swirling between his human companions, sniffed at everything and anything with a joyous abandon. Suddenly, he veered off the path with a triumphant yelp and snatched a fallen branch, its size far too large for his small snout. He proudly paraded it before his humans, the oversized stick jutting awkwardly from his jaws, tail thumping with glee. They both smiled.

They continued down the winding path, which was flanked by rows of weathered headstones, each one a silent testament to a life lived. Vibrant bouquets of flowers added splashes of color to the somber scene, each carrying its own message of love, remembrance, and longing. In the distance, a lone figure knelt, placing a single white rose on a freshly turned mound of earth.

As they approached the south exit of the cemetery, Karim regained his composure. "It was good seeing you again, Grace," he said, his voice warm again.

"Same here," Grace agreed, her heart aching for him. She was captivated by his vulnerability and wished she could soothe him, help him overcome his pain.

"Would you like to meet again tomorrow?"

She hesitated. Julius had drilled into her to not tell anyone that they were leaving town. "Maybe," she said evasively.

Karim's smile faltered, disappointment crossing his features.

"I will call you for sure," she said quickly.

His smile returned, brighter this time. "Until tomorrow, then," he said, a hint of longing lingering in his voice.

Grace forced a smile in response, the weight of her secret departure heavy on her chest. As she passed the gate and crossed the street, she saw Agent Weber already waiting in his Mercedes, the engine purring.

- 28 -

JULIUS

Friday, November 11, 2033, 6:00 p.m.

Julius slammed the trunk of the rental car shut and let out a frustrated sigh. He paced back and forth beside the car, scanning the driveway leading to the Zhang residence. Where was Grace? He checked his watch. Six p.m. He'd thought he would find her tucked in bed, recovering from the attack. Instead, he'd found an empty room, the bed meticulously made. A lone suitcase, tightly packed and zipped shut, stood sentinel in the doorway. So, she'd planned to leave with him, but now she was gone. There was no note, no explanation. Had something happened to her? A new attack? Puppy was missing, too. Had they just gone for a walk, or had they both been kidnapped? Julius paced, waiting. This woman was driving him crazy.

The last sliver of sun dipped below the horizon, casting long shadows across the deserted driveway. An unsettling chill crept into the air and coiled in Julius's gut. He couldn't wait much longer. He glanced at his watch. Fifteen more minutes. If she was not back by then, he would call the police. He tightened his grip on the car keys, the metal digging into his palm. Every rustle of leaves, every distant creak sounded amplified in the tense silence.

In the distance, two faint glows appeared and steadily grew brighter. Headlights. They pierced through the twilight, carving a path down the driveway toward him. Julius's blood ran cold. He recognized the sleek lines of the silver Mercedes behind the harsh beams. It was Angus Weber, the FBI agent. What did he want so late in the day? Did something bad happen?

The car came closer and rolled to a stop. Two people were in the car. The driver was Angus. He offered a curt nod, his expression unreadable. The passenger door opened, and a blonde woman emerged with Puppy on her arm. It was Grace. The car pulled away with a screech of tires and disappeared into the night.

"Where have you been?" Julius asked Grace with a raised voice. "I searched for you everywhere."

"I'm so sorry for the scare, Julius," Grace said with a disarming smile. "I forgot to leave a note. I had to walk Puppy. The geese were too territorial, so Agent Weber gave me a ride."

"I see," he said. She couldn't walk the dog because of the geese? That was hard to believe. The park was vast, plenty of room to avoid the birds. Besides, Grace had spent many hours here over the past few days. The geese knew her by now. They wouldn't chase her. Something else was going on.

"Are you ready to leave?" Grace asked politely.

"Yes. I got your suitcase already."

"Thank you!"

Nathanael Zhang appeared on the doorstep. He squinted into the gathering darkness, his gaze landing on Julius and Grace. "I heard a car," he said. "Are you ready to leave?"

"Yes," Julius choked out, suppressing tears that welled in his eyes. He felt overwhelmed. Rolando's visit cut short, a brutal attack on Grace, the FBI at his door, and a desperate escape ahead. Would they be safe out there? His heart pounded. He walked briskly up the stairs and emotionally embraced his father.

The sudden display of affection caught Nathanael off guard. He patted Julius's back awkwardly, his gaze shifting to Grace. "Julius is risking his life for you. Do you understand that?"

Grace swallowed. "I know," she whispered.

"Bring him back unharmed," he said slowly.

She held his gaze. "I promise."

Julius turned around and climbed into the car, pressing the start button. The engine roared to life with a low hum.

Grace joined from the passenger side, cradling the giant Labrador retriever in her lap. Puppy yipped with excitement, nuzzling the dashboard and wagging his tail against the seat.

Nathanael stood sentinel on the porch, his silhouette outlined by the warm glow of the entrance hall. He waved at them briefly, then turned around and disappeared into the house. The massive oak door of the Zhang mansion groaned shut behind him.

Julius gripped the steering wheel tighter as he reversed out of the spot and turned around. Dust swirled behind the car as he pressed the gas pedal. The headlights swept across the driveway, gliding past the geese on the lawns and turning around the corner where Grace had been attacked mere hours earlier. As they approached the gatehouse, the security guard's wide-eyed stare bored into them. They had not told anyone that they would leave. The point was to vanish without a trace. Like Rolando when he'd disappeared after a cyberhacking job. Rolando. He didn't know that Julius was coming with Grace. Hopefully he wouldn't throw a fit.

In the passenger seat, Grace gently ran her fingers through Puppy's soft fur. The dog had nestled snugly in her lap, looking up at her with adoring eyes. Her gaze drifted to the road ahead. She looked determined and a bit excited, not scared at all. That was infectious. Julius reached for the stereo. The radio crackled to life and Rihanna's "Umbrella" burst forth. Julius cranked the volume, the playful defiance of the song filling the air.

Grace and Puppy both swiveled their heads toward him, surprise etched across their faces. "Rihanna?" Grace asked with a hint of amusement. "I thought your taste ran more toward Bach and Beethoven."

Julius chuckled, a warmth spreading through his chest. "Well, Grace," he drawled, "there's a whole lot you don't know about me."

Her smile bloomed. "Intriguing," she replied, leaning forward with a playful glint in her eyes. "I can't wait to find out more."

He nodded, his eyes moving back to the road ahead. "First things first—let's lose any tails."

He directed the car down the dimly lit streets of Atherton. The silhouettes of grand mansions loomed in the night, their elegant facades barely discernible against the starless sky. They approached a solitary traffic light, its red glow enforcing a pause.

"Do you see the on-ramp sign?" he asked.

She squinted, looking ahead. "There! Right after the gas station," she said, pointing at a faded blue sign.

He cast a quick glance at the surrounding vehicles. A beat-up VW Beetle, a flashy Porsche, a black SUV with tinted windows. Were any of them a threat?

When the traffic light switched to green, he punched the gas, tires squealing as he took a sharp turn onto the US 101 on-ramp. A quick glance in the rearview mirror showed an empty ramp behind them. A thrill of relief and satisfaction washed over him. Nobody had followed them. They had done it. They had escaped. He merged onto the highway, the roar of traffic engulfing them. Here, amongst the swarm of headlights and anonymous faces, they were just another pair on the move.

- 29 -

JULIUS

Friday, November 11, 2033, 7:00 p.m.

Fueled by the rhythm of the radio, they continued down the highway toward San Francisco. As twilight descended, shadowy sentinels of trees and buildings lined the road. Every mile devoured felt like progress, an escape from unknown followers. Grace, the printed map on her lap half covering Puppy, traced their course down the highway toward the Bay Bridge signs.

"Take this exit here." She pointed ahead.

"A living navigator beats a GPS any day," Julius mused, merging them onto eastbound I-80.

"True," Grace replied with a smirk, adjusting the map to reveal Puppy's mischievous eyes peeking out. "But can we sniff out the nearest puppy stop like a GPS can?"

"We will figure that out as well." He smiled. "Are you okay with that big guy on your lap?"

"Of course." She laughed. "He's practically glued to me anyway. He wouldn't stay on the back seat."

It felt good to be on the road. As they drove on, the cityscape dwindled in the rearview mirror and was replaced by the shimmering bay on their left and a mix of fields, trees, and warehouses on their right. The traffic around them thinned.

They passed a billboard for OrchidBio. Julius recalled the rare embrace with his father—a fleeting balm for the emptiness in his chest. His father, a titan of success, had always tried to mold him into a mirror image of himself. But Julius constantly fell short of his expectations.

He stole a glance at Grace, who gently scratched the Labrador retriever behind his ear. The massive pup's eyes fluttered shut, a blissful grin spreading across his furry face. She chatted with Puppy in a playful voice. There was no hidden agenda in her eyes, no veiled expectations. When their gazes met, a wave of affection washed over him. There was genuine acceptance in her eyes, a quiet admiration for the man he was. A surprised laugh escaped his lips, a sincere reaction to the revelation in her eyes. A deep connection crackled between them, a shared vulnerability.

He turned the music off. "You must be exhausted after all you've been through today," he said gently. "We still have about three more hours ahead of us. You could take a nap if you like?"

"Believe me, I've survived worse," she said, gently stroking Puppy.

"You mean the cure from cancer? Did you expect to die?"

"That also," she said evasively, her gaze drifting out the window.

"Why did this man want to kill you, Grace?" he pressed gently. "Don't I deserve to know after an assassin came to my home today?"

She sighed. "Honestly, Julius, I have no idea. But I assume it has to do with my treatment at SUEC."

"Why would your treatment cause such a reaction?" he asked. "Who would kill a cancer survivor? Even if you were cured with a new miracle drug, it makes no sense."

He felt her gaze lingering on him. "It might shock you," she said calmly.

He scoffed. "I am a physician, Grace. I've seen it all. There's no medical mystery that would faze me."

She adjusted the turtleneck of her sweater. "Well, you haven't seen everything yet, Doctor. It wasn't a drug that saved me. It was a surgery."

"A surgery? But you had metastases in every organ!"

A guarded look settled on her face. "That's all I can tell you. The procedure is classified. Can you respect that?"

He forced a smile. "Of course." His pulse quickened. He had uncovered a piece of the secret. It was good that they were on this road trip together. He would find out the rest as well.

Grace's words echoed in his mind. *Classified . . . surgery.* What kind of surgery could eradicate metastasized cancer? His gaze drifted to her neck. The turtleneck of her sweater covered her circular scar perfectly. But he remembered it very well. It was unlike any surgical scar he'd ever seen. A breast cancer survivor with a peculiar neck scar . . . It had to be connected. Maybe an implant of some sort, a reservoir releasing a miracle drug? But then wouldn't there be a telltale bump? Her physique was flawless.

Frustration gnawed at him. His mind wasn't smart enough to figure this out. But he had plenty of experience with exploiters. If someone saw this new surgical cure as a threat to their profits or power, then the surgeon who had performed it would be the real target. Why silence Grace, the survivor, when the key to replicating the procedure resided with the surgeon?

"We need to take the exit here," Grace said, pointing at a diversion ahead.

Julius focused on the road ahead. He took the 188B exit and followed the signs toward Sierra Ville/Lake Tahoe. The road stretched out before them and they both got lost in their thoughts. The only sound was the rhythmic hum of the engine.

A flicker in the rearview mirror sent a jolt through him. A black SUV with tinted windows had taken the same exit, subtly changing lanes whenever they did. Was this the same van that had stood at the traffic light beside them in Atherton? Julius changed from the most-right to the most-left lane and accelerated. He glanced in the mirror again. The SUV kept up. There were few cars on the road. Julius made a swift turn back to the right lane, sending Puppy tumbling from Grace's lap. The mysterious van mirrored their movements.

"Hey, what are you doing?" Grace exclaimed, holding on to the startled dog.

"We're being followed," Julius said, his voice tight. "We need to find a way to lose the black SUV behind us."

Grace flipped down the sun visor and peered into the small mirror, her reflection etched with worry. Julius decelerated sharply, forcing the SUV to swerve around them. A flicker of surprise crossed the driver's face as they shot past. Julius laughed. But their victory was short-lived. The black SUV lurched toward the emergency lane, tires screeching in protest as it slammed to a halt.

"Hit the gas!" Grace exclaimed, reaching for the dashboard to steady herself.

This was their chance. Julius punched the gas, the engine roaring as they shot past the surprised driver.

Had they shaken them? No. The SUV roared back to life, merging back behind them with renewed force. It felt like a predator stalking its prey.

"They're not giving up!" Grace cried.

Julius accelerated more, but the black SUV persisted in trailing them. As they approached a sign for a rest area, Julius made a split-second decision. With a jerk of the wheel, he sent the car swerving off the main road. The tires squealed as they veered onto the exit ramp, dust billowing in their wake. The SUV missed the exit and screeched to a halt in the emergency lane a few hundred yards down the road, its brake lights a menacing glow in the distance.

Julius slowed down and drove to a rest area. For a moment, they were alone. But for how long? A veil of trees, their branches heavy with leaves, sprang up between them and the highway, offering a temporary cloak of invisibility.

Grace, chest heaving, released her grip on the dashboard. "Did we lose them?" she whispered.

Julius scanned the rearview mirror. "For now," he said grimly. "But they might wait for us to rejoin the highway."

"Or they could be bold enough to drive backward down the exit lane," Grace said. "We need to act quickly."

They slowly drove into the resting area, the crunch of gravel beneath their tires. There was only one other car—an old, dented Toyota. A coat-clad figure was walking a golden retriever a few yards away. The driver's door was slanted.

"We need to ditch the car and get a new one," Grace said firmly.

"What? Steal one?" Julius sputtered, eyes wide.

"Borrow," she corrected. "Park behind them, leave the key in the car. It'll be a fair trade, considering the circumstances."

"But that's . . . illegal!" Julius protested.

"We can worry about that later," Grace countered, urgency edging into her voice. "Right now, we need to escape."

Julius hesitated. Who was the man in the SUV? Grace had been attacked by an assassin earlier today. Better not find out.

"What about our suitcases?" he asked.

"I'm afraid, we won't be able to retrieve them from the trunk. It would risk valuable time and draw unnecessary attention. We'll have to leave them behind."

"Well, we can always buy new stuff. But how do we start the car?"

Grace smirked. "Leave that to me."

Julius stared at her. "I thought you were an honest person."

"I am," she responded. "I got survival training. And I want to stay alive as much as you do. Park behind the car."

Julius did as he was told. He felt overwhelmed, like when Annya barked orders at him in the ER.

Grace handed him the leash. "Take Puppy for a walk. But don't stray too far. When you hear the engine, grab him and jump in."

Julius' heart pounded in his chest. He took the leash, the leather cool against his sweaty palm. He pushed open the car door, a gust of wind whipping his hair. Grace opened the passenger car as well and Puppy bounded out. Julius walked around the car and clipped on the leash. The dog eagerly darted toward a patch of grass, his tail wagging tentatively as the lure of adventure pulled him forward. The man with the golden retriever gave them a cursory glance.

Puppy lunged toward the golden blur with a playful bark. Julius gently steered him in the opposite direction, looking apprehensively at Grace, who approached the other vehicle. She slipped into the driver's seat and fumbled with the front panel. Suddenly, the engine sputtered and roared to life.

Adrenaline shot through him. He bolted for the car, Puppy excitedly racing with him. Grace unlocked the passenger door. With a yank, he flung it open and scooped up the protesting puppy. A beat of indecision passed over his face as he glanced at the passenger seat. It was too small for both him and the dog.

"Get in!" Grace urged, her voice sharp.

He squeezed into the car, the puppy wriggling and yelping, landing half in Grace's lap.

The man behind them let out a guttural yell.

"Julius, for the love of God, shut the door!" Grace shrieked.

Julius shoved the pup further into her embrace and slammed the door. Grace sped off, tires squealing.

The man behind them waved frantically, launching himself into a desperate sprint, his dog following him. But their figures quickly morphed into a flailing silhouette in the rearview mirror.

Grace merged onto the highway. Julius stole a glance back. The black SUV sat in the emergency lane, waiting. But as they joined the highway, the SUV did not follow them. It shrank in the rear mirror until it was gone.

A rush of exhilaration washed over Julius. He glanced at Grace. Their eyes met in a shared burst of laughter and Puppy joined with a joyful yelp. Against all odds, they had outsmarted their pursuers in this wild ride. They had gotten away.

- 30 -

ANNYA

Friday, November 11, 2033, 7:00 p.m.

The shriek of wheels tore through the ER. A young woman in a white coat, face etched with panic, propelled a gurney carrying a patient in a doctor's coat—a jolt of white against sterile white. Every head whipped around. A code on a colleague wasn't something they saw often. Annya's breath hitched. It was Dr. Triveda.

"What happened?" Annya demanded, her voice sharp with concern, as Lu'lu, the assistant surgeon, skidded the gurney to a stop. Tears welled in Lu'lu's eyes. "I found her unconscious in her office. No idea what happened."

Dr. Triveda's face was flushed, her eyes shut. Annya leaned in. "Dr. Triveda, can you hear me?" she called, gently shaking the woman's shoulder.

She blinked briefly. "I am so tired," she responded slowly.

Annya palpated the woman's wrist. The pulse was very fast.

"Perhaps a heart attack?" Lu'lu suggested.

Annya placed her stethoscope on Dr. Triveda's chest. The heartbeat was fast and irregular. The lung excursions were shallow but clear.

Two ER nurses appeared beside them, a young woman with cascading braids and an older man with iron-gray hair.

Annya's mind raced. The fake nurse at the rehab center and the reporter at the party had both died of belladonna poisoning.

"Dark room, stat! IV and activated charcoal," she barked. The nurses sprang into action, whisking Dr. Triveda away. Annya followed them.

In the procedure room, Annya grabbed a large-bore suction catheter, tore open the packaging with a practiced snap, and shoved it through Dr. Triveda's nose down to her stomach.

"Syringe," Annya commanded. She listened intently with her stethoscope, searching for the telltale gurgle of gas in Dr. Triveda's stomach to confirm that the NG tube found its mark. Simultaneously, the young nurse secured a blood pressure cuff on Dr. Triveda's left arm. The elder nurse, his movements measured and precise, brought the charcoal solution. He handed it to Annya, then established another IV in the right arm and initiated an electrolyte drip.

Annya attached the suction catheter to a container of lukewarm water and added the appropriate dose of activated charcoal, a black, gritty mixture that resembled fine sand. She slowly pumped the fluid into the stomach and then withdrew it via suction, aiming to flush out any remaining toxins and residual belladonna. The black slurry retrieved with each cycle confirmed the presence of the charcoal absorbing the poison. After repeating this process several times, Annya monitored Dr. Triveda's gastric contents until the charcoal returned clear, indicating minimal remaining toxin in the stomach. Next, she got physostigmine from the medical cabinet and administered it slowly.

"What's that?" asked the younger nurse.

"An antidote for an intoxication," Annya explained.

"How do you know she's intoxicated?" she asked.

"I'm working based on an assumption," Annya said.

They watched Dr. Triveda's blood pressure and heart rate on the monitor.

"No effect," Lu'lu said from the back.

Annya had almost forgotten about her. "We have to be patient," she said. A sudden thought struck her. "Lu'lu, you were the junior surgeon who assisted in Grace's surgery, weren't you?"

Lu'lu blinked, surprised. "Yes, why do you ask? It's strange, actually. You're the second person to ask that today."

"Is that so? Who was the first?"

"Wassily, her ex-husband. I ran into him in the cafeteria."

"Interesting. What did he want?"

"Information. He asked how Grace recovered from her cancer. I told him I had no idea, and even if I did, patient confidentiality . . ."

"And what did he say?"

Lu'lu shrugged. "He pushed a bit, arguing he was still her husband. When I wasn't giving anything away, he just left."

Annya tried to connect the dots. Grace's ex-husband had been in the hospital prior to the poisoning attack on the woman at the party and prior to a presumed poisoning attack on Dr. Triveda. That man was suspicious. She had to inform Angus. The FBI had to check him out.

Annya's gaze flicked back to the monitors beside Dr. Triveda. The frantic beeps had morphed into a steadier rhythm. Though the surgeon's eyes remained closed, the flush on her face had receded, leaving a more natural pallor.

"We saved her," Annya announced.

"You're amazing!" Lu'lu exclaimed. "The way you handled that unknown poisoning was incredible!"

The senior nurse checked Dr. Triveda's pulse and nodded in agreement. "No doubt she's the best physician we have in the ER."

Annya felt a flicker of triumph. "It was great teamwork. Thanks, everyone!" she said.

This time, she had won. But who would be next?

- 31 -

GRACE

Friday, November 11, 2033, 9:30 p.m.

The crisp air bit at Puppy's trembling form outside the brightly lit grocery store in Truckee. Grace remembered reading somewhere that Truckee, nestled close to Lake Tahoe, held the dubious honor of being the coldest town in the nation. She leaned down and wrapped her arms tightly around the shivering dog. Thanks to the reduced sensitivity of her body, the cold held no sting for her anymore. But Puppy's shivers fueled her sense of urgency.

Beside her, Julius bounced slightly under the neon lights of the parking lot, his gaze searching the darkness. To their right, towering cedars cast long shadows that danced across the asphalt.

Grace had overheard Julius's call with Rolando. His boyfriend's voice had been sharp with anger. *Don't come to the cabin with a stolen car. Ditch it in the parking lot at the mall and wait for me at the Safeway store. I'll pick you up there.*

So, here they were, waiting. Every passing car sent a jolt of anticipation through them, headlights momentarily blinding them before slicing on into the darkness. Few shoppers weaved around them, their bulging grocery bags occasionally bumping against them as they hurried toward their cars. The silence felt heavy with anticipation.

Finally, a weather-beaten VW campervan approached slowly and stopped in front of them. Grace recognized the driver's mustache and dark eyes. Rolando looked at her with undisguised hostility.

Julius was quick to jump into the passenger seat.

Grace looked at the car, hesitant where she could go.

"Here," Rolando grunted, and pointed at the back seat. She opened the sliding door and ushered the dog in. Then she followed him into the van, sliding the door shut with a thud. The dog whimpered and put his big head in her lap.

"Did you take a photo of the stolen car's license plate?" Rolando asked.

Julius bobbed his head eagerly.

Rolando's gaze flicked to Grace. "Cell phone?"

"Just the one you gave me," Julius blurted, pre-empting Grace.

"I left mine at home," Grace said. "I mean, the Zhang residence." A flicker of defiance sparked in her eyes.

"This isn't your home," Rolando growled.

A tense silence stretched between them.

"Let's just get out of here, all right?" Julius interjected. "No need to fight."

Rolando whirled on him, his voice a sharp bark. "Shut up, Julius. You promised silence about my cabin. How much weight does your word hold? You are a constant disappointment!"

Julius flinched and shrank back in his seat.

Rolando hit the gas, the car surging forward. Grace gripped the armrest. The cedar trees blurred into a green streak as they sped past. They finally screeched to a halt in a deserted spot at the end of the parking lot, beneath the ominous shadows of the trees.

Rolando cut the engine, climbed out, and circled the car. "Out," he commanded, opening the passenger and back doors.

Grace's heart hammered against her ribs. What did he want? With a gentle nudge, she coaxed Puppy to move enough for her to wriggle out from under his bulk. Julius followed suit.

Rolando reached beneath the passenger seat and emerged with a long, glinting object. A metal detector. He swept it purposefully over Julius, the whirring machine the only sound that dared to break the suffocating silence.

"You're clean," he declared, then turned his attention to Grace. "Now you."

"I've implants from a surgery," she explained.

"Where are those?" he asked.

"In my spine," she said, pointing at the back of her neck.

He swept the metal detector over her. It beeped at the back of her neck. He moved the detector to the front, and it beeped again. He pulled down her turtleneck and stared at her scar.

"Easy there," she hissed. "That's private."

His eyes met hers, cold and calculating. "I'm your best bet of survival," he grunted. "You can walk away now. Or if you want to hide in my cabin, you'll pass my little test."

Grace instinctively retreated a step, clenching her jaw.

He shrugged. "Your choice."

The silence stretched, thick and suffocating.

"Let me do it," Julius intercepted. "What are you searching for, Rolando?"

"A small implant," Rolando explained. "Like a hard peanut, lodged under the skin."

Julius stepped closer. "May I?" he asked hesitantly.

Grace, caught off guard by his sudden proximity, managed a curt nod. Julius's fingers brushed against her skin as he pulled down the turtleneck. He gently palpated her exposed neck, the touch sending a shiver down her spine. His fingers carefully followed the exposed scar. Their eyes locked.

"There's something," he murmured, his voice low and serious. "Right under the scar, Grace. Please, feel for yourself."

He gently took her free hand and guided it to the area. She knew what he meant. A small, hard lump nestled just beneath the smooth scar tissue. She'd brushed it off before, assuming it was just scar tissue itself, part of the healing process. But now, beneath Julius's watchful eyes, a jolt of alarm ripped through her. Her fingers traced the spot again. The lump felt distinct, a definite object under the thin layer of skin. How had she missed it? Shame burned in her chest. She'd focused on letting the scar heal completely and never probed this deeply before. Or perhaps the attack earlier today had moved the object further to the surface. She looked at both men in surprise.

Rolando's hand dipped into his pocket, emerging with another glint of metal—a Swiss Army knife. "We need it out," he declared, his voice leaving little room for argument.

Grace stared at the exposed blade. What if the implant served some vital function, a key to her head–body integration? Her fingers trembled as she touched the spot again.

"If you are a study subject for SUEC's new treatment, then they marked you like a lab rat," Rolando explained. He leaned closer. "The faster we get it out, the better."

The logic was brutal yet undeniable. With a tight nod, Grace bent her neck to the left, exposing the area with the palpated object.

"Do it," she said.

Rolando tossed the knife to Julius. "Doctor, your turn."

Julius grimaced, his face etched with concern. "Any alcohol?"

Rolando leaned into the car and rummaged behind the back seat, pulling out a crumpled pack of tissues and a surprisingly decent-looking bottle of whiskey.

Julius poured a generous amount onto the tissues and the blade. The sharp bite of liquor filled the air. He dabbed the makeshift swabs at the sensitive area of her neck. Grace clenched her fists, trying to steady herself. The coolness from the alcohol aggravated her skin. She felt a sharp stab at her neck, sending a jolt of pain through her, followed by a trickle of warmth running down her skin.

Instinctively, she reached up to touch the spot, but Julius's firm grip on her hand stopped her.

"Don't touch that," he said gently. "You don't want to cause an infection."

She put her hands down.

Julius slightly squeezed the area, then held a crimson-stained tissue in front of her with a smooth, metallic object on it that glinted faintly in the dim light.

Grace gasped. It was a small metallic capsule, indeed. She wanted to reach for it, but Julius held her back again.

"One moment," he said gently. "We have to attend to your wound first." With the other hand, he reached for a clean tissue and pressed it firmly against the wound. The pain dulled slightly.

"Do you have some Band-Aids?" he asked Rolando.

Rolando leaned into the car again, rummaged in the back, and returned with two crumbled pieces.

"That'll do," Julius said. "Please place it over the tissue here."

Rolando opened the Band-Aids and secured them over the tissue on Grace's neck.

Julius stepped back and smiled. "A perfect surgery," he said.

"Thank you!" Grace smiled back.

They looked at the small metallic object in his hand.

"Can I see it?" Grace rasped.

"It's a bug." Rolando stepped between them and snatched the object from Julius's grasp. "We have to get rid of it as quickly as possible." His eyes darted around the parking lot. With a muttered curse, he strode toward a dark-gray pickup truck boasting a Montana license plate. He flung the object into the truck bed.

"Tourists," he muttered. "Hopefully on a shopping spree before vanishing on the highway. That'll buy us a few hours, maybe the night."

- 32 -

ANNYA

Friday, November 11, 2033, 10:00 p.m.

The concrete steps scraped beneath Annya's shoes as they descended into the basement of SUEC Hospital. An undercover operative for years, Annya had access to the security center. Angus followed close behind, his footsteps echoing against the bare gray walls. Harsh fluorescent lights cast the stairwell in a silvery glow.

The steps gave way to a cold, sterile corridor with a heavy metal door at the end. A glowing security panel pulsed beside it. Annya placed her ID card on the reader and the door swung open with a mournful groan.

Inside, a mosaic of monitors on the wall showed live feeds from various areas of the hospital. Two security guards sat hunched before the display. As Annya and Angus entered, they swiveled in their chairs, suspicion in their eyes.

Annya greeted them with a warm smile. "Good evening," she said. "Just a routine inspection. This is FBI Director Angus Weber."

The taller guard grunted in acknowledgment, his gaze lingering on Angus. "ID, please."

Angus produced his credentials. The guard inspected his badge with a curt nod and turned back to the monitors.

Annya and Angus pulled up chairs at a vacant workstation.

"Are you sure it was another belladonna intoxication?" Angus asked.

She nodded. "The lab results confirmed it. And the security team found a half-eaten sandwich on Dr. Triveda's desk that contained high quantities of belladonna."

"The surgeon wouldn't have stood a chance without your quick thinking," Angus said, his voice filled with admiration. "I need to talk with her as soon as she wakes up."

"It'll be a while. We gave her a strong sedative to ensure a full recovery."

"I need a timeline. Who did she come into contact with before this happened? And where did she get that sandwich?"

Annya nodded. She swiftly pulled up security footage from the hallway outside Dr. Triveda's office for the 6 to 7 p.m. window. There were no cameras inside the offices themselves. The footage showed Dr. Triveda entering at 6:15 p.m. At 6:30 p.m., Lu'lu, the assistant surgeon, rushed in. Then, a minute later, she burst back out, frantically calling for help.

"She looks genuinely distressed," Annya said.

Angus squinted at the footage. "Could be an act. She knows there are cameras, right?"

"Yeah, perhaps. She might be a bit naïve, but I cannot imagine that she would violently attack her supervisor."

"Ambition can take people to dark places," Angus countered.

"Maybe."

"Can you check where she was before?"

"Sure." Annya activated the face recognition software. A flurry of locations materialized on the screen: surgery rooms, wards, the cafeteria. Her eyes scanned through.

"There," Angus rasped, pointing at a figure in the cafeteria. "Can you zoom in on that?"

She complied. "That's Wassily," she said. "Grace's ex-husband. How does he know Lu'lu?"

Angus grinned. "Well, it seems Mr. Wassily gets around. He also dated Bianca about two years ago."

"What? I thought he cheated on Grace with another woman?"

"Yes, he did that as well."

"Disgusting!"

"Well, womanizing is not a crime," Angus said. "But his presence here, on the same day of Dr. Triveda's incident, might be a different story. Can you find Dr. Triveda in the cafeteria as well?"

Annya refocused on the face recognition software, her eyes scanning the crowd in the cafeteria. "There she is," she muttered, pointing at the screen. "Dr. Triveda, waiting in line with a sandwich. Wassily was in the cafeteria at the same time as her."

Angus leaned closer. "That was around noon, several hours earlier?"

Annya nodded. "Correct. The poison could have been slow-acting, or perhaps she didn't eat the sandwich until later. There's even a chance the sandwich was tampered with after the fact."

Angus scrutinized the footage. "Lu'lu is in the cafeteria as well. And many other SUEC employees. There, in the line behind Dr. Triveda, is the woman who made a scene at the party."

Annya checked. "Oh, that's Tina, Grace's supervisor."

"And here are you." Angus grinned. "Just a few yards away."

Annya nodded. "You are correct. This was prime lunchtime."

"Can you see if anyone put anything in Dr. Triveda's food?"

"No. I also don't see any direct contact between Wassily and Dr. Triveda. Wassily met Lu'lu for lunch in the cafeteria. Dr. Triveda walked away with her sandwich."

"There's no evidence that anyone put anything in her food in the cafeteria," Angus concluded. "Although, there are some blind spots at the checkout station. There's no camera in her office either, so crucial moments are completely blank."

Annya sighed. "What about Bianca's husband, Karim? He met Grace at the cemetery. Was that just chance or orchestrated?"

Angus rubbed his chin. "He had a better reason to be at the cemetery than Grace did. And I ran his fingerprints. Clean record—not even a parking ticket. His prints were not on any of the champagne glasses from the party. Plus, there's no security footage of him at the hospital today."

"So, no sign of him at any of the scenes." Annya scrolled through the footage again. "Lu'lu reported that she was scheduled to assist Dr. Triveda with a transplant biopsy in the late afternoon. But Dr. Triveda didn't show up. So, Lu'lu went to her office and found her on the floor."

"Why was Wassily in the hospital?" Angus wondered.

Annya shrugged. "All the others work there. But he had no reason to be there."

"Exactly. Lunch break or not, his presence just before the incident is suspicious, to say the least. We may not have a direct connection yet, but Wassily is about to get my full attention."

A cell phone buzzed. They both instinctively reached for their phones. It was Angus's that vibrated insistently. He answered.

"Really?" he said, his eyes rolling upward.

Annya watched him, trying to decipher what was going on.

Angus's grim expression deepened. "I'm on my way," he muttered, hanging up.

"Is everything all right? I thought we were heading home together?"

He pushed his glasses up his nose. "I'm sorry, Annya. Apparently Julius and Grace decided on a spontaneous Tahoe getaway." His voice was tinged with frustration. "Nathanael Zhang informed my team and we had them tailed to ensure their safety. But Julius and Grace managed to lose them. They stole a car and slipped away without a trace."

"What?" Annya couldn't believe her ears. "They are in deep danger."

Angus nodded. "Worse. Grace's chip got compromised. They discarded it on a truck somewhere near Sacramento. Our team nearly scared a honeymoon couple to death pulling them over for questioning."

"So, you have no idea where they are right now?"

"They vanished in a parking lot. Security footage in the area is wiped clean. That's Rolando's handiwork, Julius's cyberhacker boyfriend, no doubt."

Annya's voice tightened. "What a nightmare. We have to find them as soon as possible. They could be in grave danger."

Angus nodded. "My team's already on it. They'll scour the Tahoe area and its surroundings."

"Every minute counts. We need to find them before their pursuers do."

- 33 -

GRACE

Friday, November 11, 2033, 10:00 p.m.

The wind howled outside the cabin. Grace watched as Julius tended to the fire within the stone hearth, his movements deliberate and familiar. The oven hummed softly, gradually pushing back the cold that seeped through the cabin walls. The flames crackled and danced, licking their way upward, their tips brushing the heavy iron grate that held a bed of glowing embers. The logs, thick with the scent of pine, surrendered to the heat, their outer bark splitting with pops and hisses. Deeper within the fire, a mesmerizing kaleidoscope of orange, red, and yellow flickered, casting long, playful shadows across the rustic cabin. Wisps of smoke curled lazily up the chimney.

A furry puddle of contentment, Puppy dozed on the weathered leather couch, his body rising and falling with each breath. Rolando had given him a whopper of a bone—the evidence gone, devoured with joyous abandon. Now, the pup was fast asleep. Occasionally, he twitched his velvety ears and gently wagged his tail. Perhaps he dreamed of chasing squirrels through the snow-dusted woods that stretched just beyond the window. It had been a long day for him, and for all of them.

Grace arranged plates on the sturdy, rustic table. Behind her, Rolando deftly transferred a large family-sized pizza onto a wooden serving platter, the scent of melted cheese and savory toppings filling the air. Grace's stomach rumbled in anticipation, reminding her just how hungry she was. She found three wine glasses in the kitchen cabinet and placed them on the table. Rolando wrestled with a corkscrew, his brow furrowed in concentration. With a satisfying pop, the cork surrendered, and a rich, inviting aroma of red wine joined the symphony of scents. He filled the glasses with a deliberate measure.

Julius hovered nearby, hands shoved deep in his pockets. His gaze flicked between Grace and Rolando, then darting away. Perhaps it was the unfamiliar nature of this simple domestic scene that threw him off-balance, or perhaps it was the tension brewing between Rolando and Grace that made the air crackle.

"All right," Rolando announced, setting the pizza down with a slight thud. "Let's eat."

They sat down and reached for the pizza. The first bite was met with a chorus of *mmms* and nods of approval. The melty mozzarella cheese stretched in gooey strands, the tangy tomato sauce and savory toppings truly delightful. They ate in silence for a while, punctuated only by the clink of cutlery on the plates.

As the meal neared its end, Grace stole a glance at Rolando. He sat beside Julius, one arm casually draped over the back of Julius's chair. It seemed less about comfort and more about claiming territory. He met Grace's gaze, a provocative glint in his eyes, as he snatched the last slice of pizza and slowly raised it toward his mouth. No courtesy, no question—it was a ruthless grab. The unspoken challenge hung heavy in the air, a primal display of possessiveness. As he began to chew, he looked at her with a flicker of aggression, and then his eyes darted to Julius, a subtle shift that spoke volumes.

Across from her, Julius remained blissfully oblivious. He scraped the last bit of cheese from his plate with a sigh of contentment. "That was delicious, Rolando," he said, his gaze lingering on the other man. "Thank you for everything." He leaned back in his chair, the aged wood groaning softly beneath his weight, a satisfied smile on his face.

"Just doing what any friend would do," Rolando said, patting Julius's shoulder. His eyes flickered back to Grace, a cold glint replacing the warmth. "But Grace is not part of the equation."

A bitter taste filled her mouth. "With all due respect, Rolando," she interjected, "I'm the reason Julius and I are still alive. I hijacked that car and drove us away."

"Is that so?" Rolando scoffed, his gaze pinning her down. "Then perhaps you can enlighten us. Why are these people so keen on killing you? Because Julius and I seem to be in the middle of the cross fire."

Julius took a sip from his wine. "You said it had something to do with a new surgery at SUEC?" he asked Grace. "What was it, exactly? If they implanted a chip in you, it must be something groundbreaking."

Here they were again. Grace gripped her glass of wine tighter. A touch of tipsiness warmed her cheeks. "I can't say," she replied courtly.

Rolando scoffed. "What do you mean you can't say? We just risked our necks for you. What's so damn important about this surgery?"

Grace bristled. He wouldn't understand. The weight of her secret pressed down on her. It was only a matter of time that news about her surgery leaked. Media scrutiny, ethical debates, predators trying to prey on her—she would be dissected from every angle, a human guinea pig thrust into the merciless spotlight.

Her voice was tight as she countered, "Let's just say the surgery fundamentally altered who I am."

Rolando shrugged. "Change is inevitable. It's a fundamental part of life."

"Exactly," she echoed. "But some people seem to have a problem with that change."

"Which people?" Julius asked, his brow furrowed.

"I don't know," Grace admitted. "Someone powerful enough to send assassins after me. Maybe they don't like what I represent." Her gaze flickered to Rolando, a silent challenge in her eyes.

Rolando shrugged. "Who cares. Some people won't like you until it is popular to like you."

"But a cure for metastasized cancer? How could anyone oppose that?" Julius's voice crackled with disbelief.

A heavy silence descended, punctuated only by the crackling

fire. In moments like this, Grace yearned to share the weight of her miracle cure, the sheer improbability of it all. To blurt it out to Julius, her soulmate, to see the awe in his eyes. But the fantasy soured instantly. What if he reacted with fear? Disgust? What would he do if he knew about her body transplant? The risk was too high.

"I'm truly sorry," Grace finally whispered. "There are things I can't share."

"You can, but you won't," Rolando concluded.

"That's right," Grace said firmly.

The room seemed to spin around her, the weight of the conversation crushing her. An echo of Annya's words resonated in her mind: *You don't owe anyone an explanation.* Her new reality was a fragile construct. It could shatter with one wrong word. The surgery hadn't just changed her physically; it had reshaped her very essence. She wondered if she would ever feel whole again. Revealing her secret felt like an insurmountable risk.

She pushed herself to her feet. "I'm tired," she announced. "I'll go to bed."

Rolando studied her for a long moment. "Very well, Grace," he finally said, his voice low and menacing. "Consider today a courtesy. You can stay here tonight. But tomorrow morning"—his eyes hardened—"you and your problems disappear from my doorstep. I don't want any part of it."

Her eyes flickered to Julius, but he offered no solace. His gaze was fixed on the floor. With a curt nod, she acknowledged Rolando's ultimatum. She turned around and walked toward the back room, the one designated as hers upon arrival.

She pushed open the heavy wooden door with a creak and was greeted by a wave of cool air. The bedroom had a rustic charm, laced with the faint scent of pine needles. The centerpiece was a large bed piled high with fluffy comforters in a patchwork of faded blues and browns. Across the room, a weathered dresser stood under a window with simple rustic curtains on each side. Behind the window, the moonlight cast an ethereal glow through the trees.

Exhaustion pulled Grace across the room. She sank gratefully onto the mattress, which sighed beneath her weight. She reached out to the sturdy nightstand beside the bed and traced the smooth grain with her fingertips. It felt cool and reassuring.

The stress of the day came down on her. The frantic escape from the Zhang residence, the heart-pounding chase on the highway, a hijacked car, waiting in the dark, a bug discovered under her skin, Rolando's simmering hostility. This was life, raw and real. Who in their right mind would choose a second round of endless pain and suffering?

As if to rebel against her dark thoughts, her mind replayed different memories. The cool evening breeze ruffling her hair as she stood shoulder to shoulder with Julius, Puppy nestling in her arms, their laughter as they evaded the trailing van, the thrill of escape pulsing through their veins. Julius holding her close as they swirled around on the dance floor, his eyes deep and endless. These moments were everything. Even if tomorrow held nothing but a bullet with her name on it, this feeling of being alive had been worth it all.

A crumbled T-shirt hung over the back of the chair beside the bed. Perhaps Rolando, for all his faults, had a thoughtful side after all. She got up and changed.

Then, she stepped across the hallway to the small bathroom, a cramped space lit by a single flickering bulb. The walls were clad in rough wooden panels. To her left was a small, foggy mirror above a chipped porcelain sink with three toothbrushes, two nestled together in one cup, the other standing solitary. That had to be hers. She claimed it and brushed her teeth, letting her gaze meander around. To her right was an old-fashioned pull-chain toilet, and in the corner behind her was a narrow shower stall with a curtain that had seen better days. It reminded her of her shabby apartment in San Francisco.

She was used to this kind of establishment, but what about Julius? The contrast to the lavish Zhang residence, with its marble floors and glittering chandeliers, couldn't be starker. Why would a millionaire's son choose to spend his weekend in a rundown cabin? And what drew a self-proclaimed Robin Hood to the epitome of the elite? What common ground could they possibly share? With his looks and pedigree, Julius could date anyone, royalty included. What attracted him to Rolando? Was it the thrill of rebellion? A need for authenticity? She couldn't understand it.

Grace went back to her room and crawled under the rough covers of her bed. A chill clung to everything—the threadbare mattress, the scratchy blanket, even the large pillow. Clearly, this room hadn't been occupied in months. Grace moved her toes to warm up her feet and stared up at the rough-hewn wooden panels of the ceiling. Each knot and imperfection stood out in the dim moonlight. Restlessly shifting, she knew she wouldn't be able to fall asleep until she had warmed the bed with her body. A faint murmur of voices drifted to her from the living room. Rolando and Julius, their laughter muffled by the distance. The two men were clearly enjoying themselves. But what about her? Where would she go tomorrow? The silence of her bedroom felt suffocating.

She remembered Julius's burner phone on the table beside the entrance in the hallway. Almost a day had passed since her last connection with anyone besides Julius. He had Ronaldo now, but what about her? A prickle of longing snaked through her. Rising again soundlessly, she tiptoed to the hallway on her bare feet, the floorboards protesting with each silent step. She snapped the phone and slipped back into her room.

She burrowed beneath the covers, the phone a cold weight in her hand. Holding her breath, she strained to hear any sounds from the living room. Thankfully, the muffled laughter continued. They hadn't noticed. She nestled deeper under the thick blanket, grateful for its increasing warmth, and inspected the phone. It was simple, but it had an internet browser.

She opened her Gmail. Three new messages blinked accusingly on the screen, each from Tina. The first began with a brusque *Did you talk with Mr. Zhang?* A knot of apprehension tightened in Grace's stomach. The message ended with a cold *You owe me.* With a swift swipe of her finger, she deleted all three messages.

There was another message from Annya. *Hello, Grace, you and Julius went to Tahoe? I'm worried. Please let me know that you're okay.*

Grace's heart hammered against her ribs. She tried to think. Was it safe to respond? Annya was her friend, the one person who always had her back. Rolando had made it clear that he didn't want to have anything to do with her. Tomorrow, she would be on her own.

Grace's fingers trembled slightly as she typed a quick response. *No worries, I'm fine. Will be back for my follow-up exam next week.*

It had to be true. Thankfully, her week's worth of medication was tucked in her jacket pocket, a stroke of luck considering the suitcase she'd left behind. But next week, she would need refills, another challenge in her precarious situation.

Finally, she saw the message from Karim. *I really enjoyed my time with you.*

Her heart skipped a beat. She reread it and reread it again, a flicker of warmth chasing away the cold dread. She genuinely liked him. He was unlike any other man she had met. Wassily had initially been breathtakingly charming, but after they'd married, he'd switched to constant criticism. *That outfit looks dull. Why don't you put on some makeup? Can't you park the car correctly? That idea is stupid. Why bother with all that extra work?* She couldn't remember when Wassily had said anything nice to her.

Julius, on the other hand, was her soulmate, a puzzle piece in her life she hadn't even known was missing. Their conversations flew effortlessly, bound by a deep understanding. Julius was able to finish her sentences, not in an annoying way, but because their thoughts ran on similar tracks. They could sit together in comfortable silence, simply enjoying each other's presence. But Julius did not look at her body like Karim did. Julius flirted with Rolando in the living room. He had called her his new stepsister. That was how he saw her. The laughs of the two men felt like a knife twisting in her gut.

Karim was different. His gaze at her held an intensity that both captivated and unnerved her. His look seemed to devour her whole, laced with a deep visceral yearning. A connection she craved. But how could she even contemplate a relationship with the secret of her surgery festering inside her? Karim could never know the truth about Bianca. He would hate her for stealing his wife's body. That was how he would see it. That's how many people would see it. She couldn't risk that judgment. Yet, on the most primal level, she felt the acceptance of his gaze when he looked at her. There was a spark within him, a glimmer of physical acceptance she desperately needed.

With a silent sigh, she typed, *I enjoyed it as well. It's good to have a friend.* And she added a smiley face.

The door to the bedroom next to her shut with a bang. Music began to play. No more hushed voices. This was awkward. She placed the phone on the nightstand with a soft thud. *Try to sleep*, she told herself. She rubbed her icy feet. She couldn't sleep if her feet were so cold. But her exhaustion soon caught up with her. Her eyelids grew heavy, the insistent thrumming of the music from next door a strange lullaby. One by one, her thoughts drifted away, replaced with fragmented dreams and a yearning for a normalcy that seemed increasingly out of reach. As the last embers of consciousness flickered, a single tear escaped her eye, tracing a cold path down her cheek before sleep finally claimed her.

- 34 -

WASSILY

Saturday, November 12, 2033, 8:00 a.m.

The shrill ring of the doorbell shattered the peace in Wassily's apartment. He shuffled to the door, peering through the peephole. A young man beamed back, holding up a badge: Reporter, *San Francisco Chronicle.*

Wassily studied the figure for a moment. The young man looked eagerly at the closed door. Should he just ignore the intrusion? He didn't like to be disturbed that early. But the reporter might loosen his purse strings for whatever story he was chasing. The idea of some quick cash was tempting. Opportunities like this didn't come knocking every day. With a sigh, he opened the door.

The man straightened. "Good morning, Mr. Wassily," he said, "I'm Daniel Wright from the *San Francisco Chronicle.*"

Wassily stood square in the doorway, arms crossed. "Hi. What can I do for you so early on a Saturday?"

"We're putting together a piece on the passing of Ms. Petra Petrova, our colleague who died at the Zhang party. You were the last one who talked with her before she died, weren't you? Do you remember any details from her choking incident?"

"Perhaps. Depends what you're looking for. My memory isn't what it used to be for free."

The reporter hesitated, his gaze meandering from Wassily to the hallway behind him. "Could we talk inside?"

Wassily did not move an inch.

The reporter reached into his leather purse, extracted a crisp fifty-dollar bill, and held it out. "This is for your time, Mr. Wassily."

Wassily's smile broadened as he took the bill. This was serious business, indeed. "Sure, come this way," he muttered with an inviting gesture. He turned around and led the man to the kitchen. The couch in the living room could easily lull this talker into an unwanted stay.

The reporter followed, his eyes taking in the cramped room. The kitchen barely held a fridge and a counter, leaving no place to sit.

Wassily leaned against the cool metal of the stove with practiced indifference. "So what do you want to know?" he asked.

The reporter shifted nervously. "Well, we're trying to understand the circumstances around Petra's death. Did you notice anything out of the ordinary when you talked with her at the party?"

Wassily shrugged. "She choked and died. Unfortunately, that happens sometimes."

"She was young and healthy, no prior conditions whatsoever."

"Who knows," Wassily said smoothly. "Sudden deaths due to undetected cardiac issues do happen."

"That's not what happened here."

"Seems you already got your story figured out."

"As I said, Petra was completely healthy. Clean diet, regular exercise, annual checkups—there's no way she had a hidden heart condition."

The reporter's confidence grated on Wassily's nerves. The man had walked in with all the answers, as if he'd already scripted his story.

"If you know everything already, perhaps you can excuse me now. I have some work to do."

"Hold on a minute," the reporter countered, his voice firm. "We haven't discussed her choking in the security footage. You were right next to her. Can you tell me anything else that might help explain what happened?"

Wassily shrugged. "What should I tell you? She choked on champagne. I was as surprised as you."

"We deserve some straight answers, Mr. Wassily."

"Of course you do. But I didn't observe anything out of the ordinary. I'm not a detective."

The reporter leaned in, his gaze turning sharp. "Perhaps it has something to do with the miraculous recovery of your ex-wife from terminal cancer?"

Now Wassily *was* surprised. "What does my ex-wife have to do with a choking reporter?"

"You tell me. Could there be a connection between Petra's death and the secrecy about that 'wonder drug' that your ex-wife was treated with?"

"I don't know anything about a wonder drug."

"Your ex-wife was working in the lab of a prominent cancer researcher at SUEC, right? She had terminal cancer and was suddenly cured?"

"Yes, that's right," Wassily confirmed, thrown off guard by the sudden shift in topics.

"Perhaps she took a new drug that she herself developed?"

"Not that I'm aware of," Wassily said. But a sliver of doubt crept into him. "And why would that be so important?"

"Well, the researchers who cure terminal cancer will win so many Nobel Prizes that the Nobel committee will have trouble handing them out fast enough. It would be a media sensation."

Wassily eyed the man with renewed interest. "Would you pay for information about such a drug?"

"Of course. We're in the dark. Was it a drug from her own lab? Can it cure any breast cancer? And other cancer types? Information like that could be worth a fortune."

"Well, Grace—my ex-wife—did work day and night on a new cancer drug in her lab at SUEC. But she told me that it didn't work as expected."

"Could that have been a disguise?"

"I don't think so. Grace is honest to a fault. Not one to play games."

The reporter leaned back, a glint in his eyes. "Did you know that her supervisor is on the verge of signing a multimillion-dollar contract with OrchidBio? Any chance your ex-wife stood to gain from that?"

Wassily stared at the reporter. He had been on a similar trail, visiting Lu'lu for lunch at the hospital. Her guarded silence had spoken volumes. She knew an important secret about Grace's surgery, that much was clear. But she had not revealed what it was. Was Grace involved in some lucrative business he knew nothing about?

"I don't know about a business deal," he rasped. "But you can be assured that I'll find out."

The reporter placed a business card on the counter. "Call me if you do. I'm sure my editor can make it worth your while."

Wassily picked up the card, twirling it between his fingers. "Sure, just be prepared to make it an offer I can't refuse. Next time, you won't be the only reporter I offer my services to."

"Mr. Wassily"—the reporter's voice took on a more serious tone—"freelancing is a fickle business. There's no fortune to be made. But a front-page exclusive would surely produce a nice return for both of us."

"That will work for me."

He didn't want to hear more about the harsh realities of freelancing. With a firm nudge on the reporter's back, Wassily guided the man towards the door. The man mumbled a goodbye and slipped through the doorway. Wassily watched him go, shutting the door behind him with a soft click.

He glanced at the reporter's business card. Grace and a multimillion-dollar deal? Maybe the man was right. This was a story worth telling. But it wouldn't be on his terms. No, this story would be told on Wassily's terms.

He tucked the card into his pocket, the gears in his mind starting to spin. This morning had just taken an interesting turn. With a newfound spring in his step, he walked back to the living room, whistling "We are the Champions."

- 35 -

GRACE

Saturday, November 12, 2033, 8:00 a.m.

Grace stretched, the crisp mountain air nipping at her cheeks as she threw back the covers. The aroma of freshly brewed coffee wafted through the cabin. Peeking out the window, she gasped. Overnight, a thin layer of snow had transformed the tall pine trees into a pristine white wonderland. Sunlight glinted off the branches, each one a delicate sculpture against the cerulean sky.

The sounds of Rolando and Julius drifted from the kitchen—playful jabs punctuated by easy laughter. She craved that kind of easy camaraderie, the kind that came from shared experiences. But for her, the world was more complicated. She could not share her story with anyone. With a sigh, she slipped into the rustic bathroom. Turning the faucet handle with minimal resistance, Grace cranked the shower knob to its maximum setting. The blast of heat stung a bit, a welcome sensation against her numb skin. She enveloped herself in the steam, the moisture a temporary balm.

Her hands glided down her new body. She liked it better than the old one. The soft skin and even curves were flawless, beautiful. Would anybody else ever touch it? How would she explain the scar around her neck? Guarding her secret was a constant effort, a never-ending vigilance that wore her down. She couldn't afford to slip, to let her true self show. The risk was too great.

Would this go on forever? Would she ever find anyone she could trust so completely that she could share her secret? Would she ever find love again? The thought lingered as she stood under the cascading water, the steam swirling around her like the haze of secrets within.

She turned the water off, wrapped herself in a towel, and walked back to her room. She felt a pang of regret as she thought about her lost suitcase with all the new designer clothes. There was no other choice than to dress in the same clothes as yesterday. She checked herself in the mirror beside the door. The sweater looked as good as new. It *was* new; the designer for the Zhang family had just bought it earlier this week.

Julius's burner phone caught her eye. She'd meant to put it back on the table in the hallway last night. Perhaps she could do that now on the way to the kitchen. But a quick email check wouldn't hurt, would it? She tapped open the browser.

There was a new email from Karim. *Same place, same time?*

Sorry, I had to leave town, she responded. *But I could call you later today?* What would she say? She wasn't sure. She just felt an urge to talk with him.

To her surprise, an instant response appeared. *That would be nice.*

She gave it a thumbs-up and instantly felt much better. All she needed was just one good friend.

There was another email from Wassily. *I was arrested because of an alleged poisoning attack at the party. Call Agent Weber. I have nothing to do with this.*

Grace scoffed. Typical. He contacted her when he needed something. And what a sweet irony. Someone was finally blaming him. The FBI would resolve this. Wassily was a cheater, but otherwise harmless in the grand scheme of things. Her ex could sit this out. She would ignore his message.

Grace's hand hovered over the close button. But a flicker of movement at the top of the screen snagged her attention. A new text message. She hesitated. This was Julius' phone. Was it okay to look? But times were desperate. If he conversed while they were on the run, she had to know what this was about.

She clicked on the small green icon with the white speech bubble. It was a message from Nathanael Zhang. *A surgery cured Grace?*

he wrote. *That is revolutionary. Find out more. We will patent it.*

What on earth was that about? Julius's father wanted to patent her surgery? Her heart hammered against her ribs. Below it, another text, sent from Julius last night. *Grace was cured by a new surgery, not a drug.*

Disbelief flooded her. She looked at the phone screen. Julius had started the conversation. He had texted his father, directly after she had told him about the surgery. Julius, the man she'd trusted, had revealed her secret and planned to exploit it with his father. A bitter laugh escaped her lips. Wassily, the womanizer, or Julius, the false friend—what difference did it make? They were all the same: exploiters.

She stomped into the living room. Rolando glanced up from sizzling eggs, spatula poised midair. Julius, caught midsentence, swiveled his head toward the sound. A stray piece of bacon dangled from his fingers, forgotten halfway to the eager dog at his feet. Puppy whimpered in confusion. Grace stood framed in the doorway, brandishing the cell phone in her hand like a weapon.

"You wanted to sell my therapy through your father's company?" she snapped at Julius. "Is that the real reason you befriended me?"

Julius's expression shifted from nonchalant to startled. "Grace, you're misunderstanding," he stammered. "Yes, my father is interested in your treatment. He mentioned it himself. But I care about you. You know that. I am your friend."

Grace's jaw clenched so tightly her teeth ached. "Care about me?" she spat. "Is that what you call prying into my treatment and using it to line your father's pockets?"

"It's not like that, Grace," he countered, his voice strained. "My father sees the potential. He wants to help—"

"Help himself, you mean!" Grace cut him off, her voice a whip.

Rolando interjected. "Hey, let's all calm down here. What were you doing with Julius's phone, Grace?"

Before Grace could protest, he snatched the phone from her grasp with surprising speed. A quick glance at the screen sent a dark flush creeping up his neck.

"So, you decided to check your *email*?" he spat, his voice laced with a dangerous edge. "And, Julius, you texted your father? Is this your idea of hiding?"

Silence filled the room. Julius and Grace looked at him, caught.

"The text was on the highway," Julius mumbled.

"And then you brought the damn phone here?" Rolando roared, his voice tinged with disbelief. "Are we playing hide-and-seek? And you, Grace," he snapped, turning his glare on her, "you logged into your Gmail?"

She shrugged. "I thought it was a burner phone," she said, a tide of guilt settling in her stomach.

Rolando threw his hands up in exasperation. "This is beyond stupid! Your anonymity vanished the moment you accessed your Google account! That opens your entire digital footprint on Google, not just your emails! When you log in, your location is revealed based on the phone's IP address."

"Not everyone's a hacker," Julius muttered, a hint of defiance clinging to his voice.

"You're being hunted by an assassin, Julius!" Rolando scoffed. "And the FBI. Do you honestly think they can't track you? This isn't child's play, and your carelessness could get us all killed!"

"But you gave Julius a burner phone for secrecy?" Grace asked.

"Exactly. As long as its use remains unknown, it's a direct line to me—and to me only," Rolando explained. "Whoever's after you will scour your online presence for activity. The second you log in to any of your usual accounts, it's like switching on a beacon. They can track the phone's location through the IP address, and with Julius's little text, connect that to the SIM card. Finding you then becomes a simple matter of following the trail."

Rolando looked at the screen. "And Miss Genius here sent an email to the CIA," he exclaimed, throwing his arms up once more.

"What are you talking about?" Grace shrieked.

"You emailed Annya Segond. Don't you know that she is a

CIA operative? And practically in bed with the FBI director, Angus Weber? We could as well have hung a flag on our cabin: We are here!"

"Annya is CIA?" No. It couldn't be. Not Annya. The woman with whom she'd shared her deepest secrets, who had helped her get back on her feet, celebrated every milestone with her? The woman she'd thought was her friend, her rock. She had been a carefully constructed lie. All those meetings and whispered confessions had been nothing but a job—Annya keeping tabs on a national asset.

A sharp beeping sound pierced through the cabin.

"Here we go," Rolando roared, his voice tight with urgency. He jumped toward a computer screen at the entrance. With a tap, the display flickered to life, revealing two Range Rovers barreling down a dusty road lined with towering pines.

"What is that?" Grace asked.

"This is the road to our cabin," Rolando grunted. "They'll be here any minute. This way." He sprinted toward a back door that slammed shut behind him with a bang.

Julius, without hesitation, bolted after Rolando. Grace, heart pounding, scooped up Puppy and raced after them. The door led to a dimly lit garage where Rolando's pickup truck and a sleek Smart electric car sat parked.

"Take the Smart," Rolando barked to Grace, throwing a key in her direction. It landed at her feet. He pointed at the electric car. "I put a battery in that takes you about five hundred miles. We're taking the van."

Julius stood frozen, his eyes darting between Grace and Rolando.

"You're coming?" Rolando shouted at him.

"What about Grace?" Julius asked.

"Get in the car, Julius," Rolando pressed. "The FBI's on my tail. Twenty years in prison or worse. I've got to vanish."

"And you're taking me with you?"

"No," Rolando countered. "I'll duck out back at the grocery store in Truckee. You take the van, head home. Sell the car, pay me back later."

Julius looked undecided. "Where are you going?" he asked Grace.

"Nowhere you need to be," she spat, her eyes blazing. "You and your father want to exploit me. I'm better off alone."

Julius looked at her, hurt.

Grace stormed past him, shoving Puppy into the Smart's back seat. She started the car, and the engine roared to life.

Julius remained rooted to the spot.

Rolando was already in the van. He rolled the window down. "Get in the damn car, Julius! Now!"

Julius finally scrambled into the passenger side.

"Ladies first," Rolando barked, his voice tight. "Right turn. The others are coming from the left."

Grace's hand slammed down on the gear shift, shoving it into reverse. The screech of tires echoed through the garage. She caught a glimpse of Julius through the window, his gaze a mask of desperation. It didn't matter. He was a traitor. Yesterday, she'd almost told him her secret. The thought sent a fresh wave of nausea crashing over her. Another betrayal, another confidante who was quick to sell her out. And beneath the anger, a deeper ache bloomed, a slow, agonizing tear that ripped her heart apart.

She whipped the Smart right, racing down the street. Rolando peeled out after her. Grace's heart raced as she glanced in the rearview mirror. In the distance, two dark SUVs came down the street and stopped in front of the cabin. Were they new killers or FBI? She would never know. She swerved around a corner, Rolando close behind her, the vehicles parting ways at the next intersection.

- 36 -

ANNYA

Saturday, November 12, 2033, 8:00 a.m.

Dr. Triveda propped herself up in bed against a pile of fluffy pillows, a slice of plain toast balanced on her lap. A mug on the nightstand exhaled wisps of steam with the scent of chamomile. Annya quietly entered the room and closed the door behind her with a soft click. She approached Dr. Triveda with a warm smile, her footsteps barely audible against the polished linoleum floor. She reached for a chair beside the nightstand and took a seat beside her.

"Good morning, how are you feeling?" Annya asked.

"I'm feeling much better," Dr. Triveda replied. "I can't remember much, but I heard you saved my life. Thank you!"

"No worries." Annya smiled.

"You thought it was an intoxication?"

Annya nodded. "The tox screen revealed belladonna poisoning. You didn't try to harm yourself, did you?"

Dr. Triveda's eyes widened, a flicker of confusion crossing her face. "Absolutely not! Belladonna?"

Annya leaned in. "Well then, it looks like someone might have sinister intentions," she said calmly. "Can you think of any enemies?"

Dr. Triveda shook her head. "Not that I can recall. This is all very . . ." Her voice trailed off, leaving the sentence unfinished.

"I'm wondering if this could have to do with the surgery you performed on Grace. Did you happen to meet Wassily and Lu'lu yesterday?"

"Wassily who?" Triveda responded.

"Grace's ex-husband," Annya clarified.

"Sorry, I don't know him," Triveda replied.

"But you do know Lu'lu?"

"Of course, you know that."

"Did you talk with her?" Annya inquired.

"No," Triveda replied.

"What about Tina?" Annya continued.

"The scientist?" Triveda paused, a thoughtful look on her face. "She did approach me briefly in the cafeteria. She was curious about the 'wonder drug' Grace received and how it was delivered."

"How did she know you treated her?" Annya questioned further.

"We tried to keep it confidential, but it's an open secret that I operated on Grace. One person tells another, and you know how that goes. It's a miracle that nobody from the surgery team spilled the whole story. SUEC must have rewarded them very well for keeping quiet. But sooner or later, the truth will come out."

"That's not our concern," Annya responded. "The SUEC leaders just want to wait a bit longer to ensure the procedure was a success."

"Tina is not the only one curious," Triveda added. "Many colleagues from the hospital approached me, trying to piece together what was going on. Some of them have wild imaginations. Tina was on the more conservative side, suspecting some treatment involving surgical guidance, like interventional radiology or immunotherapy that requires oversight by an anesthesiologist and surgeon."

Annya chuckled.

"Exactly," Dr. Triveda said. "Her ideas weren't particularly creative. She only considered existing technologies and couldn't fathom an entirely new approach. She asked if it was some kind of vascular catheter delivering a drug directly to tumors, because then we should test her drug as well. Clever name: DIPUTS, drug-induced protection from uncontrolled tumor spread. Tina was convinced her drug would perform as well or better than previous treatments. I entertained the idea to test her drug to pacify her. She seemed desperate, and I wanted to get her off my back."

"Did you happen to see anyone out of the ordinary yesterday?" Annya asked.

"Hmm, off the top of my head . . . the Zhang manager."

"Mr. Zhang? As in Nathanael Zhang, CEO of OrchidBio?"

"The one and only. Sent his manager to see me, can you believe it? Seems like my surgery on Grace caused quite a stir. Most people believe Grace was cured by a drug, which would be worth a fortune. But if they search online, there's no new patent for cancer therapy—except for Tina's work."

"And you didn't tell him anything about the surgery?"

"No, of course not. I had already talked in detail with his boss. I informed him that the procedure was confidential, and he just left."

"It's impressive how you've maintained confidentiality about the procedure. What keeps you so committed to keeping it quiet?"

"Well, it's probably best to see how Grace fares long-term before we get ahead of ourselves." Dr. Triveda managed a weak smile as she looked at Annya. "But honestly, Annya, I'm thrilled that the procedure worked. It's the breakthrough of our generation. My parents came here with nothing, working as farmworkers. I'll make them incredibly proud."

"A true American dream. But a complex one, wouldn't you say?" Annya said.

"Absolutely. There's so much to consider. The technical details, the long-term effects. That's why I want to refine this technique, hone it to perfection. I'm not after money—SUEC pays me well. I'm fortunate enough already. I want to train a few surgeons so they can perform the procedure in the future. Perhaps for ourselves or our loved ones!"

"Well, we don't want to get ahead of ourselves. There could be issues. Starting with the supply of bodies," Annya said. "And someone clearly wasn't thrilled with your success. Someone tried to kill you!"

"Yes, every scientific leap has its share of challenges. Take space flight, for example—people thought it was madness at first! I'm prepared for the obstacles. And besides, the FBI is watching my back. They'll handle the outside threats, and I'll focus on perfecting my procedure."

"So, about your sandwich. Who had access to it? It seems a bit risky leaving it unattended."

Dr. Triveda ran a hand through her hair. "Honestly, Annya, with everything going on, I barely had time to breathe. It probably sat on my desk for a few hours. The cafeteria was packed, people everywhere. One wrong bump and who knows what could have landed in there. Then again, it could have been in my office too. Staff come and go all day."

Annya's gaze lingered on her. "Of all the people you met, did you notice this sign on anyone?" she asked, opening her cell phone and showing her the ouroboros symbol.

Dr. Triveda squinted at the image, her brow furrowing. "This symbol? Hmm, wait a minute . . ." A spark of recognition ignited in her eyes. "Yes, I've definitely seen it before. Tina has a tattoo like that."

"Tina? Grace's supervisor?" Annya asked. This was becoming more and more peculiar.

"Yes, correct. I remember noticing it during our conversation in the cafeteria. Honestly, it did catch me off guard to see a tattoo on her. Not that there's anything wrong with it, of course," she added quickly. "It just was a bit unexpected."

Annya nodded. "Thank you. I think I learned a lot."

Dr. Triveda looked at her. "Will you discharge me now?"

Annya hesitated, her gaze lingering on the surgeon. Her vital signs had returned to normal, but she would need some time to fully recover. "I would prefer to keep you under observation for a little longer," she finally responded.

"Come on, I feel much better already." The surgeon chuckled, "And besides, I'm a physician myself. I can monitor my own recovery."

"Do you have anyone who can keep an eye on you at home?" Annya asked. "A family member, perhaps?"

Dr. Triveda sighed. "I live alone. But I have a friend who could pick me up and take me home. I'll call her if anything gets worse. But that wouldn't be expected, wouldn't you say?"

Annya felt uneasy. Her gut instinct told her that this wasn't a good idea. But arguing would likely lead to Dr. Triveda discharging herself. "Where do you live?" she asked.

"I live in San Francisco, near Dolores Park."

Annya considered it for a beat. There were several hospitals close by in case Dr. Triveda encountered any further issues. She offered a small nod. "All right. If your friend picks you up and checks on you at least once daily for the next few days, I'll proceed with your discharge."

"We have a deal." Dr. Triveda grinned, a hint of triumph in her voice.

Annya met her gaze. She would have preferred to keep her in the hospital, safe and monitored. But she knew Dr. Triveda. Her stubborn streak was as legendary as her surgical skills. There was no way she'd stay put against her will. With a tight nod, Annya turned and left the patient room.

- 37 -

GRACE

Saturday, November 12, 2033, 10:00 a.m.

Grace checked her rearview mirror once again, a habit she had repeated countless times over the past two hours. There was no sign of anyone tailing her on the highway. Still, fear gnawed at her, urging her not to stop. Puppy squirmed restlessly on the back seat. Due to their hurried departure, his morning potty break had been sacrificed. Finally, the dogs restlessness became too evident to ignore. They both needed a break.

She pulled into a rest area and parked under a large oak tree. She didn't want to charge the car or use a credit card to stay untraceable. After letting Puppy attend to his needs, she placed him back in the car and headed to the restroom in the back of the nearby fuel station. A woman was washing her hands at the sink. Did she look at her suspiciously? Grace reminded herself not to become paranoid. On her way out, she grabbed a coffee, even though she had only a few dollars left. Staying alert was essential.

She got back into the car and resumed her drive down the highway. Puppy lay on the backseat, napping peacefully. The stop had been good for him. Her mind raced, trying to think of a safe haven where they could hide for a while. Since the surgery, she'd been warned to steer clear of old friends; her physical transformation was too noticeable. But these were exceptional circumstances. She needed a sanctuary, and the so-called friends from her new life had proven untrustworthy. Wassily, Julius, and Annya—they all seemed to have hidden motives, making her feel like a pawn in their games. With every passing mile, a cold emptiness grew inside her. The longing for someone she could trust felt like a physical pang in her chest.

Her friend Mona came to mind. They had been inseparable during their college days, both starting with bachelor's degrees in biology. While she pursued neurosciences, Mona had specialized in marine biology. Their paths had diverged when Mona landed her dream job at UC Santa Barbara, their inseparable bond stretching thin by distance and diverging passions.

If she called Mona and asked for her help, her old friend would help her for sure. But how should she call her without a phone? Spotting a sign for a fuel station, Grace took the exit and slowly drove into the parking lot. Her gaze darted around the empty space. An elderly couple in a VW Beetle pulled in beside her. The woman on the passenger side got out and retrieved a basket from the trunk, filled with sandwiches and sodas. Swallowing her pride, Grace approached her and spun a story about a stolen phone. The man joined them, eyeing her with suspicion, but then hesitantly offered his cell.

She dialed Mona's old number and a surge of relief washed over her when the call connected. Mona's familiar voice was like a comforting embrace on a cold morning. Grace choked back a sob, twisting the truth once more, telling her old friend a story about a breakup with Wassily. It wasn't actually lying, she reassured herself. She shared the truth about her cheating husband; she only held back that it happened more than a year ago. Relief flooded her as Mona, ever the friend, offered to join her in her home in Santa Barbara.

She forced herself to think clearly. Mona was only a temporary solution. She could hide at her place until the FBI caught the lunatic who was trying to kill her. But the reality was, she'd eventually have to return to San Francisco for her medical checkups. She needed a friend there as well, someone outside the tangled web she'd found herself in.

Karim. He'd been a beacon of normalcy, checking in on her without any strings attached. Unlike the others, Karim valued her for herself, not for what she knew or what she could offer. She dialed his number, her heart pounding. The phone rang a few times, and just as she was about to give up, he answered.

"Hi, Grace, would you like to meet again?" he asked cheerfully.

Grace's throat constricted. Did she have to lie to everyone? "I'm sorry, Karim. I'm actually still out of town. But I thought I'd touch base. I had promised to call you today."

"It's the weekend," Karim said. "If you can't come see me, perhaps I should come to you? Are you far away?"

Grace's mind raced. Mona had always enjoyed company. Back when they were students, they often invited friends over. But it had been years since they last saw each other. Grace wasn't sure if Mona was single or in a relationship now. She had to ask her first.

"I'm on my way to Santa Barbara."

"That's fantastic. I'm actually in Monterey, visiting an aunt. I can swing by when you have time."

Grace smiled. He had to like her a lot. Swinging by from Monterey meant a four-hour drive. But could she trust him? She hesitated, the phone deadweight in her hand. "I'm visiting an old friend," she finally said. "I'd love for you to meet her, but I want to make sure it's okay. I'll check with her as soon as I arrive. Perhaps we could see each other tomorrow."

"Sure, sounds great! I look forward to seeing you again!"

His easygoing response washed away the knot of apprehension that had formed in Grace's gut.

She returned the phone to the couple and went back to her car.

- 38 -

WASSILY

Saturday, November 12, 2033, 10:30 a.m.

The fluorescent lights buzzed overhead, casting a harsh glare across the interrogation room. Wassily stared at the plain wall, the white paint a mocking reminder of his innocence. He sat at a simple table with Agent Weber opposite him. A manila folder lay open between them, its contents a mystery that gnawed at Wassily's already frayed nerves.

His day had begun so well with the reporter. But it had taken a dark turn when the FBI agent had appeared at his door, whisked him away to the FBI office in San Francisco, and deposited him in this purgatory. The agent's questions bounced around: the woman at the party, a surgeon's suspicious collapse at SUEC, random acquaintances. None of it made sense. Was the FBI so desperate they'd harass innocent bystanders? Why him? He was a law-abiding citizen. A bead of sweat trickled down his temple.

"Look, Agent Weber," Wassily pressed, his voice tight with exasperation, "I've told you this before. These incidents are a pure coincidence. The woman at the California Palace? A tragic heart attack. The surgeon at SUEC? Same story. Sure, I was present at both locations. But so were hundreds of others!"

Across the table, the agent remained impassive. "Except, Mr. Wassily, witnesses placed you in direct contact with both victims shortly before their collapse." He leaned forward, pinning him with a steely gaze. "How can we be certain you weren't the one who poisoned them?"

Wassily scoffed. "With what, exactly? I can barely handle a fly swatter in my own kitchen, let alone concoct some undetectable poison and use it twice in public!" Indignation flared in his chest. He couldn't believe the situation—from chance witness to prime suspect.

The agent stared at him with grim determination. Silence stretched between them, thick and suffocating.

Wassily recognized the tactic. The agent was trying to wear him down, hoping he would crack under pressure. He forced himself to exhale slowly, willing his racing heart to calm.

Agent Weber slid a piece of paper from the envelope and held it in front of him. It showed a serpent devouring its own tail.

"Have you seen this before?"

Wassily recognized the symbol instantly. But he wasn't sure it was a good place to reveal this here. Honesty could easily be misconstrued as involvement. But this was the FBI. Surely they wouldn't hold an innocent man's knowledge against him . . . would they?

"Have you seen this before?" the agent asked again, his hawk eyes on him. He had scented blood.

"I might have," he stammered, buying himself time. "Let me think." His mind raced, a desperate scramble for the right answer.

Agent Weber's chair scraped harshly against the linoleum floor as he leaned forward, his voice dropping to a low growl. "This isn't a game, Mr. Wassily. We're investigating a homicide. Any attempt to hinder our progress will have dire consequences."

Wassily swallowed. "Well, I might have seen it on Bianca." He stole a glance at the agent, searching for a reaction on his stoic face.

"*Bianca*? Interesting," he said. Was there a flicker of genuine surprise?

"She was just a friend," Wassily added hastily, feeling a prickle of heat creep up his neck.

The agent sighed. "Mr. Wassily, I wouldn't dream of prying into your personal life. Who you choose to share your bed with is none of my concern."

Wassily let out a breath of relief.

"Where did you see it on her?" the agent asked.

Wassily tapped his chin thoughtfully. "Above her right ankle, I believe. It looked special—I couldn't help but wonder if it held some meaning."

"And what did Bianca say?"

"I don't remember, exactly. Something about a circle of life and death, I think. It was the symbol of a bible club or some such thing. Not really my scene, you know?" A nervous chuckle escaped his lips.

Agent Weber scribbled notes in his pad. "Do you happen to know where this bible club met?" he asked.

Wassily feigned deeper thought, stalling for time. "Hmm, I vaguely remember dropping her off at an old warehouse building in the Mission District in San Francisco. I live just a few blocks away, so it wasn't a big deal for me." Hopefully he hadn't done anything wrong.

"Do you have the address?" the agent asked.

"Unfortunately, no."

Agent Weber pulled up a map on his phone and slid it across the table. "Can you point out the area, perhaps?"

Wassily leaned forward. It was a map of San Francisco. He zoomed in and tapped the area. "There, around here."

"Are you sure?" The agent's gaze was on him.

"Absolutely. I know my neighborhood."

The agent made a note on his phone.

"So, obstructing the investigation has consequences," Wassily ventured cautiously. "But I provided valuable information. Surely that warrants a reward. Perhaps a trip back home?"

Agent Weber leaned back in his chair, steepling his fingers as he studied Wassily. "I have one more question," he said.

What a rollercoaster. Wassily looked at the agent. "Yes?" he asked, bracing himself.

"Grace disappeared. Do you have any idea where she might have gone? Does she have any local friends?"

Now Wassily was surprised. A strangled laugh escaped his lips. "The FBI lost Grace? I'll give her that, she's a clever one."

The agent did not react. "She could be in danger," he said with a flat voice. "It's important that we get to her as quickly as possible."

Wassily looked at the man. "If I tell you, can I then go home?"

The agent leaned back. "Let's put it this way, we'll keep you here as long as it takes to get all the information we need."

Wassily cleared his throat. "Well, she sometimes went out with a few lab colleagues, but I don't think they were close. Her work was her life, you know? Now, of course, she has her new millionaire friend. If I were you, I'd start with that guy."

The agent's face was unreadable. "Anyone else? A close friend from her past, perhaps?"

Wassily feigned concentration. "Honestly, women's conversations tend to go over my head. They can meander, you know? Like a scenic route with no destination. The trick is to appear engaged. Nod and smile. I don't follow the trail of names in these situations."

"Think hard, Mr. Wassily," the agent pressed. "Grace's life might depend on it. I'm not interested in anyone she mentioned once. I am interested in a close friend she might have mentioned multiple times."

Wassily tried to remember. "She missed an old college friend, Maria or similar. She moved to Santa Barbara, and Grace wanted to visit her. I told her that we should go. Santa Barbara is a beautiful place."

"Do you remember the woman's full name?"

"No, sorry. I only remember that they went to college together."

The agent rose, a hint of satisfaction in his posture. "Thank you for your cooperation, Mr. Wassily. You're free to go."

- 39 -

JULIUS

Saturday, November 12, 2033, 11:00 a.m.

One of the black vans had taken after them, so they had changed plans and Rolando had raced through backroads in North Tahoe until they had lost them. Now they drove down Interstate 80, nearing Sacramento. Outside, the towering pines of Lake Tahoe gave way to a tapestry of evergreens and vibrant fall foliage. As they descended into the sprawling California Central Valley, the landscape flattened and the air grew warmer. Golden fields of dried crops stretched toward the horizon. In the distance, the foothills of the Coast Ranges shimmered, a promise of a new direction.

Julius stole a worried glance at his partner. Rolando's hands were clamped around the wheel, knuckles stark white against the leather. Guilt gnawed at Julius. He'd assured Rolando this was a simple job, a way to help Grace disappear. Now, with every passing mile, the silence in the car screamed with the unspoken truth: One wrong turn and the FBI would be waiting at the next exit, ready to slam the steel door on Rolando's freedom forever.

"This is all my fault," he muttered. "I just wanted to help Grace."

Rolando slammed his fist on the steering wheel. "You did help Grace, Julius," he growled, "and you put both our necks on the line in the process."

Julius flinched, his gaze dropping to his feet. "I know, and I'm so sorry. I just . . ." Shame choked his next words.

"I don't get it, Julius," Rolando said, his voice tight with anger. "What's so special about her that you would risk everything?"

Julius shrugged. "I don't know."

He felt like a failure. His phone call had led the pursuers right to them. Rolando had every right to be upset. His father would be disappointed too. Julius pictured his father's face when he got home: a stolen car, a chase, and a missing Grace—that was far from the progress his father expected. And the secret behind her cure? Not exactly a success story either. A heavy sigh rumbled through him. There was no way he could return home empty-handed.

Rolando guided the car off the highway, pulling into a gas station. There was only one other car parked nearby, a family of four. The children were playing near the pumps while their parents attended to refueling.

"This is where I part ways," Rolando declared solemnly.

"Here?" Julius exclaimed. "Where will you go?"

Rolando gestured toward the distant skyline. "Sacramento isn't too far. I'll catch a train and lay low for a while. I need to wait until the air clears and the FBI isn't breathing down our necks."

Tears welled in Julius's eyes. "When will I see you again?"

"I can't give you a definite answer," Rolando replied. "I'll have to go underground for a bit. I'll reach out when it's safe to do so."

He leaned over and gave Julius a soft kiss. Across the pump, a child stared, wide-eyed and curious. Heat flooded Julius's cheeks. "Be safe," he managed, his voice barely a whisper.

Rolando grunted in reply, a hint of worry etching his features. He grabbed a backpack from the trunk, its contents bulging with unknown necessities. With a final lingering look, Rolando turned around and disappeared into the golden-brown fields behind the gas station.

Julius watched him walk away, the weight of their uncertain future pressing down on him. He reached into his pocket, gently touching the soft velvet of the ring box. He had planned to propose at the cabin, but the pizza dinner had left Rolando fuming over Grace. Julius had managed to cheer him up afterward, leading to a night of raw passion. Then, Grace had stomped into their breakfast, Rolando had spotted their enemies, and they had to flee.

Julius watched his figure become smaller and smaller in the distance. Would there ever be a good time to propose to him? What did he want more, to be with Rolando or marry someone else who shared his dream of building a home together? He wasn't sure.

A car behind him honked. Julius forced himself to focus on the mundane. He stepped out of the car and pumped gas, the rhythmic whoosh a counterpoint to the frantic drumbeat in his chest. Everyone he cared about was gone. His mother. Grace. Rolando. Was he cursed, destined to watch those he loved dissolve into thin air?

No, he wouldn't let fate take another person from him. Determined not to be another victim, he strode into the gas station. Inside, the fluorescent lights cast a sterile glow on the aisles of chips and candy. He grabbed a few granola bars, a water, and a new phone. He stepped out of the building, drove the car to an empty parking spot, and called Annya.

She answered right away. "Julius! Thank goodness." Her voice crackled with worry. "We've been going crazy trying to reach you. Are you all right?"

He smiled. He'd almost forgotten Annya. Fate would never be able to get rid of this woman, that much was clear. Rolando's words echoed in his mind: *CIA operative romantically involved with the FBI director* . . . If someone knew Grace's whereabouts, it was her.

"I'm fine," he said.

"Where are you?"

"At a gas station."

"Are Rolando and Grace with you?"

"I haven't seen Rolando," he lied. "And Grace left this morning. I looked for her but cannot find her. Any chance you might know where she went?"

"I'm sorry, I'm not at liberty to say. But I learned from Angus that some vehicle with a stolen license plate is chasing you. The FBI will intercept it. But there could be others. It's not safe out there. You should come back home immediately."

"What about Grace?"

"The FBI is looking after her. You should stay out of this for your own safety."

"But you just said that you have no idea where she is. How do you want to keep her safe if you don't know where she is?"

"Angus has sent an FBI team to Santa Barbara to keep an eye on her. I have to work at the ER and cannot leave the city."

"Santa Barbara?" Julius said. "Do you know the address?"

"Julius, I just said you should stay out of this and come home."

"Grace is very smart, Annya. She lost the FBI twice. If she doesn't want to be found, she will not be found. I'm her friend. I can get to her and let you know if there's any issue. Then, Angus's team can come to help."

There was a moment of silence.

"I'll text you the address."

"Thank you!"

"Be careful, Julius." Annya's voice turned serious. "If you find her first, call me right away. Remember what happened at your father's house. Don't engage, just let us know. We'll handle it from there."

"Sure, I'll call."

With trembling fingers, he punched the address into his GPS and started the car. Would Grace even see him after their fight this morning? He'd figure that out once he got there. The engine roared to life, and Julius sped off, the open highway stretching before him.

- 40 -

WASSILY

Saturday, November 12, 2033, 2:00 p.m.

Wassily shuffled forward in the line to the Mission District bakery that snaked down the sidewalk. Each breeze carried a new aroma of freshly roasted coffee, caramelized sugar, and nutty sourdough, making his stomach rumble. After being dismissed from the FBI, he'd taken the Muni to his apartment. But the confinement of his deserted home had left him craving life. Here, next door, the bakery pulsed with warmth and the comforting rhythm of activity.

Behind the window, golden baguettes were nestled against towering walnut loaves and trays of jewel-toned pastries. A chalkboard menu advertised seasonal specials. As he came closer to the counter, the barista caught his eye, a pretty woman in a crisp white apron with long chocolate-brown hair that cascaded down her shoulders. He couldn't resist deploying his charm, flashing a winning smile.

"Can I tempt you into making the most delicious tomato and cheese sandwich of the day for me, and a tall latte?" He leaned closer. "What's your name?"

The woman offered a cool smile, then her gaze returned to the task at hand. She steamed his milk, creating a mesmerizing dance of frothy white against the sleek espresso machine. A minute later, she handed him a steaming cup and a paper bag.

"Thank you!" He flashed his most winning smile.

"Enjoy!" she responded with a quick, polite smile, her focus already shifting to the next customer.

Usually, his charm yielded at least a fluttering compliment or a playful glance. This time, it landed with a thud. He felt a prickle of irritation. But the aroma of warm tomato and melted cheese from the paper bag quickly replaced it.

He found a seat by the window, the bakery's clinking cups, chattering customers, and hissing espresso machines a comforting background hum. Maybe the tomato and cheese would be enough of a win today. He took a bite, the tangy sweetness a welcome distraction. Across the counter, the pretty barista expertly crafted another latte. Wassily watched her for a moment, a playful idea forming in his mind. Perhaps he would try a different tactic tomorrow.

Back to business. He pulled up his cell phone and googled Grace's name. The reporter this morning had promised generous compensation for information about the wonder drug that had cured her. Unfortunately, the meeting with Lu'lu hadn't revealed any leads. She knew something, but she wouldn't tell him.

A headline in Google News caught his attention: *From Deathbed to Dancing: Woman Defies Terminal Cancer with New Miracle Drug.* Below it a photo of Grace with that gay new friend of hers. A bitter pang shot through Wassily. A trail of at least twenty articles echoed the story, each a digital footprint of his frustration. *Huffington Post*, *San Francisco Chronicle*, Reuters, CBS—the list sprawled across the screen. The story was only a few hours old and was going viral.

Wassily scrolled down, his gaze snagging on the article's author: It was the reporter who'd interviewed him that morning, the one who'd pressed his business card into his hand. Wassily's name wasn't mentioned anywhere in the byline. He reread the article. The reporter had taken his intel and spun it into glory for himself.

Wassily forced a wave of annoyance to recede. He needed a clear head. This reporter had played him, and the frustration was a bitter pill to swallow. But anger wouldn't solve anything. He had to outsmart this guy, reclaim control in this situation.

What exactly had cured Grace? The revelation wouldn't require a middleman. He could make a lucrative career for himself, especially if it involved an exclusive story about a first human survivor. A series of social media posts, news articles, interviews, book deals could yield a golden microphone, a Pulitzer, a career minted in history.

His gaze drifted back to the photo—Grace, alive and vibrant. Her cure was like a lottery win, he just knew it. There had to be a way to leverage this.

Wassily leaned back in his chair, taking another swig of coffee. Coffee houses had been cauldrons of innovation for centuries. From the Enlightenment philosophers hatching revolutionary ideas to the writers and artists birthing new movements, coffee houses had borne countless breakthroughs. A tapestry of historical figures flitted across his mind—Voltaire scribbling critiques in a Parisian cafe, Ben Franklin brainstorming inventions over a steaming cup in Boston, and Wassily Kandinsky meeting with his friends from the expressionist group Der Blaue Reiter in a coffee house in Munich. His namesake, Kandinsky, had translated the essence of life into colors that resonated with the soul, bypassing mere intellect.

That was it! Searching for information and facts about Grace's cure wasn't the answer. Facts and figures didn't win hearts and minds. People craved stories—narratives that painted vivid pictures, songs that evoked emotions. Nobody, he realized with a slow smile, had asked for the cold, hard truth. There was a better way to play this. He wouldn't chase sterile facts; he'd paint a picture. A story, vibrant and emotional, that would capture the public's imagination just as surely as Kandinsky's colors resonated with the soul.

- 41 -

GRACE

Saturday, November 12, 2033, 5:00 p.m.

Grace's finger pressed the gleaming brass doorbell of the small but charming hilltop villa in Santa Barbara. The house before her was a masterpiece of Spanish Revival, its elegant curves and intricate plasterwork gleaming under the golden sunlight. Simple iron grilles adorned the windows, their dark lines a stark contrast to the whitewashed walls and the vibrant red tile of the roof. Grace waited with a sliver of unease. Puppy sat down beside her and looked up at the door with his big brown eyes, his tail thumping a happy rhythm against the floor.

The rustic wooden door flung open and revealed a woman with familiar features framed by shorter, darker hair than Grace remembered from their college years. Gone were the youthful curves; time had etched lines around the eyes of her friend. Yet, a genuine smile stretched across her face, crinkling the corners of her eyes in a way that sparked a forgotten warmth in Grace's chest.

"Hello, stranger!" Mona exclaimed, her voice comfortingly familiar. "Great to see you!" Her arms shot out, pulling Grace into a tight hug.

A shaky laugh escaped Grace's lips. "Mona," she whispered. "It's so good to see you. I had no idea how much I missed you!" Why had it taken her so long to come here?

Puppy let out an excited yelp, jumping toward her. Mona crouched down to him. "Oh my gosh," she breathed, patting his fluffy fur. "You're the most adorable thing I've ever seen!" She turned to Grace. "Come on in!"

She turned around, Puppy following closely with a wagging tail. Grace trailed behind. They stepped through a modest entrance area into a spacious living room with a vaulted ceiling and an open veranda door, which provided a picturesque view of Santa Barbara and the distant ocean.

Mona pointed at a large beige leather couch adorned with a multicolored quilt and a rustic coffee table. "Have a seat, dear."

She sank into the sofa, patting the space beside her. Puppy leaped onto the cushions, landing with a happy thump. Mona reached out, scratching him behind his ear. A contented sigh rumbled through Puppy's chest as he leaned into her touch.

"Goodness, he's adorable!" Mona exclaimed.

Grace settled into the plush cushions, nodding. "Thank you for taking us in. We were on the road for eight hours."

"Of course, I was thrilled to get your call! We haven't seen each other in ages! Can I tempt you with something to drink?"

"Iced tea would be fantastic if you have some."

"Of course you still love your tea." With a gentle move, Mona got up and disappeared through a side door.

Grace leaned back, the exhaustion from the journey settling into her bones. It felt incredibly good to see her old friend again. A quiet sigh escaped her lips. In her old life, she'd gotten so caught up in the chase, she'd lost sight of what truly mattered.

"Are you living here by yourself?" she asked loudly.

"Yeah, I haven't found the right match yet. And you got divorced. Did you meet someone new?"

"It's a bit complicated," Grace said.

"I can imagine!" Her voice carried from the kitchen.

Mona reappeared, a tray laden with two iced teas, a bowl of colorful vegetable chips, and a few treats for Puppy held aloft. "Here you go," she announced, settling onto the couch beside Grace. The familiar scent of her lavender perfume carried a forgotten comfort. Grace reached for the iced tea, the condensation cool against her hand. The first sip was pure refreshment, chasing away the remnants of the long drive. She eyed the bowl of vegetable chips.

Mona chuckled. "Try one," she urged, pushing the bowl closer. "They're my latest healthy obsession."

Grace picked up a vibrant green chip and was surprised by a satisfying crunch and a burst of unexpected flavor. "Wow," she breathed. "These are delicious!" She reached for more.

"Help yourself. There's plenty more where that came from." Mona laughed. Then, her smile softened. "But seriously, Grace, what's going on? You sounded so out of sorts on the phone."

Grace looked at her friend. How much could she tell her? No way she would believe the story about her surgery. "It's a long story," she admitted.

"I saw the news article about you." Mona beamed.

"What article?"

"On Google News."

Grace looked at her, confused. "What are you talking about?"

"You didn't see it yet? You and your millionaire beau are all over the news!"

Mona reached for her phone, opened the browser, and showed her a news article with today's date. The headline read: *From Deathbed to Dancing: Woman Defies Terminal Cancer with New Miracle Drug.* Below the bold letters, a photo captured Grace mid-twirl with Julius at the gala. Their gazes were locked, a visible spark passing between them.

Mona's eyes gleamed. "Did you both take it?"

Grace stared at her, not sure what to say.

"You look amazing!" Mona beamed. "Whatever you took, I would like to try it, too. Is it a clinical trial? Can I sign up for it?"

"No, you cannot sign up for it," Grace said.

"Why is it a secret?" Mona pressed. "You could share it with your old friend?"

Grace felt nausea washing over her. Mona had her own agenda, just like everybody else.

"Come on, Grace. You can tell me, right? What was the wonder drug? I presume it includes growth hormones?"

Grace flinched. She said her usual sentence. "I'm sorry, I cannot talk about it."

Mona's smile faltered. "Okay, fine," she said. "Remember when I got a role as an extra in a movie with Ryan Gosling? Everyone under the sun asked me to arrange a meeting with him. I know how you feel."

Grace's gaze became steely. "Believe me, Mona, you have no idea how I feel right now."

"Well," she said, "I assume you just want to hide until the hype has settled?"

"Would that be possible?" Grace asked.

"Of course!" Mona straightened, regaining her usual bravado. "I'll get us some groceries for a reunion dinner. Meanwhile, feel free to take a shower. The bathroom is upstairs. You didn't bring any luggage?"

Grace shook her head.

"There are fresh sweaters in the cabinet in the bathroom. You can borrow one if you like."

"Thank you!" Grace reached for Mona's hand, the gesture feeling a bit awkward after the charged exchange. "I appreciate your hospitality."

"Of course." Mona beamed.

- 42 -

ANNYA

Saturday, November 12, 2033, 5:00 p.m.

Annya and Angus walked down the path to the SUEC research building, an octagonal limestone building with large semi-circular glass windows. After discovering that Tina wasn't home, Angus had asked Annya to show him the way to the research building. With a swipe of her ID, Annya activated the imposing glass doors. They hissed open, granting them entry. The atrium soared three stories high, culminating in a magnificent stained-glass dome. Sunlight streamed through the colorful panes, casting a kaleidoscope of light across the polished marble floor.

Annya led Angus into a sleek chrome elevator that hummed to life as they ascended. On the third floor, the doors slid open and revealed the pungent scent of chlorine bleach. They took a right turn and walked down a long hallway, passing countless frosted-glass panels that provided fleeting glimpses of lab benches, fume hoods, and Bunsen burners. The weekend quietude had settled over the facility, broken only by the low hum of unseen machinery and the occasional flicker of movement behind the opaque glass. Finally, they reached a door with a simple inscription: Faculty Office.

"Is that Tina's office?" Angus asked.

Annya nodded. "All faculty offices here are shared. That's why there is no specific name on it." She knocked.

"Come in," Tina's low voice howled from the inside.

Annya pushed open the door. "Hello, Tina!" she greeted cheerfully.

Tina, head buried in a microscope on her desk, glanced up in surprise. "Annya? What brings you to the lab on a Saturday?" Her gaze went to Angus. "And Mr. Weber? You're the FBI agent from the Zhang party, correct?"

Angus offered a confirming nod. "That's right."

"How can I help you?" she asked. "Is something wrong? It must be serious if the FBI is involved?"

Angus leaned forward, his voice low. "Dr. Triveda was attacked yesterday. An attempted poisoning."

Tina's eyes widened. "That's horrible. But why are you coming to me with that information?"

"Because you were in the cafeteria at the same time as Dr. Triveda. We are checking everyone who had contact with her."

"You think I could have poisoned her?" Tina scoffed. "With what? And why?" Her indignation seemed genuine, but a flicker of something else danced in her eyes. Fear, perhaps? Annya couldn't quite place it.

"We also saw you at the Zhang party. You seemed quite upset?" Annya said.

Tina's gaze darted from Angus to Annya. "What does that have to do with anything?" she asked, her voice sharp.

Angus took over. "We were wondering if the incident with Dr. Triveda might be somehow related to Grace's new treatment."

"I read the news," Tina said. "Grace and her wonder drug."

"You also worked on a new cancer treatment, didn't you?" Angus asked.

Tina hesitated for a beat. "Yes," she admitted, "but I didn't attempt to kill her surgeon, if that's what you're asking. I simply inquired if she'd consider delivering my drug with the same method she used on Grace."

"And what did she say?" Annya pressed.

"She said she would think about it. Which means not interested," Tina said. "She seemed completely brainwashed by it all. Just like Nathanael Zhang."

"Nathanael Zhang backing out of a promised business deal was quite a hit for you?" Annya asked.

Tina slumped in her chair. "I've poured years of my life into finding a cure for cancer. Then, our new agent, DIPUTS, showed promising results. Not a revolution, but similar efficacy as other chemotherapeutic drugs. That meant hope for a new treatment and hope for a decent payout."

"That's exciting," Annya said, feigning enthusiasm to encourage Tina to tell more. *This is the problem*, she thought. *It's all about profit. Helping people is secondary.*

"I saw my opportunity," Tina explained. "It was all a matter of marketing. I just had to sell it right. I filed a patent, worked tirelessly to produce results, and contacted OrchidBio. Nathanael Zhang was interested. The data looked good."

"But then the deal stalled?" Angus asked.

"That's right," Tina confirmed. "Nathanael requested more data. Industry style. Dose-finding studies, toxicity studies, stability of the agent for long-term storage. Data that a university grant would not fund. So, I took a loan from the bank. And another. And another."

"That was quite a financial risk," Angus said.

Tina nodded. "I told myself I would get it all back through the OrchidBio contract. Plus a nice pension for my retirement. SUEC doesn't pay pensions, and I am exhausted. It's time to settle down in a nice beach house."

"And then Grace came along," Annya concluded.

"Exactly. Grace had worked with my drug for years, but she openly criticized it. And when she was diagnosed with cancer, she refused to participate in a trial with our drug and chose a different treatment instead."

"From a business perspective, Grace's criticism was a death sentence to your drug?" Annya asked.

Tina nodded. "The moment she moved in with the Zhangs, I knew it was over. No way my drug would sell with Grace living under their roof. She wanted to sell her own drug. My OrchidBio deal was dead. Nathanael is chasing whatever cured Grace now." Her eyes flashed with a desperate certainty. "I know it."

Angus leaned forward, his gaze steady. "And that leaves you in a precarious position, financially speaking? Debt and no retirement?"

"I'm destroyed," she choked out. "After all I've done for her. I taught her everything she knows about cancer therapy. Then, she goes on a medical leave and emerges with some wonder drug that ruins me."

"And then you took revenge?" Angus asked.

Tina straightened. "Absolutely not," she said briskly. "I would love to shoot her, but that's not part of my repertoire." She glanced from Angus to Annya. "Wait a minute. You came here for the surgeon, not Grace herself. Unless . . ." Her voice dropped to a near whisper. "The woman who collapsed at the party . . . was she a target? Is *Grace* in danger?"

Annya was impressed. Tina's deduction was laser sharp. "We're trying to understand a series of events that may be connected," she said.

Angus tapped on his phone and held the screen in front of Tina. It showed the ouroboros serpent consuming its tail. "Can you enlighten us what this means?" he asked.

Tina's eyes narrowed. "Can you not leave me a bit of privacy?" she asked. "Why are you digging into my private life?"

Angus and Annya exchanged glances. "I'm sorry, we didn't want to intrude," Annya said. "A person of interest has a tattoo like this, and we noticed that you have one as well." Her eyes went to Tina's arm.

Tina's hand darted up to clutch the fabric, her jaw clenching. "Is that right?" she snapped. "Well, congratulations on finding a common tattoo. Does it mean everyone with one is a criminal now?"

Angus leaned forward, his gaze unwavering. "Not necessarily. But a coincidence can be a curious thing, wouldn't you agree?"

"Okay, I had an affair," she blurted out. "There you go. Are you happy now?"

A beat of silence followed, thick with tension. Angus remained impassive. "What does the symbol mean?" he asked.

"I don't want to talk about it," she said firmly.

Annya leaned forward, meeting Tina's gaze head-on. "Tina, I understand that this is difficult for you. But keeping things bottled up won't make them disappear. Whatever that symbol represents, it's clearly significant to you. But from what we've gathered, it might also be connected to attacks on people's lives."

Tina remained silent, her gaze fixed on the floor.

"Let's be clear, this is a homicide investigation," Angus added. "I have the authority to bring you in for questioning, if that's the route you prefer."

Annya glanced at him. He gave her a slight nod. *Don't back down.*

A heavy silence hund in the air.

"It's the Order of Balance," Tina finally said.

Annya looked at her, trying to understand. "The Order of Balance," she repeated. "Is that a group of people?"

Tina nodded.

"What does it have to do with that symbol of a snake eating itself?" Annya gestured toward the image.

"The ouroboros is an alchemical symbol that expresses the unity of all things, material and spiritual."

"You don't strike me as mystic, Tina," Annya said.

A wry smile touched Tina's lips. "The ouroboros has many ties to the sciences," she explained. "For example, the chemist Friedrich Kekulé dreamed of the ouroboros and used it to depict the structure of the benzene molecule."

"And so, the people with this symbol are a group of scientists?" Angus asked.

Tina shook her head. "No, not at all. They are from all walks of life."

"A group of people with a shared belief?"

Tina nodded. "For them, the ouroboros represents a holistic view—body, mind, and spirit are all intertwined, crucial for a sense of wholeness. Many members have faced challenges in the past and seek a path to inner peace within this community. It's about rediscovering their worth and the sacredness of their existence."

"Why didn't we find any evidence of this group online?" Annya asked.

Tina smiled knowingly. "The members of the order see the online world as a distraction that pulls them away from their inner journeys. They believe face-to-face interactions foster deeper, more authentic bonds. Staying offline helps them maintain the purity of their teachings."

Angus raised an eyebrow. "So, regular in-person meetings? How big a group are we talking?"

Tina thought for a while. "It's intimate, maybe fifty members. They value a tight-knit community. That's what appealed to me too. We met weekly."

"So, this group focuses on the body–soul connection," Annya said. "What happens at these meetings?"

"There's always an opening remark by the leader, then a speech by a member while we have a nice dinner together."

"What are the speeches about?"

"A variety of topics on holistic well-being. It could be the importance of exercise and healthy eating, or how bad habits like excess alcohol or drugs disrupt our natural balance. They also discuss herbal medicine, aromatherapy, and ways to detoxify the body."

Annya studied Tina across the table. *How could a scientist so grounded in logic be drawn to essential oils and herbal remedies?* "You found that helpful?" she asked.

Tina smiled. "Maybe not in the strictly scientific sense," she admitted. "But honestly, Annya, what I craved most was the community. Living alone for so long . . . well, who cares if we sip some funky-smelling tea if it fosters a sense of belonging?"

"Is there any member participation beyond the meetings?" Angus asked. "Donations? Volunteer work? Duties?"

Tina nodded. "During the dinners, each member meets privately with the leader. They're assigned a task to contribute to the group. Sometimes suggestions are welcome, other times the leader dictates. It starts small but gets more bizarre over time. That's what ultimately drove me away. I don't like being patronized."

"What did they ask you to do?"

"At first, it was manageable," Tina explained. "He suggested spending an hour each day in silent contemplation in nature. With my schedule, it was a stretch, but I found it surprisingly rewarding. Then, the tasks took a weird turn."

"How so?"

"One involved getting this tattoo, which made me quite uncomfortable. Next, he asked me to take a stranger to the Zhang Gala."

"You took a stranger to the Zhang gala?" Angus looked at her in surprise. "Who was it?"

"As you might guess, a stranger is precisely someone you don't know beforehand," Tina said sharply. "A young fellow from the group, dark hair, fancy clothes—that's all I remember. Tickets were not easy to get, and he was eager to get in. I got mine as a potential business lead, and it came with a plus one. So, I escorted him in, and then . . . *poof!* He disappeared into the crowd."

Angus and Annya exchanged a look. "We can check that on the surveillance cameras," he said.

"Did I do anything wrong?" Tina asked.

"We don't know yet," Annya said. "But your honesty helps us piece things together."

"So, you left the Order of Balance after this incident?" Angus asked.

Tina nodded curtly. "Taking a complete stranger to the gala felt . . . exploitative. It crossed a line for me. Who knew what they might ask next? So, I decided to stop attending the meetings altogether."

"Probably a wise move." Angus nodded. "When do these people meet?"

"Every Saturday at seven p.m.," she responded.

Angus checked his watch and looked at Annya. "All right, let's go see what this group is all about."

"Hey, you didn't ask me where they are meeting."

"We know that already." Angus smiled. "Warehouse in the Mission District of San Francisco, right?"

Tina's jaw dropped. "Impressive," she conceded. "But getting in won't be easy."

"Could you take us along?" Annya asked.

Tina nodded. "I can bring one guest, and Annya, you look unassuming enough to pass as a potential convert. But you, Mr. Weber"—she glanced at Angus—"you'd stand out like a sore thumb, law enforcement written all over you. It won't be an undercover operation if you tag along."

Angus looked from Tina to Annya, a silent debate raging behind his steely blue eyes.

Annya smiled at him. "I've got this," she declared.

"Your job is intel, not becoming a target," he countered.

"Of course. I'll get the information we need," she said. "We can decide from there what to do."

Angus's gaze lingered on Annya. With a heavy sigh, he finally conceded. "All right. You two take the lead. But remember, Annya"—his voice turned serious—"if anything feels off, if your gut tells you to run, don't hesitate. Call me, no matter what."

- 43 -

GRACE

Saturday, November 12, 2033, 6:00 p.m.

Grace had taken a seat on the weathered veranda bench with Puppy by her side, taking in the breathtaking view of the Pacific Ocean. The air was laced with the tang of salt, and a breeze gently teased her hair. Hues of yellow, orange, and red slowly descended into the vast expanse of the ocean.

Before the surgery, sunsets were just sunsets, beautiful but fleeting moments in the grand scheme of things. Now, with each fiery stroke of orange and red bleeding into the vast canvas of the sky, Grace felt a pang of bittersweet appreciation.

The key turned in the door, and a minute later, Mona emerged onto the terrace, her arms laden with two grocery bags overflowing with fresh produce. She set them down with a soft thud.

"Enjoying the show?" she said with a warm smile.

"This is breathtaking," Grace whispered.

"Are you hungry? How about I fix us a quick dinner?"

Grace turned. "That sounds amazing. Can I help?"

Mona chuckled, her hand reaching out to gently pat Grace's shoulder. "Relax, dear. You look like you could use a break. This won't take long. Still a fan of spaghetti with tomato sauce, I take it?"

Grace nodded. "More than ever," she whispered. "Thank you!"

Mona reached for a button at the wall, flicking on a string of lights that twinkled to life around them like fireflies. Retrieving her bags, she disappeared through the veranda door into the house.

Grace pivoted to admire the scenery in front of her. The salty breeze carried a whisper of a forgotten magic. Here, amidst the beauty of nature, in the serene company of Mona and Puppy, lay the true treasures she'd neglected in the pursuit of her busy life.

Her hand glided over her neck and cheeks. Nothing unusual. With their rushed escape from the cabin, she'd abandoned her jacket with the immune suppressants inside. How long could she go without them? Probably not long. What if her borrowed body rejected her head? Well, that would not happen overnight. Hopefully. She could work that out tomorrow. For now, she would enjoy this moment. She leaned back and closed her eyes.

She must have dozed off for a while. The aroma of garlic and simmering tomatoes woke her. Her stomach rumbled in anticipation. As the sound of footsteps approached, Puppy bounded toward the terrace door. With a laugh, Mona stepped out, carrying a steaming bowl of tomato-sauced noodles.

"Sorry, pup." She chuckled. "This feast is for the humans tonight."

She placed the bowls on the rustic wooden table, then knelt, offering Puppy a bone. The giant baby dog snatched the offering and began gnawing with gusto. Mona disappeared back inside, only to return moments later with a tray laden with a bowl of green salad, a bottle of red wine, glasses, cutlery, and plates.

"Alfresco dining?" she asked, setting the table.

Grace looked at her, undecided. "It might be a bit chilly?"

"I'm always prepared." Mona winked, reaching for a sleek metallic lamp beside the table. With a click, the lamp hummed to life, bathing the terrace in a warm orange glow.

The gentle heat melted away the tension in Grace's shoulders. "Perfect," she said.

The doorbell's shrill ring shattered the peaceful scene. Mona and Grace exchanged a startled glance.

"Were you expecting visitors?" Grace whispered, her voice barely a breath.

"No, I was supposed to be at my fitness class tonight. I'm not expecting anyone," Mona said.

Grace's heart hammered against her ribs. "Then it must be for me," she said, her voice tight with apprehension. "Does this house have a security camera?"

"No, it doesn't. This neighborhood is safe."

"Well, you never know. This could be dangerous, Mona."

"Aren't you overreacting?"

"Well, to be honest, it's possible that someone might have followed me here."

"What do you mean? A reporter?"

"I'm not sure."

"We could walk around the house and peek around the corner to see who it is."

Grace shook her head. "No. Let me handle it. I'm trained in self-defense."

A flicker of surprise crossed Mona's face. "Self-defense? Is San Francisco that bad now?"

"I'll be right back," Grace replied, her voice low but steady. "If you hear anything concerning concerning, anything at all . . . take Puppy and run."

"Grace, you're scaring me!" Mona protested.

"Don't worry, Mona. I've got this."

Grace rose silently and tiptoed around the house, her feet sinking into the soil of the flowerbeds. The doorbell rang again. She grabbed a big branch of a tree that had fallen on a rhododendron bush to her right. She slowly crept toward the source of the unwelcome sound and peeked around the corner.

There, bathed in the warm glow spilling from the kitchen window, stood a familiar figure, broad shoulders framing a lean frame, hands tucked casually in his pocket. His gaze lingered on the closed door, a silent plea etched into his posture, that sent a jolt through her.

"Julius," she exclaimed. "What on earth are you doing here?"

His head snapped toward her and his face lit up, a flicker of relief crossing his features as their eyes met. "Does your door have a problem?" he asked, a teasing lilt to his voice.

She had been thinking about him on the long ride to Santa Barbara. His father had made his interest in her treatment clear. Of course, Julius was caught in the middle. But he had chosen to follow her here instead of running away with Rolando. He must have really cared about her.

She ran toward him, and he embraced her. The familiar scent of him, a mix of ocean air and citrus cologne, washed over her, momentarily erasing the memory of their fight at the cabin.

A shaky laugh escaped her lips. "Oh, Julius." She sighed, clinging to him for a beat longer than necessary. "I thought . . . Well, for a second there, I thought it might be someone dangerous. How did you find me?"

"I called Annya," he said with a sheepish smile. "She has a way of knowing things."

Grace looked at him in surprise. "But I didn't call or text anyone this time. How did she manage to do that?"

He shrugged. "Perhaps they followed your car?" he suggested, nodding toward the Smart across the driveway.

"But I parked in front of a different house on purpose."

"Well, she got your address, and I'm glad I found you here. She asked me to text her that you are safe."

"We can do that later. For now, I just want some peace. And I can defend myself. I've done it twice, and I will do it again."

Their eyes met. "I'm not sure. It might be better to let them know."

"Just give us a few minutes of privacy. I feel terrible about how we left each other. You risked your life taking me to Tahoe—and your relationship with Rolando. You didn't have to do that. But you did."

He looked at her with his dark chocolate eyes. "Grace," he began, his voice thick with remorse, "I'm so sorry about the text. My father can be ruthless. He wanted to know your secret, and he asked me to find out. If he sees a good deal, he goes for it. He used me as his pawn. I promise it won't happen again. You mean much more to me than that, Grace. A lot more. You're my best friend . . ." He trailed off, his eyes pleading for her understanding. "I cannot lose you."

Tears welled up in her eyes. "I know," she whispered. The urge to kiss him, to erase the hurt and find solace in his touch, was almost overwhelming. But a stronger instinct held her back. This was not what this was. She reached for his hand. "Come," she said. "Meet my friend."

As they rounded the corner, the twinkles of the veranda lights revealed Mona on the terrace, brandishing a fork like a medieval jouster wielding a lance. Grace smothered a laugh, stealing a glance at Julius, whose lips were twitching with amusement. Clearly combat wasn't on this woman's résumé.

A blur of fur rocketed toward Julius with a high-pitched yelp. Puppy circled Julius's legs, a furry whirlwind of unbridled joy, yaps punctuated by ecstatic snorts, his wagging tail rotating like a helicopter. Julius crouched down, offering his open palm for a greeting.

"Hey there, buddy," he cooed. "Looks like someone's happy to see me!"

The pup launched himself at Julius's hand, showering it with enthusiastic licks. Julius chuckled, wrapping his arms around Puppy in a tight embrace. They clearly had missed each other. After a moment, Julius reluctantly disentangled himself, following a beaming Grace toward the table.

Mona stared at him with mouth wide open. "Wow."

"Mona, this is Julius," Grace introduced before turning to Julius. "This is my friend Grace. We've known each other since high school."

"Nice to meet you, Mona!"

Mona ran a hand through her short, spiky pixie cut and subconsciously straightened her sunflower blouse.

Julius's eyes went to the food on the table. "I'm terribly sorry to interrupt," he said with his smooth baritone voice.

"Oh, not at all." Mona scrambled to her feet. "Please have a seat. Are you hungry?"

A hint of a smile played on his lips. "Starving, actually. Just drove in from Tahoe, following Grace's lead."

Before he could say another word, Mona was already disappearing into the house. In a whirlwind, she reappeared, setting down a fresh plate, glass, fork, and spoon. "Here you go."

- 44 -

GRACE

Saturday, November 12, 2033, 6:30 p.m.

The heater on the veranda emanated a gentle hum, providing a comforting warmth against the cool evening air. Crickets chirped a rhythmic chorus around them. Mona, radiant in her element, distributed steaming spaghetti. Meanwhile, Grace uncorked the bottle of red wine. Clinking glasses, Mona, Grace, and Julius reveled in the simple meal, their conversation flowing effortlessly, punctuated by bursts of laughter. Puppy's tail thumped a frantic beat against the wooden planks of the deck, his big eyes waiting for a morsel to tumble from the table.

Grace's gaze drifted to her friends, their faces bathed in the warm lamplight, a reflection of the joy that bloomed from their shared experience. She hadn't missed her cell phone at all tonight. Julius was easy company and ridiculously attractive. And Mona was clearly captivated by him. She had always had this knack for film stars, perhaps a subconscious attempt to fill a void in her own seemingly ordinary life. But she was so much more. She was smart, hilarious, and the life of every party. It was fun to be with her. As for Julius, Grace's appreciation wasn't rooted in his looks. It was his kindness, the attentiveness in his gaze, the genuineness that radiated from him. In him, Grace found a kindred spirit, a reflection of the values she cherished most.

"Ice cream, anyone?" Mona offered, a playful glint in her eyes.

Grace groaned dramatically. "Oh my gosh, Mona. How can we ever make this up to you?"

"You can come by more often," Mona declared, tapping her

index finger playfully. "I haven't seen you in years. I missed you!"

"I missed you too," Grace responded. "This time, I promise we'll stay in touch."

"And where," Mona added with a mock frown, "have you been hiding this charming friend of yours? To mend this emotional wound, I demand another dinner soon."

Grace chuckled. "You drive a hard bargain, Mona. What do you say, Julius?"

He grinned. "My pleasure, ladies."

Mona rose, gathering the empty dishes. "All right, let's get this cleaned up."

Grace started to protest, but Mona waved her off. "Nonsense, darling. You chat with Julius. I'll just pop these in the dishwasher and grab the ice cream. No worries, I'll be right back." Mona disappeared into the house.

Julius watched her retreat until she vanished around the corner. Then, with a deep breath, he turned to Grace. "There's something I've been wanting to ask you, Grace."

Grace tilted her head. She felt a bit tipsy. "What is it?" she asked.

He hesitated, then blurted out, "Would you consider coming home with me?"

Her breath caught. "To your house in Atherton? What about your father?"

"Honestly, Grace, he likes you very much. Deep down, I think he just wanted to push both of us to reveal your secret. He'd be happy to see you again. I promise he won't bother you with his business again if you don't want to. I can handle him."

Grace's gaze met Julius's, her breath catching in her throat as she drowned in the depths of his dark eyes. "Come home with you. What does that even mean, Julius?" she finally asked, her voice barely a whisper.

He reached into his pocket, his movements betraying a hint of nervousness. With a slow flourish, he produced a small black box and placed it on the table in front of Grace.

She gasped.

"Open it," he said, a hesitant smile gracing his features.

Grace's hand trembled slightly as she reached for the box. She lifted the lid with agonizing slowness, as if afraid of what it might reveal. Nestled inside, a huge diamond sparkled with an almost blinding brilliance.

"Julius," she whispered, her voice thick with disbelief. "You can't be serious." A wave of exasperation washed over her. "We've only known each other for a week!" She closed the box.

A flicker of sadness crossed his eyes, but his jaw remained firm. "I know it seems sudden, Grace," he admitted softly, "but there's a connection between us. I know you feel it too."

Grace stared at the box, then back at Julius, a whirlwind of confusion swirling within her. "What about your boyfriend?" she finally managed, her voice barely a whisper.

Julius sighed. "Well, it's complicated. I love him too. And to be honest, I wasn't sure at first whom I want to marry. But Rolando is a wanted hacker. His dedication runs deeper than anything else for him. He will always be a free spirit."

Grace's heart ached for him, a flicker of sympathy battling with her own confusion. "Couldn't you leave, start over somewhere new? You have the resources."

He shrugged, a bitter smile twisting his lips. "Sure, that's an option for a weekend. But my father is getting old, Grace. He needs me. And eventually, the family business will be mine. In addition, there would be no place for Rolando and me to go. Many countries have agreements with the US to apprehend and extradite criminals. They will notify the CIA if they have a person of interest the US wants, and will conduct a joint operation to apprehend him."

"You could move to Russia or China."

"As gay people? And what would they do with a wanted cyber hacker? Probably not the best to find out."

A heavy silence descended upon them. Grace met his gaze, his pain mirrored in her own.

"What do you feel for me?" she asked. Her heart pounded in her chest. This was the question she'd been yearning to ask all along, yet dreading the answer.

"I don't have all the answers, Grace," he started, then faltered, searching for the right words. "What I feel for you is intense, all-consuming in a way I never thought possible. But it's different from what I have with Rolando. A different kind of love, perhaps."

A pang of jealousy shot through Grace, followed by a wave of confusion. "Different?" she echoed, her voice barely a whisper.

"Yes," he said, his gaze locking with hers. "With Rolando, it's a firestorm, a force I can't resist. But with you, Grace, it's like home."

Grace stared at him, his raw honesty leaving her breathless. This wasn't the fairytale romance she'd envisioned, but the intensity in his eyes sparked a flicker of something undeniable within her. A feeling both foreign and familiar, a yearning she couldn't quite name.

"I am not sure, Julius," she said softly, gently sliding the black box back toward him.

Mona stepped onto the veranda with three bowls of ice cream balanced on a tray, which wobbled at her arrival. Her eyes darted between Grace and Julius, taking in the box and the tense atmosphere. "Whoa, whoa, whoa, did I miss something major here?"

With a flourish, she managed to deposit the ice cream on the table, her gaze fixed on the black velvet box. She reached out and snatched it from the table, turning it over in her hands with a frown.

"What is this?" Her eyes snapped to Julius, taking in his flushed cheeks. "Did you just propose?"

"Something like that," he said, his cheeks reddening.

"And you?" She pointed at Grace. "What do you have to say?"

"I need to think about it," Grace repeated.

Mona's brow furrowed. "Think about what, exactly? Grace, you are my best friend, but . . . honey, your taste in men hasn't exactly been stellar. Remember that last one? Practically flirting with the wallpaper the moment you weren't looking. That's part of why we drifted apart, frankly. I couldn't stand the guy. But Julius? He's perfect. Handsome, charming, and clearly smitten with you. So, what on earth do you need to think about?"

Grace's eyes met Julius's in a fleeting moment, a silent exchange that sent a pang of guilt through her. Mona's words echoed in her mind. Was there truth to them? Could she marry for intellectual connection and settle for indifference in the physical realm? She was inhabiting a stranger's body. Her new body felt numb, and she didn't feel a particular urge to find out if she even had a physical desire.

She did love Julius. But would it be enough? What about Karim? He radiated an undeniable physical yearning for her that he didn't try to hide. But was it truly for her, or did he see Bianca every time he looked at her? Their first coffee had ended with a discordant note, their minds seemingly on different frequencies.

So, what did she crave more? The comfort of intellectual intimacy or the spark of physical attraction? Grace was adrift in a sea of uncertainty. She wasn't sure. She just wasn't sure.

With a weary sigh, Mona conceded. "All right, this has been a long day. Here's the deal, you take this box, consider it carefully, and hopefully Julius and I will see the rock on your finger tomorrow morning." Mona reached for Grace's sweater that she had borrowed after the shower. She slipped the box into a hidden pocket. Grace blinked, surprised by the secret compartment.

Julius had remained silent, his hand mechanically stroking the dog's head resting in his lap. Grace inched closer, her touch hesitant as she placed a hand on his arm. "Julius," she whispered, her voice thick with emotion, "you know I care about you deeply."

"Yes, I know," he mumbled, looking at the dog.

"Give me some time," she pleaded, her voice trembling slightly. "Until tomorrow."

"Of course," he said curtly, a muscle clenched in his jaw.

Grace rose from the bench, her gaze lingering on Julius.

"Puppy needs a walk," she announced, her voice strained. Puppy's ears perked up instantly, his tail thumping a happy rhythm against the bench. She reached for the leash hanging on the chair, and Puppy erupted in a frenzy of excited barks and jumps, mirroring Grace's own internal turmoil. She clipped on the leash.

"Should I join you?" Julius asked.

Grace paused. She looked back at him. "I think it's best if I have some . . . alone time," she finally replied, the words tasting like ash in her mouth.

"Right, of course," he conceded. "Please be safe."

Mona piped up. "No worries, this neighborhood is practically a retirement village. I've walked back here from neighborhood dinners a hundred times. It was never a problem. Come on, Julius, let's give her some space. We can clear away the dishes, and if by some miracle Grace hasn't made up her mind by morning"—she winked at him—"I'm happy to fill in."

A wry smile tugged at Julius's lips. "Intriguing offer, Mona."

Mona gestured toward a narrow walkway barely visible in the twilight. "That leads to a beautiful path through the hills," she said, her voice softening. "Perfect for clearing your head."

Grace offered a wan smile. "Thank you!"

The path, shrouded in the deepening shadows, seemed to mirror the turmoil within her. She walked toward it, the gravel crunching beneath her feet as Puppy tugged gently on the leash.

- 45 -

ANNYA

Saturday, November 12, 2033, 7:00 p.m.

Annya, Tina, and Angus walked down the uneven sidewalk in the Mission District in San Francisco, past quirky storefronts, graffiti-streaked lofts, and weathered Victorian buildings. Angus had parked a few blocks down from their destination, a habit honed from years of experience navigating undercover operations. In the city, it was easier to disappear by foot than to drive away on a congested street. Around them, people from all walks of life went about their evening. Hipsters with meticulously tousled hair and vintage clothing brushed shoulders with artists in paint-splattered jeans, techies glued to their phones, and families pushing strollers, their chatter a hum of a dozen languages. Across the street, a mural of a revolutionary woman adorned a corner building, her hand raised in a defiant fist.

As they rounded the corner, the old warehouse came into view. The once-grand structure bore the scars of time, with faded paint peeling from its brick walls and rusted metal beams jutting out at odd angles. Vines crept up the sides, weaving a tangled web that seemed to clasp the building in nature's embrace. High arched windows, now boarded shut, hinted at a time when light streamed through to illuminate a bustling interior.

Angus stopped. "I won't go any further," he declared. "Please be careful." He reached for Annya and embraced her.

Annya met his gaze with a smile. "I can handle myself."

"Of course you can." He squeezed her gently. "But there's no shame in strong women accepting help. Teamwork, remember?" He released her and shifted his focus to Tina. "Are there metal detectors at the entrance?"

Tina shook her head. "This is a community event. What do you think?"

"Good." He reached into his pocket, pulling out a small metallic device. "Here." He offered it to Annya. "Put this in your pocket. It's a tracker, just in case. And if you're not back by nine"—his voice firmed again—"I'm coming in to get you."

Annya took the device, a playful glint in her eyes. "Thank you, my knight," she teased. "I'll be fine." With a final parting smile, she turned around. A prickle of unease crept down her spine when they stepped into the looming shadow of the warehouse. She glanced back, expecting to see Angus's reassuring form, but he was already gone.

"Come this way," Tina said, leading her toward the open loading bay. Annya followed, taking in the scene around her. Several people of different ages hurried past, their faces etched with anticipation. A few of them waved at Tina.

"Hey, Tina!" boomed a voice beside them.

Tina smiled and waved back. "These are really nice people, you know," she said, tilting her head slightly toward Annya. "They're here for the community, to escape the tech-heavy city grind."

"I can see that," Annya responded. The excitement around her was infectious. She felt her own heart beating a bit faster as they stepped closer into this new world.

At the entrance, a young man in jeans and a dark-green sweater stood guard, shaking hands with each arriving guest. As Tina approached, his face broke into a cheerful grin. "Hello, Tina, great to see you again!"

"Hello, Karim, great to see you to," Tina replied, gesturing toward Annya beside her. "This is Annya, an ER physician and a friend from SUEC."

Karim's smile remained, but a steely glint flickered in his eyes as he scanned Annya from head to toe.

"Excellent," he said. "Welcome, Annya."

Annya's intuition screamed at her to step back, but she forced herself to stand her ground. She extended her hand and met his gaze head-on. "Great to meet you, Karim," she said calmly.

His handshake was firm, his grip lingering a beat longer than necessary. He gestured toward a bench lined with a collection of neatly arranged cell phones. Annya tried to count them. Fifty, perhaps.

"Please leave your phones here," Karim requested. "We wouldn't want any interruptions during our gatherings. Name tags are there if you'd like to add one. You can pick up your phone again when you leave."

No connection to the outside world? Annya hesitated for a moment.

As if he had sensed it, Karim said, "I'm afraid this is not optional. We just don't want any distractions while we connect with each other."

"Of course," Annya said. She placed her cell phone on the bench. So did Tina.

A genuine smile reappeared on Karim's face. "Please come in!" He gestured toward the warehouse interior, his attention already shifting to the next guest in line.

Annya exchanged a silent glance with Tina before stepping into the unknown.

Tina patted her shoulder reassuringly. "No worries. This is standard procedure."

Annya stepped through the entrance, and a wave of soft light and fragrance washed over her. The scent of fresh flowers mingled with the enticing aroma of roasted peppers, grilled meat and rosemary.

The factory hall was a cavernous space with exposed steel beams lining the walls and crisscrossing beams overhead. In the center, two long wooden tables stretched nearly wall-to-wall, adorned with strings of natural candles. The candles illuminated beautiful floral centerpieces and mirroring flower patterns on meticulously arranged plates. Chairs flanked either side, some occupied by folks already deep in conversation, chatting and laughing. Others stood, mingling in the open spaces between the tables, radiating a sense of easy camaraderie.

Annya's gaze, honed by years of scanning crowds for potential threats, did a quick sweep of the room. She mentally tallied the number of attendees, estimating about eighty people, a mix of ages and backgrounds. Her analytical mind filed away details—body language, groupings, potential exit points. Despite her vigilance, she couldn't help but feel the warm energy of the community gathering for a shared meal, a sense of camaraderie and connection filling the space.

Two young women materialized beside them with smiles as bright as the flowers on the tables. "Hi there!" chirped one, placing her arm around Tina. "Great to see you, Tina! Did you bring a guest today?"

"Yes, this is Annya, a dear friend."

The woman extended her hand. "Welcome!" she said with a broad smile. "We are about to start. Please have a seat."

"This looks amazing!" Annya marveled, tracing a fingertip along the rim of a flower-painted plate.

"This was our task this week," the other woman explained, her face beaming with pride. "It was a lot of work, but seeing everyone enjoy it makes it all worth it."

Annya's brows shot up. "You did all this? By yourselves?"

The woman shook her head, a playful glint in her eyes.

"Virginie and I," she corrected, gesturing toward her companion. "But we had a hand from everyone. Cleaning, flowers, setting tables—it's a community effort, you see. That's what makes this place special."

Annya nodded, sensing the palpable community around her. The scene in front of her was a stark contrast to the sterile efficiency of the ER, where bodies were stitched together with clinical precision. Here, amidst the laughter and conversation, souls were intertwined in a tapestry of shared humanity. The place did feel magical. But she couldn't afford to let the warmth seep in. She was here for a reason, a mission to uncover the connection between the group here and the attacks on Grace.

"Hello, is this seat taken?" A young woman with a wild afro that seemed to defy gravity appeared beside her. She pointed at the empty chair to her right.

"No, please sit," Annya responded with a smile.

"Hi, I'm Suzanna." The woman extended a hand with nails painted a bright green.

"Nice to meet you. I'm Annya." Annya returned the handshake, her gaze snagged by a flash of ink on Suzanna's wrist—an ouroboros tattoo.

Suzanna's gaze held a friendly curiosity. "I haven't seen you here before. Are you new?"

Annya nodded. "Yes, I just joined today."

"Welcome!" Suzanna beamed. "I've been part of this group for about a year now."

Annya leaned in. "Oh, that's great. So, can you tell me all about it? How do you like these meetings? Are they helpful?"

Suzanna nodded eagerly. "Hugely! I work as a nurse at San Francisco General. When I joined, I was burned-out beyond belief. But these gatherings have been a lifesaver. They helped me reconnect with myself. I feel so much better now than I did a year ago!"

"That is wonderful to hear." Annya forced a tight smile. The young woman did look radiant. Perhaps Bianca had sought solace in this same community for similar reasons. But clearly, the path to healing hadn't been quite as smooth for her.

"Is it true that everyone contributes a weekly task?" Annya inquired. "Does that feel like a burden at all?"

Suzanna shook her head. "Not at all. In fact, it's quite the opposite. We often get to choose what we can offer. I have a large garden and donate a good chunk of the produce for our dinners here."

Annya's gaze swept across the room. "For eighty people?"

She chuckled. "It might sound ambitious, but I'm hardly the only one chipping in. Besides, I recently expanded my herb and tomato collection specifically for these gatherings here. It brings me a lot of joy, knowing it helps others."

"Have you ever gotten an odd request?" Annya asked.

Suzanna paused, a flicker of hesitation crossing her face. "Well . . ." She scanned Annya cautiously.

"I'm just trying to understand what I'm getting into," Annya said with a winning smile. "I heard from a few others that they got some odd requests."

"Really?" Susanna looked at her. "Like what?"

"I'm not here to spread any rumors," Annya said. "I wouldn't share any of your experiences either. I'm just trying to understand what I might face if I join."

"Well, I don't think you need to be concerned in any way. Karim asked me to bring belladonna berries from my garden a few times. He's a hospitalist, so he knows how to handle them. Belladonna's got a long history for medicinal use—headache, breathing problems, inflammatory bowel syndromes. And no one keeled over that I know of." She let out a light laugh.

Karim collected belladonna berries from his community members? The nurse in the rehabilitation center, the woman at the Zhang party, and Dr. Triveda had all been poisoned with belladonna.

Annya studied Suzanna. Were all these people here operating under a veil of good intentions, blissfully unaware of their leader's larger purpose? Suzanna's innocent demeanor made it difficult to tell. Maybe some contributed unknowingly. But the people who had attacked Grace clearly had to know what they were doing.

Annya's attention was caught by an elderly man in a tailored suit who walked toward Tina. He bowed slightly. "Tina, my dear," he purred, his voice smooth as velvet. "What a delightful surprise to see you here."

"Hello, Carlos," Tina replied, a hint of coolness in her tone.

Annya looked at the man. She had heard that name before. But Carlos was a common name. Perhaps it was just a coincidence. Who was he? Tina and he locked eyes for far too long.

"I thought you didn't want to come anymore?" he asked. "Did you change your mind?"

Tina responded with a curt nod. "About the community, maybe. But not about you, Carlos. You lied to me. You pretended to be a company manager when in fact you are a house manager."

"My apologies, Tina. I simply wanted to impress you."

Tina's eyes narrowed. "Once a liar, always a liar," she snapped.

Carlos held up a placating hand. "You are understandably upset," he soothed. "Perhaps I could join you and your friend this evening? Make amends?"

Tina leaned forward with a grim face, ready to respond. But Annya stopped her, gently placing her hand on her arm.

"Please join us," she said, her voice friendly yet firm. "I'm Annya Segond."

His gaze snapped to Annya. "Oh, are you Dr. Annya Segond, an ER physician at SUEC Hospital?"

"Yes, that's right."

"Julius has told me a lot about you."

"Julius?"

"Dr. Julius Zhang. I am the house manager for the Zhang family."

"Oh, nice to meet you!" She remembered hearing the name from Julius. Had this man revealed Grace's location to the clan here, perhaps even let the assassin into the Zhang residence? How far did the infiltration go? "Please, have a seat," Annya said warmly, a smile playing on her lips.

Tina opened her mouth to protest. But before she could utter a word, the elderly man sank down beside her with a surprising agility that belied his years.

- 46 -

ANNYA

Saturday, November 12, 2033, 7:15 p.m.

A second, ethereal chime rang through the cavernous hall. Its musical notes seemed to stretch and deepen, more akin to a church bell than a theater's call to silence. As the final echoes faded, the last guests scurried to their seats. Annya, seated near the end of the long table, took a mental head count. About eighty heads all turned expectantly toward the front of the table where a wooden lectern stood gleaming under the soft glow of two large candles. Karim strode toward it with quiet confidence, his steps silencing the room. The gathering seemed to hold a collective breath as a palpable sense of anticipation settled over them. Guests leaned forward in their seats, a silent wave of attentiveness washing over the room.

"Welcome, members of the Order of Balance." Karim's voice rang clear and resonant. "We gather here tonight to honor the harmony of body and soul, the essence of our existence."

He paused, letting the words sink in. In the flickering candlelight, his eyes seemed to hold a timeless wisdom.

"Our bodies are temples that must be revered and respected. They are meticulously crafted vessels that allow our souls to navigate the wonders of the physical realm. Yet the practices of our modern lives—the relentless pursuit of progress, the constant barrage of stimulation—can disrupt this delicate harmony."

Did Karim's eloquence carry a coded message? Annya's instincts kicked in, dissecting each sentence.

Karim scanned the faces around him, his gaze a mix of concern and resolve. His gaze lingered on Annya for a moment, then moved on. "The imbalance of body and soul manifests in many ways—physical ailments, mental anguish, burnout, depression." He leaned forward, his voice gaining fervor. "The modern world, in its relentless pursuit of progress, forgets a fundamental truth. It tinkers with the vessel, neglecting the divine spark that resides within. These alterations, these violations, disrupt the sacred harmony between flesh and spirit. Within each of us lies a spark of the divine, yearning for wholeness. But this spark chokes if we sever the connection between the vessel and the essence it carries. We, the Order of Balance, are the guardians of this ancient truth. We will guard the harmony of body and soul. We will mend the broken covenant, reawaken the soul, and restore the harmony that allows body and spirit to flourish together!"

A flicker of something new ignited in Karim's eyes—a deeper shade that held both anger and a steely resolve. Was he railing against the ethics of modern medicine, perhaps even criticizing body transplants? Or was there something more personal fueling his fervor? His veiled message resonated with a strange unease.

Karim raised his glass high. "To the Order of Balance!"

A resounding chorus of clinking glasses echoed throughout the vast space. "To the Order of Balance!" they chanted.

With a measured incline of his head, Karim acknowledged the rapt audience. Then, he descended from the lectern with deliberate slow moves. The weight of his presence lingered when he finally settled back into his seat.

A wisp of melody, like a butterfly taking flight, drifted through the air. Annya glanced around, searching for the source. There, nestled in a corner, sat a young girl in a polka-dot dress, eighteen or nineteen years of age. In her hands, a horizontal flute sent a sweet melody through the hall. Mozart, perhaps.

Four young figures emerged from the shadows at the edge of the room. Each carried a pair of plates with a colorful display of glistening seafood, seared cuts of meat, and vegetables.

A collective gasp rippled through the room and was quickly replaced with animated murmurs, clinking silverware, and warm smiles. The servers brought more plates and then weaved through the crowd, filling glasses and clearing plates. The air buzzed with a sense of shared connection as the people at the table engaged in conversations and lighthearted banter.

Annya leaned closer to Suzanna, her voice dropping to a curious murmur. "Suzanna, I couldn't help but notice your tattoo. That's an ouroboros, right?"

Suzanna nodded enthusiastically. "Thanks for noticing! It's the symbol of our community here and it means a lot to me."

"What does it mean, exactly?"

"The ouroboros represents cycles of life and death, birth and rebirth."

"Good and evil?"

Suzanna laughed. "I'm not sure about that. To me, it is very positive. The ouroboros reminds me that all endings are beginnings. The serpent consumes its own tail to regenerate."

"Do you mean the snake is a cannibal?"

"No, not at all. The ouroboros isn't a picture of a hungry snake. It represents the idea of self-renewal."

"Self-renewal? Did that idea help you with your burnout?"

Suzanna nodded again. "Burnout feels like an endless cycle of stress and exhaustion, where body and soul are out of sync. The ouroboros reminded me that I can renew myself."

"You do look great right now."

Suzanna laughed. "I do feel renewed, indeed. Thanks to this wonderful community here."

Annya took in her radiant smile. To her, the ouroboros was more than a spiritual symbol. The order's staunch belief in the sanctity of body and soul made them likely antagonists of any form of body modification, let alone a body transplant. Such an abomination would probably have to be corrected according to the beliefs of the people here.

"What if someone disrespects the Order of Balance?" she asked.

Suzanna swirled the wine in her glass. "You ask funny questions, Annya. We strive to educate those who are unaware. Disrespect wouldn't be the word, I suppose. Perhaps naïveté is a better term. Big corporations exploit our bodies, pushing us past healthy limits. We simply want people to understand the sacred connection of body and soul, to guard against those who would take advantage of them."

"That is an interesting perspective. What if someone disagrees with the ouroboros concept and threatens one of your members? That sometimes happens with groups like this, right?"

"Well, if someone directly threatened our members . . ." Suzanna trailed off, her gaze hardening slightly. "This is hypothetical, of course . . ."

Annya nodded reassuringly.

Suzanna sliced the tomato on her plate into pieces. "We believe in unity, Annya. We wouldn't initiate conflict. But if someone were to directly threaten one of our members, we would certainly take steps to protect our community."

Annya nodded again. Was Suzanna brainwashed? These people here could be dangerous, fueled by some deeply ingrained belief system. Did they even realize the harm they could inflict?

A movement at the far end of the table interrupted her contemplations. Karim rose from his chair with a wave in their direction.

Carlos turned to Tina. "Remember, you wanted me to step up as a leader? Well, I talked to Karim about it, and . . ."—he paused, a wide grin splitting his face—"he appointed me deputy leader!"

"Really?" A flicker of admiration crossed Tina's eyes.

"If you would please excuse me." Carlos rose and walked over to the head of the table. Karim openly shook hands with him, looking around to ensure everyone witnessed the gesture.

"Dear fellows," Karim said loudly, "a pressing matter requires my immediate attention. Carlos here will commence the proceedings. Please consult with him with the same respect as you do with me."

A ripple of applause washed over the room.

Tina joined in, clapping enthusiastically as she leaned back toward Annya. "That is quite impressive, isn't' it?" She turned to the front of the table, where Karim patted Carlos's shoulder. Karim nodded at the crowd, then turned and disappeared into the back of the building.

Annya rose to her feet. She needed to know where Karim had gone. If he suddenly appointed a deputy for his weekly community meeting, it had to be something significant. "Do you know where the restrooms are?" she asked, looking first at Tina, then Suzanna.

Suzanna gestured vaguely toward the back of the room where Karim had just disappeared. "Over there, I think," she said.

Tina looked at her, irritated. "Do you want me to come with you?" she asked.

"To the restroom? No thanks." Annya feigned a chuckle and casually reached for her jacket. "Thanks anyway!"

Should she fetch her phone at the entrance? No, there was no time. She quickly stepped toward the back of the building, scanning the hallway for Karim. It was dark and empty. A young man, his face obscured by the shadow of a tray laden with plates, hustled past her. The clatter of dishes briefly broke the silence, then faded as he vanished through a swinging door on the left. To her right was a back door ajar. Annya slipped through.

The cool breeze of the San Francisco fog instantly hit her as she emerged onto a bustling side street jammed with parked cars. To her left were two Beaux Arts apartment buildings with a peeling white facade. To her right was a bar with a vibrant mural of Frida Kahlo's piercing gaze. Underneath, a man in jeans and a dark-green sweater walked down the street with long strides. It was Karim, his pace suggesting urgency and determination as he navigated through the urban throng. Annya pulled her jacket tight around herself and followed him.

- 47 -

JULIUS

Saturday, November 12, 2033, 7:30 p.m.

Julius meticulously wiped the spaghetti bowl with a towel, his mind drifting to Grace. He had never imagined experiencing such profound feelings for a woman. When she'd driven away from the cabin, her car disappearing down the road, it had felt like his heart had shattered. He loved Rolando, yes, but it was a different kind of love, fueled by passion and physical desire. With Grace, it was something deeper, a yearning that resonated in the very core of his being.

Grace had rekindled a feeling he hadn't experienced since his mother's passing, a loss that had left a gaping hole in his soul. Now, that sense of belonging was back, a fragile warmth he couldn't let extinguish again. It was too precious. This was what he truly craved. He yearned for the comfort of a warm embrace at the end of the day, a silent understanding that washed away the day's troubles. He wanted dinners filled with laughter, shared moments with his father, a life built with Grace by his side. He longed for a confidante, someone who made coming home feel like a true homecoming.

Sex was a primal urge he could still indulge in with Rolando. A fleeting pleasure. But home . . . that was something only those who'd lost it could truly appreciate. Rolando had no desire to fit in or settle down. Grace craved a home just as much as he did. And the thought of losing her again sent a fresh wave of panic through him. She hadn't returned the ring. Perhaps that was a sign that she might feel the same way. He would wait. He would do whatever it took because he knew that he had found what he'd been searching for all along. This woman was his soulmate. He just knew it.

The doorbell's shrill cry cut through Julius's pensive mood. He remembered Mona mentioning she'd take the overflowing trash to the trash cans in the garage. Had she locked herself out?

Julius strode toward the door and opened it. On the other side stood a stranger who looked at him out of sunken eyes. A man with sharp cheekbones, a hawkish nose, and a jagged scar across his jaw. Julius's hand instinctively reached for the doorknob, a desperate attempt to slam the door shut. But the man's hand shot out, a blur of muscle and determination, slamming against the wood with a force that sent splinters flying. The door flung wide open, its hinges groaning. With a swift move, the man pushed Julius backward into the room and stepped in.

Julius stumbled back, the world tilting precariously. Was this another assassin? How had he found them? His heart hammered against his ribs, a frantic drum against the sudden silence.

The man's eyes held a predatory glint. His gaze swept over Julius, taking in every detail with a chilling intensity.

"Where is Grace?" he demanded.

Julius' throat tightened. "I . . . I'm here alone," he stammered.

A fist sped forward and hit his face with a sickening crunch. A searing pain exploded in his head, the metallic tang of blood filling his mouth. He stumbled back.

"I won't ask again so politely," the man snarled.

Panic seared through Julius. Rolando's face flashed in his mind, nurturing a spark of defiance. He wouldn't go down without a fight. He wouldn't let this stranger intimidate him. His fingers brushed against the familiar cool metal of the switchblade that Rolando had given him for emergencies. In a swift, desperate move, he whipped the blade out and plunged it into the man's thigh.

A roar of pain erupted. The man staggered back, clutching at the wound, a crimson stain blooming on his muscular leg. He ripped the knife out with a snarl and flung it across the room, the clatter echoing in the tense silence.

Julius's mind raced. He had to get out. He had to warn Grace and save her from this lunatic. But before he could take a step, two hands shot out, wrapping around his throat like iron bands. His eyes darted around wildly, searching for a weapon, anything he could use to defend himself. But the room around him started to spin, his vision blurring. The man's grip tightened, cutting off his air. He gasped. His ears pounded with the frantic thud of his own heartbeat.

With trembling fingers, he clawed at the suffocating grasp, his nails digging deep into flesh in a futile attempt to break free from the suffocating embrace. He felt a slick warmth bloom on his palms—the man's blood. Yet the hands remained unyielding, a cruel vise tightening with each desperate heave of his chest. Stars danced before his eyes and the world began to fade at the edges, colors draining into a monochrome haze, his vision dissolving into swirling shadows. The darkness closed in, swallowing him whole.

- 48 -

ANNYA

Saturday, November 12, 2033, 8:00 p.m.

Annya followed Karim north on Valencia Street, careful to stay just out of his peripheral vision but close enough to track him. They passed a vibrant mix of Victorian homes, sleek apartments, bustling storefronts, and the imposing City College of San Francisco. Above the entrance, her eyes were drawn to a striking circular mosaic with colorful symbols in dominant hues of orange, yellow, blue, and green. She recalled reading about it. This was the Aztec calendar, with Tonatiuh, the sun god, at its center, surrounded by rings of symbols representing two realms: the earthly and the divine. Perhaps reminiscent of the concept of the Order of Balance.

Karim walked past without a glance and Annya followed close behind. They continued down Valencia Street, passing bustling grocery stores and a restaurant that wafted the aroma of freshly baked pizza. Around the corner, a brightly lit bicycle shop gave way to a cavernous auto repair garage. For a while, the rhythmic clang of metal on metal drowned out the sounds of conversation and traffic around them.

Karim forged ahead, his eyes focused on the path. He turned sharply at Twentieth Street, where Victorian houses clustered tightly together in a patchwork of gentle pinks, serene blues, and lemon yellows. There were fewer people on the sidewalk, making it harder to blend in unnoticed. Annya adjusted her stride to maintain her distance, seeking cover in the lengthening shadows of the ornate facades and turrets around her.

Karim turned around the corner of Twentieth and Dolores Street, where Dolores Park was sprawled before them, an expanse of green adorned with majestic palm trees that slowly swayed in the evening breeze. Laughter and music drifted from within, hinting at some gathering taking place. Beyond the park, the iconic San Francisco skyline stretched toward the horizon. Annya's gaze lingered for a moment on the vista. The Transamerica Pyramid, Bank of America Tower, and Salesforce Tower ignited, followed by a cascade of lights across countless other skyscrapers. The last remnants of daylight painted wisps of orange and pink on the sky above the cityscape, creating a scene so picturesque it felt almost surreal.

When she looked back at the sidewalk, it was empty. Karim was gone. Annya scanned the surroundings, searching for his figure. He had been there just a moment ago. Where was he? The bare sidewalk offered no clues of his whereabouts.

Annya tried to think logically. If Karim had headed into the park, she would have seen him. There was no nearby bus stop, and not enough time had passed for him to hop into a Waymo or Uber. He must have slipped into one of the nearby houses.

A warning bell went off in her mind. Who had mentioned Dolores Park to her very recently? The answer wouldn't come. It danced on the periphery of her mind, a name just out of reach.

Slow down, Annya scolded herself. *Focus on the cityscape, the houses, the park, the people, anything to snag that memory.*

Then, it hit her like a lightning strike. Dr. Triveda! Grace's surgeon. Dr. Triveda had mentioned living at Dolores Park in San Francisco. Karim was about to get her.

She had to act fast. Annya reached for her phone, but her pocket was empty. She had left it at the warehouse. How could she find Dr. Triveda's address? It had to be close. She walked from house to house, scrutinizing doorbells for the surgeon's name. The apartment buildings displayed names, but the villas remained frustratingly anonymous. A star surgeon likely resided in one of the grand single-family homes around the park.

Every second felt like a blow. Did Karim know about the body transplant? Annya remembered Karim's speech: *We, the Order of Balance, will guard the harmony of body and soul.* What would the leader of the Order of Balance do to a surgeon who had violated this order? Dr. Triveda had just survived a poisoning attack. Did Karim want to finish the job?

If the surgeon lived here, the neighbors would surely know her and could likely direct her to Dr. Triveda's residence. Annya began ringing the doorbells of the most imposing Victorian buildings lining the park. The first attempt yielded a frail elderly woman who shook her head at the mention of Dr. Triveda. The next door opened to a scowling man with a ferocious dog who barked so incessantly Annya could barely stammer out a question. The third attempt yielded a teenage girl who pointed toward a grand Victorian villa to their right.

Annya rushed toward the imposing three-story structure, its sheer size momentarily stealing her breath. The sharp silhouette of a steeply pitched roof adorned with a jagged mane of shingles pierced the twilight. Not a single light shone from within the house. Majestic columns upheld a sprawling porch, casting long shadows across the front. The silence of the place was almost deafening. Annya's heart pounded as she reached the wrought iron fence, the cold metal biting into her palms as she gripped the iron bars.

A familiar voice greeted Annya from behind. "Hello, Annya. Can I be of assistance?"

She spun around, her heart leaping. There stood Angus casually leaning against the fence, his hand in his pocket, his hair ruffled by the evening fog. Relief washed over her as she rushed into his embrace.

"How did you find me?" she gasped.

"Remember?" he said with a smile. "I placed a GPS chip in your pocket."

"But you wanted to look after me at nine p.m. It must be shortly after eight p.m. now."

"Tina called me. She was worried because you and Karim both disappeared."

Annya exhaled. Tina had truly chosen their side.

She pointed at the villa in front of them. "I believe Karim might visit Dr. Triveda. She's in danger."

"Then let's rescue her."

Annya glanced at Angus with admiration. Dating a workaholic had its challenges; late nights, missed dinners, and the occasional feeling of being second to his career. But watching him in his element made all the sacrifices worthwhile.

"How do we get in?" she asked.

Angus pushed open the creaky front gate. "Perhaps through the door?"

Annya couldn't suppress a smile. But another thought crept into her mind. "Can I have your phone?"

He looked back at her. "Now?"

"Karim said in his speech that his followers must restore the order of the universe. If he's after Dr. Triveda, another member of his clan may be after Grace. We must warn her."

Angus passed the phone to her. "An FBI team is on their way to her. Who else do you want to call?"

"Julius. He's on his way to her as well. I don't want him to run into a trap."

"My team tried to locate him, but he doesn't have his cell phone on him. Do you know how to contact him?"

Annya nodded. "He called me earlier from a burner phone. Your team can trace that call to locate him. I memorized the number on the display just in case." Her fingers flew across the screen. *Careful. Hit man may come for Grace.*

She pressed the phone back into Angus's hand.

"Do you want to join the FBI?" he teased. "You'd make an excellent field agent."

"No thanks."

They smiled at each other. She felt an urge to kiss him, but they had a colleague to rescue. Without another word, she turned toward Dr. Triveda's home. Angus followed.

The grand wooden steps stretched before them, each one polished to a gleaming reflection. Annya grabbed the iron railing that mirrored the fence around the house. It felt cold and unyielding. As they ascended, the auburn redwood door at the top loomed larger, a brass handle gleaming in the fading light.

Angus tugged it carefully, but it was locked.

"Should we breach it?" Annya asked.

"We don't know what's behind it. It might be better to enter from an unanticipated angle. Let's check for a back entrance."

They circled the house along the porch. There was a weathered wooden door nestled discreetly beneath a creaking fire escape. Angus reached into his pocket, a glint of metal catching the slivers of the blooming moonlight. With a quick flick of the wrist, he creaked the door open and slipped in first. Annya followed close behind, the faint click of the shutting door plunging them into inky blackness.

It took a moment for their eyes to adapt. Slowly, shapes began to emerge from the void—the faint gleam of stainless-steel appliances, the hard outline of a central island. They had entered a kitchen. Annya tiptoed forward and let out a hushed curse as she bumped her knee on a low counter. A soft whirring sound started somewhere to her left, barely audible—a refrigerator, perhaps, chugging away in the dark.

Angus turned toward her, holding his index finger against his mouth. Straining her ears, Annya caught it—a murmur of voices, faint but distinct, drifting from the depths of the house. A man and a woman, their conversation muffled by distance. Against her better judgment, she slowly stepped toward the sound, the floorboards groaning softly beneath her weight.

A narrow corridor swallowed them whole. Paneled wood walls, dark and polished, pressed in close on either side. Each creak under their shoes sent a slight shiver down Annya's spine. There was a heavy wooden door on their left. Angus, a shadow against the gloom, reached out and tested it. Annya leaned in close, peering over his shoulder. Inside, a sliver of moonlight sliced across a couch, two chairs, an ottoman and a piano in the background. An empty living room.

Angus pivoted slowly. "Clear," he whispered.

To their right, a sliver of light caught Annya's eye. A door, ajar by a hair's breadth, bled a ray of light on the polished floor. She reached out carefully, fingers brushing the cool metal of the doorknob. A silent prayer flickered through her mind as she nudged the door open a bit further, a faint creak feeling like a gunshot in the tense quiet.

A wave of stale air washed over them, carrying a dusty scent. The murmur of voices grew louder now, the conversation clearer. A man's voice, deep and commanding. A woman's reply, laced with a hint of urgency. Annya recognized the voices.

"Dr. Triveda and Karim," she whispered to Angus.

Angus gave her a curt nod, his jaw clenched. A metallic click echoed in the stale air. Annya's eyes darted to his hand. He held a drawn weapon. He slowly stepped past her, descending the dusty stairs into the cellar. Annya followed closely.

The stairs ended abruptly in a cramped landing. A solitary doorway gaped to their right. Annya risked a peek around the corner. Before them stretched a dimly lit space with rough brick walls and an uneven stone floor. Cobwebs, thick and dusty, draped from exposed beams overhead, shimmering faintly in the weak light. In the center of the room was Dr. Triveda, tied to a chair, tears streaming down her cheeks. Karim loomed over her, a glint of steel pressed against the surgeon's throat. A knife, perhaps. Beside the chair was a large woven bag. A strange twitch in its form made Annya's heart skip a beat. She squinted. Was it her imagination, or was something moving inside?

"So, you persuaded a young woman with incurable cancer to agree to transplant her head onto someone else's body." His voice crackled with fury. "A surgery that never even worked long-term in an *animal.* And once she agreed, you needed a donor body quickly before she changed her mind."

"Grace's agreement to the procedure was a unique opportunity," Dr. Triveda stammered.

"An opportunity for what? To play God with people's lives?" Karim scoffed. "And then you pressured your staff into becoming organ donors, a decision Bianca clearly wouldn't have made if she'd known it meant her death."

"Lu'lu and I just handed out information forms. It was your wife's decision to sign up for the transplant donor list or not."

Karim scoffed. "Of course. You exploited Bianca's kind heart. She eagerly signed up to help. And then you turned her compassion into a death warrant."

Dr. Triveda desperately shook her head. "We weren't pressuring anyone! We just checked for compatibility in case—"

"In case a twenty-eight-year-old nurse might die suddenly? What were the odds of that happening? Unless, of course, someone nudged things in that direction."

"I have nothing to do with your wife's death," Dr. Triveda cried.

Karim scoffed. "Spare your breath, you liar. One of my team members works for Amazon. He happened to deliver a package when you walked into my house on the day of Bianca's alleged suicide. He heard a gunshot shortly after that."

"That was not me!"

"I got the camera footage from the Amazon van. You went into my house and killed her!"

"You have no proof of that. I visited her because she had called in sick. I knew she suffered from severe depression and wanted to check on her. She killed herself."

"Well, let the ouroboros deliver its verdict on that," Karim said with a grim smile. He lunged toward the bag near Dr. Triveda's chair and ripped open the zipper.

A sharp hiss sliced through the air. A large snake erupted from the bag, its body a sinuous coil of muscle and scales. Karim jumped back.

"A rattlesnake!" Annya rasped at Angus.

The snake slowly moved toward Dr. Triveda, its body forming a menacing S-shape, the tip of the tail adorned with a wicked-looking rattle. Its triangular head swayed back and forth, its reptilian tongue flicking in and out. It seemed poised to strike at any moment.

Annya's gaze darted between the slithering menace and the surgeon. "Dr. Triveda is weakened from the poisoning attack," she whispered to Angus. "One bite and she could die in a few minutes."

The surgeon sat frozen in her chair, staring at the snake.

- 49 -

GRACE

Saturday, November 12, 2033, 8:00 p.m.

Grace followed the lights along the trail, her feet light on the soft ground. Puppy, a furry shadow at her side, trotted with his usual enthusiastic swagger, tail thumping happily as he investigated every rustle in the grass, every inviting tree trunk, and every suspicious squirrel hole. The wind whispered through the golden fields along the path, accompanied by the songs of chirping crickets. The city lights below them had morphed into a glittering sprawl, like a million tiny points of defiance against the encroaching darkness.

The cool evening breeze tugged playfully at Grace's hair, carrying the sweet scent of damp earth and a salty taste from the distant ocean. Goosebumps rose on her arms as her breath formed white mist puffs in front of her. Grace quickened her pace to get warmer. Here, under the vast expanse of the sky, she felt a forgotten sense of freedom, a stark contrast to the sterile hum of machines that had become her lullaby for months. Above, the night sky shimmered with a million stars, a dazzling display that seemed to go on forever. The Milky Way, a faint luminescent band, stretched across the heavens like a celestial river that guided her way. She spread her arms wide, threw back her head, and let out a soft gasp. Beside her, Puppy paused in his tracks, his ears perked up in curiosity. He cocked his head toward her and let out a soft woof as if confirming her sense of wonder.

Reaching down, Grace patted him gently. She had always craved for the companionship of a dog, a furry friend to share life's adventures with. Why had it taken so long? Puppy, sensing the shift in her mood, responded with a loving, wet kiss on her face. With a playful bark, he turned and bounced forward. Grace followed. Together, they continued along the path.

Her fingers traced the velvet box in her pocket. The box with the diamond ring. It was like a dream and a nightmare at the same time. She yearned for Julius to pull her into his arms, to push her up against a wall, to interlock his fingers with hers. She wanted him to touch her, to merge with her, to make her forget everything despite her name. But if she accepted the ring, that wasn't what this would be. He had a lover and she had a borrowed body. Redefining the word complicated.

There was no doubt that Julius was her soulmate, a man who understood her to the core, who cared for her deeply, who could understand her without speaking a word. He was ridiculously attractive and wealthy. If she married him, she could dance with him whenever she wanted to, embrace him whenever she wanted to, and kiss him whenever she wanted to. He would be loyal, supportive, and a daily source of joy. Was that not enough? Was there a man who had it all?

The wind became chilly. She didn't have a phone and had no sense how much time had gone by. She turned around. If she walked back the same path they'd come, they couldn't get lost. Puppy tilted his head, his brown eyes filled with a hint of disappointment.

"Sorry, boy," she murmured, crouching to scratch him behind his ears. "We'll find a new adventure tomorrow, okay?"

The dog looked up at her briefly. Then, with a new burst of energy, he bounded ahead with a wagging tail. Grace followed as they retraced their steps toward the warm glow of lights emanating from Mona's house.

As they came closer, Puppy's playful gait faltered. He slowed down, his ears pricking forward, his fur bristling along his spine. A low, guttural growl rumbled from his chest. He veered off the path slightly, placing himself between Grace and whatever unseen threat lurked ahead.

Grace stopped and inspected the house from a distance. The fairy lights on the terrace twinkled obliviously, casting a warm glow on the empty space. Nobody was on the terrace. But that was not unexpected. Julius and Mona had likely retreated into the house. Light spilled from the living room and kitchen windows, but the interiors remained opaque. She didn't see any movement inside. Were they on the couch, lost in conversation, or was an unsettling stillness afoot?

Puppy growled again. Something did not feel right. Grace decided to circle the house. A glimpse through a window might offer some clue as to what was going on. As they approached the building, Puppy let out yet another growl.

"Shush!" she murmured softly, gently pressing his snout together. He looked at her with a perplexed gaze, trying to decipher her intentions.

Grace inched closer to the house, her heart pounding. She crouched low and followed the path to the house, keeping to the shadows. Puppy, transformed into a silent wraith by her side, mimicked her every movement. Reaching the corner of the house, Grace paused. The light from the living room window spilled onto the ground. Carefully, she got up and peeked through the window. The living room was empty. There was nobody on the couch, nobody at the dining table. Where were they?

Grace remembered that the kitchen was in the front of the house, to the right of the entrance door. She continued cautiously, hugging the wall as she crept toward the front between the house and the garage. Puppy followed closely behind, ears perked, eyes gleaming. A damp chill clung to the air. As they pressed onward, a peculiar sight caught Grace's attention: The side door leading to the garage stood wide open. A knot of apprehension tightened in her stomach, but curiosity propelled her onward. She peeked into the garage.

There was Mona. Her body was sprawled on the floor beside the overflowing trash cans, her spiked hair drenched in a dark red pool of blood. A large, gaping wound marred her skull. Grace clamped her hand over her mouth to stifle a scream. She rushed to her friend's side, gathering Mona's limp form in a desperate embrace. But the body offered no response, falling back into a lifeless heap. Panic surged through Grace as she fumbled for a pulse at Mona's neck. Her fingers encountered only chilling stillness. Mona's eyes stared dimly at the ceiling. She was gone.

Puppy whimpered mournfully. He settled beside Grace and nudged his wet nose into her numb elbow. The warmth of his fur felt like a lifeline in the storm of emotions threatening to drown her. Tears streamed down her face, a torrent of grief for her lost friend. She buried her face in the furry warmth of her canine companion, weeping for the irreplaceable loss of her friend, the unbearable responsibility of her choices that had brought her here, and the bitter sting of death that seemed to follow her everywhere.

A burning thought clawed through her grieving mind—Julius. Where was he? She leaped to her feet. She couldn't lose him too. She had outwitted the attacker in the hospital, the attacker at the party, and the attacker at the Zhang residence. And by God, she'd wrestle down this one too. If it wasn't already too late. She sprinted toward the house, Puppy darting after her.

- 50 -

ANNYA

Saturday, November 12, 2033, 8:30 p.m.

Annya pressed herself into the rough-hewn stone, her heart hammering against her ribs. Beside her, Angus leaned closer, the warmth of his body a welcome counter to the chill of the cellar. She glanced around the corner, her breath catching in her throat.

The snake's rattle buzzed furiously, echoing against the stone walls. Dr. Triveda sat frozen in her chair, a statue carved from fear. Karim retreated slowly, his eyes fixed on the creature. The snake let out another sharp, terrifying buzz, a predator poised to strike.

Angus's large hand closed over Annya's. He pressed something cold and hard into her palm. His gun. Her fingers automatically curled around the cold steel. Her gaze snatched up to meet his, trying to decipher his intentions. He nodded at her reassuringly.

His body brushed against hers as he moved past her. He entered the room with a heavy thud of his boots, shattering the tense silence. Annya flinched. This was too dangerous. But before she could react, Angus was already in the middle of the room. He ignored the viper entirely, its furious rattle replaced with a startled hiss. With a swift motion, he grabbed Dr. Triveda on her seat, hoisted her effortlessly, and carried her out of the room. The surgeon, limp and silent, seemed weightless in his grip. He deposited her with a gentle thud at the base of the stairs.

The audacity of it all left both snake and Karim momentarily stunned. Karim stared at Angus with his mouth agape. Then, he leaped toward him. A primal instinct surged through Annya, dragging her out of her hiding spot before she even realized she was moving. She stumbled into the doorway, the barrel aimed at the charging figure. Karim's face, contorted in a snarl of rage, screeched to a halt mere inches from her. Annya's finger tightened on the trigger, the metal biting into her clammy skin. They locked eyes in a silent standoff.

"You've never shot anyone, have you?" he asked calmly.

"Yes, I have," she replied, her voice steady.

His eyes narrowed. "You're lying."

Karim leaped forward, slamming into her with enough force to knock her back. Annya pulled the trigger. The gun discharged with a deafening roar, the blast echoing through the chamber and bouncing off the rough stone walls. Annya's aim, thrown off by the struggle, had sent the bullet ricocheting off the floor. The snake let out a terrifying hiss, a primal scream of outrage.

Karim wrapped his arms around her tightly, trying to immobilize her. Panic surged in her, a hot wave washing over the cold fear. Her finger on the trigger trembled, but she squeezed it again anyway. Another deafening roar soared, followed by a choked gasp. A hot, metallic tang filled the air. Below them, a crimson stain began to form on the stone floor, spreading outward like a macabre flower.

Karim stumbled backward into the cellar, a hand flying to his leg, his face contorted in a mixture of pain and shock. There was a hole in his pant leg, the fabric singed at the edges.

The snake, capitalizing on his moment of weakness, lunged forward, sinking its fangs into the leg through the hole of his pants, just above the new wound. Karim yelped in surprise, the sound echoing in the tense silence of the room.

In the same instant, a blur of movement surged past Annya. Angus ripped the gun from her hand and stepped forward. Shots rang out in rapid succession, each one a punctuation mark in the horrifying cacophony of the moment.

The snake thrashed on the floor in a final desperate dance. Blood oozed from its mangled form, staining the stone red. The reptile let out a guttural hiss laced with fury and fading life before it went limp. The metallic tang of blood hung thick in the air.

Annya rushed to Karim's side. He clutched his leg, letting out ragged gasps. "Angus, get the chair," she called back. "And an ambulance—now!" Every second counted. She needed to get him still, needed to slow the spread of the snake's venom.

Angus untied Dr. Triveda with quick moves.

"Thank you," she whispered.

Angus didn't respond. He pulled handcuffs from his pocket, reached for the doctor's wrist, and secured her to the stair railing with a sharp snap.

"I'm the victim!" the doctor protested.

Angus ignored the surgeon and hefted the chair toward Annya.

"Sit down," Annya said to Karim. "We need to keep your leg above the level of your heart."

Karim flinched as she eased him onto the chair, a low groan escaping his lips. His eyes were clouded—perhaps from the pain. Or the venom was already taking effect.

"You need to stay as calm as possible," Annya said.

"I know," he rasped. "I'm an MD, remember?"

"MD or not, right now you are wounded and the venom is coursing through your veins."

Angus spoke in a low voice on the phone. "An ambulance will be here in a few minutes," he said.

Annya nodded. "Thank you!"

She knelt beside Karim and tore open the fabric of his pants. The sight that greeted her was alarming. A large, gaping hole marred his flesh, its edges seared black from the gunshot. Blood oozed steadily from the cavity, forming a gruesome pool on the floor beneath him. Above the gun shot wound, redness and swelling radiated in an angry halo around two puncture marks. The snakebite had already triggered a severe inflammatory response.

Annya looked at Karim. Sweat was forming on his forehead. Surely his heart was racing like hers. That would accelerate the effects of the venom spreading through his body. They were in a desperate race against time.

Karim looked at Angus. "You're Grace's bodyguard," he said. "Why are you here?"

"FBI," Angus said calmly.

"This woman," he whispered, his head tilting weakly toward Dr. Triveda, "she killed my wife."

"I know," Angus responded. "She will be brought to justice."

"SUEC is too powerful for a fair trial, even for you. They'll find a way to get their star surgeon out of this mess."

Angus shook his head. "Not under my watch," he said. "We recorded a phone call in which she selected your wife as an organ donor the day before she died. And we secured the camera footage on your computer that documents Dr. Triveda entering your and Bianca's home directly before the fatal gunshot."

A choked sob escaped Karim, his body wracked with a fresh wave of pain. "SUEC will fabricate some story to explain that away." Tears streamed down his face, carving tracks through the grime and sweat. "Bianca . . ." he rasped. "I miss her so much. She was the kindest soul I've ever known. She didn't deserve this."

"You wanted to revenge her?" Annya asked softly.

Karim nodded. "What else could I do? I begged the police to investigate, but they dismissed it. 'A clear case of depression and suicide,' they said. It was too convenient. But Bianca's depression was actually getting better. I founded the Order of Balance just for her. And it was working. She loved the community and was finally finding her way back to the light. And then . . ." His voice trailed off, choked by another wrenching sob.

Annya turned around and looked Dr. Triveda in the eye. Hell was not hot enough for this person. The surgeon had been carried away by her ambition, killing Bianca to secure a donor for the body transplant and convincing a dying scientist to a procedure that would make her wake up paralyzed.

The surgeon shifted from one foot to the other, but Annya didn't see any sign of remorse in her eyes. "The man is dying," she said calmly. "What do you have to say to him?"

Dr. Triveda blinked, her gaze darting between Annya and Karim's slumped form. A muscle clenched in her jaw. "Your wife gave her life for the greatest leap modern medicine has ever seen," she said softly.

"She did not *give* her life!" Karim exclaimed. "You took it! You are a murderer!"

Angus intercepted. "As I said, Dr. Triveda will be brought to justice. We found her fingerprints on the weapon that killed Bianca. She had tried to clean them off. But there was a print left on the barrel. The forensics team confirmed that there was no gun residue on Bianca's hand and that the angle of the gunshot had come from a second party, not herself. Together with the witness who places Dr. Triveda at the scene, we have clear evidence."

Dr. Triveda looked at the ground. "For one person to live, another had to die," she mumbled. "Sometimes we have to make sacrifices to advance humanity."

"Bianca was a beautiful young woman, *my wife!*" Karim cried out, tears running down his cheeks. "She had her whole life ahead of her and you took it away!"

Annya looked at the man. He had been so charismatic just an hour ago. And here, he was breaking down. The weight of his grief, the crushing injustice of it all, hung heavy in the air, an accusation against a world of scientific progress that had failed his beloved wife.

"And then you went after Grace?" she asked softly.

Karim grimaced, a fresh wave of pain twisting his features. He swept a hand across his forehead, wiping away sweat and a sheen of cold dread. His breath came in ragged gasps, each one a struggle against the tightening grip of the snake's venom. "One of the members of the order," he rasped, "a young man named Datu, was part of a street gang in San Francisco. He became close to Bianca and me, a fierce friend. When I told him that Bianca's 'suicide' was a carefully orchestrated murder to feed Grace's need for organs, Datu offered to serve justice."

"Was that the man who drank his own poison at the hospital?" Annya asked.

Karim nodded, his eyes fluttering closed for a moment. When he opened them again, his eyes held a steely glint of determination. "After Datu passed away, the order stepped in to finish the job he started," he said. "The order has grown beyond what I ever imagined. People need a sense of purpose. In the order, they find a loyal community and a cause to fight for."

"How many people tried to finish Datu's assassination attempt on Grace?" Annya asked.

Karim's eyes glistened. "I don't know. People at the order stick together, that's for sure."

"Everyone who attacks Grace will face criminal charges," Angus said with a grim expression.

Karim smiled. "I look forward to that trial," he said. "Imagine the surprise when they take Grace's fingerprints. Is it murder if the victim was already dead?"

"And *you* went after Dr. Triveda, not Grace?" Annya asked.

Karim grimaced, his breath coming in shallow gasps. "This woman," he rasped, his hand shaking as he gestured toward the surgeon, "she was the cause of all evil. Unchecked ambition, trampling over lives in her pursuit of glory. At first, I thought Grace was her accomplice. But later, I realized that Grace had no idea that Bianca was killed so that she could live."

"But you still didn't call your gang back?" Angus asked.

Karim paused, his eyes clouding. "There was this resemblance, a haunting echo of Bianca in Grace. I couldn't place it at first. It was very confusing. I was grieving the loss of my wife and felt an urgency to be close to this stranger. But then, when I saw the tattoo on Grace's ankle, the one that I'd placed there . . . the monstrous truth slammed into me. This wasn't just a multiorgan transplant. This *was* Bianca's body in front of me. Her beautiful body, desecrated, carrying the head of another woman. It was a shock beyond comprehension."

A shudder wracked his frame, horror etched on his face. Even the searing pain in his leg seemed momentarily forgotten.

"Bianca deserves peace," he rasped. "She should be buried whole. Nobody has the right to walk her dead body around. That is sacrilege. An insult to her soul."

Angus looked at him. "But you never attacked Grace. You had several occasions."

Karim shook his head. "I could never harm Bianca, even if her body is held hostage by a stranger's head. But she deserves peace. The Order of Balance was not made for this. But in a twist of fate, its members are serving her justice. What I couldn't do, they'll finish. By now, it's likely done." He looked at Angus and Annya with a strange serenity. "I told you this to buy them time. And for myself . . . I'm ready to join Bianca. I don't want to live without her. This is the order of the universe, after all."

He let out a choked gasp. His grip on the chair slackened, his body crumpling as he slid to the ground. He settled on the cold stone floor with a soft thud, an unsettling serenity flickering in his eyes.

"This is better," he whispered. "The venom will reach my heart faster this way." The life seemed to drain from his face, leaving pale exhaustion. His eyes turned dull, filled with deep sadness.

Annya scrambled to her feet. The ambulance. Where was the damn ambulance?

She rushed up the stairs, burst through the dark hallway, and flung open the front door. The evening fog greeted her outside, thick with humidity. A gaggle of teenagers strolled down the nearby sidewalk, chatting and laughing. But there were no sirens yet.

- 51 -

GRACE

Saturday, November 12, 2033, 8:30 p.m.

The heavy oak door hung wide open, a jagged splinter dangling from its frame like a broken tooth. An unsettling silence wafted from the twilight within. Grace rushed in, her gaze darting through the foyer. There, on the threshold to the living room, was another body on the floor. Her breath hitched.

Julius.

She leaped forward and sank on her knees beside him. Dark-red bruises marred the exposed skin of his neck. With a hand that wouldn't quite obey, she brushed a stray strand of hair from his forehead, the coolness of his skin sending a fresh wave of panic through her. Fingers trembling violently, she fumbled for his pulse. There. A faint thud, but then . . . silence. Desperation clawed at her throat. No. Not like this. Not Julius. With a ragged sob, she pressed her fingertips harder, willing a response. Was it real or imagination? There was a faint pulse. She pressed her fingers deeper. There *was* a pulse. It was weak, but it was real. Julius was alive. Unconscious but alive. Leaning closer, she strained to hear his breath. A shallow rise and fall of his chest confirmed it—he was breathing.

There was a sliver of movement at the edge of her vision, followed by a sharp metallic hiss behind her. She looked back. There, beside Julius's shoe, appeared a triangular head as wide as her fist. A rattlesnake, its diamond-patterned body moving toward her, the rattle at its tail vibrating with a menacing buzz. A new wave of terror flooded Grace's veins. The snake was too close for her to escape. The chilling buzz of the snake's warning grew louder. Its dark reptilian eyes seemed to glint with cold malice, fixed intently on her.

A low, guttural growl rumbled from somewhere to her right. Grace slowly turned around, careful not to startle the snake with sudden movements. There, Puppy stood frozen, his hackles raised, his gaze fixed on the snake. Another low growl churned in his throat.

"Puppy, stay back!" Grace said calmly.

The reptile reared up in a striking pose, its large eyes fixed on Grace. But before the strike could land, a blur of beige fur launched itself into the air. In a flash, Puppy's jaws clamped down on the rattler's neck, just inches from the viperous fangs. The room erupted in a frenzy of thrashing coils. The massive serpent whipped its body back and forth, its powerful muscles straining against Puppy's hold. Dust whirled up into the air. Grace watched in horror as Puppy held on with a tenacity born of pure instinct, a low growl rumbling deep in his chest. With a series of rapid shakes, he thrashed the snake from side to side. Finally, a sickening snap echoed through the room. The rattler's body went limp, followed by an eerie silence. Slowly, Puppy released his hold, panting heavily. The lifeless body of the snake slumped to the floor, its head detached at an unnatural angle.

Grace scrambled to her feet, rushing to Puppy's side and embracing him with a soft cry. The dog looked at her, his large brown eyes shining with fierce pride amidst his blood-stained fur. He was her protector, a hero who had saved her life.

Grace glanced back at Julius. He was still unconscious. She had to call an ambulance, but she had no phone. She patted the pockets of his blazer. There was something smooth and cool—the burner phone. With shaking hands, she pulled it free, the screen refusing to illuminate at her first frantic press. A strangled gasp escaped her lips. The phone needed a passcode, something she didn't know. She opened Julius's eyes with one hand and held the screen in front of him. It worked. The screen flickered to life. She dialed 9-1-1.

Suddenly, she noticed a large, distorted shadow stretch grotesquely across the white wall beside her. Her breath hitched. Another man. The shadow grew larger, shifting towards them. Terror locked her limbs in place. The man's silhouette loomed high above her now, his arm extended, his hand holding a long object. A gun? It clicked softly.

Grace held her breath. *Death is finally here to get me*, she thought. *Whatever I do, there is no escape.*

An ear-splitting crack shattered the silence. A gun shot. Grace squeezed her eyes shut, flinching as the sound reverberated through the room.

But the searing pain she'd expected never came. Tentatively, she cracked open an eye, a ragged breath escaping her lips. Nothing. No burning sensation, no blood blooming on her shirt. She glanced at Julius. No new wounds marred his skin, either.

A heavy thud echoed in the dead silence, making the room itself shudder.

Grace turned her head, heart hammering in her chest. There, sprawled on the floor behind her, lay a hulking figure clad in dark jeans and a black leather jacket. Who was that? Another assassin? Had he brought the snake and decided to shoot her once the reptile didn't finish the job? Puppy started barking furiously, his fur bristling. The man wasn't moving.

Another movement at the open veranda door caught Grace's eye. She looked up. In the opening stood a familiar figure with a mustache, a fuming gun in his hand. He nodded at her briefly.

"Take good care of him," he grunted.

"I will," she whispered. "How did you find us?"

"I saw that he took the highway to the south rather than to San Francisco. I tracked his online footage and followed him from a distance. When he got a text that a hitman might be on his way to him, I came as quickly as possible."

"Thank you!"

They locked eyes. His gaze hadn't gotten any friendlier.

"He proposed to me." It was perhaps the most inappropriate moment for this news. But she had to get it out.

Rolando tilted his head slightly, a gesture that could have been a nod. Then, just as abruptly as he had appeared, he turned around and vanished into the darkness beyond the garden. Only the faint scent of gunpowder lingered.

Grace looked at the gaping darkness. A faint wail in the distance pierced the oppressive silence and grew steadily louder. Ambulance sirens. Finally. Loud voices erupted from the front of the house, followed by the pounding of approaching footsteps. Two paramedics in crisp white uniforms rushed in, followed by two men in FBI jackets. Grace watched them with a mix of fear and hope. One of the paramedics knelt beside the fallen figure. A tense moment stretched. Then, he announced: "He's gone."

Grace flinched. Rolando had shot him dead before he could shoot them. Her gaze darted to Julius. The other paramedic crouched beside him, his brow furrowed.

"This one's alive," he called out. The man began a quick assessment. "Possibly a concussion, but reflexes intact." He gently slapped Julius's cheeks, the sound echoing sharply in the room. With a practiced flick, the paramedic yanked open his medic bag, retrieved a vial and cracked it beneath Julius's nose with a sharp snap. A pungent ammonia aroma, acrid and eye-watering, flooded the air as he thrust the saturated cloth under Julius's limp form.

Julius stirred, his eyelids fluttering open. Confusion clouded his gaze, and then recognition sparked in their depths as he looked at Grace. He opened his mouth to speak, but a harsh cough erupted instead.

Grace sobbed as she rushed to him, wrapping her arms around him and burying her face in his chest. The warmth of his body and the reassuring thump of his heart were the sweetest sounds she had ever heard. For a moment, the world around them faded away.

"We'll take him to the hospital," the paramedic declared, and began to prepare a stretcher. "He needs a full assessment."

Grace clung tighter to Julius, a chill meandering down her spine. "I'll come with you," she rasped. "I'm his fiancée."

The paramedic gave her a curt nod.

Grace's gaze darted toward the FBI agent at the edge of the scene, a silent observer. His head tilted slightly at her words, a flicker of something crossing his features—curiosity? Sympathy? He took a measured step forward, his voice low and controlled. "I'm Agent Miller, FBI. One of my agents will accompany you to the hospital to ensure your safety. And I'll be investigating the scene here."

Tears welled up in Grace's eyes. "There's another woman," she choked. "Dead. In the garage."

- 52 -

WASSILY

Saturday, November 12, 2033, 9:30 p.m.

Wassily leaned back on his couch, reviewing the news article that the reporter had sent to him for review before it would be published later tonight. The flickering light of Wassily's phone cast an uneven glow as he scrolled through the article draft. A satisfied smirk played on his lips as he reached the end. He let out a hearty, "Yup," that echoed off the crumbling walls around him.

He tossed the phone onto the worn cushions beside him, reached for his beer and took a long pull. The bittering hops felt good on his tongue. His new life had begun.

This article was a real gem—a captivating piece about a local researcher who'd turned her life around from incurable cancer. By now, Wassily was quite sure that Grace had a skeleton or two in her closet, but that wasn't the story that sold papers, was it? People craved happy endings, redemption arcs, comfort food for the soul.

Wassily took another swig. He had finally found his calling. With his charm and silver tongue, he could become a master storyteller, cooking up stories that people could relate to. The truth was overrated. Nobody wanted to read more about the dull, monochromatic, depressing reality around them. People craved color, a splash of the fantastical in their everyday lives. And that was where he came in, the artist wielding words like paintbrushes, coloring the world a little brighter, a touch more hopeful. After all, wasn't that what entertainment was all about? Wasn't it about weaving a temporary escape, a chance to lose yourself in an enchanting story that felt completely true?

Wassily smiled, the confines of his apartment momentarily forgotten, replaced with the warmth of a self-proclaimed mission—to be the architect of his readers' temporary realities, one article at a time.

Wassily picked up the business card, a grin tugging at his lips. He grabbed his phone and punched in the reporter's number. It rang twice before a cheery voice answered.

"Hello," Wassily greeted him. "It's Wassily, Grace's ex-husband. I just read the article. You captured everything perfectly!"

The reporter's voice boomed with satisfaction. "Fantastic! I'm glad I got the details right. Even better, the DIPUTS creator confirmed everything. Looks like we have a rock-solid story for the front page! Thanks again for the scoop, Wassily. My editor's thrilled!"

Wassily's smile widened. "I'm thrilled here too!"

"I have one last request," the reporter said. "Do you have a fresh photo of your ex-wife? The ones we used might be a bit dated."

"Sure, I have plenty. I will send one your way. By the way, about that compensation . . .?"

"I'm already on it," the reporter interrupted. "I just wired the payment. I think you'll be happy."

Wassily's fingers flew across his phone, pulling up his bank app. A low whistle escaped his lips as he saw the sum. That was more money than his account had seen in a long time. Rent wouldn't just be covered, it looked like a bigger apartment was finally within reach. Bigger and brighter, a space that reflected the newfound success he felt swirling around him.

"I'm very pleased, indeed," he said. "Here's to many more collaborations in the future!"

"Absolutely," the reporter replied, his voice buzzing with excitement. "This story is just the beginning. With your access to SUEC and the Zhang family, we could turn this into a goldmine. Keep me posted on any updates, Wassily. We could build a whole series on it—following 'cured Cinderella' navigating the world of wealth. Trust me, our readers will eat it up."

Wassily smiled. "Consider it done. You'll be hearing from me again soon."

He hung up. His gaze lingered on Grace's photo on his phone. He'd been looking at life from the wrong angle. All this time, he'd chased after fleeting appearances. But true value, he realized, lay elsewhere. Wit, for instance, aged like fine wine, becoming sharper with each passing year. His creativity, too, could blossom, transforming into a cloak of ingenuity that draped him in confidence—and a regular income. And his ability to spot opportunities? That would be honed to a razor's edge.

- 53 -

ANNYA

Sunday, November 13, 2033, 8:30 a.m.

Carlos, his tuxedo as sharp as ever, held the intricately carved door wide open. Annya and Angus stepped into the grand entrance hall of the Zhang residence , where the air was filled with the delightful aroma of freshly baked pastries, subtly intertwined with a hint of jasmine.

The house manager led them past a magnificent V-shaped marble staircase, its polished surface creating a mesmerizing interplay of light and shadow. They passed towering marble columns and entered the formal dining room, which exuded the same opulence. Soft, ambient lighting cast a warm glow on rich mahogany furnishings and intricate wall tapestries. Expensive artwork and tastefully placed sculptures hinted at a discerning eye for art. A large, polished grand piano sat in the corner to their right.

Nathanael Zhang sat at the head of a grand table, a steaming porcelain cup in front of him. He rose gracefully, acknowledged Carlos with a curt nod and extended his hand to Annya and Angus, greeting them with a firm handshake.

"May I offer you some tea, or perhaps coffee?" Carlos inquired.

Annya and Angus exchanged a glance. "No, thank you," Annya replied.

With a silent bow, the house manager retreated.

"Please, have a seat." Nathanael said, gesturing broadly to the opulent chairs around the mahogany table. Once Angus and Annya had settled in their seats, he turned to Angus. "So, the people who attacked Julius and Grace were part of a spiritual cult?"

"Something like that," Angus confirmed.

"And the attackers have been dealt with?"

Angus nodded. "The group leader died last night, and the individual who assaulted Julius and Grace was shot at the scene."

Annya stole a glance at Angus. His no-nonsense demeanor was both reassuring and intimidating. Even in a room filled with wealth and power, Angus commanded attention with his unyielding presence. He left Rolando's name unspoken, respecting Julius's wishes.

"And Carlos was part of this group?" Nathanael asked.

Angus nodded again. "Carlos cooperated fully. He played a significant role in our interrogation of the remaining cult members last night."

Annya couldn't suppress a dry smile. In her opinion, Carlos's cooperation had been fueled less by genuine remorse and more by a desperate scramble for redemption.

"He wasn't involved in the attack on Grace here at my home?" Nathanael asked. "I've known him for years and can't imagine him harming us. But after all I've heard . . ."

Angus offered a calming nod. "Understandable, Mr. Zhang. We conducted a thorough investigation, and there's no evidence Carlos was knowingly involved. He led a member of the clan to Grace's surgeon at the hospital." He paused. "However, Carlos didn't know that that individual planned a poison attack on the surgeon. Unfortunately, several members of the cult were unwittingly manipulated into assisting crimes."

Nathanael flinched. "That's terrible."

"Indeed," Angus agreed. "Fortunately, the cult has been dismantled. We've apprehended two additional suspects and believe we've neutralized all potential threats."

"I'm relieved to hear that," Nathanael said, his features softening for a fleeting moment. "Julius is my only son. I have to be sure he's safe. There cannot be another attack on my family."

"Of course," Angus said. "We've apprehended all suspects and for your complete peace of mind, we'll maintain a security detail at your residence for another week or two."

Annya smiled. This was well delivered. The surveillance wasn't a concession to a millionaire, but a move to safeguard Grace, a national treasure.

"We were notified that Julius and Grace have returned here already?" she asked.

Nathanael nodded. "Julius discharged himself from the hospital in Santa Barbara last night. His CT scan did not reveal any brain injury. He and Grace took a private jet ride home. Fresh air and familiar surroundings are the best medicine, wouldn't you agree? There's no place like home to mend."

"And you approved of Grace staying here? Didn't you want her to leave?"

Nathanael gestured toward Angus. "Well, that was before Mr. Weber here successfully drained the swamp. Now that the threat is neutralized, she's welcome to stay. She's practically family," he added with a shrug. "She's busy fussing over Julius upstairs. It strengthens the family image, wouldn't you agree? It was about time Julius came to his senses."

Angus and Annya exchanged a gaze.

"Did you see the news this morning?" Nathanael shifted the subject.

"We received a summary but haven't had the chance to read the actual article," Annya said.

With a flourish, Nathanael activated a holographic display, conjuring an online search result. A cascade of headlines flooded the screen, all variations of the same theme. The blaring headline read: "A Triumph of Science: DIPUTS Drug Offers Cure for Terminal Breast Cancer." It was accompanied by a photo of Grace, champagne flute raised high in a triumphant toast.

Nathanael leaned back in his chair, a hint of amusement flickering in his eyes. "It seems the news is a bit explosive." He gestured toward the holographic display. "The article claims that Tina's drug cured Grace. And apparently, Tina confirmed it."

"What did Grace have to say about that?" Annya asked.

A wry smile spread across Nathanael's face. "That, Annya, is the curious part. Grace will not comment on the matter. Apparently, the security team at the front gate has been fending off reporters all morning. She doesn't want to talk with any of them. She's busy holding my son's hand upstairs." He chuckled.

"So, will you now complete the pending deal with Tina for her DIPUTS drug?" Angus asked.

Nathanael shook his head. "I don't think so."

"Why not?"

Nathanael sighed. "For starters, I can't shake the feeling there's more to the cure than meets the eye. And if Grace decides to join my family, SUEC can keep their grubby mitts off her. Besides, promoting a drug with a backward name that sounds like 'stupid' isn't exactly my idea of good business."

- 54 -

JULIUS

Sunday, November 13, 2033, 9:00 a.m.

Julius sat nestled beside Grace on the cream chaise lounge, their shoulders brushing comfortably as they scrolled through the news on the tablet together. Grace smiled as he stroked her hand, her diamond ring glinting in the sunbeam that entered through the tall French windows. At their feet, Puppy chewed on a plush toy, wagging his tail.

Julius looked at Grace. "I'm glad you accepted the ring," he said with a mischievous smile.

She leaned in, brushing her lips against his ear. "I always wanted it," she confessed, planting a lingering kiss on his cheek.

"But yesterday," he pressed gently, "you weren't sure. What made you change your mind?"

She looked at him with her dark soulful eyes that stole his heart every time. "When I saw you lying on the floor, I almost lost my mind. It hit me that every moment we share could be our final one. I might leave the house for a few minutes, and when I return, you're gone." Her voice softened, her fingers reaching for his. "I couldn't bear the thought of living without you, Julius."

He smiled. He was in love with her. It wasn't the frantic flutter of butterflies or confused emotions of young love. With her, he felt a clarity, a deep sense of being accepted for who he truly was. And even though it was terrifying at first, he knew she was his soulmate.

"I remember the first time we talked at the hospital," he said. "I instantly felt understood. With you, everything feels just right."

"What about Rolando?" she asked, observing him intently.

He thought about it. "I do love him too," he said. "In a

different way. But Rolando and I can never live together. He doesn't crave that kind of relationship." He put his arm around her and stroked her back. "I have enough of adventures. I want a home, a shared life, a future built together."

She wrapped both arms around him and buried her head in his chest. "I know what you mean," she mumbled, the words vibrating through him. "But don't you think we deserve a little adventure, too?"

What adventure was she referring to? He held his breath, waiting for her to elaborate.

Finally, she pulled back, her eyes searching his. "What if I find myself a Rolando, someone I spend some spicy time with from time to time?"

He scoffed. "Well, I hope you don't."

Unthinkable. A sharp pang of jealousy twisted in his gut. His gaze lingered on her, tracing the light in her eyes, the curves of her lips. He hadn't realized how deeply his feelings for her ran.

Puppy had sensed the shift in the atmosphere. The playful wag of his tail faltered. With a worried whine, he trotted over to Grace and nudged her hand with his wet nose. Grace scooped him into her lap, gently scratching behind his ears and leaning forward to kiss him. His eyes fluttered closed in pure canine contentment.

Julius studied the way the California sun glinted off Grace's face. The scar at her neck had started to fade. "Is it possible to transplant a head on someone else's body, Grace?" he asked the question he had wanted to ask for a while.

Her smile faltered for a moment, a flicker of something unreadable crossing her eyes, before she forced a laugh. "What do you think?"

"Well, I'm counting one and one together. The scar on your neck, a year of rehab at SUEC Hospital, your ex-husband literally saying that you got a new body, a cult trying to kill you, the FBI covering for you. There seems to be only one answer."

Silence stretched between them. Finally, her dark eyes locked with his. "What if that were true?"

He took her hand with the diamond ring, outlining it with his index finger. "Performing such an audacious surgery is mind-blowing," he said. "But the idea of transferring your consciousness, your very essence, into a new body . . . that's something else entirely." He paused, his voice dropping to a whisper. "If anyone could adapt to such a challenge, it's you, Grace. You're the strongest woman I know."

Grace's gaze darted away from him for a moment, focusing on the distant California horizon behind the window. A moment of silence stretched between them. When their eyes met again, there was a vulnerability in them that tugged at his heart.

"Could you please not tell your father?" she whispered.

His breath hitched. It was true.

A blush crept up her neck under his scrutiny. The secrets she held close didn't diminish his feelings. On the contrary, they made her even more captivating.

He gently laced his fingers with hers. "Grace, whatever you've been through, whatever secrets you hold, I'm here for you. Always."

Grace leaned over and kissed him with an intensity that sent a jolt through him, a primal awakening he didn't know he craved. He surrendered to it, his own response raw and unfiltered. Her hand tangled through his hair, and he pulled her closer. Every touch, every brush of their bodies, was a revelation. No other woman had ever made him feel this way—consumed, desperate, and utterly alive.

- 55 -

GRACE

Monday, November 13, 2033, 9:00 a.m.

Grace walked through the large entrance hall of SUEC Hospital. The semicircular glass front illuminated the large hall with natural light. The air carried the familiar scent of rose water and brimmed with hurried footsteps, hushed conversations, and the occasional choked sob. A large reception desk dominated the center of the hall. Behind it, staff members in crisp uniforms answered phone calls and directed patients. Grace did not stop there. She knew the hospital inside out and directly followed the bright-red signs to the ER.

When she turned around the corner, a group of chatting nurses in starched white zipped by. A man in a SUEC uniform pushed a wheelchair steadily ahead, the woman within pale and withdrawn. Another woman on crutches, her brow furrowed in concentration, navigated the stairs with slow determination. Grace had seen it all, the worry, the pain, the suffering. A familiar ache settled in her chest.

She thought about Mona, her best friend. College days filled with laughter, Mona's infectious smile when she'd talked about her sea turtle research, the way she'd dragged Grace to every party—a whirlwind of life. The dream job at UC Santa Barbara, her chosen path of independence, her content happiness—all cut short by a cruel twist of fate.

And Bianca. Grace had read the news that Dr. Triveda had been arrested for allegedly killing Bianca to facilitate an organ transplant. Fortunately, neither Grace's name nor the fact that Bianca's entire body had been transplanted had been mentioned. SUEC was powerful. They would spin the story to minimize the damage.

But how did she feel about walking around in the body of a women who had been killed to enable her surgery? How could she reconcile the miracle of her second chance with the horrific sacrifice that had made it possible? Grace saw Bianca's face in her dreams at night, a haunting echo in quiet moments. Bianca had lived and breathed and loved, just like her. Grace hadn't known her. And she never would. Bianca was gone, a sacrifice for her survival.

Grace felt the weight of responsibility settle on her shoulders. Mona and Bianca were both murdered because of her. What could she do to honor their sacrifice? She had to do something. She owed it to them. But what? Seek justice? How? Testifying against Dr. Triveda? That wouldn't bring Bianca or Mona back. But it would put her at risk. She couldn't testify without acknowledging that she was a transplant recipient. She was a survivor, yes, but her body transplant had to remain a secret. She knew that much by now.

A sudden flash blinded her. Squinting, she squeezed her eyes shut and then opened them, momentarily disoriented. A familiar figure stood directly in her path. Speaking of nightmares. Here was Wassily, a sleek, rectangular camera with a large protruding lens cradled in his hand. Where did he get that? It looked far beyond his budget. And why had he just taken a picture of her?

"Hello, Grace," he boomed. "How are you doing today? You look radiant." His gaze swept appreciatively over her outfit. "I mean, that combo of casual jeans, high-neck cashmere sweater, and short trench coat looks really cool. Could set a new trend."

Grace gritted her teeth. She needed to get to the ER. "What do you want, Wassily?" she muttered.

"Well, I wondered if you saw my news article yesterday," he said with a large grin.

"I did."

"What did you think?"

"I have only one word for it: stupid," she spat, the pent-up frustration finally bubbling over.

"Well, if there were any misconceptions in your opinion, would you like to share your side of the story?"

"I *am* the story, Wassily," she gasped. "How did you find me, anyway?"

"Well, I still have my connections here." He smiled broadly, a picture of misplaced joviality. "And we are practically still married. You never submitted the divorce certificate."

Grace nodded. "Angus Weber reminded me of that. I submitted the papers last week. They have been filed. There are no ties between us anymore, Wassily. Now, if you'll excuse me. I have somewhere to be."

She pushed past him.

To her dismay, he turned and walked with her. "I have great news. I'm a reporter now. Do you have a comment as the new flame of the Zhang heir?"

Grace stopped dead in her tracks, a gasp escaping her lips. She whirled around, her gaze boring into his. "This," she stated fiercely, "is my message: Don't focus on your appearance, but what makes you you. Don't look for a savior. Be your own hero."

Wassily gasped. "That's well said, indeed. Anything else?"

She leaned closer, her voice dropping to a low, intense whisper. "You don't create a bond by living under the same roof or sleeping in the same bed. A true bond ignites when you can bare your soul to another, when your deepest vulnerabilities are met with understanding and acceptance."

"I like it, I like it," he muttered. "Can you give me more?"

She sighed. He hadn't understood a word. And perhaps never would. "That's all."

They had reached the ER reception area. Behind the counter, a formidable nurse peered over the bridge of her glasses, taking in the scene. "Do you belong together?" she asked.

"No," Grace responded quickly.

The nurse's gaze shifted to Wassily, her expression hardening. "Then I need you to step back, sir."

Wassily, caught off guard, glanced between Grace's steely

resolve and the imposing figure behind the counter.

"Or I will call security," the nurse added with a grim tone, leaving no doubt about her next course of action.

"Well, it was lovely seeing you again, Grace," Wassily said politely. "Until next time."

"Goodbye," Grace replied. Was it wrong to secretly hope that he would simply vanish before crossing paths with her again?

The nurse guided her back to the examination room, the same room where she had met with Annya just about five days ago. It felt like an eternity. A familiar pang of apprehension hit Grace as she sank onto the stretcher. Another nurse came in, checking her vitals and drawing a blood sample. After she left, silence stretched in the stark white room.

Then, the door swung open and Annya hurried in with her usual vibrant energy. "Grace, I'm so glad to see you all in one piece!" she exclaimed. "You were not hurt, were you?"

Grace ignored her outstretched hand. "So, you're CIA?" She asked the question she had regurgitated in her mind since Rolando had revealed this secret to her.

Annya's smile faltered. She closed the exam room door with a soft click, pulled a chair closer, and sat beside Grace. "Yes, Grace," she admitted, her voice low. "I'm with the CIA. This needs to stay between us. My cover is crucial. I can only help you if no one knows."

Grace stared at a point on the floor. "So, you were watching me all along? Spying on me? I thought you were my friend."

"It's not that simple, Grace," Annya said softly. "I'm both a CIA operative and your friend. When I found you paralyzed and alone, I was horrified. I volunteered to keep an eye on you because I knew that you needed help."

Grace looked at her, not sure what to think.

Annya brushed her bangs to the side, revealing a jagged scar that sliced across her forehead. "You're not alone, Grace. I understand the horrors of violence. Many years ago, I was hit by the bullet of a

Russian assassin. It put me in the ICU for months. I still have flashbacks."

Grace stared at the scar on her forehead, a jagged circle roughly the size of a walnut. The impact point was the most prominent, a puckered white crater where the bullet had entered. Time had softened the edges. Spiderweb lines radiated outward, a constellation of smaller craters marking its path beneath the skin. The most unsettling detail was the subtle depression beneath the scar, where the bone itself seemed to have sunken inward. Maybe Annya wasn't just some random stranger after all. She had been shot at like Mona and Bianca—and survived.

"Were you paralyzed as well?" Grace asked.

Annya shook her head. "I could move all my limbs when I woke up. But I wasn't allowed to move at first, to let my wounds heal. Then, I went through months of rehabilitation. Not the same as your ordeal, of course."

Grace looked up at her. "Thank you for sharing that," she said. "Even so, why did you spy on me?"

"I was protecting you," Annya said. "I assume my cryptic message sent Rolando to you and Julius in Santa Barbara."

For a moment, the only sounds were the faint hum of Annya's computer and the distant footsteps in the hallway.

"Thank you," Grace finally said.

Their eyes met in silent acknowledgment.

"How are you holding up, Grace?" Annya asked.

Grace sighed. "I miss Mona terribly. And I'm horrified that Bianca was murdered for my surgery. If I had known that, I would've never agreed to the body transplant."

"Of course not."

"Did *you* know that Bianca was murdered?"

Annya shook her head. "I believed that Bianca had committed suicide and signed an organ donor agreement. The truth came out only recently."

"I see."

"Does that change how you feel about your body?"

"Yes, of course. Bianca didn't choose to die. She was killed so that I could live. I am walking around in a stolen body."

"Are you angry?"

"I feel awful," she admitted, her voice barely a whisper. "Was it wrong that I wanted to live? I could've asked more questions about the surgery and the donor. But I didn't. I took the chance to live with both hands. How can I even think about being happy after what happened? It's my fault Bianca's gone. And Mona."

"Perhaps you can make it up to them."

"I wish I could turn back time and die of cancer. Then, Bianca and Mona would still be alive."

"Or someone else would be walking around with Bianca's body, and another person's friend would have been killed. Dr. Triveda would have transplanted Bianca's body on you or someone else. And another recipient might not have escaped multiple assassin attacks."

Grace nodded. "I persevered against all odds."

"You are not the victim here. You can shape this story."

"I want to honor Bianca and Mona, create a legacy for all of us."

Annya squeezed her hand gently. "Mona would want you to be happy, Grace."

"That we can agree on. "I also have good news . . ." She hesitated, then held out her hand, the diamond on her finger catching the light. "Julius proposed, and I said yes."

"Wow, congratulations!" Annya took her hand and inspected the large gleaming rock. "It's beautiful! I'm sure Mona would have cheered you on."

Tears welled up in Grace's eyes. "She did," she choked out, wiping a stray tear. "She kept telling me to accept the ring. I think she'd want me to go through with it. To marry him." Grace adjusted the turtleneck on her sweater. It felt too tight.

Annya nodded with a soft smile. "Staying with the Zhang family will be good for you," she said. "And Julius is a good guy. There are not many like him out there."

"I know. He doesn't know what I looked like before. He only knows the Grace I am now. That helps me accept my own self, even if I don't survive another year. I'm certainly aware that animals with head transplants haven't lived that long."

Annya turned to the holographic monitor beside her. "Well, your bloodwork looks good, except for a slight elevation in white blood cells. Likely a reaction to stopping the immunosuppressants. I brought you a fresh supply and wrote a prescription for refills." She handed Grace a packet of medication.

Grace took it mechanically.

"Did you talk with Tina?" Annya asked.

Grace shook her head. "No, I didn't. Tina seems happy about the attention for her new drug, and with the news out, maybe people will stop searching for the real cure."

"That is good for everyone involved."

"You were right, Annya. They're not ready for it. The cult's reaction made that clear."

Annya nodded. "New drugs come and go. This hype about your supposed cure will fade too. Then, you and Julius can move on with your lives. But if word gets out about the body transplant, you'll be a target forever."

Grace nodded. "I know that now." She paused. "What happened to Dr. Triveda?"

"She was taken into custody and will face charges for murdering an organ donor."

Grace's eyes narrowed. "Won't that lead people back to me? The missing organs?"

"SUEC provided her lawyer. Patient privacy is the official stance. No need to spook the recipients. They were innocent bystanders."

"Do you think the SUEC lawyers will get her acquitted?"

"I don't think so. The evidence is clear. SUEC lawyers prioritize the institution, not individuals. Distancing themselves from

Dr. Triveda is their best play right now. If the prosecution convinces the jury that she killed Bianca, she will face prison time."

"What about Lu'lu? I heard that she got promoted?"

Annya nodded. "Yes, that's right. We'll keep an eye on her, of course. But honestly, Grace"—her voice took on a reassuring tone—"I don't think SUEC will be considering additional body transplants anytime soon. Dr. Triveda's whole mess has put a serious damper on that."

Grace's gut clenched. She would remain the only one in the world. "I see," she said.

"So, what does the future hold for you?"

Grace took a deep breath, letting the possibilities swirl in her head. "Julius and I want to enjoy life as long as we can," she declared, the word tasting new and sweet on her tongue. "We want to live in the moment and truly experience what's left." A mischievous grin tugged at her lips. "Neither of us needs to work, with my pension and Julius's trust fund. That opens many possibilities. We are free."

Annya looked at her intently. "What options are you considering?" she asked.

"Maybe we create a rehabilitation center for people like me. Or a foundation that helps people with depression. Or an organization that flags bogus treatments, like Tina's drug. Maybe all of them!"

"All of these are wonderful ideas. I'm glad you want to give back to the community."

Excitement bubbled in Grace's chest. "And the Zhangs! The mansion next door just went on the market, and Julius put in a bid. If we get it, we'll move there. That way, we can support his father and have our own space too. And when the business gets handed down, Julius can just hire a CEO."

Annya smiled. "Sounds like true love."

Grace looked at her with gratitude. She was a dear friend after all. How many months or years did she have left? Perhaps it was better not to know. Would she and Julius get to build a new life from the ashes of the old? Only time would tell.

ACKNOWLEDGMENTS

I am profoundly grateful to everyone who played a role in the creation of this book, whether big or small. I extend sincere thanks to my colleagues and friends for sharing their honest perspectives on the academic world. Your input was indispensable. I am indebted to my team members at the Pegasus Medical Writing Group and the Stanford Medical Humanities Fellowship for their feedback on early drafts. Their critiques and insights were instrumental in shaping the plot. I would also like to thank Lauren Schoenthaler for her guidance on the legal intricacies of a medical detective story.

A special thanks to Sarah Peterson Pittock, Advanced Lecturer in the Program in Writing and Rhetoric at Stanford, who served as my coach for this project. Our regular meetings were a vital source of inspiration and support, allowing me to navigate the challenges of writing while balancing a demanding clinical and research career. Her astute observations on character development, story structure, and dialogue were instrumental in elevating this story to its full potential.

To my beloved husband, Dr. Thomas Link, whose constant encouragement and insightful feedback on crafting suspense were vital to this book's success. I am grateful to Elisabeth Daldrup and Berthold Schroeter for their feedback on the characters in the story. I would also like to extend my sincere gratitude to Hendrik Daldrup for creating the book's website and fostering connections with our readers.

A special thanks to my editor, Courtney Umphress, for her extraordinary work on this novel. Her meticulous editing and insightful suggestions have significantly enhanced the story while preserving its authentic voice. Her attention to detail in fact-checking and identifying plot holes has been invaluable and her developmental comments have guided me toward strengthening character arcs and storylines.

Finally, to the reader, thank you for choosing this book. I hope the stories within inspire reflection on identity and medical ethics. If Grace's story can change even one person's life for the better, then the long hours of writing it were worth it.

ABOUT THE AUTHOR

Elisabeth Link, MD, is a professor of radiology at Stanford University and a member of the Pegasus Physician Writers at Stanford, a group of physicians who write creatively. She lives in San Francisco, California, with her husband, Thomas Link, MD.

Dr. Link began writing creatively as a young child to entertain her grandmother in Germany. Later, as a college student, she published reflections about her life in Northern Germany and her experiences with her dog Bobby in local newsletters. After completing medical school, Dr. Link moved to the United States, where she found a supportive community of writers at the Pegasus Physician Writers group at Stanford. Intrigued by the complexities of human interaction and power dynamics within academia, she crafts detective stories that are both entertaining and thought provoking.

Dr. Link is a passionate advocate for women in STEM (science, technology, engineering, and mathematics/medicine). She is widely known for her powerful reflections and opinion pieces, such as "The Fermi Paradox in STEM—Where Are the Women Leaders?" (https://doi.org/10.1007/s11307-017-1124-4). Her novels feature strong female protagonists who conquer major obstacles in the academic world and inspire others to stand up for themselves and face their own challenges.

Dr. Link has received more than fifty honors and awards for her creative works over the past three decades, but the feedback from her students is most rewarding to her. One mentee wrote:

> *"I am aware that I cannot control the barriers that enter my life, but, like water, I will never be broken. Medicine is an intellectual journey, and I'm determined to reach my goal of becoming the best doctor my patients will ever encounter."*

A NOTE FOR THE READER

Thank you for reading an authorized copy of this book. Monasteria Press LLC is an independent publisher, and we rely on the support of our readers to continue publishing new books. By purchasing our publications, you are directly supporting our authors and enabling us to continue doing what we love.

If you enjoyed this book, please consider leaving a review on Amazon, Barnes & Noble, Powell's Books, Goodreads, or Social Media. Reviews are essential for helping us spread the word about great stories and can make a real difference in an author's life. Our authors invest significant time, effort, and heart into their writing, and knowing that their words have had a positive impact can be a great source of encouragement. Additionally, your review can be a valuable resource for fellow readers. Many people rely on peer recommendations when choosing books, making your insights a powerful tool for sharing great literature.

Please keep in mind that other readers may appreciate the joy of discovery and elements of surprise in the story. So, please avoid giving away spoilers in your review.

Thank you for being part of our community! To explore more titles from Monasteria Press, please visit our website: monasteria-press.com.

We look forward to welcoming you back soon!

The Monasteria Press Team

BOOKS BY ELISABETH LINK

Who Killed Nia Johnes?
Elisabeth Link, MD
Monasteria Press 2023

Her lifeless body was found in her wrecked car, with a bullet hole in her head. Dr. Nia Johnes, a young researcher at Silicon Valley University of Evolutionary Computation (SUEC), was murdered in cold blood. CIA Agent Dr. Annya Segond, SUEC's radiologist Dr. Lili Pham, and FBI Agent Terrel Wright believe her research on infectious diseases could have been the reason for her murder. Before they can make anything out of the few leads they have on the case, another researcher at SUEC narrowly escapes a shooting attack. Are the unexplained infections plaguing the campus somehow connected? What are the unsettling research activities that the SUEC leaders would prefer to keep quiet? With an assassin on the loose and not knowing who to trust, Agent Wright, together with Doctors Segond and Pham, must fight to save their lives and their careers as they race to uncover the shocking truth behind Dr. Johnes's assassination.

Lovers of mystery murder novels won't get enough of Elisabeth Links' *Who Killed Nia Johnes?* With an intriguing plot, the author weaves a tale of scientists, medical research, a hitman, sleuths, blackmail, and deceit. Amidst the whirlwind of pursuits and inquiries, Dr. Link skillfully incorporates the breathtaking scenery and architectural beauty of Northern California. This award-winning novel offers suspense, thrills, and adventure.

Paperback ISBN: 978-1-958277-04-1
Hardback ISBN: 978-1-958277-00-3
eBook ISBN: 978-1-958277-03-4
Library of Congress Control Number (LCCN) 2022921262

BOOKS BY ELISABETH LINK

The Stolen Brain Chip
Elisabeth Link, MD
Monasteria Press 2021

A fast-paced mystery novel with an educational twist. The story revolves around a fictional university in the hills above Redwood City, California, known as Silicon Valley University of Evolutionary Computation (SUEC). Newly developed brain chips designed to amplify cognitive abilities are stolen. Thus begins a string of events that leaves fifteen people injured, five hospitalized, and four dead. Dr. Lili Pham, Dr. Annya Segond, FBI Agent Terrel Wright, and FBI Agent Angus Weber start a race against time to rescue a young student from a ruthless killer, retrieve the brain chips, and prevent a bomb explosion.

To find the killer before he strikes again, it will take more than traditional on-the-scene evidence. The clues about the murderer revolve around various types of bone fractures that people suffer—pathological details that medical students and radiologists often have a hard time remembering. Some of the fractures provide clues to the mysteries of who the killer is and who stole the brain chips. The book also includes x-ray images showing what those different fractures look like. This is a great read for anyone interested in medicine and medical education.

The novel has a strong female protagonist and conveys the concept that we are all heroes-in-waiting. The time will come when each one of us will get a chance to step up and be the hero.

Paperback ISBN 978-1-7372582-3-0
Hardback ISBN 978-1-7372582-5-4
eBook ISBN 978-1-7372582-4-7
Library of Congress Control Number (LCCN) 2021950975

BOOKS BY ELISABETH LINK

The Claim
Elisabeth Link, MD
Monasteria Press 2024

An elite university. An abduction. An FBI investigation.

In the not-so-distant future of 2033, a gripping medical mystery unfolds in the heart of Silicon Valley. Dr. Frida Ending, a young medical insurance agent, is abducted and disappears without a trace. FBI Special Agent Angus Weber and CIA Operative Dr. Annya Segond launch an investigation that leads them to a hospital in Silicon Valley, where every pending insurance claim for children with cancer has been suddenly approved. Who is behind this? Is Frida a victim or a villain? The only witness is the parrot Caramba, who keeps his beak shut. As Annya and Angus delve deeper into the investigation, they uncover a trail of greed and betrayal that leads them closer to the truth, and finally, a shocking revelation.

In *The Claim*, readers are taken on a thought-provoking journey that reveals ruthless and manipulative practices within a profit-based healthcare system. The game out there is rigged, and everybody knows it.

Paperback ISBN 978-1-958277-05-8
Hardback ISBN 978-1-958277-07-2
eBook ISBN 978-1-958277-06-5
Library of Congress Control Number (LCCN) 2023947148

Made in United States
North Haven, CT
10 November 2024

59777266R00167